KU-667-689

Index to Fairy Tales, 1973-1977,
Including
Folklore, Legends and Myths
in Collections
Fourth Supplement

Compiled by

Norma Olin Ireland
B.A., B.S. in L.S.

The Scarecrow Press, Inc.

Metuchen, N.J., and London, 1985

DEDICATION

To my friend of over forty years, Reva Beckner Potter, who helped me through the period following my husband's passing. Reva was my first, and remains my best friend in Fallbrook, California, and was previously a classmate of Dave's, in Pendleton, Indiana. Although distance sometimes separated us, Reva remained our good friend over the years. Absolutely loyal, she is "always there" when I need a strong shoulder.

Although she "doesn't have room for more books," and "doesn't like fantasy," here is one book of fantasy she *might want!*

N.O.I.

Library of Congress Cataloging-in-Publication Data

Ireland, Norma Olin, 1907–
        Index to fairy tales, 1973–1977, including folklore, legends, and myths in collections, fourth supplement.
        Originally published: Westwood, Mass. : F.W. Faxon Co., 1979.
        "Supplement to . . . Index to fairy tales, 1949–1972 (Faxon, 1973) and the fourth supplement to Mary Huse Eastman's original Index to fairy tales, myths and legends (Faxon, 1926)"—Foreword.
        1. Fairy tales—Indexes. 2. Mythology—Indexes. 3. Folklore—Indexes. 4. Folk literature—Indexes. I. Ireland, Norma Olin, 1907–   . Index to fairy tales, 1949–1972. II. Eastman, Mary Huse, 1870–1963. Index to fairy tales, myths, and legends. III. Title.
[Z5983.F17I732 1985]   [GR550]   016.3982   85–22138
ISBN 0–8108–1855–8

Copyright © 1985 by Norma O. Ireland

MANUFACTURED IN THE UNITED STATES OF AMERICA

R
016.398
Ir21
v. V

FOREWORD

This work is a Supplement to our *Index To Fairy Tales, 1949–1972* (Faxon, 1973) and the fourth supplement to Mary Huse Eastman's original *Index To Fairy Tales, Myths and Legends* (Faxon, 1926). This volume includes collections published from 1973–1977, plus a few reprints of works not included in the earlier *Indexes,* collections of special geographic interest, (e.g., Torres Straits), and some works of interest to adults as well.

Scope and Arrangement

130 titles (collections only) have been indexed, selected on the basis of availability and favorable reviews in professional journals. Arrangement is alphabetical, primarily by title and subject; author entries have been included only when an author is specifically listed in a collection. The title entry is the main entry. Author-title abbreviations are used to locate stories as listed in the "List of Collections Analyzed And Key To Symbols Used" at the beginning of the *Index.* The "Key To Symbols Used" consists of abbreviated author-title entries and is as simple and easy-to-use as possible.

If the first word of the title is the same, or similar to the subject entry, then it is omitted under the subject classification, as redundant. We have followed ALA rules when the same word, or combination of words, is used as the heading for different kinds of entry, i.e., "Arrange the entries alphabetically by the word following the entry word; arrange personal surnames before the other entries beginning with the same word; when title and subject headings are identical, file title entries after subject entries; adopt the order: person, place, subject (other than person or place), title." We have deviated from library practice only in capitalization: story titles are capitalized as they were listed in the books themselves. There are also a few subject entries combined with title entries, and they have been indicated as such.

v

Subject Headings

More than 2,050 subject headings have been used, not including cross-references. We consulted children's librarians who urged as much "subject-indexing" as possible, not only to help them quickly locate stories (including those with unusual subjects), but also to please their young readers who request specific types of stories. The latter consideration accounts for the large number of entries under certain topics which are frequently requested, such as "Princes and Princesses."

In general, the headings used in the previous *Index* are repeated here, with some additions and a few changes. Early names of countries have been used when the stories pertain to the early years of these countries, e.g., Persia. (Cross-references from the countries' present names have been provided.) In our reading and/or scanning of every story, we have endeavored to judge the importance of subjects. Certain subjects which had only small mention have been omitted.

Acknowledgements

Once again, we wish to thank the librarians of the Fallbrook branch of the San Diego County Library who worked so diligently to obtain as many books requested as possible through interlibrary loan. We also wish to thank various nearby libraries (Oceanside, Carlsbad), for the use of their excellent collections, as well as for their "telephone reference service" for double-checking bibliographic information.

We hope this Supplement, compiled over a period of five years, will be helpful to all libraries, both large and small, which contain fairy tales, folklore, legends, and myths in their collections.

Mrs. Norma Olin Ireland

LIST OF COLLECTIONS ANALYZED
IN THIS WORK
AND
KEY TO SYMBOLS USED

AARDEMA — BEHIND
Aardema, Verna. *Behind the Back of the Mountain: Black Folktales from Southern Africa.* Illus. by Leo and Diane Dillon. New York: The Dial Press, 1973. 86p.

AIKEN — NECKLACE
Aiken, Joan. *A Necklace of Raindrops and Other Stories.* Illus. by Jan Pienkowski. Garden City, N.Y.: Doubleday & Co., 1968. 95p.

ALEXANDER — FOUNDLING
Alexander, Lloyd. *The Foundling and Other Tales of Prydian.* Pictures by Margot Zemach. New York: Holt, Rinehart and Winston, 1973. 88p.

ALPERS — LEGENDS
Alpers, Antony. *Legends of the South Seas: The World of the Polynesians Seen Through Their Myths and Legends, Poetry and Art.* New York: Thomas Y. Crowell Co., 1970. 416p.

ANDERSON — HAUNTING
Anderson, Jean. *The Haunting of America: Ghost Stories from Our Past.* Illus. by Eric von Schmidt. Boston: Houghton Mifflin Co., 1973. 171p.

BAGLEY — CANDLE
Bagley, Julian. *Candle-lighting Time in Bodidalee.* Illus. by Wallace Tripp. New York: American Heritage Press, 1971. 128p.

BAIN — COSSACK
Bain, Robert Nisbet, ed. and trans. *Cossack Fairy Tales and Folk Tales.* Illus. by Noel L. Nisbet. New York: Frederick A. Stokes Co., Inc., 1894; rpt. Millwood, N.Y.: Kraus Reprint Co., 1973. 53p.

BAKER — AT
Baker, Betty. *At the Center of the World: Based on Papago and Pima Myths.* Illus. by Murray Tinkelman. New York: Macmillan Publishing Co., Inc., 1973. 53p.

BAMBERGER — MY
Bamberger, Richard. *My Second Big Story-Book.* Trans. by James Thin. Irvington-on-Hudson, N.Y.: Harvey House, Inc., 1969. 220p.

BANG — GOBLINS
Bang, Molly. *The Goblins Giggle, and Other Stories.* New York: Charles Scribner's Sons, 1973. 57p.

BANG — MEN
Bang, Garrett. *Men from the Village Deep in the Mountains, and Other Japanese Folk Tales.* New York: Macmillan Publishing Co., Inc., 1973. 84p.

1

BAUM — MOTHER
Baum, Lyman Frank. *Mother Goose in Prose.* Illus. by Maxfield Parrish. New York: Bounty Books 1897; rpt. New York: Scholarly Reprints, Inc., 1976. 265p.

BECHSTEIN — RABBIT
Bechstein, Ludwig. *The Rabbit Catcher, and Other Fairy Tales.* Trans. by Randall Jarrell. Illus. by Ugo Fontana. New York: Macmillan Publishing Co., Inc., 1962. 34p.

BELPRÉ — ONCE
Belpré, Pura. *Once in Puerto Rico.* Illus. by Christine Price. New York: Frederick Warne & Co., Inc., 1973. 96p.

BELTING — WHIRLWIND
Belting, Natalia. *Whirlwind Is a Ghost Dancing.* Illus. by Leo and Diane Dillon. New York: E.P. Dutton & Co., Inc., 1974. n. pag.

BIRD — PATH
Bird, Traveller. *The Path to Snowbird Mountain: Cherokee Legends.* New York: Farrar, Straus and Giroux, 1972. 87p.

BLAND — COMPLETE
Bland, Edith Nesbit. *The Complete Book of Dragons.* Illus. by Eric Blegvad. New York: Macmillan Publishing Co., Inc., 1973. 198p.

BOMANS — WILY
Bomans, Godfried Jan Arnold. *The Wily Wizard and the Wicked Witch, and Other Weird Stories.* Trans. by Patricia Crampton. Illus. by Robert Bartelt. New York: Franklin Watts, Inc., 1970. 180p.

BROWN — BOOK
Brown, Abbie Farwell. *The Book of Saints and Friendly Beasts,* Illus. by Fanny Y. Cory. Boston: Houghton Mifflin Co., 1928; rpt. Greatneck, N.Y.: Core Collections, 1976. 225p.

CALHOUN — THREE
Calhoun, Mary. *Three Kinds of Stubborn.* Illus. by Edward Malsberg. Champaign, Ill.: Garrard Publishing Co., 1973. 48p.

CAREY — BABA
Carey, Bonnie, trans. *Baba Yaga's Geese, and Other Russian Stories.* Illus. by Guy Fleming. Bloomington, Ind.: Indiana University Press, 1973. 128p.

CARLE — ERIC
Carle, Eric. *Eric Carle's Storybook: Seven Tales by the Brothers Grimm.* Illus. and retold by Eric Carle. New York: Franklin Watts, 1976. 94p.

CARPENTER — PEOPLE
Carpenter, Frances. *People from the Sky: Ainu Tales from Northern Japan.* Illus. by Betty Fraser. Garden City, N.Y.: Doubleday & Co., Inc., 1972. 108p.

CARRICK — WISE
Carrick, Malcolm. *The Wise Men of Gotham.* Illus. by Malcolm Carrick. New York: The Viking Press, 1973. n. pag.

CARTER — ENCHANTED
Carter, Dorothy Sharp. *The Enchanted Orchard, and Other Folktales of Central America.* Illus. by W.T. Mars. New York: Harcourt Brace Jovanovich, Inc., 1973. 126p.

CARTER — GREEDY
Carter, Dorothy Sharp, ed. *Greedy Mariani and Other Folktales of the Antilles.* Illus. by Trina Schart Carter. New York: Atheneum, 1974. 133p.

COLWELL — ROUND
Colwell, Eileen H. *Round About and Long Ago: Tales from the English Counties.* Illus. by Anthony Colbert. Boston: Houghton Mifflin, 1974. 124p.

CORRIGAN — HOLIDAY
Corrigan, Adeline. *Holiday Ring: Festival Stories and Poems.* Illus. by Rainey Bennett. Chicago: Albert Whitman and Co., 1975. 256p.

COTT — BEYOND
Cott, Jonathan, comp. *Beyond the Looking Glass: Extraordinary Works of Fairy Tale and Fantasy.* New York: The Stonehill Publishing Co., 1973. 519p.

COURLANDER — FOURTH
Courlander, Harold. *The Fourth World of the Hopis.* Decorations by Enrico Arno. New York: Crown Publishers, Inc., 1971. 239p.

CURTIN — MYTHS
Curtin, Jeremiah. *Myths and Folk-Tales of the Russians, Western Slavs, and Magyars.* New York: Benjamin Blom, Inc., 1890; rpt. New York: Arno Press, Inc., 1971. 555p.

DARRELL — ONCE
Darrell, Margery, ed. *Once Upon a Time: The Fairy-Tale World of Arthur Rackham.* New York: The Viking Press, 1972. 296p.

DE BOSSCHERE — CHRISTMAS
DeBosschere, Jean. *Christmas Tales of Flanders.* Illus. by Jean DeBosschere. New York: Dodd, Mead, 1917; rpt. New York: Dover Publications, 1972. 145p.

DE ROIN — JATAKA
DeRoin, Nancy, ed. *Jataka Tales.* Illus. by Ellen Lanyon. Boston: Houghton Mifflin Co., 1975. 82p.

DOLCH — ANIMAL
Dolch, Marguerite P. *Animal Stories from Africa.* Illus. by Lee J. Morton. Champaign, Ill.: Garrard Publishing Co., 1975. 168p.

DUONG — BEYOND
Duong van Quyen. *Beyond the East Wind: Legends and Folktales of Vietnam.* Written by Jewell Reinhart Coburn. Thousand Oaks, Calif.: Burn, Hart and Company, Publishers, 1976. 96p.

FAIRY TALES
Fairy Tales from Many Lands. Illus. by Arthur Rackham. New York: The Viking Press, 1974. 121p.

FEHSE — THOUSAND
Fehse, Willi. *The Thousand and One Days.* Trans. by Anthea Bell. Illus. by Erich Holle. New York: Abelard-Schuman, 1971. 213p.

FICOWSKI — SISTER
Ficowski, Jerzy. *Sister of the Birds and Other Gypsy Tales.* Trans. by Lucia M. Borski. Illus. by Charles Mikolaycak. Nashville, Tenn.: Abingdon, 1976. n. pag.

GARDNER — DR.
Gardner, Richard A. *Dr. Gardner's Fairy Tales for Today's Children.* Illus. by Alfred Lowenheim. Englewood Cliffs, N.J.: Prentice-Hall, Inc., 1974. 96p.

GARDNER — DRAGON
Gardner, John C. *Dragon, Dragon, and Other Tales.* Illus. by Charles Shields. New York: Alfred A. Knopf, 1975. 75p.

GARDNER — GUDGEKIN
Gardner, John C. *Gudgekin, the Thistle Girl, and Other Tales.* Illus by Michael Sporn. New York: Alfred A. Knopf, 1976. 60p.

GARDNER — KING
Gardner, John C. *The King of the Hummingbirds and Other Tales.* Illus. by Michael Sporn. New York: Alfred A. Knopf, 1977. 58p.

GINSBURG — HOW
Ginsburg, Mirra, ed. and trans. *How Wilka Went to Sea and Other Tales from West of the Urals.* Illus. by Charles Mikolaycak. New York: Crown Publishers, Inc., 1975. 128p.

GINSBURG — LAZIES
Ginsburg, Mirra, ed. and trans. *The Lazies: Tales of the Peoples of Russia.* Illus. by Marian Parry. New York: Macmillan Publishing Co., Inc., 1973. 70p.

GINSBURG — ONE
Ginsburg, Mirra, ed. and trans. *One Trick Too Many: Fox Stories from Russia.* Illus. by Helen Siege. New York: The Dial Press, 1973. 40p.

GREAT CHILDREN'S
Great Children's Stories: The Classic Volland Edition. Illus. by Frederick Richardson. Northbrook, Ill.: Hubbard Press, 1972. 160p.

GREEN — CAVALCADE
Green, Roger Lancelyn. *A Cavalcade of Dragons.* Illus. by Krystyna Turska. New York: Henry Z. Walck, 1970. 256p.

GREENE — CLEVER
Greene, Ellin, comp. *Clever Crooks: A Concoction of Stories, Charms, Recipes and Riddles.* Illus. by Trina Schart Hyman. New York: Lothrop, Lee & Shepard Co., 1973. 154p.

GREENE — RAT. *See* HOUSMAN — RAT

GRIMM BROS. *See* CARLE — ERIC; SEGAL — JUNIPER (I), (II)

HARRIS — SEA MAGIC
Harris, Rosemary. *Sea Magic and Other Stories of Enchantment.* New York: Macmillan Publishing Co., 1974. 178p.

HARRISON — BOOK
Harrison, David L. *The Book of Giant Stories.* Illus. by Philippe Fix. New York: American Heritage Press, 1972. 44p.

HAUFF — BIG
Hauff, Wilhelm. *The Big Book of Stories by Hauff.* Illus. by Januez Grabianski. New York: Franklin Watts, Inc., 1971. 224p.

HAUTZIG — CASE
Hautzig, Esther, trans. *The Case Against the Wind, and Other Stories,* by I.L. Peretz. New York: Macmillan Publishing Co., 1975. 96p.

HAVILAND — FAIRY
Haviland, Virginia, ed. *The Fairy Tale Treasury.* Illus. by Raymond Briggs. New York: Coward, McCann & Geohegan, Inc., 1972. 191p.

HAVILAND — FAVORITE INDIA
Haviland, Virginia. *Favorite Fairy Tales Told in India.* Illus. by Blair Lent. Boston: Little, Brown & Co., 1973. 95p.

HAYES — HOW
Hayes, William D. *How the True Facts Started in Simpsonville and Other Tales of the West.* New York: Atheneum, 1972. 94p.

HEADY — SAFIRI
Heady, Eleanor B. *Safiri the Singer: East African Tales.* Illus. by Harold James. Chicago, Ill.: Follett Publishing Co., 1972. 96p.

HIGGINSON — TALES
Higginson, Thomas Wentworth. *Tales of the Enchanted Islands of the Atlantic.* Illus. by Albert Herter. New York: Macmillan Publishing Co., 1898; rpt. Greatneck, N.Y.: Core Collections, 1976. 259p.

HIGONNET-SCHNOPPER — TALES
Higgonnet-Schnopper, Janet, trans. *Tales from Atop a Russian Stove.* Illus. by Franz Altschuler. Chicago: Albert Whitman and Co., 1973. 160p.

HOKE — GHOSTS
Hoke, Helen, comp. *Ghosts and Ghastlies.* New York: Franklin Watts, Inc., 1976. 181p.

HOKE — MONSTERS
Hoke, Helen, comp. *Monsters, Monsters, Monsters.* Pictures by Charles Keeping. New York: Franklin Watts, Inc., 1974. 187p.

HOPKINS — WITCHING
Hopkins, Lee Bennett. *Witching Time: Mischievous Stories and Poems.* Illus. by Vera Rosenberry. Chicago: Albert Whitman, 1977. 128p.

HOUSMAN — RAT
Housman, Laurence. *The Rat-Catcher's Daughter.* Selected and with an afterword by Ellin Greene. Illus. by Julia Noonan. New York: Atheneum, 1974. 169p.

JAGENDORF — FOLK, SOUTH
Jagendorf, Moritz A. *Folk Stories of the South.* Illus. by Michael Parks. New York: The Vanguard Press, Inc., 1972. 355p.

JAGENDORF — NOODLE
Jagendorf, Moritz A. *Noodlehead Stories from Around the World.* Illus. by Shane Miller. New York: The Vanguard Press, Inc., 1957. 302p.

JONES — COYOTE
Jones, Hettie. *Coyote Tales.* Illus. by Louis Mofsie. New York: Holt, Rinehart and Winston, 1974. 51p.

JUNNE — FLOATING
Junne, I.K. *Floating Clouds, Floating Dreams: Favorite Asian Folktales.* Garden City, N.Y.: Doubleday & Co., Inc., 1974. 134p.

KINGSLEY — SESAME
Kingsley, Emily Perl, David Korr, and Jeffrey Moss. *The Sesame Street Book of Fairy Tales.* Illus. by Joseph Mathieu. New York: Random House, 1975. 41p.

KRYLOV — FABLES
Krylov, Ivan H. *Kriloff's Fables.* Trans. from the Russian by C. Fillingham Coxwell. Rpt. New York: E.P. Dutton & Co., 1970. 176p.

LAWRIE — MYTHS
Lawrie, Margaret, comp. and trans. *Myths and Legends of Torres Strait.* New York: Taplinger Publishing Co., 1970. 372p.

LEACH — WHISTLE
Leach, Maria. *Whistle in the Graveyard: Folktales to Chill Your Bones.* Illus. by Ken Rinciari. New York: The Viking Press, 1974. 128p.

LESTER — KNEE
Lester, Julius. *The Knee-High Man and Other Tales.* Illus. by Ralph Pinto. New York: The Dial Press, 1972. 32p.

LEVINE — FABLES
Levine, David, ed. *The Fables of Aesop.* Illus. by David Levine. Boston: Gambit, 1975. 103p.

LIFE — TREASURY
Life, Editors of. *The Life Treasury of American Folklore.* Illus. by James Luwicki. New York: Time Inc., 1961. 348p.

LITTLEDALE — STRANGE
Littledale, Freya, ed. *Strange Tales from Many Lands.* Illus. by Mila Lazarevich. Garden City, N.Y.: Doubleday & Co., Inc., 1975. 146p.

LYONS — TALES
Lyons, Grant. *Tales the People Tell in Mexico.* Illus. by Andrew Antal. Consulting ed. Doris K. Coburn. New York: Julian Messner, 1972. 94p.

McDOWELL — THIRD
McDowell, Robert E., and Edward Lavitt, eds. *Third World Voices for Children.* Illus. by Barbara Kahn Isaac. New York: The Third Press — Joseph Okpaku Publishing Co., Inc., 1971. 147p.

MacFARLANE — MOUTH
MacFarlane, Iris. *The Mouth of the Night: Gaelic Stories Retold.* Illus. by John Lawrence. New York: Macmillan Publishing Co., 1976. 147p.

McGARRY — GREAT
McGarry, Mary, comp. *Great Fairy Tales of Ireland.* Illus. by Richard Hook. New York: Avenel Books, 1973. 127p.

McHARGUE — IMPOSSIBLE
McHargue, Georgess. *The Impossible People: A History of Natural and Unnatural, of Beings Terrible and Wonderful.* Illus. by Frank Bozzo. New York: Holt, Rinehart and Winston, 1972. 170p.

MANLEY — SISTERS
Manley, Seon, and Gogo Lewis. *Sisters of Sorcery: Two Centuries of Witchcraft Stories by the Gentle Sex.* New York: Lothrop, Lee & Shepherd Co., Inc., 1976. 220p.

MANNING — CHOICE
Manning-Sanders, Ruth. *A Choice of Magic.* Illus. by Robin Jacques. New York: E.P. Dutton & Co., Inc., 1971. 319p.

MANNING — MONSTERS
Manning-Sanders, Ruth. *A Book of Monsters.* Illus. by Robin Jacques. New York: E.P. Dutton & Co., 1976. 128p.

MANNING — OGRES
Manning-Sanders, Ruth. *A Book of Ogres and Trolls.* Illus. by Robin Jacques. New York: E.P. Dutton & Co., Inc., 1973. 127p.

MANNING — SORCERERS
Manning-Sanders, Ruth. *A Book of Sorcerers and Spells.* Illus. by Robin Jacques. New York: E.P. Dutton & Co., Inc., 1974. 125p.

MANNING — TORTOISE
Manning-Sanders, Ruth. *Tortoise Tales.* Illus. by Donald Chaffin. New York: Thomas Nelson Inc., 1974. 95p.

MARTIN — RAVEN
Martin, Fran. *Raven-Who-Sets-Things Right: Indian Tales of the Northwest Coast.* Illus. by Dorothy McEntee. New York: Harper & Row, Publishers, Inc. 1975 90p.

MINARD — WOMENFOLK
Minard, Rosemary, ed. *Womenfolk and Fairy Tales.* Illus. by Suzanna Klein. Boston: Houghton Mifflin Co., 1975. 163p.

MOREL — FAIRY
Morel, Eve, ed. *Fairy Tales and Fables.* Illus. by Gyo Fujikawa. New York: Grosset & Dunlap, 1970. 124p.

NESBIT — COMPLETE. *See* BLAND — COMPLETE

NOVÁK — FAIRY
Novák, Miroslav. *Fairy Tales from Japan.* Illus. by Jaroslav Serych. New York: Hamlyn, 1970. 196p.

OLENIUS — GREAT
Olenius, Elsa. *Great Swedish Fairy Tales.* Illus. by John Bauer. Trans. by Holger Lundbergh. New York: Delacorte Press/Seymour Lawrence, c.1966, 1973. 239p.

OPIE — CLASSIC
Opie, Iona, and Peter, comps. *The Classic Fairy Tales.* London, New York: Oxford University Press, 1974. 255p.

ORCZY — OLD
Orczy, Emmuska, Baroness. *Old Hungarian Fairy Tales.* Illus. by Montague Barstow and Baroness Emmuska Orczy. New York: Dover Publications, Inc., 1969. 95p. paper.

PERRAULT — FAIRY
Perrault, Charles. *Perrault's Fairy Tales.* Trans. from the French by Sasha Moorsom. Illus. by Lande Crommelynck. Garden City, N.Y.: Doubleday & Co., 1972. 96p.

PICARD — TALES
Picard, Barbara Leonie. *Tales of Ancient Persia: Retold from the Shah-Nama of Firdausi.* New York: Henry Z. Walck, Inc., 1972. 270p.

PIPER — STORIES
Piper, Watty, ed. *Stories That Never Grow Old.* Illus. by George and Doris Hauman. New York: Platt and Munk Publishers, Inc., 1959. n. pag.

PROVENSEN — BOOK
Provensen, Alice, and Martin. *The Provensen Book of Fairy Tales.* New York: Random House, 1971. 140p.

PUGH — MORE
Pugh, Ellen. *More Tales from the Welsh Hills.* Illus. by Joan Sandin. New York: Dodd, Mead & Co., 1971. 125p.

RANSOME — OLD
Ransome, Arthur. *Old Peter's Russian Tales.* Illus. by Faith Jaques. London: Thomas Nelson and Sons, Ltd., c.1916, 1971. 243p.

RASKIN — GHOSTS
Raskin, Joseph, and Edith. *Ghosts and Witches Aplenty: More Tales Our Settlers Told.* Illus. by William Sauts Bock. New York: Lothrop, Lee & Shepard Co., 1973. 128p.

ROBERTS — GHOSTS
Roberts, Bruce. *Ghosts and Specters: Ten Supernatural Stories from the Deep South.* With photographs by Bruce Roberts. Garden City, N.Y.: Doubleday & Co., Inc., 1974. 95p.

ROBINSON — SINGING
Robinson, Adjai. *Singing Tales of Africa.* Illus. by Christine Price. New York: Charles Scribner's Sons, 1974. 80p.

ROCKWELL — THREE
Rockwell, Anne. *The Three Bears and Fifteen Other Stories.* Illus. by Anne Rockwell. New York: Thomas Y. Crowell, 1975. 117p.

ROY — SERPENT
Roy, Cal. *The Serpent and the Sun: Myths of the Mexican World.* Illus. by Cal Roy. New York: Farrar, Straus and Giroux, 1972. 119p.

RUGOFF — HARVEST
Rugoff, Milton Allan, ed. *A Harvest of World Folk Tales.* New York: Viking Press, 1949; rpt., ibid., 1968. 734p. paper.

SCHWARTZ — WHOPPERS
Schwartz, Alvin. *Whoppers: Tall Tales and Other Lies Collected from American Folklore.* Illus. by Glen Round. Philadelphia: J.B. Lippincott Co., 1975. 128p.

SEGAL — JUNIPER (I)
Segal, Lore, trans. *The Juniper Tree and Other Tales from Grimm.* Selected by Lore Segal and Maurice Sendak. Vol. I. Illus. by Maurice Sendak. New York: Farrar, Straus and Giroux, 1973. 168p.

SEGAL — JUNIPER (II)
Segal, Lore, trans. *The Juniper Tree and Other Tales from Grimm.* Selected by Lore Segal and Maurice Sendak. Vol. II. Illus. by Maurice Sendak. New York: Farrar, Straus and Giroux, 1973, pp. 169-332.

SEKOROVÁ — EUROPE
Sekorová, Dagmar, ed. *European Fairy Tales.* Illus. by Mirko Hanák. New York: Lothrop, Lee and Shepard Co., 1971. 176p.

SERWADDA — SONGS
Serwadda, W. Moses. *Songs and Stories from Uganda.* Transcribed and edited by Hewitt Pantaleoni. Illus. by Leo and Diane Dillon. New York: Thomas Y. Crowell Co., 1974. 80p.

SHAW — CAT
Shaw, Richard, comp. and ed. *The Cat Book.* Illus. by various artists. New York: Frederick Warne & Co., Inc., 1973. 48p.

SHAW — FROG
Shaw, Richard, comp. and ed. *The Frog Book.* Illus. by various artists. New York: Frederick Warne & Co., Inc., 1972. 48p.

SHAW — MOUSE
Shaw, Richard, comp. and ed. *The Mouse Book.* Illus. by various artists. New York: Frederick Warne & Co., 1975. 47p.

SHAW — OWL
Shaw, Richard, comp. and ed. *The Owl Book.* Illus. by various artists. New York: Frederick Warne & Co., 1970. 48p.

SHAW — WITCH
Shaw, Richard, ed. *Witch, Witch! Stories and Poems of Sorcery, Spells and Hocus-Pocus.* Illus. by Clinton Arrowood. New York: Frederick Warne & Co., 1975. 205p.

SHEEHAN — FOLK
Sheehan, Ethna. *Folk and Fairy Tales from Around the World.* Illus. by Mircea Vasiliu. New York: Dodd Mead & Co., 1970. 152p.

SHERLOCK — EARS
Sherlock, Philip Manderson, and Hilary Sherlock. *Ears and Tails and Common Sense: More Stories from the Caribbean.* Illus. by Aliki. New York: Thomas Y. Crowell Co., 1974. 125p.

SLEIGH — STIRABOUT
Sleigh, Barbara. *Stirabout Stories.* Illus. by Victor Ambrus. Indianapolis, Ind.: Bobbs-Merrill, 1971. 144p.

SPERRY — SCAND.
Sperry, Margaret, trans. *Scandinavian Stories.* Illus. by Jenny Williams. New York: Frederick Watts, Inc., c.1938, 1971. 288p.

SPICER — 13 DRAGONS
Spicer, Dorothy Gladys. *13 Dragons.* Illus. by Sofia. New York: Coward, McCann & Geoghegan, Inc., 1974. 159p.

SPICER — 13 RASCALS
Spicer, Dorothy Gladys. *13 Rascals.* Illus. by Sofia. New York: Coward, McCann & Geoghegan, Inc., 1971. 128p.

STORIES FROM WORLD
Stories from Around the World. Ed. and Introd. by Marguerite Henry. Illus. by Krystyna Stasiak. Northbrook, Ill.: Hubbard Press, 1974. 156p.

STUART — WITCH'S
Stuart, Forbes. *The Witch's Bridle and Other Occult Tales.* New York: E.P. Dutton & Co., Inc., 1974. 135p.

VOGEL — RAINBOW
Vogel, Ilsa-Margret. *The Rainbow Dress and other Tollush Tales.* New York: Harper & Row, Publishers, Inc., 1975. 48p.

WAHL — MUFFLETUMP
Wahl, Jan. *The Muffletump Storybook.* Illus. by Cyndy Szekeres. Chicago: Follett Publishing Co., 1975. 127p.

WHITNEY — IN
Whitney, Thomas P., trans. *In a Certain Kingdom: Twelve Russian Fairy Tales.* Illus. by Dieter Lange. New York: Macmillan Publishing Co., 1972. 136p.

WOJCIECHOWSKA — WINTER
Wojciechowska, Maia. *Winter Tales from Poland.* Illus. by Laszlo Kubinyi. Garden City, N.Y.: Doubleday & Co., Inc., 1973. 65p.

WOLKSTEIN — LAZY
Wolkstein, Diane. *Lazy Stories.* Illus. by James Marshall. New York: The Seabury Press, 1976. 39p.

WYNESS — LEGENDS
Wyness, Fenton. *Legends of North-East Scotland: Stories for the Young and Not So Young.* New York: Gramercy Publishing Co., 1970. 139p.

YOLEN — GIRL
Yolen, Jane. *The Girl Who Cried Flowers and Other Tales.* Illus. by David Palladini. New York: Thomas Y. Crowell Co., 1974. 56p.

A

A — hill (Wanted — a king)
Cott — *Beyond* p.239-241

AARDEMA, VERNA
Aardema — *Behind* p.85

ABBOTS AND ABBEYS
The convent free from care
The joyful abbot
Saint Cuthbert's peace
The thoughtless abbot
The wonders of Saint Berach

Abdallah the ungrateful
Fehse — *Thousand* p.15-23

Abdul Kasim the rich
Fehse — *Thousand* p.24-65

"ABOMINABLE SNOWMEN"
Big people
The mystery of Bigfoot

Abraham and the idols
Rugoff — *Harvest* p.550-551

Abraham Lincoln (1809-1865)
Corrigan — *Holiday* p.32-33

Abraham Lincoln, a mourning figure, walks
Anderson — *Haunting* p.40-48

Abrahams, Peter
Joseph the Zulu

ABSENCE
The long wait

ABUSE. See Cruelty

ABYSSINIA. See Africa — Ethiopia

ACCEPTANCE
The weaver of tomorrow

ACCIDENTS
The story of Little Boy Blue

ACCUMULATIVE STORIES. See Repetitive rhymes and stories

ACCUSATIONS
The obsession with clothes

ACTORS AND ACTRESSES
Patches

ADAM AND EVE (Biblical). See Creation

ADAMS, ABIGAIL
White House ghosts

Adba
Lawrie — *Myths* Pt. 1 — p.357;
Pt. 2 — p.358

ADRAMELECH
Workers of evil — and a few good spirits

ADVENTURE
The boy and the trolls, or
The adventure

An adventure of Digenes the Borderer
Green — *Cavalcade* p.58-60

An adventure with Evesgika
Carey — *Baba* p.103-108

The adventures of Billy MacDaniel
Manning — *Choice* p.191-199

The adventures of Little Peachling
Fairy Tales p.84-86
Junne — *Floating* p.66-67

The adventures of Renard
Rugoff — *Harvest* p.304-314

ADVICE
Good advice
Lesson for lesson
The lonely witch
Picking mountain pears
Three bits of advice

Advice from a caterpillar
Darrell — *Once* p.91-96

A-e-oina, the demon, and the tattle-tale
dog
Carpenter — *People* p.9-15

AES SIDHES. *See* Sidhe (Sidhean*)*

AESOP'S FABLES
The bear and the fox
The crab and his mother
The fox and the grapes
The frog and the ox
The frogs asking for a king
The gnat and the bull
The hound and the hare
The kid and the wolf
The kingdom of the lion
The lion, Jupiter, and the elephant
The mice in council
The miller, his son, and their
donkey
The north wind and the sun
The ox and the frog
The quack frog
The sun and the wind
The town mouse and the country
mouse

Aesop's fables
Darrell — *Once* p.235-247

Afanasjev, A.N.
The little golden fish

AFFECTION. *See* Friendship; Love

Afrãsib
Picard — *Tales* p.132-142

AFRICA
Burial of a titled man
The faery folk
The foolish lion and the silly rooster
Halfway people
How the Milky Way came to be
The Isinyandende
The legend of the elephant
Leopard hunt

Little people
The Lord helpeth man and beast
Lullaby
Marandenboni
My wish
No witchcraft for sale
Nyangara, the python
The old woman
People can't be made from iron
People of the sea
The seven monsters
Song of an unlucky man
Takise
Talk
The two wizards
Visit to the village
Wakaima and the clay man
When Noodlehead marries Noodle-
head
Why the spider has a small head
Workers of evil — and a few good
spirits
- *Algeria*
The frog's saddle horse
- *Angola*
Big people
, *Central*
Goat and lion and snake
Lizard who was always right
Rabbit and antelope
The tortoise
, *East*
The coucal's voice
The crocodile's cousin
The deceitful leopard
Dirty hands
The doctor's servant
Gathering salt
The giraffe's neck
The hunter's bargain
The jumper
King of the mice
Lion and hyena and rabbit
The monkey princes
The monkey's heart
Rabbit and big rat and lion
Rabbit and elephant
Rabbit and tortoise and lion
A safe home
Spots
The strong chameleon
Tortoise and elephant
True tears
Visitor

- *Ethiopia*
  Hare's ears
- *Ghana*
  Ayele and the flowers
- *Kenya*
  Big people
  "Leave it there!"
- *Nigeria*
  Breaking in a kola nut
  Hallabau's jealousy
  The stepchild and the fruit
    trees
  Why there is death in the world
  Wrestling in Iboland
, *North*
  Lion and jackal
- *Sierra Leone*
  "Mother-in-law, today is shake-
    head day!"
  Ojumiri and the giant
  Why the baboon has a shining
    seat
, *South*
  The bird that would not stay
    dead
  Elephant wants to be king
  The smart rabbit
- *Tribes*
  - *Ashanti*
    Talk
  - *Bantu*
    How the frog lost his tale
      (tail)
    Sebgugugu the glutton
  - *Bushmen*
    The trick on the trek
  - *Hottentot*
    How blue crane taught
      jackal to fly
  - *Pygmies*
    Little people
  - *Zulu*
    The house in the middle
      of the road
    Joseph the Zulu
    Little hen eagle
    Tusi and the great beast
    The winning of Kevelanga
- *Uganda*
  Akanyonyi
  Awo!
  Kaleeba
  Keenene
  Nnoonya Mwana Wange
  Nnyonyi

Nsangi
Purre Ce!
Ttimba
Tweriire
Wavvuuvuumira
Woowooto
- *Language, pronunciation of*
    Serwadda — *Songs* p.ix
, *West*
  The crocodile and the hen
  Dog and leopard
  Elephant and tortoise
  The foolish monkeys
  Hippopotamus and elephant
  The lion and the goat
  Lu-bo-bo
  The spider and the sky god's
    stories
  Why the bat flies at night
  The zebras who spoke the
    truth

Africa — folktales
  Rugoff — *Harvest* p.4-41

AFRITS (Arab. evil spirits)
  Workers of evil — and a few good
    spirits

Afternoon by a pond in the heart of
  Vermont
  Shaw — *Frog* p.30-31

Afterword
  Whitney — *In* p.131-136

AGARES (a devil)
  Workers of evil — and a few good
    spirits

Agburug
  Lawrie — *Myths* p.186-188

The aged lion
  Krylov — *Fables* p.108-109

**AGE. *See* Birthdays; Old Age; Time;
  Youth**

The ages of man
  Levine — *Fables* p.48

AGOGWE
  Little people

AGREEMENTS (Bargaining)
  See also **Devils**
  The devil's bridge

AGREEMENTS (Bargaining) *(continued)*

The hunter's bargain
The iron wolf
Ten miles at each step
The terrible stranger
The woman who flummoxed the
fairies

AGRICULTURE. *See* **Country Life;
Farmers; Ploughs and Ploughing**

Ah-Dunno Ben
Jagendorf — *Folk, South* p.216-218

Ahu ula: The first feather cloak
Alpers — *Legends* p.262-268

Aib
Lawrie — *Myths* p.288

AIKEN, JOAN
Aiken — *Necklace* p.95

AILBE, SAINT
The wolf mother of Saint Ailbe

Aili's quilt
Jagendorf — *Noodle* p.196-201

Ainu tales (Japanese)
Carpenter — *People* p.1-108

AIR
The small kingdom

AIRPLANES. *See* **Aviation**

AITUTAKI
Lament on losing a kite

Aiwali of Muri
Lawrie — *Myths* p.13-15

Akanyonyi
Serwadda — *Songs* p.53-59

ALABAMA
The battle of Bay Minette
Don't drop into my soup
The face in the courthouse window
False alarm
Fearless Emma
The first tale of Alabama
How far is it to Jacob Cooper's?
Railroad Bill

The smartest one in the woods
- *Name origin*
The first tale of Alabama

Aladdin
Manning — *Choice* p.108-127

ALARMS
False alarm

Alas for Theodosia
Life — *Treasury* p.169-171

ALASKA
See also **Aleutian Islands; Eskimos**
The raven brings light
Workers of evil — and a few good
spirits
- *Flag*
Benny's flag

ALCOHOLISM
, *Pretended*
The great fishbowl contest
The river-road ramble
The woman married to a
drunkard

ALDERMAN
The stone people and the alderman
The story of Tommy Tucker

ALE. *See* **Beer**

Alenoushka and her brother
Ransome — *Old* p.168-175

ALEUTIAN ISLANDS
- *Umnak Island*
The outside man

ALEXANDER, LLOYD
Alexander — *Foundling* p.88

ALEXANDER THE GREAT
The Lord helpeth man and beast

ALGERIA. *See* **Africa — Algeria**

Ali Baba
Stories from World p.10-29

Alice's adventures in Wonderland
Darrell — *Once* p.71-138

Alice's evidence
Darrell — *Once* p.133-138

All is well (The day boy and the night
girl)
Cott — *Beyond* p.462-463

All on a summer's day
Jagendorf — *Folk, South* p. 302-304

ALLEGIANCE. See Loyalty

Alleyne, Leonora
The frog

The alligator and the jackal
Haviland — *Favorite India* p.53-62

ALLIGATORS AND CROCODILES
Abdul Kasim the rich
The crocodile and the hen
Crocodile play
The crocodile's cousin
The doomed prince
The great goldfish contest
The little pig's way out
Lookit the little pig!
The monkey and the crocodile
Nobody sees a mockingbird on
Friday
Old Mister Smoothback
The pet crocodile
The river-road ramble
The three dooms
The trick on the trek

Allingham, William
The fairies
The leprechaun; or, Fairy shoe-
maker

The alms tale
Carrick — *Wise* n. pag.

Alone with God
Rugoff — *Harvest* p.575-576

ALONENESS. See Loneliness

ALPHORNS
The shepherd's choice

ALTARS
Negotium perambulans

Alyosha Popovich
Higonnet-Schnopper — *Tales* p.129-
140

Amagi
Lawrie — *Myths* p.199-200

Amapola and the butterfly
Belpré — *Once* p.29-33

AMAZON RIVER
Little people!

AMAZONS
The islands of the Amazons

AMBITION
Elephant wants to be king

AMERICA
See also names of countries and
states; **Eskimos; Indians of North
America; Tall Tales; United States**
I hear America singing!
- *Colonists*
The angel of Hadley
Black Sam and the haunted
treasure
The blacksmith of Brandywine
Drop Star
Evangeline
Father Marquette and the
manitou
Ichabod, Crook-jaw and the
witch
The monster of Leeds
The pirate woman
The pirates and the Palatines
Tom Quick, the Indian slayer
The white doe
The witch of Wellfleet
, *Discovery of*
Land! Land — sight!
- *Folklore and myths*
Life — *Treasury* p.78-109
Rugoff — *Harvest* p.43-91
Big John the conqueror
Davy Crockett: Sunrise in his
pocket
Dicey and Orpus
Jack and the varmints
Jack's hunting trips
John Henry and the machine in
West Virginia
The man and his boots
Old Gally Mander
Paul Bunyan's big griddle
Paul's cornstalk
The tar baby
Why women always take ad-
vantage of men

AMERICA (continued)
- *Maps*
  Map of myths of early
  America
- *Frontiersmen*
  See also names of frontiersmen
  Brady's Leap
  Corpse maker and Calamity's
  child
  Davy Crockett's boast
  How Daniel Boone met his
  wife
  Johnny Appleseed
  Mike Fink, last keelboatman
  The tragedy of Potts' Hill

AMERICAN INDIAN DAY
  Corrigan — *Holiday* p.176-186
  Thunderbird
  The war god's horse song —
  Navaho Indians

Amipuru
  Lawrie — *Myths* p.109

AMON (a devil)
  Workers of evil — and a few good
  spirits

Anansi and turtle and pigeon
  McDowell — *Third* p.72-74

"ANANSI" STORIES
  From tiger to Anansi; a Jamaican
  tale
  The grass-cutting races
  Lizard and a ring of gold
  Why the spider has a small head

The ancient curse
  Carter — *Enchanted* p.105-108

Andersen, Hans Christian
  The Emperor's new clothes
  Five in a pod
  Flying trunk
  The little match-girl
  The nightingale
  The real princess
  The swine-herd
  The tinder-box
  The ugly duckling

Andrusz who disliked beans
  Ficowski — *Sister* n. pag.

Anfy and his landlord
  Higonnet-Schnopper — *Tales* p.34-
  44

The angel
  Wojciechowska — *Winter* p.1-7
The angel of Hadley
  Life — *Treasury* p.105-107

ANGELS
  Bontcha the silent
  John O'Hara's lantern
  The princess's slippers
  The Tsar and the angel
  Workers of evil — and a few good
  spirits

ANGER
  See also **Temper**
  The eruption of Pele's anger

ANGIRAS
  Workers of evil — and a few good
  spirits

ANGOLA. *See* Africa — Angola

Aniello
  Manning — *Choice* p.95-107

Animal friendship
  Ginsburg — *One* p.29-30

ANIMAL RACES. *See* Races, Athletic

ANIMALS
  See also names of animals
  Alice's adventures in Wonderland
  The big bamboo boat race
  The dance of rubber baboon
  The going-home mix-up
  Halfway people
  The high-low jump
  The house in the forest
  How fire came to the earth
  How the animals obtained fire
  The legend of the elephant
  The little fisherman
  The Lord helpeth man and beast
  The rascal crow
  The river-road ramble
  Rumors
  The run of the forest
  Saint Blaise and his beasts
  The search for Little Water
  The story of Little Tsar Novishny,

the false sister, and the faithful
  beasts
The tricks of Hunahpú and
  Ixbalanqué
The turnip
Who lived in the skull?
- *Counting*
    The sly fox
, *Talking*
    The master cat; or Puss in
      boots

Animals and insects
    Schwartz — *Whoppers* p.71-81

Animals from heaven
    Carpenter — *People* p.16-23

ANNAM. See Vietnam

Anne Boleyn
    Leach — *Whistle* p.22-23
                      .
Anointing of a new-born child
    Alpers — *Legends* p.185

Anpu and Bata
    Rugoff — *Harvest* p.200-208

Answer to a child's question
    Corrigan — *Holiday* p.42

Ant
    Krylov — *Fables* p.123-125
    Levine — *Fables* p.68

The ant and the dung beetle
    Levine — *Fables* p.74

The ant and the grasshopper
    Morel — *Fairy* p.53

The antelope boy of Shongopovi
    Courlander — *Fourth* p.139-146

ANTELOPES
    Rabbit and antelope
    Sweet tooth
    Trickery

ANTILLES (Islands)
    See also names of islands
    Brer Rabbit's trickery
    Brother Annancy fools brother
      Fire
    Compae Rabbit's ride
    The goat and the tiger
    Greedy Mariani

How El Bizarrón fooled the devil
How the clever doctor tricked
  death
How the moonfish came to be
Juan Bobo
Malice, Bouki and Momplaisir
Man-crow
The miser who received his due
Rabbit's long ears
The shepherd and the princess
Snake the postman
The three fairies
The tortoise who flew to heaven
Wheeler
Why dog lost his voice
Why misery remains in the world

Antillia, the island of the seven cities
    Higginson — *Tales* p.143-167

ANTS
    The aunts

"ANYHOW STORIES"
    Wooden Tony; an anyhow story

The ape
    Krylov — *Fables* p.135-136

Apelles and the young ass
    Krylov — *Fables* p.80

APES. See Baboons; Gorillas; Monkeys

APHRODITE
    The cat and Aphrodite
    The ugly slave girl and Aphrodite

Apinini and Sidipuar
    Lawrie — *Myths* p.300

APOTHECARIES. See Pharmacists

An apparition
    Hoke — *Ghosts* p.157-165

The apple tree
    Hoke — *Ghosts* p.166-181

APPLE TREES
    See also **Apples**
    The dreamer
    The enchanted apple tree
    Khavroshechka
    The old witch
    , *Golden*
        The golden apple-tree and the
          nine peahens

APPLE TREES *(continued)*
, *Singing*
The singing tree

APPLES
The black bull of Norroway
The cat sat on the mat
The juniper tree
A red, ripe apple, a golden saucer
Snow-White and the seven dwarfs
The sporran full of gold
, *Diamond*
The serpent Tsarevich and
his two wives
- *Dumplings*
A pot of trouble
, *Golden*
East of the sun and West of
the moon
The firebird
The golden bird
Hercules: the eleventh task
, *Magic*
Prince Ahmed and the fairy
Peribanou
- *Pies*
There's some sky in this pie
, *Transparent*
The tale of the silver saucer
and the transparent apple

APPLESEED, JOHNNY
Johnny Appleseed

APPRECIATION. *See* **Gratitude**

APPRENTICES
The poor miller's boy and the
little cat
, *Sorcerer's*
Workers of evil — and a few
good spirits

April
Corrigan — *Holiday* p.87

APSARAS
Halfway people

Apukura's mourning for her son
Alpers — *Legends* p.171-182

ARABIA
Aladdin

The barber's tale of his sixth
brother
The cow and the thread
The first Kalandar's tale
Khusrau and the fisherman
The magic horse
The ruined man who became rich
again through a dream
Tale of the devout Israelite
- *Folk tales*
Rugoff — *Harvest* p.131-164

ARBITRATION. *See* **Judges and Justice**

ARBOR DAY
Corrigan — *Holiday* p.78-84
Come out and look!
Tommy

ARCHANGELS. *See* **Angels**

The archer and the king
Rugoff — *Harvest* p.671-672

ARCHERY
See also **Arrows**
Bukia
The fire-bird, the horse of power
and the Princess Vasilisia
The frog
Go I know not whither and fetch
I know not what
King Malcolm and the herd-boy
The magic egg
Metarawai
- *Bows*
Rama, the bow that could
not be bent
Turtles of gold and bitter
regrets

ARCHES
, *Magic*
Geinau and Jeiai

ARCTIC
See also **Alaska; Eskimos; North
Pole**
The ice dragon

ARGENTINA
The incubus

ARGONAUTS
Jason and the dragon of Colchis

ARGUMENTS. *See* **Persuasion; Quarreling**

ARISTOCRATS
Tahaki of the golden skin

ARITHMETIC. *See* **Mathematics**

ARIZONA
Eerie iron horse of the Arizona desert
Little head, big medicine

ARKANSAS
See also **Eureka, Arkansas**
The bull didn't have a chance
The Colonel teaches the judge a lesson in good manners
The daring of yellow doc
How red strawberries brought peace in the woods
In Arkansas stick to bears; don't mess with swampland skeeters
The judge and the baseball-pitching Indian chief
The lost treasure
The proud tale of David Dodd
The sad-lonely end of Wilhelmina Inn
Sam Hudson the Great
A tale of steep-stair town
- *Ozarks*
High winds and funny weather
Sam Hudson the Great
Snipe hunters
The talking turtle

The Arkansas traveler
Jagendorf — *Folk, South* p.29-33

ARMADILLOS
Big for me, little for you
Riddles one, two, three

ARMENIA
The Princess who learned to work
Saint Blaise and his beasts

ARMOR. *See* **Girdles (Armor); Shields and Shield-makers; Swords**

The army of the dead
Life — *Treasury* p.181-183

Arnason, Jón
The boy in the secret valley

Arnott, Kathleen
Unanana and the elephant

The arrival of the Tewas
Courlander — *Fourth* p.164-174

ARROGANCE. *See* **Pride**

ARROWS
The eagle wounded by an arrow
The frog
The frog princess

ARSON
The witch's wish

ARTHUR, KING
Galahad, the Holy Grail
The half-man
The history of Tom Thumb
King Arthur at Avalon
Merlin the enchanter
Sir Lancelot of the Lake
- *Death*
King Arthur at Avalon

ARTISTS
See also **Painters and Paintings; Portraits**
A Chinese fairy tale

As the tadpole said
Shaw — *Frog* p.48

Asbjornsen, Peter Christian, and Jorgen Engerbretsen Moe
The Christmas bear
East of the sun and West of the moon
The hen that saved the world
The husband who was to mind the house
The rooster that fell in the brew vat
The three billy-goats-gruff
The three sisters who were entrapped into a mountain
Why the bear's tail is so short
Widow Fox and her four sisters

ASH TREES
The can with a will of its own

ASHES
Cinderella

Ashes for sale
Lyons — *Tales* p.71-79

ASIA
See also names of countries
Little people
, *Central*
Ea and Eo

The ass and nightingale
Krylov — *Fables* p.151-152

The ass and the lapdog
Levine — *Fables* p.4

The ass and the load of salt
Levine — *Fables* p.40

The ass bearing an idol
Levine — *Fables* p.76

The ass carrying salt
Rugoff — *Harvest* p.419

The ass who passed for a lion
Levine — *Fables* p.74

The assault (Petsetilla's posy)
Cott — *Beyond* p.117-122

ASSES. See Donkeys

The asses complain to Zeus
Levine — *Fables* p.90

The ass's shadow
Rugoff — *Harvest* p.421

ASSYRIA
Workers of evil — and a few
good spirits

ASTAROTH
Workers of evil — and a few
good spirits

ASTROLOGY
The three Ivans
Turtles of gold and bitter regrets

The astronomer
Levine — *Fables* p.24

ASXATHAX (ghost)
The outside man

At the court of China. *See* **Turandot**

Ataraga at the pool
Alpers — *Legends* p.83-91

ATHENA
Heracles and Athena

ATHENIANS
The rich Athenian in distress

ATHLETES AND ATHLETICS
See also **Baseball; Races,
Athletic;** etc.
The flea and the athlete
The ice dragon
The ice dragon, or Do as you
are told
Three strong women

ATHRACTA, SAINT
The ballad of Saint Athracta's stags

ATIU
By whose command?
Canoe-launching song

ATLANTIS
The lost continent of Atlantis
The story of Atlantis

ATOLLS AND OUTLIERS
- *Kapingamarangi*
The Eitu who went as a
man's wife
The lobster and the flounder
- *Tikopia*
The women and the bats
- *Tokelau*
The basket of souls
How counting came to be
from one to ten

ATONEMENT. See Punishment

Aukam
Lawrie — *Myths* p.195

Aukam and Tiai
Lawrie — *Myths* p.24-27

The aunts
Roy — *Serpent* p.110-119

Aurora (The day boy and the night
girl)
Cott — *Beyond* p.425-426

AURORA BOREALIS
The ice dragon, or Do as you are
told

Ausi and Dubua
Lawrie — *Myths* p.234-235

Auslander, Joseph
Prayer for Thanksgiving

AUSTRALIA
See also **Torres Strait**
Nuinumma — Kwiten
Workers of evil — and a few
good spirits

AUSTRALOPITHECUS
Little people

AUSTRIA
Luck for fools
- *Tyrol*
The haunted room
Schnitzle, Schnotzle
The singing leaves

Author's note (Safiri the singer)
Heady — *Safiri* p.7-9

AUTUMN
October
The rainbow dress

AVAR TALES
The miller's sons

AVARICE. *See* **Greed**

AVIATION
The last of the dragons
- *Disappearances*
The horror of the heights
Awo!
Serwadda — *Songs* p.41-43

AXES
Boiled axe
The clever soldier and the stingy
woman

AXLES
The oxen and the axle

Ayaymama
Rugoff — *Harvest* p.603-607

Ayele and the flowers
Robinson — *Singing* p.44-49

Ayoga
Ginsburg — *Lazies* p.59-63

AZERBAIDZHAN TALES
Sheidulla

AZTEC TEPICTOTON
Little people

B

B — B — (Wanted — a king)
Cott — *Beyond* p.302-307

BAAL
Workers of evil — and a few good
spirits

Baba Yaga
Leach — *Whistle* p.86
Ransome — *Old* p. 58-70
Shaw — *Witch* p.158-168

Baba Yaga's geese
Carey — *Baba* p.92-95

Babaia and Sagewa
Lawrie — *Myths* p.238-240

BABIES
Blood Clot boy
The dragon tamers
Fiti au mua, who was born in
the sea
For the anointing of a new-born
child
Gaibida
The Island of the Nine Whirlpools
Saint Keneth of the gulls
The stolen bairn and the Sidh
- *Freaks*
The freak

BABOONS
The dance of rubber baboon
Dirty hands
Halfway people
The monkey princes
Why the baboon has a shining
seat

BABYLON
Daniel and the dragon of Babylon

BAD LUCK. *See* **Luck, Bad**

The badger and the fox
Novák — *Fairy* p.16-21

BADGERS
The crusty old badger
The fox and the badger
The mat-maker's adventure

Badi and the sabei
Lawrie — *Myths* p.275

BAEL (a devil)
Workers of evil — and a few
good spirits

BAGDAD
Abdul Kasim the rich
The Caliph turned stork
Semrude the Fair and the Cadi

BAGPIPES
Hans my hedgehog

BAGS. *See* **Sacks**

Bahhh!
Jagendorf — *Noodle*

Bai
Lawrie — *Myths* p.366-367

Bailey, Carolyn Sherwin
Li'l' Hannibal

The bailie's daughter
Rugoff — *Harvest* p.262-266

BAKERS
See also **Bread; Cakes;** etc.
Semrude the Fair and the Cadi
The theft of a smell
The woman who flummoxed the
fairies
The woodpecker

The baker's cat
Aiken — *Necklace* p.65-73

The baker's son and the king's
daughter
Spicer — *13 Rascals* p.90-100

BALAN (a devil)
Workers of evil — and a few
good spirits

BALANJI (musical instrument)
Ojumri and the giant

The bald knight
Rugoff — *Harvest* p.420

BALDNESS
Diogenes and the bald man
Don't marry two wives
Susui and Dengam
The traveller's shoes

Ball, Charles
Fifty years in chains

BALL GAMES
See also names of ball games
How the rabbit lost his eye

The ballad of Saint Athracta's stags
Brown — *Book* p.69-76

The ballad of Saint Felix
Brown — *Book* p.108-113

The ballad of Saint Giles and the deer
Brown — *Book* p.183-189

BALLADS
Get up and bar the door
Our goodman
, of *"Forty-niners"*
Sweet Betsy

BALLOONS
The last balloon

BALLS
The king's nose
The little red hairy man
The three kingdoms — the cop-
per, the silver, and the golden
, *Crystal*
The crystal ball
, *Golden*
The frog king, or Iron Henry
The frog prince
, *Iron*
Prince Monkey
, *Magic*
The magic ball
, *Silver*
Go I know not whither and
fetch I know not what

BALLS (Dancing). *See* **Dancers and
Dancing**

Balten and the wolf
De Bosschere — *Christmas* p.61-68

The bamboo cutter
Bagley — *Candle* p.26-33

BANANA TREES AND BANANAS
Ausi and Dubua
Burumnaskai
Dugama, maker of dugong magic
Wamin Ngurbum

BANDITS
See also individual names; **Outlaws**
Ashes for sale
Good advice
Hats to disappear with
, *Western*
Black Bart, bandit and "Po8"

BANNOCKS
The ship that sailed on sea and
land

BANSHEES
Earl Desmond and the banshee
Workers of evil — and a few
good spirits

The banyan deer
Haviland — *Favorite India*

BANYAN TREES
The oldest of the three

BAOBAB TREES
Marandenboni

Baptismal chant
Alpers — *Legends* p.186

BAPTISMS
See also **Christenings**
Hine and Tinirau
Little Lapp

The barber's tale of the sixth brother
Rugoff — *Harvest* p.140-144

BARDS. *See* **Minstrels**

Barefoot in bed
Jagendorf — *Noodle* p.43-44

BARGAINING. *See* **Agreements**

BARLEYCORN
Thumbelina

BARNUM, P. T.
Little people
People of the sea

The barracuda
McDowell — *Third* p.59-65

The barrel
Krylov — *Fables* p.95-96

The barrel bung
Olenius — *Great* p.29-37

BARRELS
Balten and the wolf
The rabbit and the barrel

Barrie, J.M.
Peter Pan in Kensington Gardens

Bartek the doctor
Wojciechowska — *Winter* p.8-21

BARTER. *See* **Agreements**

BASEBALL
John McGraw's jinx killer
The judge and the baseball-pitching
Indian chief

BASHKIR TALES
The clever Durmian

Basho
Haiku

The basilisk
Stories from World p.40-47

The basket of souls
Alpers — *Legends* p.308-310

BASKETS AND BASKET-WEAVERS
Foxglove
The girl in the basket
The three wishes
The treasure of Li-Po

BASS, SAM
Sam Bass, Texas Robin Hood

Bastianelo
Rugoff — *Harvest* p.540-542

The bat, the bramblebush, and the
gull
Levine — *Fables* p.10

Bata
Harris — *Sea Magic* p.59-80

BATHS AND BATHING
Ataraga at the pool
Diana and Actaeon
The goblins at the bath house
The story of Meidu

BATS
Why the bat flies at night
The women and the bats
- *Skins*
Forget-me-not

The bats of Ru-pe-shi-pe
Carpenter — *People* p.81-85

BATTERING RAMS
The wall and the battering ram

The battle of Bay Minette
Jagendorf — *Folk, South* p.19-22

The battle of the birds
Fairy Tales p.15-27

BATTLES
Cuchullin and Fardia
Goba
The Kiwai raiders
Naga
The white buffalo

BAUER, JOHN
Olenius — *Great* p.ix-x

Beale Street folks
Jagendorf — *Folk, South* p.260-265

BEAN, ROY
Only in Texas

BEANS
Andrusz who disliked beans
Brer Rabbit, businessman
Jack and the beanstalk
The origin of corn and beans

The bear among the bees
Krylov — *Fables* p.43-44

The bear and the fox
Darrell — *Once* p.242

BEARDS
Im
Mannikin Spanalong
People from the sky
- *Hairs*
The three golden hairs

BEARS
Animal friendship
The boy who was never afraid

The brown bear of the green glen
The cat who became head-
forester
Cesarino and the dragon
The children on the pillar
The Christmas bear
Daughter and stepdaughter
Foni and Fotia
Goldilocks and the three bears
"Good-by, dear little bear god"
The great bear of Orange
The hermit and the bear
Homolovi and the journey north-
ward
The lion, the bear, and the fox
The little house
The little pig's way out
Masha and the bear
Mike Hooter and the smart bears
in Mississippi
Mr. Rabbit and Mr. Bear
Not long after the earth was
made . . .
The old man and the bears
The ordeal of Hugh Glass
The peasant and the bear
The peasant, the bear, and the
fox
The right drumstick
Rose Red
Snow-white
The story of the three bears
The tailor, the bear, and the devil
The three bears
The travelers and the bear
What is trouble?
Why the bear sleeps all winter
Widow Fox and her four suitors
- *Tails*
Why the bear has a stumpy
tail
Why the bear is stumpy-
tailed
Why the bear's tail is so short
, *White*
East of the sun and West of
the moon

The bear's revenge
Spicer — *13 Rascals* p.82-89

Bearskin
Segal — *Juniper (II)* p.217-227

BEASTS. See Animals; Monsters; etc.

Beaumont, Madame de
  Beauty and the beast

The beautiful birch
  Ginsburg — *How* p. 45-51

BEAUTY
  Ayoga
  Cupid and Psyche
  The earth will have its own
  Forget-me-not
  Go I don't know where and bring
    back I don't know what
  Go I know not whither and fetch
    I know not what
  The peacock and the jackdaw
  The princess with freckles
  Punished pride
  Rabbit's long ears
  The rat catcher's daughter
  The reed maiden
  Ricky with the tuft
  The sleeping beauty
  The sleeping beauty in the wood
  The sunshade
  The three fairies
  Three golden oranges
  Turandot
  Vassilissa golden tress, bare-
    headed beauty

Beauty
  Bamberger — *My* p.98-102

BEAUTY AND THE BEAST (subject)
  Opie — *Classic* p.137-138

Beauty and the beast
  Opie — *Classic* p.139-150
  Provensen — *Book* p.33-48
  Sekorová — *Europe* p.121-135

Bechstein, Ludwig
  Beauty
  King Golden
  Oda and the snake

A bed for the night
  Aiken — *Necklace* p.74-83

BEDS
  Goldilocks and the three bears
  The three bears
  - *Mattresses*
    The real princess

BEECH TREES AND BEECHNUTS
  The magic box
  The three riddles
  Uletka and the white god

BEELZEBUB
  The master and his pupil
  Workers of evil — and a few
    good spirits

BEER
  The field of Boliauns
  The rooster that fell in the brew
    vat

BEES
  The bear among the bees
  The bear's revenge
  The eagle and the bee
  The fly and the bee
  Johnny and the three goats
  The thrush girl

The bees in the well
  Jagendorf — *Noodle* p.72-73

Beetle
  Sheehan — *Folk* p.51-60

BEETLES
  The brave beetle
  , *Dung*
    The eagle and the dung
    beetle

BEGGARS
  The fig-tree beggar, and the will-
    ful princess
  Fortune and the beggar
  How the beggars came to town
  The longest story in the world
  The man who couldn't get married
  Mons Tro
  The rich woman and the poor
    woman
  Robin Hood and the beggar

The beginning of it all (Wanted — a
    king)
  Cott — *Beyond* p.219-221

The beginning of maize
  Carter — *Enchanted* p.46-49

Beizan
  Lawrie — *Myths* p.321

BELGIUM
The last adventure of Thyl Ulen-
spiegel
- *Flanders*
Batten and the wolf
The boy who always said
the wrong thing
The convent free from care
Donkey and scholars
The dwarf and the blacksmith
The Emperor's parrot
The enchanted apple-tree
Farmer broom, farmer leaves,
and farmer iron
The frying-pan
The giant of the causeway
Hop-o'-my-thumb
The key-flower
The little blacksmith Verholen
Little Lodewyk and Annie the
witch
The mermaid
The ogre
Percy the wizard, nicknamed
Snail
The rich woman and the
poor woman
Simple John
The story of Seppy who
wished to manage his
own house
The story of the little half-
cock
The two chickens or the two
ears
The witches' cellar
The wonderful fish

Bell, Anthea, trans.
Beauty and the beast
Cinderella or The little glass
slipper
Little Red Riding Hood
Puss in Boots or The master cat
Sleeping Beauty
Snow White

BELLS
Catch-the-wind
Don't foul the well — you may
need its waters
Fools' bells ring in every town
The great bell of Bosham
, *Silver*
The silver bell

The silver bell of Chênière
Caminada

Belmont antics
Jagendorf — *Noodle* p.229-232

Belpré, Pura
The three magii

BELTING, NATALIE
Natalie Belting (subject)
Belting — *Whirlwind* n. pag.

Benét, Stephen Vincent
Abraham Lincoln (1809-1865)
Nancy Hanks

Bennett, Rowena
The Witch of Willowby Wood

Benno and the secret code
Sleigh — *Stirabout* p.122-123

Benny's flag
Corrigan — *Holiday* p.115-118

Benson, E.F.
Negotium perambulans

BEOWULF
The water monster

Beowulf and the dragon
Green — *Cavalcade* p.45-53

BERACH, SAINT
The wonders of Saint Berach

Berger, Josef
Ichabod, Crook-jaw and the witch

BERRIES
The fairy tree

BES (Egyptian dwarf god)
Little people

Beskow, Elsa
When Mother Troll took in the
king's washing

The best food
De Roin — *Jataka* p.8-9

The best laugh is the last laugh
Jagendorf — *Folk, South* p.234-
236

Beston, Henry
The lost half-hour

BETEL
The legend of the betel

BETRAYAL
See also **Deception; Traitors; Trickery**
Blodeuwed the betrayer
The fox and the goat
The incubus
The treacherous brothers

BETS. See Wagers

Beug and the sarap
Lawrie — *Myths* p.74-75

Beware
Hopkins — *Witching* p.15

The bewitched cat
Sperry — *Scand.* p.49-59

Bia
Lawrie — *Myths* p.49-52

BIBLE
See also names of Biblical characters
The meeting
The Tsar and the angel

Bierce, Ambrose
A jug of syrup
Moxon's master

The big bamboo boat race
Bagley — *Candle* p.120-128

Big Bird's story hour
Kingsley — *Sesame* p.5-41

BIG COLUGO (monster)
In the Avu observatory

Big for me, little for you
Sherlock — *Ears* p.37-51

"BIG HEADS"
Halfway people

Big John the conqueror
Rugoff — *Harvest* p.67-71

Big Mose, the bowery boy
Life — *Treasury* p.152-153

BIG PEOPLE
See also **Giants and Giantesses;**
names of big people, e.g.,
Amazons

McHargue — *Impossible* p.1-26

Big sixteen
Jagendorf — *Folk, South* p.247-249

BIGAMY
The man with three wives

"BIGFOOT"
The mystery of Bigfoot

Bigfoot Wallace and the hickory nuts
Life — *Treasury* p.210-214

Bila
Lawrie — *Myths* p.359-360

Bill is with me now
Leach — *Whistle* p.66-67

Billy Goat Gruff
Piper — *Stories* n. pag.

"BILLY THE KID"
The death of Billy the Kid

Bimini and the fountain of youth
Higginson — *Tales* p.220-227

BIRCH TREES
The beautiful birch

The bird that would not stay dead
Littledale — *Strange* p.83-89

The bird, the mouse, and the sausage
Ginsburg — *One* p.46-48

The bird witch
Bomans — *Wily* p.93-98

BIRDS
See also names of birds
Alice's adventures in Wonderland
Answer to a child's question
Ayaymama
The battle of the birds
The cat and the birds
Deumer
Father bird and the fledgelings
The four worlds
How fire came to the earth
King Solomon's ring
Kuaka
The monkey's Buddha
Paimi a Nawanawa
Peter Pan in Kensington Gardens

BIRDS (continued)

The rascal crow
Saint Francis of Assisi
The savage birds of Bald Mountain
The sharp gray sheep
Sister of the birds
The son of the king of the city of straw
Sui
The tortosie who flew to heaven
Tritl, Litil, and the birds
Wakai and Kuskus
Why the sea-slug has two mouths
, Artificial
    The nightingale
, Brown
    Bila
- Colors
    How the finch got her colors
, Dancing
    The garden of magic
, Dead
    The happy prince
- Feathers
    The sporran full of gold
, Fiery
    The crystal ball
, Golden
    The golden bird
    The man and the wife in the vinegar jug
, Green
    The green bird
    The killing pot
- "Honey-guides"
    The bird that would not stay dead
- Houses
    Gora and the buk
- Kings
    Ten miles at each step
    What came of picking flowers
, Magic
    Purr Ce!
-Nests
    The magpie's nest
, Nine-headed
    The nine-headed bird
- Songs
    The juniper tree
    Kaleeba
    Tweriire

, Useless
    The poorest man in the world
The birth and boyhood of Rustem
    Picard — Tales p.61-66
The birth of Simnel cake
    Greene — Clever p.130-133
The birth of the princess (Petsetilla's posy)
    Cott — Beyond p.43-47

BIRTHDAYS
See also Gifts
    Corrigan — Holiday p.156-158
How the beggars came to town
The patchwork quilt
Pippi celebrates her birthday
Uncle James or the Purple stranger
Who wants a birthday?
The witches' birthday party

BIRTHMARKS
Hallabau's jealousy
The psaltery that played by itself

BISHOPS
The three hermits

BITTERNESS
See also Unhappiness
The blind singer, Saint Hervé

BIU
Lawrie — Myths p.194-195

Bizhan and Manizha
    Picard — Tales p.203-223

Bjarni Sveinssen and his sister Salvör
    Rugoff — Harvest p.689-694

BLACK ANNIS (a hag)
Workers of evil — and a few good spirits

Black Bart, bandit and "Po8"
    Life — Treasury p.198-201

The Black brothers
    Cott — Beyond p.1-37

The black bull of Norroway
    Sekorová — Europe p.106-110

The black cat's eyes
    Leach — Whistle p.95-97

The black charger
Stories From World p.106-111

The black colonel
Wyness — Legends p.1-6

The black ghost dog
Jagendorf — Folk, South p.308-312

Black Sam and the haunted treasure
Life — Treasury p.95-99

The black sheep
Baum — Mother p.55-61

Blackbeard's treasure
Leach — Whistle p.45-46

Blackberries in February
MacFarlane — Mouth p.112-122

BLACKBIRDS
Coyote rescues the ring-girl
Sing a song o' sixpence
The story of Ait Kadal
Uletka and the white lizard
, White
The white blackbird: an
Easter story

Blackmail
De Roin — Jataka p.16-19

BLACKS
See also **Africa;** etc.
Ah-dunno Ben
Beale street folks
Big Sixteen
Black Sam and the haunted
treasure
Daddy Mention
De witch woman
Direy and Orpus
Fifty years in chains
Guess who!
John Henry
John Henry and the machine in
West Virginia
My people
Thank you M'am
- Children
Li'l' Hannibal
-Freedom
I have adream
- Heroes and heroines
Bras coupé

- Mulattoes
Yuisa and Pedro Mexias

The blacksmith of Brandywine
Life — Treasury p.84-86

BLACKSMITHS
Devil-may-care
Dewi and the devil
The dragon tamers
The dwarf and the blacksmith
Horns for a rabbit
The little blacksmith Verholen
Mimer, the master
Osborn, the smith
The sad victory
The smith, the weaver, the harper
The witch's bridle
The wolf's eyelashes
The young witch-horse

The blacksmith's tale
Carrick — Wise n. pag.

Blair, Lee
Beware

BLAISE, SAINT
Saint Blaise and his beasts

BLAME
Responsibility

Bland, Edith Nesbit
The fiery dragon

BLESSINGS
The ship that sailed on sea and
land

BLIND
The brown bear of the green glen
The deceived blind men
The destruction of Palatkwapi
Footless and blind champions
The footless and the blind
The hero
The old woman
The old woman and the physician
The purchased miracle
The seven blind brothers
Sister of the birds
Tahaki of the golden skin
Vesper

The blind man, the deaf man, and the
donkey
Haviland — Favorite India p.35-52

The blind singer, Saint Hervé
Brown — *Book* p.126-147

Block Island wreckers
Life — *Treasury* p.137-138

Blodeuwed the betrayer
Stuart — *Witch's* p.45-53

BLOOD
The origin of corn and beans

Blood Clot boy
Life — *Treasury* p.57-60

Blood stoppers
Life — *Treasury* p.271-273

"BLOODY BONES"
Workers of evil — and a few good
spirits

BLOWING
The six who went together
through the world

The Blue beard
Opie — *Classic* p.106-109

The blue falcon
MacFarlane — *Mouth* p.46-56

Blue Johnny and the pilot
Life — *Treasury* p.179

"BLUE MEN OF THE MINCH"
The people of the sea

BLUEBEARD
See also Bluebeard
Bluebeard (subject)
Opie — *Classic* p.103-105
Fitcher's feathered bird
Mr. Fox

Bluebeard
Perreault — *Fairy* p.13-19

BLUEBIRDS
The book of beasts

BLUFFING
Beetle
Jack and the varmints

Blunck
Little step-mother

BOARS. See Hogs

Boastful Aulus and the sly thief
Spicer — *13 Rascals* p.27-33

BOASTFULNESS. See Braggarts

A boasting chant in war
Alpers — *Legends* p.194

BOAT RACES
The big bamboo boat race

BOATMEN
A soccer game on Dung-ting Lake

BOATS
See also **Ships and Shipbuilding**
Peter Pan in Kensington Gardens
Smartness for sale
- *Sailing vessels*
The ship that sailed on sea
and land
, *Stone*
The witch in the stone boat

Bob o' the carn
Colwell — *Round* p.117-121

BODACH (Scottish spirit)
Workers of evil — and a few good
spirits

The boggart and the farmer
Colwell — *Round* p.57-60

BOGGARTS
Little people
Workers of evil — and a few good
spirits

BOGIES
Nuiumma-kwiten
Raw head and Bloody Bones
Workers of evil — and a few good
spirits

BOGLE-BO
Workers of evil — and a few good
spirits

BOGLES. See Ghosts

BOHEMIA
See also **Czechoslovakia**
The cunning cat
Dunber
Johnny and the witch-maidens

Boigu
Lawrie — *Myths* p.207-208

Boiled axe
Carey — *Baba* p.73-74

BOILERS
, *Rotary*
Snake Magee's rotary boiler

BOLES, CHARLES E. ("Black Bart")
Black Bart, bandit and "Po8"

BOLEYN, ANNE
Anne Boleyn

BONES
The dog and the bone
Teeny-Tiny
The teeny-tiny woman

BONNETS. See Hats

BONNEY, ANNE
The pirate women

BONNEY, WILLIAM H.
The death of Billy the Kid

Bontcha the silent
Hautzig — *Case* p.65-73

BOOBY ISLAND
- *Origin*
Pötikain and Ngiangu

The book
Manley — *Sisters* p.185-204

The book of beasts
Bland — *Complete* p.1-21

BOOKCASES
The book

BOOKS AND READING
Benno and the secret code
The foundling
The wizard of Long Sleddale
- *Collections*
The "spirited" librarian
, *Secret*
The master and his pupil

BOONE, DANIEL
How Daniel Boone met his wife

BOOTS. See Shoes — Boots

Boots
Schwartz — *Whoppers* p.56-59

BORDEN, LIZZIE
The legend of Lizzie Borden

BORIQUEN. See Puerto Rico

BORSKI, LUCIA M.
Lucia M. Borski (subject)
Ficowski — *Sister* n. pag.

BOSTON, MASSACHUSETTS
The lady in black of Boston harbor

Bottle Hill
Manning — *Choice* p.54-62

BOTTLES
Don Demonio's mother-in-law
The soldier with the wooden leg
Women
, *Magic*
Bottle Hill
, *Silver*
The fiery dragon

BOULDERS. See Rocks and Stones

Bowen, Elizabeth
The apple tree

BOWLS
Lisalill

BOWS AND ARROWS. See Archery

BOXES
See also **Caskets; Chests**
King Solomon and the Queen of
Sheba
The master thief and the dragon
The months
Raven's deed
- *Beechwood*
The magic box
- *Ebony*
The lost half-hour

The boy and his pa
Corrigan — *Holiday* p.122-130

The boy and the dragon
Green — *Cavalcade* p.11-15

The boy and the North Wind
Piper — *Stories* n. pag.

The boy and the snake
Krylov — *Fables* p.139

The boy and the trolls, or The adventure
Olenius — *Great* p.203-210

Boy Blue and the crab-catcher
McDowell — *Third* p.66-71

The boy in danger of drowning
Levine — *Fables* p.78

The boy in the secret valley
Littledale — *Strange* p.103-109

The boy who always said the wrong thing
De Bosschere — *Christmas* p.25-28

The boy who cried "Wolf"!
Piper — *Stories* n. pag.

The boy who wanted to learn to shudder
Bang — *Goblins* p.15-27

The boy who was never afraid
Olenius — *Great* p.141-152

The boy with the hand of fire
Carter — *Enchanted* p.24-26

BOYD, BELLE
The merry tale of Belle Boyd
The rebel belle

Boyislav, youngest of twelve
Curtin — *Myths* p.273-294

BOYS
See also titles beginning with Boy
The little boy who wanted pancakes
The little bull-calf
Momotaro, the peach boy
Momotaro, the peach sprite
The story of Little Boy Blue

BOZZO, FRANK
Frank Bozzo (subject)
McHargue — *Impossible* p.170

Bradbury, Ray
The foghorn

BRADY, SAM
Brady's leap

Brady's leap
Life — *Treasury* p.121-122

BRAGGARTS
Boastful Aulus and the sly thief
A boasting chant in war
Davy Crockett's boast
The girl in the basket
Seven with one blow
Three strong women
, *Reverse*
High winds and funny weather

BRAHMA AND BRAHMANS (Brahmins)
Devabhuti and the foolish magistrate
The false accusation
Harsh words
The lion makers
The loyal mongoose
The three fastidious men
The tiger, the Brahman, and the jackal
The wicked Sankhashurni

The Brahman and the pot of rice
Rugoff — *Harvest* p.450-451

Bran the blessed
Higginson — *Tales* p.32-38

BRANCHES. See Trees — Branches

BRANDAN, SAINT
The voyage of St. Brandan

BRANDENBERG, ALIKI
Aliki Brandenberg (subject)
Sherlock — *Ears* p.125

BRANWEN, QUEEN
Bran the blessed

Bras coupé
Life — *Treasury* p.180-181

The brave beetle
De Roin — *Jataka* p.12-13

The brave drummer boys
Life — *Treasury* p.163-164

The brave flute-player
Bechstein — *Rabbit* p.13-21

The brave men of Austwick
Jagendorf — *Noodle* p.119-121

BRAVERY. *See* **Courage**

BRAZIL
  Why the sea moans
  The Yara

BREAD
  The case against the wind
  Easy bread
  I ate the loaf
  The rabbit catcher
  The woodpecker
  , *and milk*
    The dragon tamers
  , *Griddle*
    Clever Oonagh

BREADTH
  Broad, Tall and Sharp-eyes

Breaking in a kola nut
  McDowell — *Third* p. 9-10

The breakup of Oraibi
  Courlander — *Fourth* p.194-200

A breath of air
  Leach — *Whistle* p.105

Brechannock of Monymusk
  Wyness — *Legends* p.16-20

BREEZES. *See* **Wind**

The Bremen town musicians
  Great Children's p.104-112
  Haviland — *Fairy* p.110-113
  Piper — *Stories* n. pag.

BRENDAN, SAINT
  St. Brendan's Isles of the Blest

Brennan, Joseph Payne
  The calamander chest
  Slime

Brentano
  Witzenspitzel

Brer Rabbit, businessman
  Rugoff — *Harvest* p.607-611

Brer Rabbit's trickery
  Carter — *Greedy* p.30-34

Brewery of eggshells
  Greene — *Clever* p.28-31

Briar Rose
  Darrell — *Once* p.51-54

BRIARS. *See* **Trees — Branches**

The bridal chamber of Silver Springs
  Jagendorf — *Folk, South* p.82-86

The bridal ghost dinner
  Jagendorf — *Folk, South* p.135-137

BRIDEGROOMS
  Bearskin
  Pinto Smalto
  Prince Bajaja
  What happened to a young man
    on his wedding day
  Yelena the wise

BRIDES
  The bailie's daughter
  Bastianelo
  The bridal ghost dinner
  Broad, Tall and Sharp-eyes
  The footless and the blind
  The forest bride
  The frog (by Leonora Alleyne)
  The frog princess
  The goblins giggle
  How Thor found his hammer
  Punished pride
  The river monster
  The three fairies
  The twelve huntsmen
  The witch's daughter
  - *Names*
    Silly Matt
  - *Replacements*
    Maui and Usuru

BRIDGES
  Crossing the bridge
  The devil's bridge
  The dreamer
  The frog
  , *Abacus*
    The goblins giggle

BRIDGET, SAINT
  Saint Bridget and the king's wolf

BRIGANDS. *See* **Bandits; Outlaws**

BRITISH COLUMBIA. *See* **Canada — British Columbia**

BRITISH ISLES. *See* **Great Britain;**
  names of individual countries

Broad, Tall and Sharp-eyes
  Sekorová — *Europe* p.153-163

BRONWEN, QUEEN. *See* **Branwen,**
  Queen

The brook
  Krylov — *Fables* p.86-88

Brooks, Gwendolyn
  Tommy

Broome, Dora
  The water-bull

Broomstick train
  Shaw — *Witch* p.51-57

BROTH. *See* **Soup**

Brother and sister
  Segal — *Juniper(I)* p.42-54

Brother Annancy fools brother Fire
  Carter — *Greedy* p.68-72

Brother Gaily
  Segal — *Juniper(I)* p.129-149

Brother Mike
  Colwell — *Round* p.68-69

Brother sun and sister moon
  Roy — *Serpent* p.101-109

BROTHERS
  See also **Sons; Twins**
  Anpu and Bata
  Aukam and Tiai
  Ausi and Dubua
  Babaia and Sagewa
  The barber's tale of the sixth
    brother
  Bata
  Boyislav, youngest of twelve
  Burumnaskai
  Cannibal
  Constantes and the dragon
  The cunning cat
  Dag and Daga, and the flying
    troll of Sky Mountain
  Deibui and Teikui
  Deumer
  Donkeys and camels
  The dragon of Macedon

Dugama, maker of dugong magic
Esben and the witch
The five-brothers Li
The forest bride
The four silly brothers
Ganomi and Palai
Gifts of love
The golden bird
Hallabau's jealousy
Hansel and Gretel
The Judas tree
Kiba
King Golden
The King of Scotland's sons
The King of the Golden River, or
  The Black brothers
Kos and Abob
"Leave it there!"
The legend of the betel
The little man in green
Little Master Misery
Lludd and Llewelys
Maiwasa
Malo
Markep and Sarkep
Mau and Matang
Maui and Usuru
The miller's sons
The months
The mouse-hole, and the under-
  ground kingdom
Mutuk
Nima and Poipoi
The ogre's breath
Picking mountain pears
The pig with gold bristles, the
  deer with golden horns, and
  the golden-maned steed with
  golden tail
Podepode and Ngukurpodepode
Prince Bajaja
Prince Monkey
Salt
Sammelkin
The sea maiden
Seven black crows
The seven blind brothers
The seven Simeons, full brothers
Sigai
Simeli Hill
The story of little Tsar Novishny,
  the false sister, and the faithful
  beasts
The story of the forty-first brother
The story of the wind

The story of three shepherds
Strong-man
Susui and Dengam
Syre-Varda
The table, the pack, and the bag
The tall tales
The three brothers
The three fastidious men
The three feathers
The three kingdoms
The treacherous brothers
The treasures of Rhampsinitus
Tritel, Litel, and the birds
The twelve brothers
The twelve months
The twelve wild ducks
The two princes
The two wizards
Ubir
The untamed shrew
Wad and Zigin
Waii and Sobai
Why the sea is salt
The wonderful-working steeds
The Zamay who hid his life

The brown bear of the green glen
  MacFarlane — *Mouth* p.102-111

"BROWN MAN OF THE MOORS"
  Workers of evil — and a few good
    spirits

Brown owl plans a party
  Sherlock — *Ears* p.1-9

Browne, Maggie
  Wanted — a king

BROWNE, MAGGIE
  Maggie Browne (subject)
    Cott — *Beyond* p.216

BROWNE, THOMAS, SIR
  People of the sea

BROWNIES
  Little people

BRUSHES
  The firebird

Bryant, Sara Cone
  The gingerbread boy
  The little red hen and the grain
    of wheat
  The sun and the wind

BRYCE CANYON
  The rocks of Bryce Canyon

BUCA
  Workers of evil — and a few good
    spirits

BUCCANEERS. See Pirates

Buck, Pearl S.
  The adventures of Little Peachling
  Hok Lee and the dwarfs

Budulinek
  Haviland — *Fairy* p.92-99

BUFFALO BILL. See Cody, Will

BUFFALOS
  Coyote rescues the ring-girl
  The white buffalo

BUGBEAR
  Workers of evil — and a few good
    spirits

BUGABOO
  Workers of evil — and a few good
    spirits

BUGS. See Insects; names of insects

"BUK". See Ghosts

BUKIA
  Lawrie — *Myths* p.224-225

The bull and the wild goats
  Levine — *Fables* p.72

The bull didn't have a chance
  Jagendorf — *Folk, South* p.42-43

BULLETS
  , *Silver*
    The silver bullet
    Ubir

BULLFINCHES
  Sister of the birds

BULLS
  Anpu and Bata
  Bata
  The black bull of Norroway
  The bull didn't have a chance
  The giant and the rabbit
  The gnat and the bull
  The knee-high man

BULLS *(continued)*
The lion and the bull
Monster copper forehead
Rake up!
Takise
- *Calves*
The little bull-calf

Bulwer-Lytton, Edward
The haunted and the haunters

BUM-CLOCKS. *See* **Beetles; Cockroaches**

BUMBLEBEES. *See* **Bees**

BUNS. *See* **Bread**

BUNYAN, PAUL
Paul Bunyan
Paul Bunyan's big griddle
Pecos Bill meets Paul Bunyan

Burg, Marie, trans.
Broad, Tall, and Sharp-eyes
The firebird
Prince Bajaja
Punished pride
The twelve months

BURGLARS AND BURGLARY. *See*
Thieves and thievery

BURGOMASTERS. *See* **Lawyers**

Burial of a titled man
McDowell — *Third* p.11-12

BURIALS
, *Sea*
Tonga's lament on burying
his daughter while at sea
The buried money
Rugoff — *Harvest* p.574-575

The buried moon
Pugh — *More* p.55-65

BURMA
The fisherman and the gatekeeper
The tall tales

BURR, THEODOSIA
Alas for Theodosia
The mystery of Theodosia Burr

BURROS. *See* **Donkeys**

Burum
Lawrie — *Myths* p.38-39
Burumnaskai
Lawrie — *Myths* p.34-36
Burun-Teges
Ginsburg — *How* p.117-128

BUSES
The cat sat on the mat

BUSH DEVILS
Wawa

BUSHES
The sparrow and the bush
, *Bramble*
The bat, the bramblebush
and the gull
The fir tree and the bramblebush

BUTCHERS
Robin Hood and the butcher

BUTTER
Come, butter, come
Peter's adventures
When Noodlehead marries
Noodlehead

Butter cookie (recipe)
Greene — *Clever* p.27

BUTTERCUPS
The prince of the flowery meadow

BUTTERFLIES
Amapola and the butterfly
The book of beasts
The giant who was afraid of butterflies
The nose of the Konakadet
The three butterflies
- *Collectors*
The ice dragon
- *Wings*
Gammelyn, the dressmaker

BUTTERMILK
Jack Buttermilk

BUZZARDS
Coyote drowns the world
Earth magician
The first war

The killing of Eetoi
The monster eagle

By whose command?
Alpers — *Legends* p.363

BYELORUSSIAN TALES
Easy bread

BYRARY (forest giant)
The clever Durmian

BYRD, EVELYN
Virginia's ghostly aristocrat

BYZANTIUM
An adventure of Digenes the
Borderer

C

Ca, ca, ca
Serwadda — *Songs* p.77-80

CABBAGES
The little girl and the hare
The princess who lived in a kailyard
Rabbit's bride

CACTI
People of the heron and the hummingbird

CAGES
The great fishbowl contest
The river-road ramble
The tiger, Brahman, and jackal

CAILLEACHES
Workers of evil — and a few good
spirits

CAKES
Ubir
The woman who flummoxed the
fairies
, *Rice*
The rice cake that rolled
away
, *Simnel*
The birth of Simnel cake
Simnel cake (recipe)
- *Tarts*
Alice's adventures in Wonder-
land

, *Vietnamese*
Hung Vuong and the earth
and sky caves

CALABASHES
The doctor's servant

The calamander chest
Hoke — *Ghosts* p.9-19

**"CALAMITY JANE". See Canary,
Martha Jane**

Calamity Jane, the loud canary
Life — *Treasury* p.222-225

CALDRONS. See Cauldrons

A calendar of Saint's days
Brown — *Book* p.226

CALIFORNIA
Black Bart, bandit and "Po8"
The evil eye
In the beginning there was no
earth
- *Avalon* (Island)
King Arthur at Avalon
- *Death Valley*
The hole in the back wall
- *Santa Clara Valley*
The mansion of the dead

The Caliph turned stork
Hauff — *Big* p.7-27

CALIPHS
Abdul Kasim the rich

Calvert, C.
Tokutaro

CAMBODIA
The fish with hooked noses

CAMELS
The dancing camel
Donkeys and camels
Man's first sight of the camel
The patchwork quilt
Saint Fronto's camels

CAMPHOR TREES
The magic listening cap

CANADA
The ghostly spools
Noodlehead Pat

38

CANADA *(continued)*
Workers of evil — and a few good
spirits
- *British Columbia*
Digger boy was hunting
clams . . .
A man sits in the ice . . .
Moon sits smoking his
pipe . . .
Not long after the earth was
made . . .
- *Holidays. See* **Dominion Day**
-*Nova Scotia*
The man on Morvan's road
- *Acadia*
Evangeline
- *Barrington Passage*
The ghost on Brass's Hill
- *Bear Point*
Grandpa — Joe's brother
- *Halifax*
Sunrise
- *Shelburne*
The sea captain at the
door

CANARY, MARTHA JANE
Calamity Jane, the loud canary

CANDLESTICKS
, *Iron*
Abdallah the ungrateful

The cane with a will of its own
Sperry — *Scand.* p.146-158

Cannibal
Martin — *Raven* p.45-51

CANNIBALS
See also **Amizemus**
Adba
Kaperkaper the cannibal
Rao's dirge for herself
- *Polynesia*
Alpers — *Legends* p.20-21

CANNINESS. *See* **Cleverness**

Canoe-launching song
Alpers — *Legends* p.362

CANOES
Mukeis
Naga
Rebes and Id

The saga of Kuiam
Sigai
Tagai
The unlucky fisherman
The Yara
, *Magic*
The legend of Rara

Can't rust
Leach — *Whistle* p.43-44

The canyon
Schwartz — *Whoppers* p.83-84

Cap o' rushes
Minard — *Womenfolk* p.77-82
Stuart — *Witch's* p.105-118

The cap that mother made
Corrigan — *Holiday* p.98-101

Capella, Francisco de Paula
The wish that came true

CAPS. *See* **Hats — Caps**

CAPTAINS, SEA
Bill is with me now
The cat and the Captain
The ghost of Captain Flint
Grandpa Joe's brother
The harp player of Pitcher's Point
Ichabod, Crook-jaw and the witch
The sea captain at the door

The captive Piper
McGarry — *Great* p.25-28

CAPUCHINS. *See* **Monkeys — Capuchins**

CARABAOS. *See* **Water Buffalo**

CARAVANS
Holding the truth

CARDS, PLAYING
The great golloping wolf
Little Lodewyk and Annie the
witch
- *King and queens*
Alice's adventures in Wonderland

CARE. *See* **Trouble**

CARIBBEAN SEA
Anansi and turtle and pigeon

The barracuda
Big for me, little for you
Boy Blue the crab-catcher
Brown owl plans a party
Ears and tails and common sense
Forty men I see, forty men I do
  not see
The grass-cutting races
Horns for a rabbit
How the moonfish came to be
Living in the forest
Lizard and a ring of gold
Madam crab loses her head
Makonaima returns
Riddles one, two, three
Workers of evil — and a few good
  spirits

CARNIVALS. *See* **Fairs**

Carol of the brown jug
  Corrigan — *Holiday* p.246

CARPATHIA RUTHENIA. *See* **Cossacks;**
  Russia

Carpenter, Frances
  The bird that would not stay dead

CARPENTER, FRANCES
  Frances Carpenter (subject)
    Carpenter — *People* p.108

CARPENTERS
  The three butterflies

CARPETBAGGERS
  The sad tale of the half-shaven
    head

CARPETS
  Go I know not whither and fetch
    I know not what
  The three feathers
  , *Magic*
    The patchwork quilt
    Sigurd the King's son

Carr, Rosemary
  Abraham Lincoln (1809-1865)
  Nancy Hanks

Carroll, Lewis
  Alice's adventures in Wonderland
  Jabberwocky

CARTER, DOROTHY SHARP
  Dorothy Sharp Carter (subject)
    Carter — *Greedy* p.133

CARTS
  The wild ride in the tilt cart

The case against the wind
  Hautzig — *Case* p.75-83

Casey Jones
  Life — *Treasury* p.262-263

CASKETS
  Snow-White (and variants)
  , *Ebony*
    King Solomon's ring

CASKS
  Two casks

CASTAWAYS
  Beug and the sarap
  Dugama

The Castillas at Oraibi
  Courlander — *Fourth* p.158-163

The castle in the silver wood
  Sheehan — *Folk* p.8-13

The castle of Ker Glas
  Harris — *Sea Magic* p.39-58

The castle of the active door
  Higginson — *Tales* p.39-47

CASTLES
  Aurora
  East of the sun and West of the
    moon
  The King of Cauliflower's castle
  The leprechaun of Carrigadhroid
  The little red hairy man
  The magpie with salt on her tail
  The maiden in the castle of rosy
    clouds
  Mons Tro
  Puss in boots
  The sea maiden
  , *Golden*
    The golden bird
  , *Spanish*
    Spectre of the Spanish castle
  , *Underground*
    The dancing princesses
    The twelve dancing princesses

Cat! (Eleanor Farjeon)
Shaw — *Cat* p.32-33

Cat (J.R.R. Tolkein)
Shaw — *Cat* p.26

The cat and Aphrodite
Levine — *Fables* p.28

Cat and mouse in partnership
Shaw — *Mouse* p.12-16

The cat and the birds
Levine — *Fables* p.6

The cat and the Captain
Stuart — *Witch's* p.9-15

The cat and the fiddle
Baum — *Mother* p.45-51

The cat and the mice
Levine — *Fables* p.54

The cat and the mouse
Great Children's p.147-152

The cat and the parrot
Haviland — *Favorite India* p.27-34

The cat and the she-fox
Higgonnet-Schnopper — *Tales*
p. 82-90

A cat for a cow
Sperry — *Scand.* p. 170-178

The cat heard the cat-bird
Shaw — *Cat* p.25

The cat sat on the mat
Aiken — *Necklace* p.21-34

The cat, the cork, and the fox
Bain — *Cossack* p.191-194

The cat who became head-forester
Ransome — *Old* p.71-80

Catalogue, by Rosalie Moore
Shaw — *Cat* p.13-14

CAT-BIRDS
The cat heard the cat-bird

Catch-the-wind
Carey — *Baba* p.27-32

CATERPILLARS
Alice's adventures in Wonderland
The princess's slippers
, *Hairless (monster)*
Negotium perambulans

**CATHEDRALS. See Churches and
Cathedrals**

CATHOLICISM
See also **Nuns; Priests;** etc.
The Castillas at Oraibi

CATS
The bewitched cat
Blackmail
The Bremen town musicians
The cunning cat
The Cyprian cat
Dick Whittington
The dragon tamers
The fiddling cat
Forty men I see, forty men I do
not see
The fox and the cat
Gigi and the magic ring
The history of Little Mook
Hurrah for cats!
The king o' the cats
The kitten
The kitten and the falling leaves
Lat takes a cat
Little cat and little hen
The little red hen
The master cat
The master cat or Puss in boots
Maud's story
The mice and the cat
The midnight voyage of the Sea-
gull
The monster in the mill
Ms. Cat and I
My cat Jeoffry
Not one more cat
Old Sultan
Old Tom comes home
The pig that went to court
The pike and the cat
The poor miller's boy and the
little cat
The protector of the mice
Puss in boots
Puss leaves home
Pussy-cat Mew
The ring with twelve screws

Squatter's rights
That cat
To a cat
Two cats of Kilkenny
The unwelcome cat
Wheeler
Why cats always wash themselves
  after eating
Why dogs hate cats
The widow and her daughters
The wolf and the cat
, *Black*
  The black cat's eyes
  The enchanted cat
  The lonely witch
  Maraboe and Morsegat
  Yukiko and the little black cat
, *Cheshire*
  Alice's adventures in Wonder-
    land
, *Demon*
  Schippeitaro
- *Giants*
  The baker's cat
- *Kitchens*
  The three little kittens who
    lost their mittens
, *Ship's*
  Moggie Mewling
, *Siberian*
  The seven Simeons and the
    trained Siberian cat
, *Tabby*
  The wandering monk and
    the tabby cat
, *Tortoiseshell*
  Knurremurre
, *White*
  The trail of the white cat

Cats
  Schwartz — *Whoppers* p.71-72

The cat's choice
  Shaw — *Cat* p.18

Cat's menu
  Shaw — *Cat* p.42

CATTLE. *See* Cows

A caucus-race and a long tale
  Darrell — *Once* p.81-85

Cauld, cauld, forever cauld
  Leach — *Whistle* p.53

CAULDRONS (pots*)*
  See also **Kettles; Teakettles**
  The Hodja and the caldron
  Taliessin of the radiant brow

Causley, Charles
  A local haunting

**CAVALIERS. *See* Knights and Knight-
  hood**

"CAVE-IN-ROCK" GANG
  The tragedy of Potts' Hill

CAVES (Caverns)
  Amapola and the butterfly
  The ballad of Saint Giles and the
    deer
  The deliverers of their country
  The dragon of Macedon
  The fish who helped Saint Gudwall
  Gabai
  The golden key
  The green children
  Hag-of-the-mist
  The island of the nine whirlpools
  Kind little Edmund
  The nine-headed bird
  Nsangi
  Peter Klaus
  The piper of Keil
  The weaver of tomorrow
  What came of picking flowers

Caves and the cockatrice. *See* Kind
  little Edmund

The Cegua
  Carter — *Enchanted* p.97-101

CEIBA TREES
  The legend of the Ceiba of Ponce
  The wagers

CELEBRATIONS
  See also **Feasts; Festivals**
  The treasure of Nosara

CELLARS
  The witches' cellar
  , *Wine*
    Hie over to England

CELTS
  The faery folk
  Usheen on the Island of Youth
  Workers of evil — and a few good
    spirits

CEMETERIES
See also **Burials**
An apparition
The ghost challenger
Invitation to a ghost
Mary Culhane and the dead man
Sunrise
Tain't so
The wonderful-working steeds

CENTAURS
The halfway people

CENTIPEDES
Texas centipede coffee

CENTRAL AMERICA
See also individual countries
Workers of evil — and a few good
    spirits

Cesarino and the dragon
Fairy Tales p.66-76

CEYLON
Little people
People of the sea

Ceylon sillies
Jagendorf — *Noodle* p.72-74

Chafetz, Henry
Thunderbird

CHAIN TALES. *See* **Repetitive Rhymes
    and Stories**

CHAINS
, *Golden*
Dunber

CHAIRS
Goldilocks and the three bears
The story of the three bears
Ten miles at each step
The three bears
, *Rocking*
The journey in the dark

CHAMELEONS
The strong chameleon

CHAMOIS
The lion, the chamois and the fox

CHAMPLAIN, SAMUEL D.
The guardians of the St. Lawrence

Chang, Isabelle C.
The Chinese red riding hoods

CHANGEABILITY
The man and the satyr

CHANGELINGS. See Foundlings

The changelings
Olenius — *Great* p.153-169

Chant for a new tooth
Alpers — *Legends* p.187

A chant of creation
Alpers — *Legends* p.76-77

Chant on the dying of an only child
Alpers — *Legends* p.195-196

Chant to dump a surfer
Alpers — *Legends* p.193

Chant to Io
Alpers — *Legends* p.364

**CHANTICLEERS. See Chickens —
    Roosters**

CHANTS
- *Chatham Islands*
    The offspring of the sky and
        earth
, *Polynesian*
    Anointing of a new-born child
    Baptismal chant
    A boasting chant in war
    Confirmation of a warrior
    Lament on losing a kite
    Onokura laments his old age
    Tonga's lament for his daugh-
        ter
    Two love songs
    A widow's funeral chant

The chapel on Cristo street
Belpré — *Once* p.60-63

Chapkin the scamp
Rugoff — *Harvest* p.167-171

A chapter of fish
Ransome — *Old* p.146-150

**CHARCOAL AND CHARCOAL
    MAKERS**
The match
The stone-cold heart
The wolf's eyelashes

CHARIOTS AND CHARIOTEERS
Hermes' chariot
The Judas tree
, *Gossamer*
Gudgekin, the thistle girl

CHARLEMAGNE, EMPEROR
The Emperor's parrot

CHARMS
Come, butter, come

CHATHAM ISLANDS
Apukura's mourning for her son
Hine and Tinirau
The offspring of the sky and
earth
- *Rekohu*
Manaii and the spears
Ugly-ugly! Frizzled-heads,
frizzled-heads!

CHATTEES
The valiant chattee-maker

Chaucer, Geoffrey
Lat take a cat

CHEATING
Chickens come home to roost
The merchant

CHEERFULNESS
See also **Laughter**
The jolly miller
Old King Cole

CHEESE
The farmer and the cheeses
The lazy farmer's tale
The wise man of Gotham

The cheese
Carrick — *Wise* n. pag.

CHEMISTS. *See* **Pharmacists**

CHEMOSIT (demon)
Workers of evil — and a few
good spirits

CHEROKEE ROSE
The legend of the Cherokee sweet
shrub
The song of the Cherokee rose

CHERRUVE (snake-people)
Halfway people

Cherry dumplings (recipe)
Greene — *Clever* p.39

CHESS
Edain the queen
How the Great Turisgale met his
death

The chest
Krylov — *Fables* p.48-49

Chesterton, G. K.
The dragon at hide-and-seek

The chestnut tree
Novák — *Fairy* p.61-65

CHESTS
See also **Boxes; Caskets**
Beauty and the beast
The calamander chest
The wife who talked too much

Chicken Licken
Great Children's p.81-91

CHICKENS
Aniello
Brer Rabbit, businessman
The cock and the mouse and the
little red hen
The cock, the mouse and the little
red hen
The crocodile and the hen
The hen that laid golden eggs
The hen that saved the world
Henny-Penny
How Matt Carney retired and
raised chickens
Little cat and little hen
The little red hen
The little red hen and the
grain of wheat
Little Tuppens
A new way to boil eggs
Repaying good with evil
Song of a hen
The three sisters who were en-
trapped into a mountain
The time lightning struck little
Ida's umbrella
The two chickens or the two ears
The white hen

CHICKENS (continued)

- *Roosters*
  See *also* titles beginning
  with word Cock
  Beetle
  The cat, the cock, and the
  fox
  The cockerel-stone
  The foolish lion and the silly
  rooster
  The fox, the rabbit and the
  rooster
  The golden cock
  The golden cockerell
  The half-chick
  The hen that saved the world
  The lion, Jupiter, and the
  elephant
  The monster in the mill
  The rooster and the bean
  The rooster that fell in the
  brew vat
  The rooster who couldn't
  crow
  The story of the little half-
  cock
  Two roosters and the eagle
  The voices at the window
- *Horns*
  The cock and the dragon

Chickens come home to roost
  Jagendorf — *Folk, South* p.213-
  215

CHILDE OF LAMBTON
  The Lambton worm

CHILDLESSNESS
  The juniper tree
  Momotaro, the peach sprite
  (and variants)
  Rapunzel
  Tokutaro

CHILDREN
  See *also* **Babies; Boys; Girls;
  Twins**
  The basilisk
  Burumnaskai
  Monster copper forehead
  Nnoonya Mwana Wange
  The Pied Piper of Hamelin
  Stan Bolovan
  Stan Bolovan and the dragon

Tortoise and the children
Ugly-ugly! Frizzled-heads, frizzled-
  heads!
The ungrateful children and the
  old father who went to school
  again
, *Abandoned*
  Little Poucet
, *Good-luck*
  The devil and his three
  golden hairs
, *Green*
  The green children
, *Naughty*
  Maraboe and Morsegat
  The princess and the three
  tasks
The children on the pillar
  Manning — *Ogres* p.44-52

CHILDREN'S LITERATURE
  The book of beasts
  The elves in the shelves

CHILE
  The good nab and the kind mouse
  Halfway people

CHIMNEY SWEEPS
  The last piece of light
  Moon snow

CHIMNEYS
  A tale of steep-stair town

CHIMPANZEES. See Monkeys

CHINA
  See *also* titles beginning with
  word Chinese
  Big people
  The cinnamon tree in the moon
  The cock and the dragon
  Dragon thieves of Peking
  False dragon wife
  The five brothers Li
  The fox's daughter
  The golden-horned dragon
  Halway people
  Hok Lee and the dwarfs
  The inn that wasn't there
  Like master, like servant
  The maid in the mirror
  The mystery maiden from heaven
  The nightingale

Painted skin
Planting a pear tree
Retribution
The sad victory
The sorcerer of the White Lotus
  lodge
A Taoist priest
The thunder god
The treasure of Li-Po
White orchid, red mountain
Women
Workers of evil — and a few good
  spirits
- *Folk tales*
  Folk tales (subject)
    Rugoff — *Harvest* p.179-
    196
- *Peking*
  Turandot
- *Wall* (Peking)
  Dragon thieves of Peking

CHINA SEA
The dragon and the monkey

The Chinese dragon
  Green — *Cavalcade* p.161-164

A Chinese fairy tale
  Housman — *Rat* p.130-142

The Chinese red riding hoods
  Minard — *Womenfolk* p.14-19

CHIREÑOS (Indians of Chira)
The treasure of Nosara

CHIRON
Halfway people

CHIVALRY
See also **Knights and Knighthood**
The princess and the three tasks

Chocolate butter icing (recipe)
  Greene — *Clever* p.88

Chocolate potato cake (recipe)
  Greene — *Clever* p.87

CHOROTEGAS
The treasure of Nosara

The christening in the village
  Ransome — *Old* p.230-245

CHRISTENINGS
Godfather to skunks
The sleeping beauty
- *Gifts*
  Mons Tro

CHRISTIANS
Ballad of Saint Giles and the deer
Big people
The faery folk
Saint Prisca, the child martyr
Workers of evil — and a few good
  spirits

CHRISTMAS
Christmas (subject)
  Corrigan — *Holiday* p.232-253
Carol of the brown king
The cloak of friendship
The daring of yellow doc
The elves and the shoemaker
The fir tree
George Washington, the torch-
  bearer
The ghost wedding in Everhope
Little Bun Rabbit
The magic mill
The mummer's play
Now every child
The rich woman and the poor
  woman
Schnitzle, Schotzle, and
  Schnootzle
The three Magi
Through the fire
The trolls and the youngest Tomte
The warlock
Watch
What Jack Horner did
Why the sea is salt

The Christmas bear
  Sperry — *Scand.* p.29-37

A Christmas carol, by Charles Dickens
  Darrell — *Once* p.171-234

The Christmas gift
  Vogel — *Rainbow* p.33-48

A Christmas wish
  Corrigan — *Holiday* p.253

CHULLACHAQUI (forest evil spirit)
Ayaymama

Chunky's fight with the panters
Schwartz — *Whoppers* p.66-70

CHURCHES AND CATHEDRALS
The ancient curse
Belmont antics
Fair, brown, and trembling
The ghost who wasn't a ghost
Halfway people
Not on the Lord's Day
People of the sea
The ways of the Lord
The witch's wish
Worker's of evil — and a few good
spirits
- *Building*
How the devil constructed a
church
- *Congregations*
The parishioner

CHURCHYARDS. See Cemeteries

CHURNS
Come, butter, come

CHUVASH TALES
How three mighty heroes saved
the sun and the moon from the
dragon

Ciardi, John
The cat heard the cat-bird

Cinderella
Bamberger — *My* p.119-127
Haviland — *Fairy* p.138-145
Morel — *Fairy* p.28-31
Sheehan — *Folk* p.84-92

Cinderella, or The little glass slipper
Perrault — *Fairy* p.33-41
Sekorová — *Europe* p.13-19

"CINDERELLAS"
Cinderella (subject)
Opie — *Classic* p.117-121
Cinderelma
Diem and Siem!
Fair, brown, and trembling
The golden shoe
The golden slipper
Gudgekin, the thistle girl
The little scarred one

Cinderelma
Gardner — *Dr.* p.74-96

Rugoff — *Harvest* p.337-342

Cinderilla: or, The little glass slipper
Opie — *Classic* p.122-127

The cinnamon tree in the moon
Rugoff — *Harvest* p.193-195

CIRCLES
Ten miles at each step

The cistern of San Cristóbal
Belpré — *Once* p.64-65

The city mouse and the garden
Shaw — *Mouse* p.9

**CIVIL WAR. See United States —
History — Civil War**

CLAMS
Digger boy was hunting clams . . .

CLAWS
Linda-Gold and the old king

CLAY
Pemtalina
Wakaima and the clay man

Clayton, Ed
The prize is won

Cledog and the "Ceffyl-dwr"
Pugh — *More* p.115-121

CLEMENS, SAMUEL
Corpse maker and Calamity's
child

CLERGYMEN
The curse of Lorenzo Dow
Ivan the fool and St. Peter's fife
The magical spectacles
The meeting
Nas-ed-Din Hodja in the pulpit
Old Hildebrand
The proud pastor
, *Itinerant*
Lorenzo Dow raises the devil

The clever Durmian (A Bashkir tale)
Ginsburg — *How* p.91-99

Clever Grethel
Greene — *Clever* p.109-114
Minard — *Womenfolk* p.71-76

Clever Manka
Minard — *Womenfolk* p.146-155

Clever Oonagh
Greene — *Clever* p.41-54

The clever soldier and the stingy
woman
Higonnet-Schnopper — *Tales* p.45-48

The clever thief
Ginsburg — *Lazies* p.28-32

CLEVERNESS
See also **"Anansi" stories;
Trickery**
Anfy and his landlord
The boggart and the farmer
Boiled axe (and variants)
The cunning cat
The devil's bridge
The dragon and the monkey
The dragon and the peasant
The farmer and the devil
Farmer Broom, Farmer Leaves,
and Farmer Iron
The fox and the crow
The fox and the lion
The frog's saddle horse
From tiger to Anansi; a Jamaican
tale
The giant and the rabbit
Greedy and Speedy
Hansel and Gretel (and variants)
How El Bizarrón fooled the devil
How the clever doctor tricked
death
Hudden and Dudden and Donald
O'Neary
Hungry-for-battle
If you don't like it, don't listen
Jack Buttermilk
John O'Hara's lantern
The joyful abbot
The jumper
The lady and the unjust judge
A legend of Knockmany
A little peace of mind
The little pig's way out
Little Poucet
The little shepherd boy
The master cat
Molly Whuppie
The monkey's heart
Nail broth (and variants)

Nail stew
The old dog
The old man, the wolf, and the
vixen
Old Sultan
The princesses who lived in a
kailyard
The proud pastor
Puss in boots
Semrude the Fair and the Cadi
A shrewd woman
The smartest one in the woods
The soldier's fur coat
Stalo and Kauras
The strong chameleon
The thoughtless abbot
The three little pigs
The three rascals and the magic
cap
The three sisters who were en-
trapped into a mountain
The tiger and the cow
The tiger and the hare
The tinder box
Tortoise and elephant
The treasures of Rhampsinitus
Trickery
Vassilissa the cunning and the
Tsar of the sea
Visitor
The vixen and her cub
What happened to Hadji
The wise rogue
A witty answer
Witzenspitzel
The woman who flummoxed the
fairies

CLIFFORD, LUCY LANE
Lucy Lane Clifford (subject)
Cott — *Beyond* p.148

CLIMBING
The wagers

CLIPPING
The wizard's revenge

The cloak of friendship
Housman — *Rat* p.86-99

CLOAKS. See Clothes — Coats

The clock that walked by itself (Luck
or wisdom)
Perry — *Scand.* p.200-211

CLOCKS
See also **Watches**
Hickory, Dickory, Dock
The king who did not want to die
Wooden Tony; an Anyhow story

CLOG-MAKERS. *See* **Shoemakers**

CLOTH
See also **Linen**
The invisible cloth
The rich woman and the poor
    woman
The white crane

The cloth of a thousand feathers
    Bang — *Men* p.47-53

CLOTHES
The dwarf and the blacksmith
The Emperor's new clothes
The Hadja visits Halil
The North wind and the sun
The obsession with clothes
- *Capes*
    The magician's cape
- *Coats*
    The cloak of friendship
    The kitchen pooka
    The magician's cloak
    The North wind and the sun
    The stolen bairn and the Sidh
    The sun and the wind
    Trishka's coat
    , *Feather*
        Ahu ula: The first feather
            cloak
    , *Fur*
        Many-Fur
        The soldier's fur coat
- *Goose down*
        Turtles of gold and bitter
            regrets
- *Dresses*
    Gammelyn, the dressmaker
    The rainbow dress
    , *Lavender*
        The girl in the lavender
            dress
- *Jackets*
    Belmont antics
    , *King's*
        The Emperor's new clothes
- *Shirts*
    Kibbe's shirt

The three shirts of Cannach
    Colton
The wonderful shirt
- *Slippers*
    Cinderella (and variants)
- *Underwear*
    Uncle Davy Lane loses his
        underwear

The cloud
    Krylov — *Fables* p.111

The cloud tree
    Bomans — *Wiley* p.51-56

CLOUDS
Deibui and Teikui
Ialbuz
The maiden in the Castle of rose
    clouds
The mother of the sun

CLOWNS
See also **Trickery**
The jester who learned to cry

CLUBS. *See* **Sticks**

CLURICAUNES
The field of Boliauns

COACHES AND COACHMEN
Room for one more

Coat o' clay
    Rugoff — *Harvest* p.227-231

Coatsworth, Elizabeth
    Give my love to Boston
    The mouse

COBBLERS. *See* **Shoemakers**

COBWEBS. *See* **Spiders — Webs**

The cock and the dragon
    Green — *Cavalcade* p.157-160

The cock and the mouse and the little
    red hen
    Rockwell — *Three* p.17-32

The cock and the pearl
    Krylov — *Fables* p.66

The cock, the mouse and the little
    red hen
    Great Children's p.92-103

COCKATRICES
Kind little Edmund, or The Caves and the cockatrice

The cockerel-stone
Bamberger — *My* p.168-171

The cockleshell
Harris — *Sea Magic* p.135-142

COCKROACHES
The doctor's servant

COCKS. See Chickens — Roosters

Coconut kisses (recipe)
Greene — *Clever* p.100

COCONUTS AND COCONUT TREES
Gedor of Leiwag
Hina and the eel
Iaalbuz
Maui and Tuna
Mibu and the coconut
- *Spirits*
Girbar

CODES
, *Secret*
Benno and the secret code

COFFEE
Texas centipede coffee

COFFINS
The brave flute-player
The wandering monk and the tabby cat

COINS
Blackmail
Gohei and the god of poverty

COLD
Cauld, cauld, forever cauld
Frost
The outside man

The cold
Schwartz — *Whoppers* p.90-92

Coleridge, Samuel Taylor
Answer to a child's question

COLLEN, SAINT
The faery folk

The Colonel teaches the judge a lesson in good manners
Jagendorf — *Folk, South* p.59-61

COLONELS
The Arkansas traveler

COLORADO
- *Leadville*
Fur-bearing trout

COLORS
See also **Birds — Colors**
Red, in Polynesia
Alpers — *Legends* p.16-18

Colum, Padraic
The white blackbird: an Easter story

COLUMBIA RIVER
The mystery of Bigfoot
- *Valley*
The day the devil tried to be good

COLUMBUS, CHRISTOPHER
The great discovery
Land! Land in sight!

COMBS
The firebird
Pentalina
The water-nixie

Come and laugh with Bobby Gum
Jagendorf — *Folk, South* p.240-244

Come, butter, come
Greene — *Clever* p.26

Come out and look!
Corrigan — *Holiday* p.80-83

COMGALL, SAINT
Saint Comgall and the mice

COMICS. See Clowns; Fools and Foolishness

The coming of the Hopis
Courlander — *Fourth* p.9-13

The coming of Tute
Alpers — *Legends* p.353-356

Compae Rabbit's ride
  Carter — *Greedy* p.41-45

COMPANIONS. *See* **Friendship**

The company you keep
  De Roin — *Jataka* p.45-47

COMPASSION. *See* **Mercy**

COMPLAINING. *See* **Grumbling**

CONCEIT. *See* **Pride**

CONFEDERATES
  The lady in black of Boston harbor

Confirmation of a warrior
  Alpers — *Legends* p.190

The conflict of the gods
  Alpers — *Legends* p.64-67

CONFUSION
  The flower of happiness on Sunnymount Crest

CONJURERS. *See* **Magicians;**
  Witches; Wizards

CONNECTICUT
  - *New Haven*
      The witch who spoke in
      many tongues
  - *Wethersfield*
      Voices in the night

Conrad and the dragon
  Green — *Cavalcade* p.213-245

The consequence
  Alpers — *Legends* p.285-288

CONSTANCY. *See* **Loyalty**

Constantes and the dragon
  Manning — *Choice* p.235-245

CONSTELLATIONS
  See also **Moon; Stars; Sun;** etc.
  Beizam
  Tagai
  - *Magellan clouds*
      The origin of the Magellan
      clouds

CONTENTMENT
  The stone-cold heart

The three wise men

CONTESTS
  See also **Races, Athletic**
  The first flute
  - *Vietnam*
      Hung Vuong and the earth
      and sky cakes

CONTRARINESS. *See* **Stubbornness**

The convent free from care
  De Bosschere — *Christmas* p.18-20

CONVENTS
  The little blue light

CONVERSATION. *See* **Talk**

CONVICTS. *See* **Prisons and Prisoners**

COOK, JAMES, CAPTAIN
  The coming of Tute
  Visitor's song

COOKS AND COOKERY
  Clever Grethel
  Dwarf long nose
  Henrietta's story
  Longnose the dwarf
  The miller, his cook, and the king
  The one-legged crane
  The right drumstick
  The spice woman's basket
  The three Ivans

COOLIDGE, CALVIN
  - *Humor*
      Silent Cal

Cooper, George
  Twenty froggies

Cooperation
  De Roin — *Jataka* p.74-77

COOPERS
  Gratitude

"COOYOKOS" (giant monsters)
  Homolovi and the journey northward

COPPER AND COPPERSMITHS
  The giant of the causeway
  The king of the hummingbirds

The sad victory
The three kingdoms

"CORANIANS" (race)
Lludd and Llewelys

CORCORAN, MARK
Mark Corcoran (subject)
Shaw — *Mouse* p.27

CORD. *See* **String**

CORN
The beginning of maize
Brer Rabbit, businessman
Do what you can
The high-low jump
Lesson for lesson
The origin of corn and beans
Paul's cornstalk
The Phouka
The seven Simons (and variants)
, *Beginning of (Guatemala)*
The beginning of maize
- *Cribs*
The right drumstick
- *Dances*
The dance of rubber baboon
Full moon a-shining
The right drumstick
, *Grain of*
The golden slipper
- *Maidens*
The dance of the corn
maidens

The cornflower
Krylov — *Fables* p.66-68

CORNMEAL
The giant and the rabbit

Coronado and the Indian guide
Life — *Treasury* p.33-36

"CORPO SANTO"
St. Elmo's fire

Corpse maker and Calamity's child
Life — *Treasury* p.119-121

CORPSES. *See* **Dead; Death —
Corpses**

CORRIGANS
Little people

CORSICA
Golden hair

COSSACKS
The cat, the cock, and the fox
The fox and the cat
The golden slipper
The iron wolf
Ivan the fool and St. Peter's fife
The magic egg
Oh: The Tsar of the forest
The old dog
The origin of the mole
The serpent-Tsarevich and his
two wives
The serpent-wife
The sparrow and the bush
The story of Ivan and the daugh-
ter of the sun
The story of little Tsar Novishny,
the false sister, and the faithful
beasts
The story of the forty-first brother
The story of the unlucky days
The story of the wind
The story of Tremsin, the bird
Zhar, and Nastasia, the lovely
maid of the sea
The story of unlucky Daniel
The straw ox
The three brothers
The Tsar and the angel
The two princes
The ungrateful children and the
old father who went to school
again
The vampire and St. Michael
The voices at the window
The wondrous story of Ivan Golik
and the serpents

COSTA RICA
The ancient curse
The boy wtih the hand of fire
Brer Rabbit, businessman
The Cegua
The drowned mine of Santa Ana
Jack and the varmints
Nandayure and his magic rod
The Sisimiqui
The treasure of Nosara

The costly feast
Jagendorf — *Noodle* p.105-110

Cott, Jonathan
    Notes on fairy faith and the idea
      of childhood

COTTERS
    The saga of two trees

COTTINGLEY FAIRIES
    Little people
    - *Photographs*
        Cott — *Beyond* p.xvii-xx

COTTON
    Leap the elk and Little Princess
      Cottongrass
    The Muiar

The coucal's voice
    Heady — *Safiri* p.27-30

COUGHING
    Little Tuppens

COUNTING
    Donkeys all
    The four silly brothers
    How counting came to be from
      one to ten

COUNTRY LIFE
    See also **Farmers**
    Little Bun Rabbit
    Little Miss Muffet

The country mouse and the city mouse
    Morel — *Fairy* p.23-24

Country-under-wave
    McGarry — *Great* p.63-75

COUNTY SEATS
    , *Battle for*
        The battle of Bay Minette

COURAGE
    See also **Heroes and Heroines**
    The boy who was never afraid
    The brave beetle
    The brave drummer boys
    The brave men of Austwick
    Hoozah for fearless ladies and
      fearless deeds
    How Kate Shelley saved the ex-
      press
    The hungry old witch
    Jack and the varmints
    The knight of the red shield

Mau and Matang
The proud tale of David Dodd
Shingebiss
The sister queens
The sleeper
The story of the brave little rab-
    bit, Squint Eyes — Flop Ears —
    Stub Tail
The three brothers
The three riddles
The valiant chattee-maker
The valiant little tailor
, *Moral*
    The princess and the three
      tasks
- *Women*
    Fearless Emma
    Fearless Nancy Hart

COURTESY
    The Colonel teaches the judge a
      lesson in good manners
    How the sheriff's posse and the
      hold-up men sat down to dinner
      together

COURTHOUSES
    The face in the courthouse
      window

COURTS
    - *Trials*
        Nollichucky Jack

COURTSHIP
    See also **Love; Suitors**
    The golden goose
    Guess who!
    Hine and Tu
    "Leave it there!"
    One pair of blue satin slippers
      and four clever maids

Cousins, Margaret
    Down-to-earth dreamer

COUSINS
    The first Kalandar's tale
    Tortoise and elephant

COVENS
    See also **Witches**
    Workers of evil — and a few good
      spirits

COVERLETS
Esben and the witch

COVETOUSNESS. See Jealousy

The cow and the thread
Jagendorf — *Noodle* p.68-71

Cow Bu-cola
Manning — *Ogres* p.75-79

COWARDICE
The tailor and the giant

The cowardly hunter and the woodcutter
Levine — *Fables* p.8

COWBOYS
Dry farming
Fair, brown, and trembling
The ghosts of Stampede Mesa
How Joe became Snaky Joe
Pecos Bill meets Paul Bunyan

COWS
See also **Bulls**
Bottle Hill
The boy who was never afraid
A cat for a cow
Fisherman's dream
Ivan the fool and St. Peter's fife
Khavroshechka
The King of Scotland's sons
The lazy farmer's tale
Mr. and Mrs. Vinegar
The pig that went to court
Rake up!
Saint Launomar's cow
The tiger and the cow
- *Heifers*
The golden slipper
- *Hides*
The magic pot
- *Milking*
The barrel bung

COWSLIPS
The key-flower

The coyote and Juan's maguey
Rugoff — *Harvest* p.595-598

Coyote conquers the Iya
Jones — *Coyote* p.41

Coyote drowns the world
Baker — *At* p.8-15

Coyote loses his dinner
Jones — *Coyote* p.15

Coyote rescues the ring-girl
Jones — *Coyote* p.23

Coyote steals the summer
Jones — *Coyote* p.1-13

COYOTES
Brer Rabbit, businessman
Earth magician
The killing pot
The monster eagle
Repaying good with evil
The rocks of Bryce Canyon

The crab and his mother
Darrell — *Once* p.238-239

CRABS
Biu
Ialbuz
Madam Crab loses her head
- *Catchers*
Boy Blue the crab-catcher
, *Land*
The cat and the parrot

CRADLES
The cloud tree

CRAFTINESS. See Cleverness; Trickery

CRAFTS AND CRAFTSMEN
See also individual crafts
The smith, the weaver, and the
harper

Crafty Yasohachi and the flea medicine
Bang — *Men* p.7-9

Crafty Yasohachi climbs to heaven
Bang — *Men* p.2-4

Crane, Walter, illus.
The wanderings of Arasmon

CRANES
The christening in the village
The cloth of a thousand feathers
The heron and the crane
The one-legged crane
Thousands of ideas

CRANES *(continued)*

The white crane
The wolf and the crane
, *Blue*
    How blue crane taught jackal
    to fly

Crawford, Winifred
    Cat's menu

CRAYFISH (CRAWFISH)
The squirrel and the crawfish race
The swan, the pike and the cray-
    fish

CREAM. *See* **Milk — Cream**

CREATION
See also **God; Man**
A chant of creation
The conflict of the gods
Coyote drowns the world
The Cycle of A'Aisa
Earth magician
Escape from the Underworld
The four worlds
Havaiki the land
Hina and the eel
In the beginning there was no
    earth . . .
Legend of the perfect people
The monster we live on
The offspring of the sky and
    earth
People from the sky
The place of the beginning
Rabbit's long ears
Sky woman
Tangaroa maker of all things
Tiki the first man
Tuttle, fowl and pig
Uncle James or the purple
    stranger
When the sky lay on the earth
The woman in the moon
- *Chatham Islands*
    The offspring of the sky and
      earth
- *Easter Island*
    A chant of creation
- *Mangaia*
    Hina and the eel
- *New Zealand*
    Creation

When the sky lay on the
    earth
- *Porapora*
    Turtle, fowl and pig
- *Tahiti*
    Havaiki the land
    Tangaroa maker of all things
    The woman in the moon
- *Tuamotu*
    The conflict of the gods

Creation
    Alpers — *Legends* p.55-56

The creation of man
    Carter — *Enchanted* p.57-61

The creation of men
    Rugoff — *Harvest* p.96-98

CREEKS
Staring at you!

CREOLES
The bridal ghost dinner
Hyena and hare

CRETE
Halfway people

CRICKETS
How the snake lost his voice

CROCKETT, DAVY
Davy Crockett: sunrise in his
    pocket
Davy Crockett's boat

The crocodile and the hen
    Dolch — *Animal* p.1-5

Crocodile play
    Lawrie — *Myths* p.120

CROCODILES. *See* **Alligators and
Crocodiles**

The crocodile's cousin
    Heady — *Safiri* p.17-21

CROFTERS
The boy who was never afraid
The old troll of Big Mountain

Croker, T. Crafton
    The lady of Gollerus

Crommelynck, Landa
    Perrault — *Fairy* p.96

CRONES. *See* Witches

The crooked Mary
    Wyness — *Legends* p.76-79

A crooked stream
    Schwartz — *Whoppers* p.84

CROPS
    The bear's revenge
    The boggart and the farmer

CROQUET
    Alice's adventures in Wonderland

CROSSES
    The fiddlers of Tomnafurach
    Pablo and the pirate's ghost

Crossing the bridge
    Leach — *Whistle* p.75

The crow and the fox
    Levine — *Fables* p.52

The crow and the pitcher
    Morel — *Fairy* p.55

The crow and the snake
    Levine — *Fables* p.88

CROWNS
    The princess with unruly thoughts
    , *Golden*
        King Golden

CROWS
    Anfy and his landlord
    Animals from heaven
    The dove and the crow
    The fox and the crow
    The greedy crow
    The hermit Mitsina
    The magical spectacles
    Man-crow
    Maraboe and Morsegat
    The panther and the crow
    The poor man, and the king of
        the crows
    The rascal crow
    Seven black crows
    The travelers and the crow
    - *Eggs*
        The swan maiden

CRUELTY
    See also Evil; Wickedness

The bird that would not stay dead
The knight with the stone heart
Hine and Tinirau
The princess and the three tasks

The crusty old badger
    Bang — *Men* p.39-45

CRYING. *See* Tears

The crystal ball
    Bamberger — *My* p.50-53

Crystal love
    Duong — *Beyond* p.45-49

CUBA. *See* West Indies — Cuba

CUCHULAIN (Cuculain; Cucullin;
        Cuchulainn; Chuchullin; etc.)
    Clever Oonagh

Cuchullin and Fardia
    Rugoff — *Harvest* p.478-483

The cuckoo
    Carrick — *Wise* n. pag.

The cuckoo and the eagle
    Carey — *Baba* p.17
    Krylov — *Fables* p.125-126

The cuckoo in the hedge. *See* The
    Wise men of Gotham

The cuckoo of Borrowdale
    Colwell — *Round* p.30-33

CUCKOOS
    Irani and the cuckoos
    Kuduluk and Kui
    The wise men of Gotham

CUCULAIN. *See* Cuchulain

CUDGELS. *See* Sticks

The cuirassier and the horned princess
    Curtin — *Myths* p.356-369

CUMINS (CUMMINGS) FAMILY
    The Cumins of Culter

The Cumins of Culter
    Wyness — *Legends* p.7-10

Cummings, E. E.
    In just / Spring

CUMULATIVE STORIES. *See* **Repetitive Rhymes and Stories**

CUNNING. *See* **Cleverness; Trickery**

The cunning cat
    Rugoff — *Harvest* p.520-524

Cupid and Psyche
    Rugoff — *Harvest* p.405-410

CUPIDS
    Peter Pan in Kensington Gardens

CUPS
    , *Golden*
        The twelve dancing princesses

CURES. *See* **Healing**

CURIOSITY
    Bluebeard
    Cupid and Psyche
    Good advice
    Uletka and the white lizard

CURLEWS (Birds)
    Kuduluk and Kui

CURRENCY. *See* **Money**

The curse of Lorenzo Dow
    Jagendorf — *Folk, South* p.105-107

CURSES
    The ancient curse
    The bird witch
    Briar Rose
    Dancing stones
    The sleeping beauty in the wood

Cushy cow, Bonny
    Greene — *Clever* p.89

CUTHBERT, SAINT
    Saint Cuthbert's peace

CUTTLEFISH
    Mr. Cuttlefish's love story

The cycle of A'Aisa
    McDowell — *Third* p.134-135

CYCLOPS
    Big people

The Cyprian cat
    Manley — *Sisters* p.13-28

CZARS. *See* **Tzars.**

CZECHOSLOVAKIA
    See also **Bohemia; Moravia**
    Boyislav, youngest of twelve
    Broad, Tall and Sharp – eyes
    The cuirassier and the horned princess
    The firebird
    The king of the toads
    The mouse-hole, and the underground kingdom
    Punished pride
    The table, the pack, and the bag
    The treacherous brothers
    - *Prague*
        Big people

D

Daddy Mention
    Life — *Treasury* p.162-163

Daddy Mention and Sourdough Gus
    Jagendorf — *Folk, South* p.87-89

Daedalus, Icarus, and the wings
    Rugoff — *Harvest* p.403-404

Dag and Daga, and the flying troll of Sky Mountain
    Olenius — *Great* p.185-194

Dagmet
    Lawrie — *Myths* p.200-203

DAIRYING
    The match

Damak and Daram
    Lawrie — *Myths* p.214-215

Dan McGirth and his gray goose mare
    Jagendorf — *Folk, South* p.95-97

DANA, PEOPLE OF (The Danaans)
    The faery folk

The dance of rubber baboon
    Bagley — *Candle* p.101-107

The dance of the corn maidens
    Life — *Treasury* p.52-53

Dance of the ghosts
  Roberts — *Ghosts* p.25-31

DANCERS AND DANCING
  See also **Corn — Dances; Indians
  of North America — Dancers
  and Dancing**
  Blood Clot boy
  Cinderella (and variants)
  The gladiator, the belle, and the
    good snowstorm
  Hok Lee and the dwarfs
  Igowa
  Ivan the fool and St. Peter's fife
  Kate Crackernuts
  The kid and the wolf
  The mad dancers of Upo-pou-shi
  Muta
  The old man's wen
  Rabbit and the wolves
  Sadko
  The silver bell
  Terer
  The twelve dancing princesses
  Tyll Ulenspiegel. The tale of a
    merry dance
  Zub and the lamar
  - *Minuet*
    Dance of the ghosts

The dancing camel
  Levine — *Fables* p.102

The dancing princesses
  Bamberger — *My* p.70-75

Dancing stones
  Raskin — *Ghosts* p.51-59

"DANDIES"
  Lepuha and the widow of Utuma-
    lama

DANES
  The great bell of Bosham
  The water monster

DANGER
  The flower of happiness on Sunny-
    mount Crest

Daniel and the dragon of Babylon
  Spicer — *13 Dragons* p.79-87

Darak and Göidan
  Lawrie — *Myths* p.227-228

DARE, VIRGINIA
  The silver doe
  The white doe

DAREDEVILS
  Jumping Sam Patch

DA RIFF, ANDREA
  Andrea Da Riff, illus. (subject)
    Shaw — *Mouse* p.11

The daring of yellow doc
  Jagendorf — *Folk, Song* p.54-57

DARKNESS
  The journey in the dark
  Kabai
  The last piece of light
  Nycteris

Darrell, Margery
  Rackham, Arthur

DART GAMES
  Tu'i Tofus

DATES (fruit)
  The shepherd and the sea

Dauan
  Lawrie — *Myths* p.196-197

Daughter and stepdaughter
  Higonnet-Schnopper — *Tales*
    p.109-117

DAUGHTERS
  The black bull of Norroway
  Cap o' rushes
  Fanta-Ghiro
  A feather of Finist the bright fal-
    con
  The four beautiful daughters
  Frost
  The grateful toad
  The great bear of Orange
  Ialbuz
  Kapukaper the cannibal
  The lady and the lion
  The lion and the farmer's daugh-
    ter
  Oda and the snake
  The old man and death
  The sleeper
  What came of picking flowers
  The widow and her daughters

58

David and Goliath. The shepherd boy
and the giant
Stories From World p.96-99

Davis, Mary Gould
Wakaima and the clay man

Davy Crockett: sunrise in his pocket
Rugoff — *Harvest* p.74-79

Davy Crockett's boast
Life — *Treasury* p.126-127

DAWN
The goblins at the bath house

Dawn-strider
Yolen — *Girl* p.11-21

DAY. See Daylight

The day boy and the night girl
Cott — *Beyond* p.421-463

The day the devil tried to be good
Raskin — *Ghosts* p.16-21

**DAY DREAMING. See Absent-minded-
ness**

DAYLIGHT
See also **Dawn**
Photogen
Raven lets out the daylight
Raven's deed

DAYS OF THE WEEK
The Sunday child

de la Mare, Walter
Clever Grethel
I saw three witches
The listener
Molly Whuppie
The ride-by-nights

de Morgan, Mary
Through the fire
The wanderings of Arasmon

DE MORGAN, MARY
Mary de Morgan (subject)
Cott — *Beyond* p.164

De Morgan, William, illus.
Through the fire

De witch woman
Life — *Treasury* p.173-174

DEAD
See also **Death — Corpses**
The army of the dead
Island of the dead
Maski, the land of the dead
The shroud of Mari-Yvonne
The vampire of Tempassuk
, *Images of*
The story of the wooden
images

The dead hand
Pugh — *More* p.95-105

Dead man
Leach — *Whistle* p.111-112

DEAF
The blind man, the deaf man, and
the donkey

DEATH
See also **Burials; Cemeteries;
Dead; Funerals**
Bartek the doctor
Devil-may-care
The enchanted apple-tree
Godfather Death
The graveyard rose
How the clever doctor tricked
death
The king who did not want to die
Koshchéi without-death
Kuduluk and Kui
The little blacksmith Verholen
The nightingale
The old man and death
Orpheus and Eurydice
The rascal crow
The smith, the weaver, the harper
The soldier and the demons
The sphinx
Why misery remains in the world
Why there is death in the world
Xibalba
, *Acceptance of*
The weaver of tomorrow
, *Child's*
Chant on the dying of an
only child
- *Corpses*
Impulse
Mary Culhane and the dead
man
Teig O'Kane and the corpse

- *Platforms*
  Kawai
, *Frozen*
  Frozen death
- *Heads*
  The sphinx
, *Water of*
  Water of youth, water of life,
    water of death

The death of Billy the Kid
  Life — *Treasury* p.232-235

The death of Rustem
  Picard — *Tales* p.263-270

Death's messengers
  Rugoff — *Harvest* p.363-364

DEBTS
  The strange folding screen

**DECEIT. See Betrayal; Deception;
  Hypocrisy; Trickery**

The deceitful leopard
  Heady — *Safiri* p.75-81

The deceived blind man
  Rugoff — *Harvest* p.127-129

DECEPTION
  See also **Betrayal; Hypocrisy;
    Trickery**
  The boy who cried "Wolf!"
  Gigi and the magic ring
  Hermes' chariot
  Old Hildebrand
  Pinto Smalto

Decide for yourself
  De Roin — *Jataka* p.78-79

DECISIONS
  The poorest man in the world

A declaration of war, and battle royal
  Cott — *Beyond* p.76-83

DEDANNANS (fairy race)
  The fairy tree

DEER
  See also **Antelopes; Elk;** etc.
  The ballad of Saint Giles and the
    deer
  Brother and sister
  How Wilka went to sea

The pig with gold bristles, the
    deer with golden horns, and
    the golden-maned steed with
    golden tail
The smartest one in the woods
, *Banyan*
  The banyan deer
- *Does*
  The doe and the vine
  The silver doe
  The white doe
-*Hunts*
  The miller's mule
  Sergevan
, *Monkey*
  The banyan deer
- *Stags*
  A ballad of Saint Athracta's
    stags
  Learn and live
  The Tsar and the angel

The defeat of Persia
  Picard — *Tales* p.173-185

DEFORMITIES. See Handicapped

Deibui and Teikui
  Lawrie — *Myths* p.87

Deidre
  Rugoff — *Harvest* p.464-475

**DEITIES. See God; Gods and God-
  desses; Jesus Christ;** names of
  gods and goddesses

DELAWARE
  - *Dover*
    The most haunted house
  - *New Castle*
    Tick, tick, tick

DELAY
  The goblins at the bath house

The deliverers of their country
  Bland — *Complete* p.47-67

Demedes the politician
  Levine — *Fables* p.36

DEMIGODS. See Gods and Goddesses

DEMONS
  A-e-oina the demon, and the tat-
    tletale dog

DEMONS (continued)

Animals from heaven
Devil-may-care
The flying sword
How the devil constructed a
  church
The island of demons
Jack the giant-killer
Momotaro, the peach sprite
The princess's slippers
The rabbit huntress
Sankichi's gift
The soldier and the demons
Ten miles at each step
The wicked Sankhashurni
Workers of evil — and a few good
  spirits
, of sickness
  The bats of Ru-pe-shi-pe
, Water
  Big people
- Women
  The midnight voyage of the
    Seagull

Demyán's fish soup
  Krylov — *Fables* p.64-65

DENMARK
See also **Danes**
The castle in the silver wood
The clock that walked by itself
  (Luck or wisdom)
Elf hill
The Emperor's new clothes
Esben and the witch
Mons Tro
Nils in the forest
People of the sea
Peter's adventures
The princess on the pea (and
  variants)
Rake up!
A sensible suitor?
Sigurd the dragon-slayer
Sven and Lilli
Ten miles at each step
The tinderbox (and variants)
The troll's little daughter
The ugly duckling

DENTISTRY
Pulling teeth

The departure of Khosroes
  Picard — *Tales* p.224-227

DERVISHES (Clergymen)
Abdallah the ungrateful

DESERT
Eerie iron horse of the Arizona
  desert
The patchwork quilt
The three travelers
- *Fairies*
  The yellow dwarf

DESTINY. See Fate

The destruction of Awatovi
  Courlander — *Fourth* p.175-184

The destruction of Palatkwapi
  Courlander — *Fourth* p.56-71

The destruction of the Sampo
  Rugoff — *Harvest* p.280-286

DETECTIVES
Chapkin the scamp

DETERMINATION
The crow and the pitcher
The little engine that could

DETROIT, MICHIGAN
I will leave it to the devil

Deumer
  Lawrie — *Myths* p.345-346

Devabhuti and the foolish magistrate
  Rugoff — *Harvest* p.452

The devil and his three golden hairs
  Segal — *Juniper (I)* p.80-93

Devil-may-care
  Rugoff — *Harvest* p.321-330

DEVILS
See also **Beelzebub**
Andruez who disliked beans
Bearskin
Big sixteen
The Cegua
Dancing stones
The day the devil tried to be good
Dewi and the devil
Don Demonio's mother-in-law
The farmer and the devil
How El Bizarrón fooled the devil
How Sam Hart beat the devil

How the devil constructed a
    church
I will leave it to the devil
The incubus
The Isle of Satan's hand
Jack the giant-killer
John O'Hara's lantern
John Travail and the devil
The little blacksmith Verholen
Lorenzo Dow raises the devil
The obsession with clothes
The old woman
A shrewd woman
The silver bullet
The soldier and the demons
The stolen heart
The story of little Tsar Novishny,
    the false sister, and the faithful
    beasts
The tailor, the bear, and the devil
Ten miles at each step
The three golden hairs
White orchid, red mountain
Why the sea is salt
Why women always take advan-
    tage of men
Wine and the devil
The witch of Wellfleet
The wizard of Long Sleddale
- *Kings*
        Workers of evil — and a few
            good spirits
- *Tails*
        The day the devil tried to be
            good

The devil's bridge
    Colwell — *Round* p.23-26

The devil's granny
    Spicer — *13 Dragons* p.47-57

DEVOTION. *See* **Love**

Dew eagle, at night . . .
    Belting — *Whirlwind* n. pag.

Dewi and the devil
    Pugh — *More* p.77-87

DIALECT
    , *Negro*
        Big Sixteen

The diamond fish
    Lawrie — *Myths* p.246

DIAMONDS
    The noblest deed
    Uletka and the white lizard

Diamonds and toads (subject)
    Opie — *Classic* p.98-99

Dana and Actaeon
    Rugoff — *Harvest* p.401-403

Dicey and Orpus
    Rugoff — *Harvest* p.64-65

Dick Whittington
    Rugoff — *Harvest* p.236-241

Dickens, Charles
    A Christmas carol

Dickinson, Emily
    I'm nobody

Dickison, John J.
    Dixie, the knight of the silver
        spurs

Didipapa and Gorarasiasi
    Lawrie — *Myths* p.289-290

Diem and Siem
    Junne — *Floating* p.129-132

DIFFERENCES
    The ugly duck

Digger boy was hunting clams . . .
    Belting — *Whirlwind* n. pag.

DIJNS (Djinns; Jinns; Genies)
    Workers of evil — and a few good
        spirits

DILLON, LEO AND DIANE
    Leo and Diane Dillon (subject)
        Aardema — *Behind* p.85
        Belting — *Whirlwind* n. pag.

**DINAS, EMRIS (WALES) (Merlin's
    castle)**
    The red dragon of Wales

DINNERS
    See also **Feasts**
    The bridal ghost dinner

Diogenes and the bald man
  Levine — *Fables* p.94

Dirty hands
  Heady — *Safiri* p.40-45

DISAPPEARANCES
  Alas for Theodosia
  Drop Star
  The mat-maker's adventure

DISASTERS
  See also types of disasters, e.g.,
    Earthquakes
  , *Marine*
    Ghost ship of the Great Lakes

DISBELIEF. *See* **Doubt**

DISCERNMENT
  The three fastidious men

DISCONTENT
  See also **Grumbling**
  The fox and the grapes
  The pig that went to court

The discontented grass plant
  Rugoff — *Harvest* p.103-108

DISCOURTESY
  The months

The discovery of the garden land of
    Padrin
  Lawrie — *Myths* p.222

DISGUISES
  See also **Impersonations; Trans-
    formations**
  The ass who passed for a lion
  The crusty old badger
  Fanta-Ghiro
  The forest inn
  The gnome and the dragons
  Irani and the cuckoos
  Little Red Riding Hood (and
    variants)
  Merlin the enchanter
  Oh: the Tsar of the forest
  The old woman in the cottage
  The proud pastor
  Punished pride
  The serpent-Tsarevich and his
    two wives
  The twin sisters

DISHES
  See also **Cauldrons;** etc.
  - *Saucers*
    A red, ripe apple, a golden
      saucer
    The tale of the silver saucer
      and the transparent apple

DISHONESTY
  See also **Cheating**
  The cow and the thread
  The Emperor's new clothes
  The lady and the unjust judge
  Only in Texas

DISLIKE. *See* **Enmity**

DISOBEDIENCE
  Bob o' the Carn
  The ice dragon or Do as you are
    told
  How the moonfish came to be
  King Solomon and the Queen of
    Sheba
  Mrs. Gertrude
  The test
  Why dog lost his voice

DISORDER. *See* **Confusion**

The dispersal from Sikyatki
  Courlander — *Fourth* p.118-126

DISPUTES. *See* **Quarreling**

DISSATISFACTION. *See* **Discontent**

DISTRUST
  The deceived blind men

DIVERS AND DIVING
  High diving

The division
  Krylov — *Fables* p.150-151

Dixie, the knight of the silver spurs
  Jagendorf — *Folk, South* p.77-78

Do as you are told. *See* The ice
    dragon

Do what you can
  Morel — *Fairy* p.44

Do you know?
  Jagendorf — *Noodle* p.37-39

DOBIE
Little people

DOBRIN, ARNOLD
Arnold Dobrin (illustrator)
Shaw — *Mouse* p.42

Dobsinsky, Pavo
The twelve months

DOCTORS. *See* **Healing; Physicians;**
Witch-doctors

The doctor's servant
Heady — *Safiri* p.36-39

The doe and the vine
Levine — *Fables* p.28

Dog and leopard
Dolch — *Animal* p.71-79

The dog and the bones
Rockwell — *Three* p.100-101

The dog and the horse
Carey — *Baba* p.20

The dog and the hunter
Bird — *Path* p.47-50

The dog and the piece of meat
Levine — *Fables* p.54

DOG-HEADED MEN
Halfway people

The dog who wanted to be a lion
De Roin — *Jataka* p.32-34

Dogai I
Lawrie — *Myths* p.101-104

Dogai Metakurab
Lawrie — *Myths* p.210-211

The dogai of Zurat
Lawrie — *Myths* p.65-67

DOGAIS
Dagmet
Gabai
Ganalai Dogai
Gigi
Kawai
Kusa Kap
Maiwasa
Saurkeka
Uzu, the white dogai

DOGS
A-e-oina, the demon, and the
tattle-tale dog
The ass and the lapdog
The boy in the secret valley
The Bremen town musicians
The castle of the active door
The doomed prince
The dragon of Loschy Hill
Forty men I see, forty men I do
not see
Gigi and the magic ring
The history of Little Mook
Horns for a rabbit
The house dog and the wolf
Impulse
The laird's man
The Lamehva people
The little red hen
The little tailor and the three
dogs
Lu-bo-bo
The man bitten by a dog
Momotaro (and variants)
The monster in the mill
The mysterious fig tree
The old dog
The old man who made the
trees blossom
Old Sultan
The pheasant, the bear, and the fox
The ring with twelve screws
Schippeitaro
The sea maiden
Sesere
The sheep and the dogs
The stone dog
The three dooms
The tinder box (and variants)
Why dogs hate cats
Why there is death in the world
Yelub and his dog

- *Barking*
Why dog lost his voice
- *Ghosts*
The black ghost dog
The ghost dog
, *Guide*
The blind singer, Saint
Hervé
- *Hounds*
The hound and the hare
- *Poodles*
Mons Tro

DOGS (*continued*)
- *Pugs*
 The elephant and the pug
- *Training*
 The frog (by Leonora Alleyne)
, *Wild*
 The dog who wanted to be
  a lion

Dogs
 Schwartz — *Whoppers* p.73-74

Dokere
 Lawrie — *Myths* p.56-57

DOLLS
Aniello
The little girl and the hare
Tokutaro
The toys
Vasilisa the beautiful
, *Victorian*
 Edward's story
 Elsie's story
 Henrietta's story
 Maud's story

The dolphins at Fagasa
 Alpers — *Legends* p.296-297

DOMANIA
Little people

DOMINICAN REPUBLIC
How the clever doctor tricked
 death

DOMINION DAY
Dominion day (subject)
 Corrigan — *Holiday* p.132-142
Once upon a great holiday

A Dominion Day to remember
 Corrigan — *Holiday* p.135-142

DOMOVOI
Little people

Don Demonio's mother-in-law
 Rugoff — *Harvest* p.716-722

Donald Oig of Monaltrie
 Wyness — *Legends* p.45-49

Donkey and scholars
 Jagendorf — *Noodle* p.175-179

The donkey of Abdera
 Jagendorf — *Noodle* p.40-42

Donkey skin
 Perrault — *Fairy* p.84-95

DONKEYS
Ali Baba
Apelles and the young ass
The ass carrying salt
The ass who passed for a lion
The asses complain to Zeus
The ass's shadow
The Bremen town musicians
The dragon and the peasant
Ea and Eo
The farmer, her son, and their
 donkey
Lazy Jack
Lesson for lesson
The lion and ass go hunting
The lion and the wild ass
The lion, the ass, and the fox
The miller, his son, and their
 donkey
The moon in the donkey
The nine doves
Old King Cole
The old man, his son, and the
 donkey
The ox and the ass
The rabbit catcher
Saint Gerasimus and the lion
Wise, wise burros
, *Golden*
 The magic table, the gold-
  donkey, and the cudgel in
  the sack
- *Skins*
 The little donkey

Donkeys all
 Jagendorf — *Noodle* p.63-67

Donkeys and camels
 Bomans — *Wily* p.39-45

Don't drop into my soup
 Jagendorf — *Folk, South* p.10-12

Don't foul the well — you may need
 its waters
 Carey — *Baba* p.99-102

Don't marry two wives
 Jagendorf — *Noodle* p.24-29

Don't try the same trick twice
 De Roin — *Jataka* p.66-67

The Doodang
  Life — *Treasury* p.280-281

The doomed prince
  Rugoff — *Harvest* p.212-215

"DOOMS"
  See also **Fate**
  The three dooms

DOORS
  Bran the blessed

DORMICE
  Prince Rabbit

The dormouse
  Shaw — *Mouse* p.20

DOUBT
  The purchased miracle

D'Outremeuse, Jean
  Sir John Maundeville's dragon

The dove and the crow
  Levine — *Fables* p.100

DOVES
  Cinderella (and variants)
  Go to the verge of destruction
    and bring back Shmat-Razum
  How blue crane taught jackal to
    fly
  The lady and the lion
  The old woman of the forest
  A safe home
  - *Feathers, gold and silver*
    Esben and the witch

DOW, LORENZO
  Lorenzo Dow raises the devil

Down the rabbit-hole
  Darrell — *Once* p.72-75

Down the well — (Wanted a king)
  Cott — *Beyond* p.286-291

Down-to-earth dreamer
  Corrigan — *Holiday* p.172-175

Doyle, Arthur Conan
  The horror of the heights

Doyle, Richard, illus.
  The King of the Golden River or
    The Black brothers

DRACS
  The people of the sea

The dragon and his grandmother
  Green — *Cavalcade* p.120-124

The dragon and the monkey
  Morel — *Fairy* p.40-43

The dragon and the peasant
  Green — *Cavalcade* p.23-25

The dragon and the square-round
  Parkin
  Spicer — *13 Dragons* p.139-149

The dragon at hide-and-seek
  Green — *Cavalcade* p.204-212

Dragon, dragon
  Gardner — *Dragon* p.1-17

The dragon king and the twin horses
  Spicer — *13 Dragons* p.113-127

The dragon of Loschy Hill
  Spicer — *13 Dragons* p.13-22

The dragon of Macedon
  Green — *Cavalcade* p.16-20

The dragon of Shervage Wood
  Colwell — *Round* p.110-113

The dragon of the North
  Green — *Cavalcade* p.125-132

The dragon, sliced-in-two
  Spicer — *13 Dragons* p.88-100

The dragon speaks
  Green — *Cavalcade* p.249-251

The dragon tamers
  Bland — *Complete* p.95-117

Dragon thieves of Peking
  Spicer — *13 Dragons* p.23-31

DRAGONS
  An adventure of Digenes the
    Borderer
  Alyosha Popovich
  Beowulf and the dragon
  The book of beasts
  The boy and the dragon

DRAGONS (continued)
Cesarino and the dragon
The Chinese dragons
The cinnamon tree in the moon
The cock and the dragon
Conrad and the dragon
Constantes and the dragon
Daniel and the dragon of Babylon
The deliverers of their country
The devil's granny
The enchanted princess
Epilogue
False dragon wife
The fiery dragon
The fiery dragon, or the Heart of stone and the Heart of gold
The fox and the dragon
The gnome and the dragons
The golden apple-tree and the nine peahens
The golden-horned dragon
The hoard
How three mighty heroes saved the sun and the moon from the dragon
The ice dragon, or Do as you are told
The Island of the nine whirlpools
Jabberwocky
Jason and the dragon of Colchis
Kind little Edmund, or the Caves and the cockatrice
The Lady Dragonissa
The Laidly worm
The laidly worm of Spindlestone Heugh
The Lambton worm
The last balloon
The last half-hour
The last of the dragons
The little bull-calf
Lludd and Llewelys
The magic egg
The magic spider box
The master thief and the dragon
The miller's sons
The mummer's play
The nine doves
The nine-headed bird
The prince and the dragon
Prince Bajaja
The princess and the three tasks
Ragnar Shaggy Legs and the dragons
The Red Cross knight and the dragons
The red dragon of Wales
The sacred sword
St. George and the dragon
The shepherd of the Giant Mountains
Sigurd the dragon-slayer
Sir Launcelot and the dragon
Sir Maundeville's dragon
Sir Tristram in Ireland
The song of Orpheus; The song that Orpheus sang to charm the dragon
Stan Bolovan
Stan Bolovan and the dragon
The story of little Tsar Novishny, the false sister, and the faithful beasts
The two princes
Uncle James, or the Purple stranger
The wonderful shirt
The Zamay who hid his life
, *Ancient*
   Ancient dragons (subject)
      Green — *Cavalcade* p.1-33
- *Burns*
   The fiery dragon
- *Dark ages*
   Dark ages (subject)
      Green — *Cavalcade* p.35-100
- *Draklings*
   Kind little Edmund
- *Folklore*
   Dragon folklore (subject)
      Green — *Cavalcade* p.101-164
, *Ice*
   The ice dragon, or Do as you are told
- *Palaces*
   The fisherman and the Sea King's daughter
, *of later days*
   Dragons of later days (subject)
      Green — *Cavalcade* p.165-252

Dragons and elephants
   Green — *Cavalcade* p.28-33

The dragon's egg
Green — *Cavalcade* p.26-27

The dragons of Rhodes, Lucerne and
    Somerset
Green — *Cavalcade* p.96-100

DRAGOONS. See Soldiers

DRAMA
The mummer's play

The draper who swallowed a fly
Novák — *Fairy* p.119-123

The dreamer
Provensen — *Book* p.125-131

DREAMS AND DREAMING
Alice's adventures in Wonderland
Barefoot in bed
The castle in the silver wood
Hung Vuong and the earth and
    sky caves
Ivan the peasant's son and the
    little man himself one-finger
    tall, his mustache seven versts
    in length
The King's choice
Little Eva
A midsummer night's dream
The peddler of Ballaghadereen
The pedlar of Swaffham
Rocking-horse land
The ruined man who became rich
    again through a dream
The salesman who sold his dream
The serpent and the peasant
Water of youth, water of life, and
    water of death

DRESS. See Clothes; Hats

DRESSMAKERS
See also **Sewing**
Gammelyn, the dressmaker

DRIUTHS (enchanted caps)
The Lady of Gollerus

Drop Star
Life — *Treasury* p.83-84

DROUGHT
The tar baby
The two wizards

The drowned mine of Santa Ana
Carter — *Enchanted* p.102-104

DROWNINGS
The lagoon of Masaya
, *Mass*
    The song in the sea

DRUIDS
The Faery folk
The swan-children of Lir
Workers of evil and a few good
    spirits

The drum
Corrigan — *Holiday* p.121

DRUMS
The Little people
Naga
Parradiddle Pete
Ttimba
Waiat

DRUNKARDS. See Alcoholism

Dry farming
Life — *Treasury* p.281-282

DRYADS
See also **Hamadryads**
Workers of evil — and a few good
    spirits

The ducat
Krylov — *Fables* p.72-73

The Duchess of Houndsditch
Sleigh — *Stirabout* p.132-138

DUCKS
The hen that saved the world
Horns for a rabbit
The little man and his little gun
The little red hen
The princess under the earth
The two journeymen
The ugly duckling
, *Wild*
    Shingebiss
    The traveling frog
    The twelve wild ducks

DUELS
Donald Oig of Monaltrie

68

Dugama
  Lawrie — *Myths* p.260-266

Dugama, maker of magic
  Lawrie — *Myths* p.236-237

DUGONGS
  Babaia and Segawa
  Dugama, maker of dugong magic
  Gelam
  Kiba
  Tawaka, the greedy man
  Waiaba
  - *Hunters and hunting*
  Ganalai Dogai
  Kawai
  Kusa Kap
  Sesere

DUKES AND DUCHESSES
  Longnose the dwarf

DULCIMERS
  Sadko

Dull-witted Hikoichi and the duck soup
  Bang — *Men* p.9-12

Dull-witted Hikoichi, the mortar and
  the worn-out horse
  Bang — *Men* p.6-7

DUMB. *See* **Fools and Foolishness**

DUMPLINGS
  The adventures of Little Peachling
  The old woman and her dumpling
  The old woman who lost her
  dumpling

Dunber
  Manning — *Monsters* p.67-74

DUNGEONS
  The dragon tamers

Dupul and Mumag
  Lawrie — *Myths* p.12-13

"DUST BOWL" (of 1930's)
  Dry farming

Duvoisin, Roger
  The knight with the stone heart

DUVOISIN, ROGER
  Roger Duvoisin (Illus.) (subject)
  Shaw — *Mouse* p.30

DVOROVOI
  Little people

The dwarf and the blacksmith
  De Bosschere — *Christmas* p.81-
  85

DWARF KAPPA
  Little people

Dwarf long nose
  Greene — *Clever* p.56-86

DWARFS
  The adventures of Billy MacDaniel
  Dag and Daga, and the flying
  troll of Sky Mountain
  The echo well
  The giant of the causeway
  The girl who picked strawberries
  The history of Little Mook
  Hok Lee and the dwarfs
  How Thor found his hammer
  The King of the Golden River or
  The Black brothers
  Knurremurre
  Little people
  Longnose the dwarf
  The making of the hammer
  Metarawai
  Nils in the forest
  Princess Finola and the dwarf
  The princess with unruly thoughts
  Rip Van Winkle
  Rose Red
  The sleeping beauty (and var-
  iants)
  Snow-White (and variants)
  The stone
  , *Rain*
  The king and the rain dwarfs
  , *Sealskin*
  The ice dragon or Do as
  you are told
  , *Yellow*
  The yellow dwarf

E

Ea and Eo
  Ginsburg — *Lazies* p.56-58

The eagle
  McDowell — *Third* p.133

The eagle and the bee
    Krylov — *Fables* p.55-56

The eagle and the dung beetle
    Levine — *Fables* p.16

The eagle and the fowls
    Krylov — *Fables* p.106-108

The eagle and the mole
    Krylov — *Fables* p.41-42

The eagle and the spider
    Krylov — *Fables* p.74-76

Eagle boy
    Martin — *Raven* p.75-81

The eagle, the jackdaw, and the
        shepherd
    Levine — *Fables* p.12

The eagle with clipped wings and the
        fox
    Levine — *Fables* p.50

The eagle wounded by an arrow
    Levine — *Fables* p.100

EAGLES
    Blodeuwed the betrayer
    The cuckoo and the eagle
    Dew eagle, at night . . .
    The hermit Mitsina
    The magic egg
    The monster eagle
    The owl and the eagle
    People of the heron and the
        hummingbird
    The place of the beginning
    Saint Prisca, the child martyr
    The Sisimiqui
    Thunder appoints the eagle of
        earth
    The tortoise who flew to heaven
    The two roosters and the eagle
    Vassilissa the cunning and the
        Tsar of the sea
    The wishing-ring
    , *American bald*
        "Old Abe" American eagle
    - *Feathers*
        Rabbit's long ears
    , *Fish*
        Gathering salt
    , *Golden*
        The hen that laid golden eggs

- *Nests*
    Blackberries in February

Earl Desmond and the banshee
    McGarry — *Great* p.116-118

Earl Gerald
    Leach — *Whistle* p.20

The earliest kings
    Picard — *Tales* p.1-6

EARS
    See also **Hearing**
    How the Short-ears conquered
        the Long-ears
    The two chickens or the two ears

Ears and tails and common sense
    Sherlock — *Ears* p.19-35

EARTH
    See also **Creation**
    Coyote drowns the world
    Havaiki the land
    Hung Vuong and the earth and
        the earth and sky cakes
    In the beginning there was no
        earth
    The place of the beginning
    When the sky lay on the earth

EARTH DAY
    Earth day (subject)
        Corrigan — *Holiday* p.78-84
    Come out and look!
    Tommy

Earth magician
    Baker — *At* p.1-7

EARTH-OVENS
    Kultut
    Wawa

The earth will have its own
    Rugoff — *Harvest* p.647-649

EARTHQUAKES
    The destruction of Palatkwapi

EAST. *See* **Far East; Middle East**

EAST INDIES
    Workers of evil — and a few good
        spirits

East of the sun and West of the moon
    Minard — *Womenfolk* p.111-126

EASTER
Easter (subject)
Corrigan — *Holiday* p.86-94
April
In just / Spring
The rat-catcher's daughter
The white blackbird: an Easter
story

EASTER ISLAND
A chant of creation
Chant to dump a surfer
The fight with Oroi and the killing
of Oroi
How the Short-ears conquered
the Long-ears
The story of the wooden images
Two love songs
A widow's funeral chant
- *Founding*
How Hoto Matua found this
land

Easy bread
Ginsburg — *Lazies* p.12-17

EATING
See also **Cooks and Cookery;
Dinners, Feasts; Food;** etc.
El Enana

EAVESDROPPING. *See* **Listening**

Eberhard, Wolfram
The witch's daughter

The echo well
Bomans — *Wily* p.57-63

ECONOMY. *See* **Thrift**

Edain the queen
McGarry — *Great* p.112-115

EDELWEISS
Wooden Tony: an Anyhow story

EDEN, GARDEN OF
Way deep down in the Okefenokee swamps

Edgell, John
Old wine in new bottles

EDISON, THOMAS ALVA
Down-to-earth dreamer

Edom o'Gordon
Wyness — *Legends* p.121-127

Edward's story p.9-37

EELS
Hina and the eel
Tiki the first man

Eerie iron horse of the Arizona desert
Anderson — *Haunting* p.150-155

EETOI (earth magician)
Coyote drowns the world
Earth magician
The first war
The killing of Eetoi
The killing pot
The monster eagle

EEYEEKALDUK
Little people

EGGS
A bed for the night
The crystal ball
Dogai Metakurab
Fitcher's feathered bird
Humpty Dumpty
The iron wolf
The magic egg
A new way to boil eggs
The Zamay who hid his life
, *Golden*
The golden eggs
- *Shells*
Brewery of eggshells

EGRETS
True tears

EGYPT
Anpu and Bata
Bata
The doomed prince
Halfway people
King Solomon's ring
Little people
Saint Fronto's camels
The shipwrecked sailor
The story of Almansor
The three dooms
The treasure of Rhampsinitus
- *Folk tales*
Folk tales (subject)
Rugoff — *Harvest* p.197-
219

EINSEL, NAIAD
Naiad Einsel, illus. (subject)
Shaw — *Mouse* p.35,39

The eitu who went as a man's wife
Alpers — *Legends* p.311-313

The elephant and the pug
Krylov — *Fables* p.154

Elephant and tortoise
Dolch — *Animal* p.97-101

The elephant as governor
Krylov — *Fables* p.53-54

Elephant wants to be king
Dolch — *Animal* p.113-121

ELEPHANTS
The brave beetle
The company you keep
The coucal's voice
The dog who wanted to be a lion
Dragons and elephants
Ears and tails and common sense
Fearing the wind
The frog's saddle horse
The giant and the rabbit
Hippopotamus and elephant
The house in the middle of the
   road
The jumper
The legend of the elephant
The lion, Jupiter, and the elephant
The oldest of the three
Rabbit and elephant
The strong chameleon
Tortoise and elephant
The trick on the trek
Unanana and the elephant
Wakaima and the clay man

ELEVATORS
Room for one more

The elf and the doormouse
Shaw — *Mouse* p.46-47

Elf hill
Sperry — *Scand.* p.212-223

ELIJAH (Biblical)
The seven good years

ELIJAH OF CHELM, Rabbi
Big people

ELK
Leap the elk and Little Princess
Cottongrass

Elsie's story
Wahl — *Muffletump* p.97-125

ELVES
The hoard
Little people
The pear tree
The shoemaker and the elves
The wanderings of Arasmon
- *Singing*
Foxglove

The elves and the shoemaker
Haviland — *Fairy* p.118-121
Morel — *Fairy* p.81-83

The elves in the shelves
Aiken — *Necklace* p.44-54

EMBROIDERY
The three fairies

Emily's famous meal
Jagendorf — *Folk, South* p.210-213

EMPERORS
The convent free from care
Figs for gold, figs for folly
The nightingale
The seven Simons (and variants)
The shapesshifters of Shorm
The singing leaves
The small kingdom

The Emperor's new clothes
Haviland — *Fairy* p.174-179
Stories From World p.34-39

The Emperor's parrot
De Bosschere — *Christmas* p.36-41

(El) Enano
Littledale — *Strange* p.117-125

The enchanted apple-tree
De Bosschere — *Christmas* p.14-17

The enchanted cat
Orczy — *Old* p.73-82

The enchanted fisherman
    Colwell — *Round* p.19-22
The enchanted island
    McGarry — *Great* p.76
The enchanted orchard
    Carter — *Enchanted* p.13-17
The enchanted prince
    Manning — *Choice* p.183-190
The enchanted princess
    Colwell — *Round* p.34-39
    Curtin — *Myths* p.238-248

ENCHANTERS
    See also **Witches; Wizards;** etc.
    The foundling
    The true enchanter

ENCHANTMENT. *See* **Magic**

The end of it
    Darrell — *Once* p.229-234

ENEMIES. *See* **Enmity**

Engel, Lyle Kenyon
    The adventures of Little Peachling
    Hok Lee and the dwarfs
    The little engine that could

ENGINES
    The Duchess of Houndsditch
    The little engine that could

ENGLAND
    See also **London, England**
    The Bailie's daughter
    Big people
    The brave men of Austwick
    Coat o'clay
    Dick Whittington
    The dragon and the square-round
        parkin
    The dragon of Loschy Hill
    The Faery folk
    Galahad. The Holy Grail
    Get up and bar the door
    The giants of Castle Treen
    Halfway people
    The Hedley Kow
    Jack and the beanstalk
    Jack the giant-killer
    The king o' the cats

    Knucklehead John
    The laidly worm of Spindlestone
        Heugh
    Little people
    The master and his pupil
    Myself
    The old witch
    Our goodman
    The piskeys on Selena Moor
    Robin Hood and the beggar
    Robin Hood and the butcher
    Sneezy Snatcher and Sammy
        Small
    The three heads of the well
    The widow and her daughters
    The wise men of Gotham
    Workers of evil — and a few good
        spirits
    - *Bosham*
        The great bell of Bosham
    - *Cambridgeshire*
        The giant of the Fens
    - *Cheshire*
        The wizard of Alderley Edge
    - *Cornwall*
        Cornwall (subject)
            McHargue — *Impossible*
                p.28,47-48,51,59,149,159
        Bob o' the Carn
        The Faery folk
        Little people
        People of the sea
        Skillywidden
    - *Cumberland*
        The cuckoo of Borrowdale
    - *Derbyshire*
        The little red hairy man
    - *Devonshire*
        The Faery folk
        Halfway people
        Little people
        The pixie visitors
    -*Durham*
        The fairies of Midridge
    - *Folk tales*
        Folk tales (subject)
            Rugoff — *Harvest* p.222-
                276
    - *Gotham*
        The wise men of Gotham
    - *Herefordshire*
        Jack and the white cap
    - *Lancashire*
        The enchanted fisherman

- *Lincolnshire*
  The boggart and the farmer.
- *Norfolk* .
  The pedlar of Swaffham
- *Northamptonshire*
  The little man in green
- *Northumberland*
  The enchanted princess
- *Nottinghamshire*
  The farmer and the cheeses
  Jack Buttermilk
- *Shropshire*
  The giant and the wrekin
- *Somerset*
  The dragon of Shervage
  Wood
  The dragons of Rhodes,
  Lucerne and Somerset
- *Suffolk*
  Brother Mike
  The green children
- *Sussex*
  The great bell of Bosham
  The piglet and the fairy
- *Warwickshire*
  The king and the witch
- *Westmoreland*
  The devil's bridge
  The wizard of Long Sleddale
- *Yorkshire*
  The fish and the ring
  The mysterious traveller
  The tailor and the fairies

ENMITY
The noblest deed
The two enemies

ENOS, RANDY
Randy Enos, illus. (subject)
Shaw — *Mouse* p.23

ENVY. See Jealousy

Epilogue
Green — *Cavalcade* p.252

EQUALITY
The kingdom of the lion

ERASMUS, SAINT
St. Elmo's fire

Erben, K. J.
Broad, Tall and Sharp-eyes
The firebird

ERIN. See Ireland

The eruption of Pele's anger
Alpers — *Legends* p.253-256

Esau and the gorbey
Life — *Treasury* p.139-140

ESBATS
Esbats (subject)
McHargue — *Impossible* p.101

Esben and the witch
Manning — *Choice* p.128-143

Escape from the Underworld
Life — *Treasury* p.65

ESKIMOS
Little people
The outside man
Sedna and the fulmar
- *Bering Straits*
  The discontented grass plant

ESTABAN, STEPHEN
The search for the Golden Cities

ESTONIA
The goblins at the bath house

ETERNITY. See Immortality

ETHIOPIA. See Africa — Ethiopia

EUROPE
See also names of countries
Big people
Halfway people
Workers of evil — and a few good
spirits
, *Northern*
  The Faery folk

EURYDICE
Orpheus and Eurydice

Evangeline
Life — *Treasury* p.99-102

EVENING. See Night

EVENK TALES
Who will row next?

The everlasting house
Martin — *Raven* p.83-88

EVIL
See also **Cruelty; Wickedness**
The buried moon
The day the devil tried to be good
The destruction of Palathwapi
Gudgekin, the thistle girl
Judgment by fire at Pivanhonkapi
The old woman
Repaying good with evil
The tale of the silver saucer and
the transparent apple
Tiger woman
Zohak and Feridun

The evil eye
Raskin — *Ghosts* p.98-105

Evil-minded and good-minded
Life — *Treasury* p.50

An evil nurse
Cott — *Beyond* p.452-453

EVIL SPIRITS. See Spirits, Evil

EXCHANGES. *See* **Traders and Trading**

EXPEDIENCY
The farmer, his son, and their
donkey

EXPLORERS AND EXPLORATION
See also names of explorers
Coronado and the Indian guide
The fountain of youth
The Islands of the Amazons
The lost continent of Atlantis
Madoc
A map of myths of early America
Mermaids
St. Brendan's Isles of the Blest
St. Elmo's fire
Sea of Darkness
The search for the Golden Cities
The Vikings and their traces
- *Folklore*
Folklore (subject)
Life — *Treasury* p.12-45

EXTRAVAGANCE
The obsession with clothes

EYE-GLASSES. *See* **Glasses, Eye**

EYES
See also **Blind**
The basilisk
The deliverers of their country
The incubus
Johnny and the witch-maidens
Mirko, the king's son
The Queen
The wond'rous wise man
- *Cats*
The black cat's eyes
- *Eyelashes*
The wolf's eyelashes
, *Fairies in*
The girl who got a fairy in her
eye
, *Glass*
The evil eye
, *Sharp*
Broad, Tall and Sharp-eyes
, *Staring*
The lad who stared everyone
down

F

FABLES. See Aesop's Fables; Animals;
names of animals

Fables
Rugoff — *Harvest* p.415-421

Fables of animals and friends
Life — *Treasury* p.278-280

FABRICS. See Cloth; Linen

The fabulous Wilson Mizner
Life — *Treasury* p.245-248

The face in the courthouse window
Jagendorf — *Folk, South* p.16-17

FAERIES (Faery Folk). See Fairies

The Faery folk
McHargue — *Impossible* p.27-46

Fair, brown and trembling
McGarry — *Great* p.43-51

FAIR FOLK
The stone

FAIR PLAY. See Judges and Justice

FAIRIES
See also **Fairyland**
Fairies (subject)
McGarry — *Great* p.5-8
Briar Rose
Brother Mike
The captive piper
The cat sat on the mat
The cunning cat
Forget-me-not
Gudgekin, the thistle girl
Guleesh
The harp of the Dagda Mor
Hie over to England
The history of Tom Thumb
Jamie Freel and the young lady
The King's choice
The leprechaun, or, Fairy shoe-
  maker
A midsummer night's dream
Myself
Peter Pan in Kensington gardens
The Phouka
The piglet and the fairy
Prince Ahmed and the fairy Peri-
  banou
Prince Lindworm
Princess Finola and the dwarf
The seven wishes
The sleeping beauty
The sleeping beauty in the wood
The story of the little half-cock
The tailor and the fairies
Teig O'Kane and the corpse
The three wishes
Tinykin's transformations
The twin hunchbacks
Uletka and the white wizard
Wanted — a king
The woman who flummoxed the
  fairies
- *Cottingley photographs*
  Cott — *Beyond* p.xvii-xx
- *Dances and dancing*
  Lock-out time
  The twin hunchbacks
- *Doctors*
  Tokaetaro
- *Fire*
  Through the fire
, *Forest*
  The fiddlers of Tomnafurach
- *Godmothers*
  Cinderella (and variants)

- *Kings*
  The suitors of Princess Fire-
    fly
, *Maori*
  Te Kamawa and the visitors
    by firelight
- *Princesses*
  The suitors of Princess Fire-
    fly
- *Queens*
  Gudgekin, the thistle girl
  Lac Long Quan and Au Co
  A midsummer night's dream
- *Wings*
  The girl who got a fairy in her
    eye

The fairies
  McGarry — *Great* p.11-17
  Perrault — *Fairy* p.20-24

The fairies of Midridge
  Colwell — *Round* p.40-42

FAIRNESS. See Judges and Justice

FAIRS
  Mr. and Mrs. Vinegar

The fairy
  Opie — *Classic* p.100-102

Fairy cake (recipe)
  Greene —*Clever* p.25-26

FAIRY TALES
- *History* (subject)
  Cott — *Beyond* p.xi-xx,xxi-l

The fairy thorn
  McGarry — *Great* p.83-85

The fairy tree
  McGarry — *Great* p.77-82

Fairy web for Mr. Durand's daughters
  Jagendorf — *Folk, South* p.125-128

FAIRYLAND
  The golden boy
  Petsetilla's pony
  The twin hunchbacks
  The woman who flummoxed the
    fairies

FAITH
  Saint Fronto's camels

Faithful legs and lazy head
Jagendorf — *Noodle* p.156-158

FAITHFULNESS. See Loyalty

**FAITHLESSNESS. See Disloyalty;
Hypocrisy**

FAKES
See also **Hoaxes**
A breath of air
The ghost on Brass's Hill
Next turn to the right
Sunrise

FAKIRS. See Holy Men

FALCONS
The blue falcon
King of his turf
Monster copper forehead
- *Feathers*
The feather of Bright Finist
the falcon

FALL. See Autumn

The false accusation
Krylov — *Fables* p.126-128

False alarm
Jagendorf — *Folk, South* p.24-26

False dragon wife
Spicer — *13 Dragons* p.150-157

The false shaman
Martin — *Raven* p.69-73

FALSEHOOD
See also **Deception; Tall Tales**
The liar
The origin of the mole
"That's not true"
The three fairies
Who can tell the bigger lie?

**FALSENESS. See Betrayal; Deception;
Disloyalty; Hypocrisy; Traitors;
Trickery**

"FAMILIARS"
Workers of evil — and a few good
spirits

FAMINE
Eagle boy
The everlasting house

The princess who learned to work
Saint Comgall and the mice

Fancy clothes, and narrow escape
Schwartz — *Whoppers* p.46-70

Fang, Wang Mou
The flute

Fanta-Ghiro
Sekorová — *Europe* p.164-170

FAR EAST
See also names of countries
Halfway people

Farjeon, Eleanor
Cat!
Good Bishop Valentine
The great discovery
Now every child
A round for the New Year

The farmer and the cheeses
Colwell — *Round* p.85-86

The farmer and the devil
Bamberger — *My* p.46

The farmer and the poisonous snake
Levine — *Fables* p.32

The farmer and the snake
Lester — *Knee* p.42-46

The farmer and the ungrateful snake
Levine — *Fables* p.64

The farmer, his son, and their donkey
Morel — *Fairy* p.92-93

Farmer Broom, Farmer Leaves, and
Farmer Iron
De Bosschere — *Christmas* p.118-
122

FARMERS
See also **Dairying; Ploughs and
Ploughing**
The boggart and the farmer
The brave flute-player
Clever Manka
Do what you can
Hudden and Dudden and Donald
O'Neary
The lazy farmer's tale
Lookit the little pig!
The monkey's Buddha

Oda and the snake
The old man who made the trees
  blossom
The Phouka
The pixy visitors
A sensible suitor?
The singing tree
Skillywidden
Sorcerer Kaldoon
Three bits of advice
Tom the piper's son
Wakaima and the clay man
Why dog lost his voice
The wishing-ring
The wizard of Alderley Edge
The wizard's gillie

The farmer's secret
  Jagendorf — *Noodle* p.100-101

Farming
  Schwartz — *Whoppers* p.22-26

FARQUHARSON, JOHN, COLONEL
  The black colonel

The farthing rushlight
  Rugoff — *Harvest* p.417

The fast
  Hautzig — *Case* p.39-43

Faster than thunder
  Bagley — *Candle* p.82-84

FATE
  See also **"Dooms"; Fortune; Fortune Tellers; Luck; Prophets and Prophecies**
  The doomed prince

Father bird and fledgelings
  Rugoff — *Harvest* p.582-583

"FATHER FROST"
  Frost

Father Marquette and the manitou
  Life — *Treasury* p.80-82

"FATHER TIME"
  The lost half-hour

FATHERS
  Beauty and the beast
  The thoughtful father
  The ungrateful children and the old
    father who went to school again

FATHER'S DAY
  Father's day (subject)
    Corrigan — *Holiday* p.119-131
  A boy and his pa
  The drum
  A pavane for the nursery

FAUNS
  The halfway people

FAY, MIRIAM
  They called her a witch

FEAR
  See also **Cowardice**
  The story of one who set out to
    study fear
  , Lack of
    Don't drop into my soup

Fearing the wind
  De Roin — *Jataka* p.6-7

Fearless Emma
  Jagendorf — *Folk, South* p.4-9

Fearless Nancy Hart
  Jagendorf — *Folk, South* p.118-120

FEARLESSNESS. See Courage

FEASTS
  The costly feast

A feather of Finist the bright falcon
  Whitney — *In* p.85-94

A feather of Bright Finist the falcon
  Curtin — *Myths* p.47-58

Feather o' my wing
  Provensen — *Book* p.49-56

FEATHERS
  See also **Birds — Colors; Birds —
    Feathers**
  Muta
  The three feathers
  The tortoise who flew to heaven
  Tritl, Litil, and the birds
  - *Burning*
    Seven black crows
  - *Cloaks*
    Ahu Ula: the first feather cloak
  - *Cloth*
    The cloth of a thousand
      feathers

FEATHERS (continued)
, Golden
The firebird and Princess
Vasilisa
The fire-bird, the horse of
power and the Princess
Vasilissa
Mons Tro
, Magic
The seven blind brothers

FEBOLDSON, FEBOLD
Febold Feboldson (subject)
Life — Treasury p.286-287

FEET
- Toes
The tale of the hairy toe

FELIX, SAINT
The ballad of Saint Felix

FENCES
How the ranchers of Windy Canyon
built the biggest fence the West
has ever seen

FENRI (race)
Usheen in the island of youth

Ferdinand Faithful and Ferdinand
Unfaithful
Segal — Juniper (II) p.298-309

Ferguson, Sir Samuel
The fairy thorn

FERNS
Karakarkula

Ferra-Mikuia
The sunshade

FERRETS
The cloak of friendship

FERRIES AND FERRYMEN
Happy returns

FESTIVALS
See also Feasts
The water festival
, Bear
"Good-by, dear little bear god"

FEUDS
, American
The Hatfields and McCoys

FIANNA (FIANS). See Finn MacCool

FICOWSKI, JERZY
Jerzy Ficowski (subject)
Ficowski — Sister n. pag.

FIDDLERS. See Violinists
The fiddlers of Tomnafurach
Stuart — Witch's p.127-135

Fiddler's rock
Jagendorf — Folk, South p.236-239

Fiddling
Schwartz — Whoppers p.27

The fiddling cat
Shaw — Cat p.41

FIDELITY. See Loyalty

FIELD MARSHALS
The wonderful shirt

The field of boliauns
Rugoff — Harvest p.475-477

FIELDS AND STREAMS
King of his turf
The origin of the mole

FIENDS
See also Demons; Devils; etc.
The day the devil tried to be good
Workers of evil — and a few good
spirits

The fiery dragon
Green — Cavalcade p.185-203

The fiery dragon, or the Heart of stone
and the heart of gold
Bland — Complete p.119-140

FIESTAS. See Festivals

FIFES
Ivan the fool and St. Peter's fife

FIFINELLAS (wives of gremlins)
Little people

The fifth son
Roy — Serpent p.21-29

The fifth voyage of Sindbad the seaman
Rugoff — Harvest p.148-157

Fifty years in chains
  McDowell — *Third* p.93-97

The fig-tree beggar, and the willful
    princess
  Wolkstein — *Lazy* p.24-35

FIG TREES AND FIGS
  The history of Little Mook
  Mister Lazybones
  The mysterious fig tree

The fight with Oroi and the killing of
    Oroi
  Alpers — *Legends* p.237-241

Fighting
  Schwartz — *Whoppers* p.27-31

Fighting fires
  Schwartz — *Whoppers* p.32-33

FIGHTS AND FIGHTING
  See also **Quarreling**
  Maida
  Maigi
  Pitai
  Waiaba
  Waii and Sobai

Figs for gold, figs for folly
  Jagendorf — *Noodle* p.59-62

FILIPINOS. *See* **Philippine Islands**

Fillmore, Parker
  Budulinek
  Clever Manka
  The forest bride

The finch and the pigeon
  Krylov — *Fables* p.157-158

FINCHES
  - *Colors*
    How the finch got her colors

FINGAL. *See* **Finn MacCool**

Finger, Charles J.
  (El) Enano
  The magic ball

FINGERS
  Clever Oonagh
  , *Ghostly*
    The calamander chest

, *Pricked*
  Briar Rose

FINK, MIKE
  Mike Fink, last keelboatman

FINLAND
  Aili's quilt
  The destruction of the Sampo
  Fisherman's dream
  The kalevala
  Kultani, the noodle gossip
  The last adventure
  Lippo and Tapio
  Lisalill
  Maraboe and Morsegat
  The pig-headed wife
  Rabbit and our old woman
  The saga of two trees
  The tailor from the sea
  Workers of evil — and a few good
    spirits
  - *Folk tales*
    Folk tales (subject)
      Rugoff — *Harvest* p.277-
        300

FINN MacCOOL (including Fianna)
  The fairy tree

FIONN. *See* **Finn MacCool**

The fir tree
  Morel — *Fairy* p.45-48

The fir tree and the bramble-bush
  Levine — *Fables* p.76

FIR TREES
  Deidre

FIRE
  See also **Arson**
  Brother Annancy fools brother Fire
  The half-chick
  How fire came to the earth
  How fire took water to wife
  How the animals obtained fire
  Judgment by fire at Pivanhonkapi
  The last balloon
  Not bad — but it could be better
  Paslag
  The suitors of Princess Fire-fly
  Through the fire
  Tokutaro

FIRE *(continued)*

- *Fairies. See also Fairies — Fire*
Saint Blaise and the beasts
The treasure
- *Origin*
How fire was brought to
Torres Strait

FIREBALLS
"Spook Light" of Devil's Promenade

The firebird
'Higonnet-Schnopper — *Tales* p.93-
108
Sekorová — *Europe* p.136-152

The firebird and Princess Vasilisa
Whitney — *In* p.71-76

The firebird, the horse of power and
the Princess Vasilissa
Ransome — *Old* p.176-188

FIREBIRDS
Ivan Tsarevich, the fire-bird, and
the gray wolf

FIRECRACKERS. *See* **Fireworks; Fourth
of July**

FIREFLIES
How the animals obtained fire
Out
Riddles, one, two, three

The fireplace
Hoke — *Ghosts* p.53-70

FIREWOOD. *See* **Wood**

FIREWORKS
See also **Fourth of July**
The ice dragon or Do as you are
told
Fireworks
Corrigan — *Holiday* p.154

The first flute
Carter — *Enchanted* p.50-56

The first Kalandar's tale
Rugoff — *Harvest* p.134-140

The first man at Saibai
Lawrie — *Myths* p.153
(Version A); p.153-155 (Version B)

The first of the three spirits
Darrell — *Once* p.187-200

The first tale of Alabama
Jagendorf — *Folk, South* p.3-4

The first war
Baker — *At* p.43-49

The first woman
McDowell — *Third* p.119-129

FISH
An adventure with Eveseika
Aukam and Tiai
Big for me, little for you
A chapter of fish
Dagmet
Dupul and Mumag
Happy returns
Kos and Abob
Malo ra Gelar
Mons Tro
The most beautiful of all
Nageg and Geigi
The rose of the Konakadet
A taste of his own medicine
Tortoise and ogre
The two terrible fish
Why the sea-slug has two mouths
The wonderful fish
- *Barracuda*
The barracuda
- *Dance, Inside of*
Blood Clot boy
- *Devilfish*
The perpetual motion in the
sea
- *Diamond*
The diamond fish
- *Eyes*
Nageg and Geigi
- *Flounder*
The fisherman and his wife
The lobster and the flounder
, *Golden*
The fisherman and his wife
The golden fish
The little golden fish
- *Goldfish*
Forget-me-not
- *Herrings*
The nose of the Konakadet
- *Minnows*
The boy who wanted to learn
to shudder

The fisherman and the minnow
- *Noses*
   The fish with hooked noses
- *Pike*
   A chapter of fish
   The pike
   The swan, the pike and the
     crayfish
   The three Ivans
- *Pitching contests*
   The great fishbowl contest
, *Silver*
   How the moon came to be
- *Traps, Stone*
   The snake of Apro
- *Trout, Fur-bearing*
   Fur-bearing trout
- *Unicorn*
   Badi and the sabei
- *Yersh*
   A chapter of fish

The fish and the ring
   Colwell — *Round* p.46-50

The fish tale
   Carrick — *Wise* n. pag.

The fish who helped Saint Gudwall
   Brown — *Book* p.176-182

The fish with hooked noses
   Junne — *Floating* p.11-13

Fisher, Aileen
   The witch in the wintry wood

The fisherman and his soul
   Shaw — *Witch* p.58-115

The fisherman and his wife
   Carle — *Eric* p.39-48

The fisherman and his wife
   Segal — *Juniper (I)* p.94-112

The fisherman and the gatekeeper
   Junne — *Floating* p.6-7

The fisherman and the minnow
   Levine — *Fables* p.18

The fisherman and the Sea King's
   daughter
   Novák — *Fairy* p.85-93

Fisherman's dream
   Sperry — *Scand.* p.224-237

FISHERMAN AND FISHING
   See also **Fish; Ice-fishing; Whales**
     and Whaling
   Aiwali of Muri
   The barracuda
   Crystal love
   The enchanted fisherman
   The everlasting house
   Gabai
   Going fishing
   The golden fish
   Grandpa Joe's brother
   Ivanhko and the witch
   Khusrau and the fisherman
   The little fisherman
   The little golden fish
   Markep and Sarkep
   Miracles on the sea
   The nose of the Konakadet
   Pablo and the pirate's ghost
   The perpetual motion in the sea
   A red, ripe apple, a golden saucer
   The sea maiden
   The stolen heart
   The stone dog
   The unlucky fisherman
   , *Spear*
     Deibui and Teikui

Fishing
   Schwartz — *Whoppers* p.34-35

Fitcher's feather bed
   Segal — *Juniper (I)* p.71-79

Fiti au mua, who was born in the sea
   Alpers — *Legends* p.293-295

The five brothers Li
   Bamberger — *My* p.195-200

Five in a pod
   Bamberger — *My* p.171-174

Five peas in a pod
   Piper — *Stories* n. pag.

The five strange ghosts
   Novák — *Fairy* p.165-175

FLAG DAY
   Flag day (subject)
     Corrigan — *Holiday* p.112-118
   Benny's flag
   Not of school age

FLAILS
, *Threshing*
The months

FLAT HOLME
Big people

FLATTERY
The fox and the crow
The owl and the grasshopper

FLAX
The golden slipper

The flea
Lyons — *Tales* p.67-70

The flea and the athlete
Levine — *Fables* p.90

FLEAS
Crafty Yasohachi and the flea
medicine
Louse and flea go fishing

FLEMISH. *See* **Belgium — Flanders**

FLIES
See also titles beginning with "fly"
The draper who swallowed a fly
Giufá and the judge
Hungry-for-battle
The man, the woman, and the fly
Seven with one blow (and variants)
Ivan the fool

The flight from Huckovi
Courlander — *Fourth* p.127-132

FLOODS
Gratitude
The meeting
Raven lets out the daylight

FLORIDA
A boy and his pa
The bridal chamber of Silver
Springs
Daddy Mention and Sourdough
Gus
Dixie, the knight of the Silver Spurs
The fountain of youth
The great conjure-alligator-man
of Florida
Nobody sees a mockingbird on
Friday
The tale of Lura Lou

Way deep down in the Okefenokee
swamps
- *St. Augustine*
Specter of the Spanish castle

FLOUR MILLS
The miller's sons

The flower of happiness on Sunnymount
Crest
Olenius — *Great* p.175-184

FLOWERS
See also names of flowers
Ayele and the flowers
The girl who cried flowers
Little step-mother
Mistress Mary
Thumbelina
The wooing of the maze
- *Picking*
What came of picking flowers
, *Red*
The feather of Finist the bright
falcon
Jorinda and Joringel
The legend of the humming-
bird
, *Singing*
The garden of magic

The flute
Corrigan — *Holiday* p.102

FLUTES AND FLUTISTS
The brave flute-player
Crystal love
The great golloping wolf
Guani
The kid and the flute-playing wolf
The monkey musicians
The three brothers
Tortoise and the children
, *First*
The first flute

The fly
Levine — *Fables* p.42

The fly and the bee
Krylov — *Fables* p.69-70

FLY-WHISKS
Painted skin

FLYING
  See also **Aviation**
  A pair of wings
  The tortoise who flew to heaven
  The witches' cellar

The flying fool
  Jagendorf — *Noodle* p.111-114

"FLYING FOXES"
  Möibu and Bazi
  The story of the rat and the flying-fox

The flying sword
  Carpenter — *People* p.92-97

The flying trunk
  Bamberger — *My* p.155-161

FOALS. *See* **Horses**

The foam maiden
  Manning — *Sorcerers* p.?7-44

FOG
  Hine and Tinirau

The fog
  Schwartz — *Whoppers* p.93-94
  - King
    Where blonde people came from

The foghorn
  Hoke — *Monsters* p.42-52

FOLK HEROES. *See* **Heroes and Heroines**

FOLKTALES
  Folk tales (subject)
    Rugoff — *Harvest* p.xi-xviii
  , American (Glossary and index)
    Guide to persons, places and events in American folklore
      Life — *Treasury* p.301-343
    A regional guide to American folklore
      Life — *Treasury* p.297-299
  , Modern
    Modern folklore (subject)
      Life — *Treasury* p.236-267
  - Origin
    Introduction *(Impossible people)*

Foni and Fotia
  Manning — *Sorcerers* p.91-98

FOOD
  See also **Dinners; Feasts;** names of foods
  The best food
  Hung Vuong and the earth and sky cakes
  King of the mice
  Lu-bo-bo
  The story of Tommy Tucker
  , Lack of
    Lludd and Llevelys

The fool of the world and the flying ship
  Ransome — *Old* p.45-57

The foolish lion and the silly rooster
  Jagendorf — *Noodle* p.89-92

The foolish monkeys
  Dolch — *Animal* p.39-45

The "foolish people"
  Jagendorf — *Noodle* p.271-273

The foolish weathercock
  Morel — *Fairy* p.107

FOOLS AND FOOLISHNESS
  See also **Gotham, Wise Men of**
  Ashes for sale
  Bartek the doctor
  Bastianelo
  The boy who always said the wrong thing
  Coat o' clay
  Country-under-wave
  Didipapa and Gorarasiasi
  Dull-witted Hikoichi and the duck soup
  Dull-witted Hikoichi, the mortar and the worn-out house
  The Emperor's new clothes
  Esben and the witch
  The four silly brothers
  The golden goose
  The good ogre
  Half of everything
  Iawar
  Ivan the fool
  Ivan the fool and St. Peter's fife
  King Johnny
  The king of the hummingbirds

FOOLS AND FOOLISHNESS *(continued)*

Know before you criticize
Knucklehead John
Lazy Jack
Lizard who was always right
The lost half-hour
The miller, his son, and their
  donkey
The monkey gardeners
Next turn to the right
The nine doves
Now I should laugh if I were not
  dead
The owl and the grasshopper
The peasant, the bear, and the
  fox
The pig with gold bristles, the
  deer with golden horns, and the
  golden-maned steed with golden
  tail
The poor miller's boy and the
  little cat
The ring with twelve screws
Salt
The seven wishes
Simple John
The small kingdom
The three brothers
The three rascals and the magic
  cap
Three wise men of Gotham
Two foolish friends
The wonder-working steeds

Fools' bells ring in every town
Jagendorf — *Noodle* p.164-172

The footless and blind champions
Curtin — *Myths* p.82-96

The footless and the blind
Curtin — *Myths* p.149-164

FOOTSTEPS
The haunted and the haunters
Kahukura and the net-makers

FORCE. See Power; Strength

**FORESIGHT. See Fortune; Fortune
Tellers; Prophets and Prophecies**

The forest bride
Provensen — *Book* p.83-92

The forest inn
Hauff — *Big* p.119-165

A forest mansion
Carey — *Baba* p.63-66

FORESTERS. See Woodsmen

FORESTS
Ayaymama
The four sacred scrolls
The going home mix-up
Hans and Greta
Hansel and Gretel (and variants)
The house in the forest
How straws were invented
The hut in the forest
Leave well enough alone
The little daughter of the snow
The little man in green
The Little People
Little Poucet
Little Red Riding Hood (and
  variants)
Living in the forest
The mountain lad and the forest
  witch
The ogre
Oh: the Tsar of the forest
The old woman of the forest
Peter and the Witch of the wood
The run of the forest
Spring in the forest
The tea house in the forest
The three brothers
Thumbelina
, *Enchanted*
    The flower of happiness on
      Sunnymount Crest
, *Silver*
    The castle in the silver wood

Forget-me-not
Orczy — *Old* p.51-71

FORT LARAMIE, WYOMING
The galloping ghost of Laramie

FORTUNE
Master Money and Madame Fortune

Fortune and the beggar
Krylov — *Fables* p.116-118

FORTUNE TELLERS
Deidre

Gratitude
Workers of evil — and a few good
spirits
Yukiko and the little black cat

Forty men I see, forty men I do not see
Sherlock — *Ears* p.53-67

"FORTY NINERS"
Sweet Betsy

The forty thieves
Minard — *Womenfolk* p.51-64

Forud of Kalāt
Picard — *Tales* p.156-172

The founding of Moencopi
Courlander — *Fourth* p.191-193

The foundling
Alexander — *Foundling* p.1-15

FOUNDLINGS
See also titles beginning with
"Changeling"
Brewer of eggshells
The devil and his three golden
hairs
The faery folk
The goblins
The jolly miller

FOUNTAIN OF YOUTH
Bimini and the fountain of youth

The fountain of youth
Life — *Treasury* p.26-27

FOUQUÉ. See Smedley, Menella Bute.
The shepherd of the Giant
Mountains

The four beautiful daughters
Lawrie — *Myths* p.55-56

The four big trolls and Little Peter
Pastureman
Olenius — *Great* p.59-77

The four golden guinea-pigs
Sleigh — *Stirabout* p.18-27

The four sacred scrolls
Novák — *Fairy* p.22-30

The four silly brothers
Carrick — *Wise* n. pag.

The four wizards
Bomans — *Wily* p.168-173

The four worlds
Courlander — *Fourth* p.17-33

FOURTH OF JULY
Fourth of July (subject)
Corrigan — *Holiday* p.143-154
Fireworks
Independence Day

FOWLERS
King Golden
Little Hiram

FOWLS
See also names of fowls
The eagle and the fowls
Turtle, fowl and pig

The fox
Krylov — *Fables* p.97-98

The fox and the badger
Ginsburg — *One* p.14-16

The fox and the cat
Bain — *Cossack* p.133-135
Bamberger — *My* p.37

The fox and the crow
Rugoff — *Harvest* p.420

The fox and the dragon
Green — *Cavalcade* p.21-22

The fox and the geese
Rugoff — *Harvest* p.358

The fox and the goat
Levine — *Fables* p.8
Piper — *Stories* n. pag.

The fox and the grapes
Darrell — *Once* p.242
Levine — *Fables* p.12
Morel — *Fairy* p.108

The fox and the leopard
Levine — *Fables* p.10

The fox and the lion
Ginsburg — *One* p.9

The fox and the marmot
Krylov — *Fables* p.50-51

The fox and the monkey who was
  elected king
  Levine — *Fables* p.84

The fox and the quail
  Ginsburg — *One* p.31-37

The fox and the rolling pin
  Carey — *Baba* p.39-41

The fox and the stork
  Piper — *Stories* n. pag.

The fox in the hole
  Jagendorf — *Noodle* p.45-47

Fox magic
  Carpenter — *People* p.71-75

The fox, the rabbit, and the rooster
  Carey — *Baba* p.45-48

The fox who lost his tail
  Levine — *Fables* p.14

FOXES
  The adventures of Renard
  Animal friendship
  Animals from heaven
  The badger and the fox
  The bamboo cutter
  The bear and the fox
  The bear's revenge
  The blue falcon
  Brer Rabbit, businessman
  Budulinek
  The cat, the cock, and the fox
  The cat and the she-fox
  The cat who became head-forester
  The children on the pillar
  The clever Durmian
  The cloak of friendship
  The cock and the mouse and the
    little red hen (and variants)
  Compae Rabbit's ride
  Coyote loses his dinner
  Coyote steals the summer
  The crow and the fox
  The dragon and the peasant
  The eagle with clipped wings and
    the fox
  (El) Enano
  The gingerbread man
  Going fishing
  The golden bird
  Grasshopper and fox

Gratitude
The hares and the foxes
The hen that saved the world
The hyena and the fox
The jackdaw and the fox
The lion and the fox
The lion and the grateful mouse
The lion, the ass, and the fox
The lion, the bear, and the fox
The lion, the chamois and the fox
The lion, the wolf, and the fox
The lioness and the fox
The little fox
Little head, big medicine
Little sister fox
The new law
The noodlehead tiger
The old lion and the fox
The old man, the wolf, and the
  vixen
The old woman in the cottage
Ole Sis Goose
One trick too many
Pan'ambe and pen'ambe
The peasant, the hen, and the fox
The rabbit and the barrel
The raven and the fox
The red fox and the walking stick
The right drumstick
The sly fox
The terrapin and the possum out-
  wit the fox
Thousands of ideas
The travels of a fox
Two foxes
The useless wagoner
The vixen and her cub
Why the bear has a stumpy tail
  (and variants)
Widow Fox and her four suitors
The wolf and the fox
The Zamay who hid his life
- *Tails*
    One trick too many
    Pan'ambe and pen'ambe

The fox's daughter
  Junne — *Floating* p.37-39

The fox's wedding
  Fairy Tales p.87-88

Foxglove
  Bamberger — *My* p.86-90

FRANCE
France (subject)
McHargue — *Impossible* p.44,
45,92,139
The adventures of Renard
Bahhh!
Beauty and the beast
The blind singer, Saint Hervé
The castle of Ker Glas
Cinderella (and variants)
Devil-may-care
The magic pot
The master cat (and variants)
The men who wouldn't stay dead
The miller, his son, and their
donkey
The needle crop of Sainte-Dodo
Our lady's tumbler
Puss in boots (and variants)
Ricky with the tuft
The shroud of Mari-Yvonne
The sleeping beauty (and variants)
The story of Almansor
Tales from Tartari-Barbari
The theft of a smell
- *Folk tales*
Folk tales (subject)
Rugoff — *Harvest* p.301-
341

FRANCIS OF ASSISI, SAINT
Saint Francis of Assisi

FRANCISCANS
The little blue light

Frankie and Albert
Life — *Treasury* p.242-245

Fraser, Betty, illus.
People from the sky

**FRAUD. See Deception; Dishonesty;
Hoaxes; Trickery**

FRAUNCES TAVERN, (New York City)
George Washington, the torch-
bearer

The freak
Wojciechowska — *Winter* p.55-60

FRECKLES
The princess with freckles

Frederick and his Katelizabeth
Segal — *Juniper (II)* p.187-200

FREEDOM
The house dog and the wolf

FRIARS
The little blue light

Friends and neighbors
De Roin — *Jataka* p.22-26

FRIENDSHIP
See also **Loyalty**
The chestnut tree
The cloak of friendship
The company you keep
A strange and rare friendship
Trust not a new friend
Two foolish friends
- *Animals*
Animals friendship
, *False*
The travelers and the bear

The frog
Manning — *Choice* p.26-38

The frog (anonymous)
Shaw — *Frog* p.11

The frog, by Hilaire Belloc
Shaw — *Frog* p.39

The frog, by Leonora Alleyne
Shaw — *Frog* p.32-38

The frog, by Oliver Herford
Shaw — *Frog* p.42

The frog and the ox
Krylov — *Fables* p.153
Shaw — *Frog* p.28-29

The frog-king, or Iron Henry
Rugoff — *Harvest* p.346-349
Segal — *Juniper (II)* p.169-177

"FROG PRINCE"
The frog prince (subject)
Opie — *Classic* p.183-184

The frog prince
Darrell — *Once* p.43-46
Haviland — *Fairy* p.114-117
Opie — *Classic* p.185-187

The frog princess
Whitney — *In* p.37-43

FROGS
Afternoon by a pond in the heart
    of Vermont
The doctor's servant
The draper who swallowed a fly
Go I know not whither and fetch
    I know not what
Haiku
Hopping frog
How the frog lost his tale (tail)
I'm nobody
A legend of Lake Okeefinokee
The little house
Old Mister Smoothback
The ox and the frog
The quack frog
The seven wishes
The strange folding screen
A tale of two frogs
A taste of his own medicine
The traveling frog
Twenty froggies
Two frogs
- *"Frog play"*
    Möibu and Bazi
- *Tadpoles*
    As the tadpole said
    Who but a tadpole?

The frogs asking for a king
    Darrell — *Once* p.244-245

The frog's saddle horse
    Shaw — *Frog* p.12-14

The frog's tattoo
    Carpenter — *People* p.55–60

The frogs who wanted a king
    Levine — *Fables* p.70

The frogs who wished for a king
    Shaw — *Frog* p.15-20

From tiger to Anansi; a Jamaican tale
    Haviland — *Fairy* p.86-91

From twelve o'clock to one o'clock
    Cott — *Beyond* p.242-246

FRONTO, SAINT
Saint Fronto's camels

Frost, Frances
Mice under snow

Frost, Robert
Not of school age

FROST
See also **"Father Frost"**
Coyote steals the summer
The little daughter of the snow
Why evergreens keep their leaves

Frost
Fairy Tales p.92-99
Ransome — *Old* p.33-44
Whitney — *In* p.27-34

FROST GIANTS
Big people
How Thor found his hammer

Frozen death
Schwartz — *Whoppers* p.62-65

Frozen people
Life — *Treasury* p.288-289

FRUIT
See also names of fruit
The dogai of Zurat
Goblin market
The wonders of palace life

The frying-pan
De Bosschere — *Christmas* p.115-
117

FUATHS
The people of the sea

Full moon a-shining
Bagley — *Candle* p.94-100

FULMARS (birds)
Sedna and the fulmar

The funeral
Krylov — *Fables* p.149-150

FUNERALS
A widow's funeral chant

Fur-bearing trout
Life — *Treasury* p.290-291

FUR COATS. See Clothes — Coats

Furlong, Alice
Country-under-wave
The harp of the Dagda Mor

Furniss, Harry, illus.
Wanted — a king

FUTURE
The ant and the grasshopper
The weaver of tomorrow

Fyleman, Rose
Mice

G

G — G —
Cott — *Beyond* p.247-251

Gabai
Lawrie — *Myths* p.134-137

Gabriel — Ernest
Hoke — *Monsters* p.153-163

GAELIC TALES
Blackberries in February
Blue falcon
The brown bear of the green glen
How the great Turisgale met his
death
The knight of the red shield
The man who couldn't get married
The old gray man of Spring
The sea maiden
The sharp gray sheep
The ship that sailed on sea and
land
The son of the king of the city of
straw
The sporran full of gold
The three shirts of Cannach Cotton
The wizard's gillie

Gaer, Joseph
Greedy and Speedy
The hermit and the mouse
The monkey gardeners

Gag, Wanda
Gone is gone

GAHONGAS
Little people

Gaibida
Lawrie — *Myths* p.247

Galahad. The Holy Grail
Stories From World p.138-143

The galloping ghost of Laramie
Anderson — *Haunting* p.143-49

GALLOWS
The two journeymen

GALSTER, ROBERT
Robert Galster, illus. (subject)
Shaw — *Mouse* p.45

GAMEKEEPERS
The lonely witch

GAMES AND RHYTHMS
Dead man
Konggasau
Nnoonya Mwana Wange
Wameal

Gammelyn, the dressmaker
Housman — *Rat* p.24-32

Ganalai Dogai
Lawrie — *Myths* p.218

GANCONER, THE
The faery folk

GANDAYAKS
Little people

GANHARVAS
The halfway people

GANGS
How Bart Winslow single handed
wiped out the Jinson gang,
which was known as the scourge
of the West

Ganomi and Palai
Lawrie — *Myths* p.360-363

GA —OH
Big people

Gar-room!
Manning — *Tortoise* p.47-50

The garden
Cott — *Beyond* p.442-34

**GARDEN OF EDEN. See Eden,
Garden of**

The garden of magic
Pugh — *More* p.29-37

GARDENS AND GARDENING
See also **Flowers**
Abdul Kasim the rich
The discovery of the garden land
  of Padrin
The fox in the hole
Iawar
Mistress Mary
The monkey gardeners
Peter Pan in Kensington Gardens
Responsibility
Sweet tooth
Three golden oranges
The three Ivans
Wakaima and the clay man
The wooing of the maze
, *Magic*
    The garden of magic

GARDNER, EDWARD L.
Little people

GARDNER, JOHN C.
John C. Gardner (subject)
    Gardner — *Dragon* p.75
    Gardner — *Gudgekin* p.60
    Gardner — *King* p.58

GARTERS
The field of Boliauns

Garuge
Lawrie — *Myths* p.240

GATEKEEPERS
The fisherman and the gatekeeper

GATES
The king of the hummingbirds
The sword

Gathering salt
Heady — *Safiri* p.87-92

"GEATS"
Beowulf and the dragon

Gedor of Leiwag
Lawrie — *Myths* p.324

GEESE
See also **Gooseherds**
Ayoga
Baba Yaga's geese
Coyote loses his dinner
Dwarf long nose
The fox and the geese
The golden eggs
The golden goose
The hen that saved the world
John in the storeroom
Longnose the dwarf
Ole Sis Goose
Saint Rigobert's dinner
Shish and the innkeeper
The swan-geese
The tortoise who talked too much
The wondrous wonder
- *Ganders*
    Lazy Hanz
, *Wild*
    Saint Werburgh and her goose
The geese
Krylov — *Fables* p.99-100

GEIGER, EMILY
Emily's famous meal

Geinau and Jeiai
Lawrie — *Myths* p.212-213

Gelam
Lawrie — *Myths* p.297-299

GEMS. *See* **Jewels**

GENEROSITY
See also **Kindness**
Abdul Kasim the rich
Hag-of-the-mist
How the finch got her colors
Saint Fronto's camels
The shared reward
The star money

GENET CATS
The deceitful leopard

GENIES
Aladdin (and variants)
The woman of the well
, *Evil*
    "Leave it there!"

GENTILES
Revealed

"GENTLE ANNIE"
Workers of evil — and a few good
  spirits

GEOGRAPHY. *See* **Earth; Mountains;
Rivers; Sea;** etc.

GEORGE, SAINT
The deliverers of their country
St. George and the dragon

George Piney-Woods peddler
Jagendorf — *Folk, South* p.99-105

George Washington, the torch-bearer
Corrigan — *Holiday* p.57-62

GEORGIA
The curse of Lorenzo Dow
Dan McGirth and his gray goose mare
Fearless Nancy Hart
George Piney-Woods peddler
Hoozah for fearless ladies and fearless deeds
The song of the Cherokee rose
The tale of the daughters of the sun
- *Savannah*
The ghost of Captain Flint
The haunted plantation house

GERALD, 4TH EARL OF DESMOND
Earl Gerald

GERASIMUS, SAINT
Saint Gerasimus and the lion

GERMANY
See also stories by Grimm, Jacob & Wilhelm
Big people
The Bremen town musicians
Death's messengers
The devil's granny
Dwarf long nose
The elves and the shoemaker
The fox and the geese
The frog-king, or Iron Henry
The girl who picked strawberries
The golden goose
The graveyard rose
Hansel and Grethel (and variants)
Knoist and his three sons
Little people
Little Red Riding Hood (and variants)
The little tailor and the three dogs
Mimer, the master
Old Hildebrand
Peter Klaus
The pirates and the Palatines
Richmuth of Cologne

The Schilda town hall
The Schildbürger build a council house
Snow-White (and variants)
Spindle, shuttle, and needle
The stove and the town hall
The tale of a merry dance
Tyll proves to fools how great is their folly
Tyll Ulenspiegel; the tale of a merry dance
Tyll's last prank
The valiant little tailor
The wife who talked too much (and variants)
The wolf and the seven little kids
Word, wit, and merry game
Workers of evil — and a few good spirits
- *Bavaria*
The forest inn
- *Black Forest*
The stone-cold heart
- *Folk tales*
Folk tales (subject)
Rugoff — *Harvest* p.342-381

GESNER, CONRAD
Halway people

Get up and bar the door
Rugoff — *Harvest* p.270-272

GHANA. See Africa — Ghana

The ghost challenger
Raskin — *Ghosts* p.118-127

The ghost dog
Roberts — *Ghosts* p.81-87

The ghost of Captain Flint
Roberts — *Ghosts* p.15-23

Ghost of the governor's mansion
Roberts — *Ghosts* p.75-80

Ghost of the Old Gold Mine
Roberts — *Ghosts* p.59-66

The ghost on Brass's Hill
Leach — *Whistle* p.106-107

Ghost ship of the Great Lakes
Anderson — *Haunting* p.126-132

92

The ghost that came to stay
Raskin — *Ghosts* p.106-117

The ghost the whole town knew
Jagendorf — *Folk, South* p.250-253

The ghost wedding in Everhope
Jagendorf — *Folk, South* p.153-155

The ghost who wasn't a ghost
Jagendorf — *Folk, South* p.244-247

Ghostly goddess of the volcano
Anderson — *Haunting* p.165-171

The ghostly spools
Leach — *Whistle* p.76-77

GHOSTS
Abraham Lincoln, a mourning
    figure, walks
Aiwali of Muri
Anne Boleyn
An apparition
The apple tree
The army of the dead
Ausi and Dubua
Baba Yaga
Bill is with me now
Blackbeard's treasure
The brave flute-player
A breath of air
The bridal ghost dinner
The calamander chest
Can't rest
Cauld, cauld, forever cauld
A Christmas carol
Crossing the bridge
Dance of the ghosts
Darak and Göidan
Dead man
Didipapa and Gorarasiasi
Don't drop into my soup
Dugama, maker of dugong magic
Earl Gerald
Eerie iron horse of the Arizona
    desert
The eitu who went as a man's wife
The fireplace
Gaibida
The galloping ghost of Laramie
Gi of Dabangai
The girl in the lavender dress
Goat castle
The golden girl of Appledore Island

Golden hair
Gora and the buk
Grandpa Joe's brother
The gray man
The gray man's warning
The harp player of Pitcher's Point
The haunted and the haunters
The haunted mill
The haunted palace
The haunted plantation house
The haunted room
Igowa
I'm coming up the stairs
Im
The inexperienced ghost
The inn that wasn't there
Invitation to a ghost
It
Jenny Green Teeth
Joe Baldwin's light
A jug of syrup
Kabai
Kama
The lady in black of Boston harbor
The listeners
The little people
(La) Llorona
A local haunting
The man on Morvan's road
The mansion of the dead
Marie Laveau, queen of the
    voodoos
The markai of Tawapagai
Mau and Matang
Meeting with a double
The mistress in black
The most haunted house
Muta
The mysterious Ticonderoga curse
The mystery of Bigfoot
Next turn to the right
Nilar Makrem
Nobody here but you and me
Nuiumma-kürten
Ocean-born Mary
"Old Hickory" and the Bell witch
Old Tom comes home
The old wife and the ghost
Old wine in new bottles
One handful
The open window
The outside man
Pablo and the pirate's ghost
Paslag

The phantom of the loch
The phantom vaquero of the
  Texas plains
Pot-Tilter
Pumpkin
Raw head and Bloody Bones
The sea captain at the door
Sik
The silver doe
Skull race
The soldier with the wooden leg
Specter of the Spanish castle
The specter of the tower
The "spirited" librarian
"Spook Light" of Devil's Prom-
  ade
Staring at you!
The strange, sad spirit of the Scioto
Sunrise
'Tain't so
The tale of the hairy toe
Terer
The three brothers
Tick, tick, tick
The tired ghost
Tony and his harp
The two spirit women of Daoma Kes
Ug
Usius
Virginia's ghostly aristocrat
What's the matter?
The white crane
White ghosts
White House ghosts
The wicked Sankhashurni
The wild ride in the tilt cart
Willie Winkie
The wizard's revenge
Zalagi and the mari
Zub and the lamar
- *Bogles*
  Lincolnshire moon
- *Cape Cod, Mass.*
  A telltale seaweed
- *Dogs*
  The ghost dog

The ghosts in the White House
  Life — *Treasury* p.264-266

The ghosts of Gibbet Island
  Raskin — *Ghosts* p.89-97

The ghosts of Stampede Mesa
  Jagendorf — *Folk, South* p.277-280

Gi of Dabangai
  Lawrie — *Myths* p.123-124

"GIANT" (raven)
  Raven's deed

The giant and the rabbit
  Lyons — *Tales* p.40-48

The giant and the wrekin
  Colwell — *Round* p.95-96

The giant of the causeway
  De Bosschere — *Christmas* p.126-
  133

The giant of the Fens
  Colwell — *Round* p.64-67

The giant who threw tantrums
  Harrison — *Book* p.33-44

The giant who was afraid of butterflies
  Harrison — *Book* p.19-32

GIANTS
  The baker's son and the king's
    daughter
  The battle of the birds
  Big people
  Blackberries in February
  Bran the blessed
  Cannibal
  The clever Durmian
  Cuchullin and Fardia
  David and Goliath; The shepherd
    boy and the giant
  Dawn-strider
  The dragon, sliced-in-two
  The dragon tamers
  The fairy tree
  The frog
  The green bird
  Halfway people
  Hercules of Virginia
  How the Great Turisgale met his
    death
  Jack and the beanstalk
  Jack the giant-killer
  Karakarkula
  King Johnny
  The King of Scotland's sons
  King Solomon's ring
  A legend of Knockmany
  The little boy's secret
  Little people

GIANTS *(continued)*

The little red hairy man
Lludd and Llevelys
Molly Whuppie
Mons Tro
Odin's search for wisdom
Ojumiri and the giant
Pedro the trickster
Pötikain and Ngiangu
Prince Ivan, the witch baby and
the little sister of the sun
Prince Loaf
The princess and the three tasks
The princess who lived in a kail-
yard
Salt
Sea magic
Seven with one blow
Sneezy Snatcher and Sammy Small
The son of bad Counsel
The son of the king of the city
of straw
The sorcerer of the White Lotus
Lodge
Stalo and Kauras
The Sunday child
The tailor and the giant
Thunderbird
The valiant little tailor
Wawa
Witzenspitzel
The youth who wanted to shiver
(and variants)
, *Frost*
Big people
, *Irish*
Clever Oonagh
, *Iroquois*
Big people

The giants of Castle Treen
Rugoff — *Harvest* p.251-255

GIANTS' CAUSEWAY
Big people

GIFTS
The Christmas gift
The Lady of the Lake
The merchant
Monsoon
The mouse-hole, and the Under-
ground kingdom
Oda and the snake

Samoan gift, Tongan payment
The singing leaves
The talema
The treasure of Li-Po
Uncle James, or the Purple
stranger
The wondrous wonder

Gifts of love
Junne — *Floating* p.76-78

GIGGLING. See Laughter

Gigi
Lawrie — *Myths* p.113-115

Gigi and the magic ring
Sheehan — *Folk* p.72-83

GILBERT, HUMPHREY, SIR
The search for Norumbega

GILES, SAINT
The ballad of Saint Giles and the
deer

"GILLIES"
The wizard's gillie

GINGERBREAD
Hans and Greta
Hansel and Gretel (and variants)

The gingerbread boy
Haviland — *Fairy* p.7-11
Morel — *Fairy* p.66-68

The gingerbread man
Rockwell — *Three* p.33-44

Gingersnap crumb crust (recipe)
Greene — *Clever* p.144

GINGHO NUTS
The Chinese red riding hoods

GINSBURG, MIRRA
Mirra Ginsburg (subject)
Ginsburg — *One* p.40

Giovanni, Nikki
The drum

GIPSIES. See Gypsies

The giraffe's neck
Heady — *Safiri* p.82-86

Girbar
  Lawrie — *Myths* p.190-191

GIRDLES (Armor)
  Hine and Tu
  Rake up!

The girl in the basket
  Manning — *Ogres* p.66-74

The girl in the lavender dress
  Life — *Treasury* p.252-256

The girl who cried flowers
  Yolen — *Girl* p.1-10

The girl who got a fairy in her eye
  Sleigh — *Stirabout* p.9-17

The girl who picked strawberries
  Manning — *Choice* p.291-294

GIRLS
  See also **Princesses; Sisters**
  Little Eva
  The origin of mosquitoes
  , *Sleeping*
    King Solomon's ring
    Sleeping beauty (and variants)

Giufá and the judge
  Jagendorf — *Noodle* p.173-174

Give my love to Boston
  Corrigan — *Holiday* p.213-222

Gladiator, the belle, and the good
    snowstorm
  Jagendorf — *Folk, South* p.257-259

GLAISTIG, THE
  Halfway people

GLANTOKIANS (monsters)
  Impulse

GLASS, HUGH
  The ordeal of Hugh Glass

GLASSES, EYE
  The magical spectacles
  The monkey and the spectacles

GLOOM
  The last piece of light
  The merchant's son who never
    smiled

GLOSSARIES
  Glossary of S. Africa (subject)
    Aardema — *Behind* p.81-82

The Gloucester sea serpent
  Life — *Treasury* p.136

GLOWWORMS. *See* Fireflies

GLUTTONY
  Song for a gluttonous owl

The gnat and the bull
  Darrell — *Once* p.244
  Levine — *Fables* p.56
  Morel — *Fairy* p.25

The gnat and the shepherd
  Krylov — *Fables* p.47-48

GNATS
  The lion, Jupiter, and the elephant

The gnome and the dragons
  Gardner — *King* p.45-58

GNOMES
  The flower of happiness on Sun-
    nymount Crest
  The golden slippers
  Little people
  The rat-catcher's daughter
  The stone-cold heart
  Tinykin's transformations
  Uletka and the white wizard

Go, I don't know where and bring
    back I don't know what
  Whitney — *In* p.1-24

Go I know not whither and fetch I
    know not what
  Manning — *Sorcerers* p.9-23

Go to the verge of destruction and
    bring back Shmat-Razum
  Curtin — *Myths* p.179-202

Goat and lion and snake
  Dolch — *Animal* p.47-53

The goat and the tiger
  Carter — *Greedy* p.35-40

Goat castle
  Anderson — *Haunting* p.78-84

GOATHERDS
  Peter Klaus

GOATS
Big people
Billy Goat Gruff
The boy and the North Wind
The fox and the goat
The gnome and the dragons
The grass-cutting races
Guani
Halfway people
The Helm goat mystery
Johnny and the three goats
Johnny and the witch-maidens
The lion and the goat
The magic table, the gold-donkey, and the cudgel in the sack
The old troll of Big Mountain
Peter Pan in Kensington Gardens
The princess's slippers
The sparrow and the bush
The stolen turnips, the magic tablecloth, the sneezing goat and the wooden whistle
The tailor and the treasure
Tatterhood
The three billy goats gruff
Widow Fox and her four suitors
Workers of evil — and a few good spirits
Zlateh the goat
- *Kids*
  The kid and the flute — playing wolf
  The kid and the wolf
  Song of the kid
  The wolf and the seven little kids
- *Skin*
  Malice, Bouki and Momplaisir
, *Mountain*
  The mountain goats
, *Wild*
  The bull and the wild goats

Goba
Lawrie — *Myths* p.45-46

Goblin market
Cott — *Beyond* p.465-519

GOBLINS
Brewery of eggshells
Hats to disappear with
Holding the truth
Little people
The magic hammer

The old man's wen
Schnitzle, Schnotzle, and Schnootzel
Workers of evil — and a few good spirits
The goblins
Segal — *Juniper (I)* p.150-151
The goblins at the bath house
Manning — *Choice* p.74-80
The goblins giggle
Bang — *Goblins* p.47-57

GOD
The fisherman and his wife
Why dog lost his voice
Why there is death in the world
The wisdom of the Lord

"GOD OF POVERTY"
Gohei and the god of poverty

Godfather Death
Segal — *Juniper (II)* p.228-235

Godfather to skunks
Lyons — *Tales* p.34-39

GODFATHERS
The christening in the village
Ferdinand Faithful and Ferdinand Unfaithful
Mons Tro
A necklace of raindrops
The three riddles

GODMOTHERS
The christening in the village
The last balloon

GODS AND GODDESSES
See also names of gods and goddesses
The badger and the fox
The beginning of maize
Cupid and Psyche
The eruption of Pele's anger
Gohei and the god of poverty
Hercules: the eleventh task
Hermit into scorpion
The hermit Mitsina
The impious
Jason and the dragon of Colchés
The making of the hammer
Medea

The monster we live on
Odin's search for wisdom
People of the sea
The spider and the sky god's
   stories
The thunder god
The wind's bride
Workers of evil — and a few good
   spirits
- Africa — Uganda
   Akanyonyi
- Bears
   "Good-by, dear little bear god"
, Boy
   The message
   The mission ended
   The revenge
   The tricks of Hunahpú and
      Ixbalanqué
- Guatemala
   The revenge
, Indian
   Father Marquette and the
      manitou
   Tuamotu
   The conflict of the gods

Gohei and the god of poverty
   Novák — Fairy p.39-43

Going fishing
   Carey — Baba p.67-70

The going home mix-up
   Bagley — Candle p.70-76

GOLD
   See also Coins, Gold
   Ali Baba
   Ashes for sale
   The dreamer
   Hans and his master
   Hans in luck
   The harp player of Pitcher's Point
   Hudden and Dudden and Donald
      O'Neary
   The king who was fried
   Kultano, the noodle gossip
   The Lady of the Lake
   The magic pot
   Mary Culhane and the dead man
   The miser who received his due
   The mountain lad and the forest
      witch

One handful
The peddler of Ballaghadereen
The rat-catcher's daughter
The shared reward
The sporran full of gold
Stan Bolovan and the dragon
The three brothers
The three kingdoms
The traveller's shoes
- Dresses
   Gammelyn, the dressmaker

The gold knob
   Manning — Sanders p.38-43

GOLD MINES AND MINING
   See also "Forty Niners"
   The drowned mine of Santa Ana
   Ghost of the Old Gold Mine

The golden apple-tree and the nine
      peahens
   Fairy Tales p.100-111

The golden bird
   Segal — Juniper (II) p.201-216

"GOLDEN CITIES OF CIBOLA"
   The search for the Golden Cities

The golden cock
   Rugoff — Harvest p.622-630

The golden cockerell
   Littledale — Strange p.63-73

The golden eggs
   Morel — Fairy p.25

The golden fish
   Ransome — Old p.151-163

GOLDEN FLEECE
   Jason and the dragon of Colchis

The golden girl of Appledore Island
   Anderson — Haunting p.1-6

The golden goose
   Bamberger — My p.53-58
   Haviland — Fairy p.58-65
   Morel — Fairy p.116-117
   Rugoff — Harvest p.435-436

Golden hair
   Manning — Choice p.231-234

The golden horned dragon
Spicer — *13 Dragons* p.101-112

The golden key
Cott — *Beyond* p.391-420

The golden mare
Carpenter — *People* p.86-91

The golden shoe
Sperry — *Scand.* p.277-288

The golden shoes
Jagendorf — *Noodle* p.48-52

The golden slipper
Bain — *Cossack* p.147-155

The golden slippers
Bomans — *Wily* p.28-38

The golden touch
Morel — *Fairy* p.32-33

The golden valley
Manning — *Monsters* p.29-40

Goldenhair
Corrigan — *Holiday* p.54

GOLDFISH. See Fish — Goldfish

"GOLDILOCKS"
Goldilocks and the three bears
(subject)
Opie — *Classic* p.199-200
The story of the three bears
The three bears

Goldilocks and the three bears (and
variants)
Kingsley — *Sesame* p.17-19
Morel — *Fairy* p.54-57

GOLDSMITHS
The forest inn
Gammelyn, the dressmaker
The juniper tree

GOLEMS
Big people

GOLIATH (Biblical)
Big people

Gone is gone
Haviland — *Fairy* p.48-55

GONZALES, PETER
Halfway people

Good advice
Lyons — *Tales* p.58-66

Good Bishop Valentine
Corrigan — *Holiday* p.41

GOOD LUCK. See Luck, Good

Good luck and bad luck
Bamberger — *My* p.133-136

The good man and the kind mouse
Shaw — *Mouse* p.32-41

A good name gives strength
Wyness — *Legends* p.11-15

The good ogre
Manning — *Ogres* p.9-19

"Good-by, dear little bear god"
Carpenter — *People* p.24-32

GOOD-NATUREDNESS. See Cheerfulness

GOODNESS
See also **Generosity; Kindness**
Evil-minded and good-minded
Gudgekin, the thistle girl
Repaying good with evil
The two journeymen

GOOSEHERDS ("Goose girls")
The prince and the goose girl
Tattercoats

Gora and the buk
Lawrie — *Myths* p.44-45

GORGONS
Halfway people

Gorgorian, Nancy
What is a witch?

GORILLAS
Ears and tails and common sense
Nsangi

Gossamer wedding
Life — *Treasury* p.178-179

GOSSIP
Kultani, the noodle gossip

GOTHAM
The alms tale
The blacksmith's tale
The cheese
The cuckoo
The fish tale
The four silly brothers
The hare
The lazy farmer's tale
The marriage tale
The miller's tale
Three wise men of Gotham (and
  variants)
The wives' tale

GOURDS
The grateful toad
Hine and Tu
The nine-headed bird

GOVERNORS
The evil eye
It's a long time between drinks

GRABBIST GIANT
Big people

Grace Sherwood, the woman none
  could scare
  Jagendorf — *Folk, South* p.312-314

GRAIN
The miller's tale
The sack of grain
Saint Comgall and the mice

GRAND CANYON
The Lalakon dance at Shongopovi

The grand tour of the gardens
  Darrell — *Once* p.250-255

GRANDCHILDREN
Tattercoats

The grandee
  Krylov — *Fables* p.159-160

GRANDFATHERS
Ghost of the Old Gold Mine
The hunter and his wife
The hut in the forest
Lisalill
Sister of the birds
The tale of the silver saucer and
  the transparent apple

GRANDMOTHERS
Brother sun and sister moon
Budulinek
The Chinese red riding hoods
The devil's granny
The ghostly spools
Kind little Edmund, or the Caves
  and the cockatrice
Koshchei without — death
The last balloon
Little Red Riding Hood
The maid in the mirror
The message
The monkey musicians
The origin of corn and beans
The patchwork quilt
The Sunday child
The thrush girl
The tricks of Hunahpu and
  Ixbalanqué
The woman who lived in a shoe
Xibalba
- *Dragons*
  The dragon and his grand-
    mother

Grandpa Joe's brother
  Leach — *Whistle* p.64-65

GRANDPARENTS
See also **Grandfathers; Grand-
  mothers**
Old Verlooka
The turnip

Granér, Cyrus
  The four big trolls and Little
    Peter Pastureman

GRANT, THE
Halfway people

GRAPES AND GRAPE-VINES
The doe and the vine
The fox and the grapes

GRASS
The discontented grass plant
Rake up

The grass-cutting races
  Sherlock — *Ears* p.105-121

Grasshopper and fox
  Manning — *Tortoise* p.83-89

GRASSHOPPERS
The ant and the grasshopper
Karboi and Pukat
The owl and the grasshopper

The grateful toad
Bang — *Men* p.27-31

GRATITUDE
See also **Ingratitude**
The boy and the dragon
The cloth of a thousand feathers
The elves and the shoemaker
The good man and the kind mouse
The lion and the grateful mouse
The little fox

Gratitude
Novák — *Fairy* p.100-107

The graveyard rose
Harris — *Sea Magic* p.20-38

GRAVEYARDS. See Cemeteries

GRAVITY
Jim Bridger overcomes gravity

The gray man
Anderson — *Haunting* p.64-70

The gray man's warning
Roberts — *Ghosts* p.41-49

Gray Moss on green tree
Jagendorf — *Folk, South* p.133-135

GREASE (Fat)
Takise

The great bear of Orange
Manning — *Sorcerers* p.45-64

The great bell of Bosham
Colwell — *Round* p.105-107

GREAT BRITAIN
See also names of individual
     countries
Big people
The faery folk
Halfway people
Little people
Sea magic

The great conjure-alligator-man of
     Florida
Jagendorf — *Folk, Song* p.67-69

The great discovery
Corrigan — *Holiday* p.190

The great fishbowl contest
Bagley — *Candle* p.57-61

The great golloping wolf
Manning — *Monsters* p.85-97

GREAT LAKES
Ghost ship of the Great Lakes

The great lamp
Cott — *Beyond* p.436-439

GREAT PLAINS. See Plains

The great traveler of Chelm
Jagendorf — *Noodle* p.53-58

GREECE
The ass carrying salt
The ass's shadow
The bald knight
Barefoot in bed
Big people
Boastful Aulus and the sly thief
Constantes and the dragon
Cupid and Psyche
Daedalus, Icarus, and the wings
Diana and Actaeon
Do you know?
The donkey of Abdera
Fables
The farthing rushlight
The fox and the crow
The girl who cried flowers
Halfway people
Hercules: the eleventh task
The house dog and the wolf
Jason and the dragon of Colchis
The lion and ass go hunting
The man and the satyr
The master thief and the dragon
Medea
Narcissus
The nine doves
Nobody and Polyphemus
The old man and death
The old woman and the physician
The old woman and the wine jar
Orpheus and Eurydice
The princess under the earth
The story of Atlantis
Tantalus
The travelers and the bear

The wolf and the crane
Workers of evil — and a few good
spirits
- *Arcadia*
The boy and the dragon
- *Colchis*
Jason and the dragon of
Colchis
- *Folk tales*
Folk tales (subject)
Rugoff — *Harvest* p.383-
421
- *King*
How the Great Turisgale met
his death

GREED
See also **Misers**
The fish with hooked noses
The fisherman and his wife
The golden fish
The golden touch
A handful of peas
The little golden fish
The loyal mungoose
Lu-bo-bo
Mukeis
The rat-catcher's daughter
Sebgugugu the glutton
Simili Hill
Tawaka, the greedy man
Why dogs hate cats
The wonderful fish

Greedy and Speedy
Junne — *Floating* p.45-47

The greedy crow
De Roin — *Jataka* p.62-65

Greedy Goba
Lawrie — *Myths* p.73

The greedy jackal caught
Rugoff — *Harvest* p.436-437

Greedy Mariani
Carter — *Greedy* p.99-105

Green, Charles, illus.
Tinykin's transformations

The green bird
Manning — *Ogres* p.80-90

The green children
Colwell — *Round* p.70-73

GREENE, ELLIN
Ellin Greene (subject)
Greene — *Clever* p.157

"GREENIES" (fairies)
The enchanted fisherman

Gregory, Lady
Herb-healing

GREGORY, LADY
Lady Gregory (subject)
Manley — *Sisters* p.65-66,218

GREMLINS
Little people

GRENDEL (giant)
Big people

Gretchen and the white stallion
Life — *Treasury* p.196-198

Griddle bread (recipe)
Greene — *Clever* p.55

GRIDDLES
Paul Bunyan's big griddle

GRIEF
Apukura's mourning for her son
Narcissus
The rich man and the hired
mourners

Grierson, Elizabeth W.
The seal catcher and the merman

"GRIFFIN" (ship, 1679)
Ghost ship of the Great Lakes

The griffin and the wise old
philosopher
Gardner — *Gudgekin* p.21-39

GRIFFINS
Alice's adventures in Wonderland
The island of the nine whirlpools
The lady and the lion
The shepherd of the Giant Moun-
tains

GRIFFITHS, FRANCES
Little people

Grimelda
Hopkins — *Witching* p.20-25

Grimm, Jakob, and Wilhelm
Bearskin
The Bremen town musicians
Briar Rose
Brother and sister
Brother Gaily
Cat and mouse in partnership
Cinderella (and variants)
The crystal ball
The dancing princesses
The devil and his three golden
hairs
The dragon and his grandmother
The elves and the shoemaker
The farmer and the devil
Ferdinand Faithful and Ferdinand
Unfaithful
The fisherman and his wife
Fitcher's feathered bird
The fox and the cat
Frederick and his Katelizabeth
The frog king, or Iron Henry
The frog prince
The goblins
Godfather death
The golden bird
The golden goose
Hans in luck
Hans my hedgehog
Hansel and Gretel (and variants)
The house in the forest
Jorinda and Joringel
The juniper tree
The lady and the lion
The little donkey
Little Red Riding-Hood (and
variants)
The little shepherd boy
Lucky Hans
The magic table, the gold-donkey,
and the cudgel in the sack
Many-Fur
The master thief
Mrs. Gertrude
Old Sultan
The old woman of the forest
The poor miller's boy and the
little cat
Rabbit's bride
Rapunzel
Rumpelstiltskin
The seven ravens
The seven Swabians
Seven with one blow (and variants)
Simeli Hill

The six who went together through
the world
Sleeping Beauty (and variants)
Snow-White and the seven dwarfs
(and variants)
Spindle, shuttle, and needle
The story of one who set out to
study fear
The three feathers
The three golden hairs
Tom Thumb
Twelve brothers
The twelve huntsmen
The two journeymen
The wolf and the seven little kids
The youth who wanted to shiver

Griswold, Gwendolyn
"Not a creature was stirring . . ."
Puss leaves home

GROCERS
The haunted room

GROUCHINESS. See Grumbling

The grouchy old owl
Shaw — *Owl* p.28

GROUSE
The ice dragon or Do as you
are told
The new law

GRUMBLING
The cock and the mouse and the
little red hen
The grouchy old owl
The stolen turnips, the magic
tablecloth, the sneezy goat and
the wooden whistle

Gruntvig, Svend
The clock that walked by itself
(Luck or wisdom)
Elf hill
A sensible suitor?
Ten miles at each step

Guani
Belpré — *Once* p.18-24

The guardians of the St. Lawrence
Higginson — *Tales* p.196-204

GUATEMALA
The beginning of maize

The creation of man
The first flute
How the moon came to be
The message
The mission ended
The revenge
The tricks of Hunahpú and
   Ixbalanqué

Gudgekin, the thistle girl
   Gardner — *Gudgekin* p.1-20

GUDWALL, SAINT
   The fish who helped Saint Gudwall

Guerber, Helene Adeline
   The shepherd's choice

Guernsey, Clara Florida
   The silver bullet (a story of old
   Nantucket)

GUERNSEY, CLARA FLORIDA
   Clara Florida Guernsey (subject)
      Manley — *Sisters* p.45-46,218

Guess who!
   Jagendorf — *Folk, South* p.168-171

GUILE. *See* **Cleverness; Trickery**

GUINEA FOWLS
   The tortoise who flew to heaven

GUINEA PIGS
   Dwarf long nose
   The four golden guinea-pigs

Guleesh
   Fairy Tales p.34-51

GULLS. *See* **Sea Gulls**

GULPING
   The ship that sailed on sea and
   land

GUNS AND GUNNERY
   Go to the verge of destruction
      and bring back Shmat-Razum
   The little man and his little gun
   - *Blowguns*
      How the moon came to be

GUSHTĀSP
   Picard — *Tales* p.228-239

GUY FAWKE'S DAY
   The ice dragon or Do as you are
   told

GYMNASIUMS
   The donkey of Abdera

GYPSIES
   Gypsies (subject)
      Ficowski — *Sister* n. pag.
   Andrusz who disliked beans
   Faithful legs and lazy head
   The foam maiden
   How a tailor became a king
   The magic box
   Macpherson's lament
   The mother of the sun
   The reed maiden
   The rose and the violinist
   Sister of the birds
   The stolen bairn of the Sidh'
   Where blonde people came from
   - *Words*
      , Pronunciation of
         Ficowski — *Sister* n. pag.

H

HABIT
   The half-man

HADES. *See* **Hell**

HADROPITHECUS
   Little people

The hag
   Shaw — *Witch* p.157

Hag-of-the-mist
   Pugh — *More* p.39-54

HAGS. *See* **Witches**

Haiku
   Shaw — *Frog* p.46

HAIR
   The bird witch
   Don't marry two wives
   The magician's cape
   The traveller's shoes
   , Blonde
      Where blond people come
      from

HAIR (continued)
- *Brushes*
    The water-nixie
- *Cloaks*
    The mermaid
, *Girls'*
    The lagoon of Masaya
, *Golden*
    A ballad of Saint Athracta's
      stags
    The devil and his three golden
      hairs
    Golden hair
    King Golden
    The making of the hammer
    Many-Fur
    Rapunzel
    Vassilissa goldentress, bare-
      headed beauty
, *Long*
    Rapunzel
- *Tufts*
    Ricky with the tuft
, *White*
    Karbai and Pukat

HAITI
    The goat and the tiger
    Greedy Mariani
    Why dog lost his voice

The half-chick
    Haviland — *Fairy* p.66-71

The half-man
    Higginson — *Tales* p.74-82

Half of everything
    Bamberger — *My* p.17-19

Halfway
    Schwartz — *Whoppers* p.56

Halfway people
    McHargue — *Impossible* p.105-134

Hall, Elizabeth P.
    The witch: a tale of the Dark
      Ages

HALL, ELIZABETH P.
    Elizabeth P. Hall (subject)
    Manley — *Sisters* p.105-106,
      219

Hallabau's jealousy
    Stories From World p.130-137

HALLETT, GOODY
    The witch of Wellfleet

HALLOWE'EN
    Hallowe'en (subject)
    Corrigan — *Holiday* p.202-208
    Dead man
    Jamie Freel and the young lady
    Knurremurre
    Ol' Clackety teeth
    The warlock of Glen Dye
    Workers of evil — and a few good
      spirits

Haltrich
    Half of everything
    Who can tell the bigger lie?

HAMADRYADS
    People of the sea
    Workers of evil — and a few good
      spirits

Hames, Inez and A. W. Reed
    The monster of Caukaudrove

HAMILTON HOUSE (South Carolina)
    Shake hands with a Yankee

HAMMERHEADS (birds)
    A safe home

HAMMERS
    How Thor found his hammer
    The magic hammer
    The making of the hammer
    One-inch fellow
    The smith, the weaver, and the
      harper
    Stingy Kichiyomu and the iron
      hammer

HAMS
    Why dogs hate cats

Hamsun, Kurt
    An apparition

A handful of peas
    De Roin — *Jataka* p.20-21

HANDICAPPED
    Babaia and Sagewa
    A Christmas carol
    The destruction of Palatkwapi
    The echo well
    The history of Little Mook

The soldier with the wooden leg
Through the fire
Through the needle's eye

HANDMILLS. See Mills, Hand

HANDS
The dead hand
The fiery dragon, or the Heart of
  stone and the heart of gold
, *Satan's*
  The Isle of Satan's hand

HANKS, NANCY
Nancy Hanks

HANNER DYN (the half-man)
The half-man

Hans and Greta
  Gardner — *Dr.* p.38-56

Hans and his master
  Manning — *Choice* p.224-230

Hans in luck
  Carle — *Eric* p.11-24

Hans my hedgehog
  Segal — *Juniper (I)* p.11-22

HANSEL AND GRETEL
Hansel and Gretel (subject)
  Opie — *Classic* p.236-237

Hansel and Grethel (and variants)
  Darrell — *Once* p.59-65
  Opie — *Classic* p.238-244
  Piper — *Stories* n. pag.
  Rugoff — *Harvest* p.364-371
  Segal — *Juniper (I)* p.152-168

HANUKKAH
Hanukkah (subject)
  Corrigan — *Holiday* p.224-231
Zlateh the goat

HAPPINESS
See also **Cheerfulness**
The Chinese dragons
The first flute
The girl who cried flowers
The three wise men
The time of the ugly
The wind man
, *Flower of*
  The flower of happiness on
    Sunnymount Crest

The happy prince
  Provensen — *Book* p.133-140

Happy returns
  Housman— *Rat* p.143-152

Harald the Viking
  Higginson — *Tales* p.168-185

Harchand the Just
  Fehse — *Thousand* p.98-103

The hare
  Carrick — *Wise* n. pag.

The hare and the tortoise
  Morel — *Fairy* p.15

The hare at the hunt
  Krylov — *Fables* p.119

Hare running
  Manning — *Tortoise* p.60-66

HARES. See Rabbits

The hares and the foxes
  Levine — *Fables* p.48

Hare's ears
  Manning — *Tortoise* p.80-82

Haroun al Raschid's ride to Basra. *See*
  Abdul Kasim the rich

The harp of the Dagda Mor
  McGarry — *Great* p.119-126

The harp player of Ritchie's Point
  Anderson — *Haunting* p.71-77

HARPERS. See Harps and Harpists

HARPIES
The halfway people

HARPS AND HARPISTS
The blind singer, Saint Hervé
David and Goliath, The shepherd
  boy and the giant
Orpheus and Eurydice
The smith, the weaver, and the
  harper
The stolen bairn of the Sidh
Tony and his harp
The wanderings of Arasmon
, *Golden*
  Jack and the beanstalk

Harsh words
De Roin — *Jataka* p.29-31

Hart, Henry H., tr.
The flute

HART, NANCY
Fearless Nancy Hart

HART, SAM
How Sam Hart beat the devil

Hartley, L. P.
Conrad and the dragon

HARTS. *See* Deer

HARVEST AND HARVESTERS
The field of boliauns

The Hatfields and the McCoys
Life — *Treasury* p.183-185

HATRED. *See* Enmity

HATS
Anfy and his landlord
The stone statue and the grass hat
- *Caps*
The cap that mother made
- *Hoods*
The sporran full of gold
, *Magic*
The magic listening cap
The three rascals and the
magic cap
, *of darkness*
The cloak of friendship
, *Reed*
New Year's hats for the
statues
- *Sombreros*
The sombreros of the men
of Lagos
, *White*
Jack and the white cap
, *Wishing*
The crystal ball

Hats to disappear with
Junne — *Floating* p.74-75

Hauff, Wilhelm
The story of Caliph Stork

HAUGHTINESS. *See* Pride

The haunted and the haunters
Hoke — *Ghosts* p.20-42

HAUNTED HOUSES
See also **Ghosts**
The most haunted house
The riddle of the room upstairs
What's the matter?

The haunted mill
Hoke — *Ghosts* p.47-52

The haunted palace
Novák — *Fairy* p.125-130

The haunted plantation house
Roberts — *Ghosts* p.33-40

The haunted room
Bamberger — *My* p.27-29

HAUSA TALES
The old woman
Takise

Havaiki the land
Alpers — *Legends* p.57-62

Haviland, Virginia
One-inch fellow

HAWAIIAN ISLANDS
- *Hawaii*
The eruption of Pele's anger
Lonopuha, or the origin of
Healing: and the story of
Milu
- *Maui*
Ahu ula: The first feather cloak
- *Oahu*
Ghostly goddess of the volcano

HAWKS
Coyote steals the summer
Turandot

HAWTHORN
The fairy thorn

HAY AND HAYMAKERS
The story of Little Boy Blue

HAZEL TREES
Cinderella

He who digs a pit for others. *See*
Semerude the Fair and the Cadi

He who likes to bite and kiss will
    always go astray and miss
    Carey — *Baba* p.49

HEADS
    Kasakuik
    The King of Colchester's daughter
    Sagerwazer
    Tusi and the great beast
    The yellow ribbon
    , *Enchanted*
        Bran the blessed
    , *Golden*
        The three heads of the well

HEALING
    See also **Medicine; Ointment;
        Physicians**
    Blood stoppers
    The brown bear of the green glen
    Don Demonie's mother-in-law
    Herb-healing
    Hok Lee and the dwarfs
    Lonopuha, or the origin of healing:
        and the story of Milu
    The magic listening cap
    No witchcraft for sale
    The wandering monk and the
        tabby cat
    Through the fire
    The Well of D'yerree-in-Dowan
    The woman of the well

HEARING, SENSE OF
    The ship that sailed on sea and
        land

Hearn, Lafcadio
    The old woman and her dumpling
    The story of O-Tei

Heart of stone and the heart of gold.
    See The fiery dragon

HEARTS
    See also names of animals, sub-
        division **Hearts**
    The stolen heart
    , *Golden*
        Leap the elk and little Princess
            Cottongrass
    , *Leaden*
        The happy prince

Hearty soup (recipe)
    Greene — *Clever* p.153-154

The heat
    Schwartz — *Whoppers* p.88-89

HEAVEN
    See also **Paradise**
    Bontche the silent
    John O'Hara's lantern
    The little blacksmith Verholen
    The tortoise who flew to heaven
    - *Keys*
        The key-flower

The heavenly sandwich
    Vogel — *Rainbow* p.13-20

HEBREWS. See Jews

HEBRIDES, SCOTTISH
    Blackberries in February
    The blue falcon
    The brown bear of the green glen
    How the Great Turisgale met his
        death
    The knight of the red shield
    The man who couldn't get married
    The old gray men of Spring
    The sea maiden
    The sharp gray sheep
    The ship that sailed on sea and
        land
    The son of the king of the city of
        straw
    The sporran full of gold
    The three shirts of Cannah Cotton
    The wizard's gillie

HECATONCHEIRS
    Big People

The hedgehog, the merchant, the king,
        and the poor man
    Curtin — *Myths* p.517-545

HEDGEHOGS
    Hans my hedgehog

The Hedley Kow
    Rugoff — *Harvest* p.224-226

HEIGHT
    Broad, Tall and Sharp-eyes

HEINZELMANNCHEN
    Little people

HELL
    John O'Hara's lantern
    Maski, the land of the dead

HELL-DIVERS (birds)
Manabozho, the trickster

The Helm goat mystery
Rugoff — *Harvest* p.560-564

The hen that laid golden eggs
Levine — *Fables* p.44

The hen that saved the world
Sperry — *Scand.* p.21-26

Henderson, Bernard
Tokutaro

Henny-Penny (Chicken Little)
Haviland — *Fairy* p.12-15
Rockwell — *Three* p.63-70

Henrietta's story
Wahl — *Muffletump* p.65-95

HEN-WIVES
Fair, Brown, and Trembling

HENRY, JOHN
John Henry and the machine in
West Virginia

HENRY, PATRICK
Thanks to Patrick Henry

HENS. See Chickens

Heracles and Athena
Levine — *Fables* p.26

Heracles and Ploutos
Levine — *Fables* p.20

HERAKLES
Halfway people
Workers of evil — and a few good
spirits

Herb-healing
Manley — *Sisters* p.67-70

HERBS
The blind singer and Saint Hervé
Dwarf long nose
Longnose the dwarf

Hercules of Virginia
Jagendorf — *Folk, South* p.297-
301

Hercules: the eleventh task
Rugoff — *Harvest* p.411-415

The herdsman and the lion
Levine — *Fables* p.26

HERDSMEN
The cane with a will of its own

Herford, Oliver
The elf and the doormouse
The frog

HERMES
The statue vendor
Zeus and men

Hermes' chariot
Levine — *Fables* p.80

The hermit and the bear
Krylov — *Fables* p.103-106

The hermit and the mouse
Junne — *Floating* p.48-49

Hermit into scorpion
Roy — *Serpent* p.30-35

The hermit Mitsina
Rugoff — *Harvest* p.111-119

HERMITS
The ballad of Saint Giles and the
deer
Cesarino and the dragon
Dewi and the devil
King Johnny
Saint Cuthbert's peace
The sea gulls
The three hermits

The hero
Jagendorf — *Noodle* p.212-215

HEROD, KING
Ragnar Shaggy-Legs and the
dragons

HEROES AND HEROINES
See also names of heroes and
heroines
Heroes and heroines (subject)
Higonnet-Schnopper — *Tales*
p.91-160
Alyosha Popovich
The curse of Lorenzo Dow
Deidre

The destruction of the Sampo
Footless and blind champions
The forest inn
How Kate Shelley saved the express
How three mighty heroes saved
  the sun and the moon from the
  dragon
The proud tale of David Dodd
The Kalevala
The last adventure
Sam Hudson the Great
Seven with one blow
Sigurd the dragon-slayer
The three kingdoms
Vasilisa and Prince Vladimir
, Folk
    Daddy Mention and Sour-
      dough Gus
    The great conjure-alligator-
      man of Florida
    Lafitte's great treasure
    The life of Annie Christmas
    Way deep down in the Oke-
      fenokee Swamp
- Polynesia
    Apukura's mourning for her son
    Ataraga at the pool
    Hine and Tinirau
    How Tahaki lost his golden
      skin
    The legend of Rara
    Maui and Tuna
    Maui-of-a-thousand-tricks
    Tahaki of the golden skin
- Revolutionary War
    They called her a witch

The heron and the crane
    Carey — Baba p.42-43

HERONS
    The christening in the village
    Karbai and Pukat
    Lizard and a ring of gold
    The wolf and the heron

Herrick, Robert
    The hag

HERVÉ, SAINT
    The blind singer, Saint Hervé

HEUVELMANS, BERNARD, DR.
    Workers of evil — and a few good
      spirits

HEXES
    See also **Curses; Magic; Witch-
      craft; Witches**
    The time Blue Louisey put a hex
      on the house

Hiawatha
    Life — Treasury p.54-56

HIBERNATION
    Frozen people

HICKOK, JAMES BUTLER ("Wild Bill')
    The McCanles fight as Hickok told
      it

Hickory, dickory, dock
    Baum — Mother p.141-147
    Cott — Beyond p.292-296

A hickory tree
    Schwartz — Whoppers p.85-86

HID-FOLK
    Faery folk

Hie over to England
    McGarry — Great p.18-24

High diving
    Schwartz — Whoppers p.36-38

The high-low jump
    Bagley — Candle p.19-25

High winds and funny weather
    Life — Treasury p.276-277

Higher mathematics in Helm
    Rugoff — Harvest p.565

HIGHWAYMEN. See Bandits

Hill, Pati
    The dormouse

HILLS
    Apinini and Sidipuar

HIMALAYAS (Mts.)
    The monkey and the crocodile
    The oldest of the three
    The wonders of palace life

Hina and the eel
    Alpers — Legends p.73-75

HINDUS AND HINDUISM
Workers of evil — and a few good spirits

Hine and Tinirau
Alpers — *Legends* p.113-117

Hine and Tu
Alpers — *Legends* p.337-341

HIPPOGRIFFS (winged horses)
The book of beasts

HIPPOPOTAMI
The fiery dragon
Takise

Hippopotamus and elephant
Dolch — *Animal* p.55-61

Hiroko
Wolkstein — *Lazy* p.7-13

His very best friend
Sperry — *Scand.* p.159-169

The history of Jack and the bean-stalk
See also Jack and the bean-stalk
Opie — *Classic* p.164-174

The history of Jack and the giants
See also Jack the giant-killer
Opie — *Classic* p.51-65

The history of Little Mook
Hauff — *Big* p.29-59

The history of Tom Thumb(e)
Haviland — *Fairy* p.72-77
Opie — *Classic* p.33-46

HIVA OA
Kae and the whale
Tahia the fragrant girl

The hoard
Green — *Cavalcade* p.246-248

HOARDING. See Greed; Misers

HOAXES
Manhattan hoax
Paslag

HOBGOBLINS
Little people

HOBHOLE HOB
Little people

The Hodja and the burglar
Rugoff — *Harvest* p.176

The Hodaj and the caldron
Rugoff — *Harvest* p.175-176

The Hodja visits the Halil
Rugoff — *Harvest* p.176-178

HOES
Awo!

HOGS
The best food
Burum
The castle in the silver wood
The fiery dragon
The great fishbowl contest
Juan Bobo
The Kiwai raiders
Lazy Hans
The little pig's way out
Lookit the little pig!
The old woman and her pig
The pig that went to court
The pig with gold bristles, the deer with golden horns and the golden-maned steed with golden tail
The piglet and the fairy
Route taken by Nima in Binihin
The story of the three little pigs (and variants)
"That's not true"
The three brothers
Tom, the piper's son
Turtle, fowl and pig
The witches' cellar
- Boars
The draper who swallowed a fly
The lion and the wild boar
Old Sultan
The wild boar and the fox
- Gold and silver bristles
Esben and the witch

HOHOKAM (ancient ones)
Baker — *At* p.51-53

Hok Lee and the dwarfs
Junne — *Floating* p.32-36

HOKKAIDO
The "little people"
People from the sky

Holding the truth
  Rugoff — *Harvest* p.426-431

The hole in the back wall
  Life — *Treasury* p.217

HOLES
  The buried money
  The fox in the hole
  The strong chameleon
  Thousands of ideas

HOLIDAYS
  See also names of holidays
  The field of boliauns

HOLLAND, PHILEMON
  People of the sea

HOLLAND. See Netherlands

Holmes, Oliver Wendell
  Broomstick train

HOLY GRAIL
  Galahad. The Holy Grail

HOLY MEN
  The king who was fried
  Mouse-maid made mouse

HOLY VIRGIN. See Mary, Virgin

HOMES
  Zeus and the tortoise

HOMO SAPIENS
  Big people
  Workers of evil — and a few good
    spirits

Homolovi and the journey northward
  Courlander — *Fourth* p.72-81

HONDURAS
  The enchanted orchard
  How the devil constructed a church
  The purchased miracle
  The warrior who shot arrows at a
    star

HONESTY
  See also **Truth**
  The poorest man in the world
  The shepherd who could not lie

HONEY
  The bird that would not stay dead

The fox and the badger
Goblin market
The rabbit and the honey-gum slide
Sweet tooth
Toast and honey
Utua Ninia

Honey butter (recipe)
  Greene — *Clever* p.129

HONOR
  A mother shames her son,
    Mapukutoora

Hood, Tom
  Petsetilla's posy

HOOD, TOM
  Tom Hood (subject)
    Cott — *Beyond* p.40

HOODS. See Hats — Hoods

Hoozah for fearless ladies and fearless
    deeds
  Jagendorf — *Folk, South* p.108-117

HOP O' MY THUMB
  Hop-o'-my thumb (subject)
    Opie — *Classic* p.128-129

Hop-o'-my-thumb (Little Poucet)
  De Bosschere — *Christmas* p. 29-
    35

HOPE
  The foundling

Hope-Simpson, Jacynth
  The water monster

Hopkins, Lee Bennett
  This witch

Hopping frog
  Shaw — *Frog* p.42-43

The horned woman
  Manley — *Sisters* p.62-64

HORNS
  The tale of the huntsman
  , *Magic*
    The small red ox

Horns for a rabbit
  Sherlock — *Ears* p.77-87

The horror of the heights
Hoke — *Monsters* p.132-152

"HORRORS" (evil ones)
The buried moon
The dead hand

The horse and the soldier
Levine — *Fables* p.102

The horse-egg
Jagendorf — *Noodle* p.19-21

HORSE-RACES
The chapel on Cristo street

Horse trading in Wichita Falls
Jagendorf — *Folk, South* p.290-292

HORSEMEN AND HORSEMANSHIP
The galloping ghost of Laramie
The prince and the goose girl
The steed and his rider

HORSES
A ballad of Saint Athracta's stags
The bear's revenge
The Cegua
The clever thief
The dog and the horse
The dragon king and the twin horses
The fire-bird, the horse of power and the Princess Vasilissa
The "foolish people"
Gohei and the god of poverty
The golden shoe
Halfway people
Hoozah for fearless ladies and fearless deeds
Ivan the peasant's son and the little man himself one-finger tall, his mustache seven versts in length
The knee-high man
The little fox
Little sister fox
The merchant's son who never smiled
Mirko, the king's son
The pig that went to court
The poor miller's story and the little cat
Prince Bajaja
The steed and his rider

The story of Tremsin the bird Zhar, and Nastasia, the lovely maid of the sea
"That's once" (and variants)
Usheen in the island of youth
The white fairy horse
The witch's bridle
A witty answer
The wonderful shirt
The wonderful working steeds
The young witch-horse

, *Black*
The black charger
, *Blind and deaf*
Catch-the-wind
, *Colts*
How the Great Turisgale met his death
Rescue of Ivan Tsarevich and the winning of the colt (variant)
The story of the forty-first brother
The two journeymen
, *Golden*
The golden bird
The golden mare
The pig with gold bristles, the deer with golden horns, and golden-maned steed with golden tail
, *Grey*
Mons Tro
, *Magic*
The magic horse
- *Mares*
Dan McGirth and his gray goose mare
The golden mare
How Sam Hart beat the devil
Marya Moryevna
- *Mustangs*
The phantom vaquero of the Texas plains
, *Palomino*
Lesson for lesson
- *Thieves and thievery*
The phantom vaquero of the Texas plains
, *Water*
Cledog and the "Ceffyl-dwr"
, *White*
Ferdinand faithful and Ferdinand unfaithful

The great bell of Boshan
Gretchen and the white
　　stallion
The man, the white steed and
　　the wondrous wood
The wizard of Alderley Edge
, *Winged*
　　Little Hiram

HOSPITALITY
　　The mysterious traveller

The hound and the hare
　　Darrell — *Once* p.240

HOURS. See Time — Hours

The house dog and the wolf
　　Rugoff — *Harvest* p.416-417

The house in the forest
　　Bamberger — *My* p.103-107

The house in the middle of the road
　　Aardema — *Behind* p.74-80

The house on the hill
　　Great Children's p.153-160

The house that Jack built
　　Rockwell — *Three* p.45-52

HOUSES
　　The Schildbürger build a council
　　　house
　　The story of the three little pigs
　　The woman who lived in a shoe
, *Brick*
　　　The three little pigs
, *Building*
　　　The goat and the tiger
, *Indian*
　　　The hole in the back wall

HOUSEWIVES
　　A tale of Steep-stair town

HOUSEWORK
　　Gone is gone
　　The husband who was to mind the
　　　house
　　The story of Seppy who wished
　　　to manage his own house

HOUSMAN, LAURENCE
　　Afterword (subject)
　　　Housman — *Rat* p.164-169
　　Golden market

How a tailor became a king
　　Wojciechowska — *Winter* p.32-40

How a wolf reforms
　　De Roin — *Jataka* p.60-61

How ailments were put in their proper
　　place
　　Hayes — *How* p.70-80

How Baira got a wife
　　Lawrie — *Myths* p.185-186

How Bart Winslow single handed
　　wiped out the Jimson gang,
　　which was known as the scourge
　　of the West
　　Hayes — *How* p.10-23

How blue crane taught jackal to fly
　　Aardema — *Behind* p.26-33

How counting came to be from one to
　　ten
　　Alpers — *Legends* p.305-307

How Daniel Boone met his wife
　　Life — *Treasury* p.111-112

How El Bizarrón fooled the devil
　　Carter — *Greedy* p.23-29

How far is it to Jacob Cooper's?
　　Jagendorf — *Folk, South* p.17-19

How fire came to the earth
　　Life — *Treasury* p.72-73

How fire took water to wife
　　Carey — *Baba* p.81-83

How fire was brought to Torres Strait
　　Lawrie — *Myths* p.83-84

How hoop snakes can sting
　　Life — *Treasury* p.287-288

How Hotu Matua found this land
　　Alpers — *Legends* p.233-236

How it all came right in the end
　　Cott — *Beyond* p.139-144

How Joe became Snaky Joe
　　Jagendorf — *Folk, South* p.271-
　　275

How Kate Shelley saved the express
　　Life — *Treasury* p.229-231

How man began
McDowell — *Third* p.131-132

How Matt Carney retired and raised
chickens
Hayes — *How* p.54-69

How Merle found the stolen packet
Cott — *Beyond* p.267-272

How Nycteris grew (in the day boy and
the night girl)
Cott — *Beyond* p.430-431

How Photogen grew (in the day boy
and the night girl)
Cott — *Beyond* p.428-430

How red strawberries brought peace
in the woods
Jagendorf — *Folk, South* p.33-35

How Rustem found Raksh
Picard — *Tales* p.67-74

How Sam Hart beat the devil
Life — *Treasury* p. 149-150

How straws were invented
De Roin — *Jataka* p.51-53

How Tahaki lost his golden skin
Alpers — *Legends* p.130-139

How the animals obtained fire
Bird — *Path* p.17-20

How the beggars came to town
Baum — *Mother* p.183-196

How the clever doctor tricked death
Carter — *Greedy* p.9-13

How the devil constructed a church
Carter — *Enchanted* p.109-114

How the finch got her colors
Piper — *Stories* n. pag.

How the frog lost his tale (tail)
Shaw — *Frog* p.21-23

How the Great Turisgale met his death
MacFarlane — *Mouth* p.38-45

How the Milky Way came to be
McDowell — *Third* p.23-24

How the moon came to be
Carter — *Enchanted* p.40-45

How the moonfish came to be
Carter — *Greedy* p.3-8

How the posy changed hands
Cott — *Beyond* p.90-96

How the rabbit lost his eye
Bird — *Path* p.67-69

How the raccoon got rings on his tail
Bird — *Path* p.51-53

How the ranchers of Windy Canyon
built the biggest fence the
West has ever seen
Hayes — *How* p.37-53

How the sheriff's posse and the hold-
up men sat down to dinner
together
Hayes — *How* p.81-94

How the Short-ears conquered the
Long-ears
Alpers — *Legends* p.247-250

How the snake lost his voice
Novák — *Fairy* p.81-84

How the sneaky waterstealer set the
cattlemen and the sheepmen
against each other
Hayes — *How* p.24-36

How the true facts started in Simpsonville
Hayes — *How* p.1-9

How Thor found his hammer
Rugoff — *Harvest* p.666-671

How three mighty heroes saved the sun
and the moon from danger
Ginsburg — *How* p.69-77

How to become a witch
Leach — *Whistle* p.98-99

How Wilka went to sea
Ginsburg — *How* p.29-41

How wise is an owl
Shaw — *Owl* p.44

Howard, Mrs. Volney E.
The midnight voyage of the
Seagull

HOWARD, MRS. VOLNEY E.
Mrs. Volney E. Howard (subject)
Manley — *Sisters* p.144-145,
219

Howitt, Mary, and William
The golden shoe

HROTHGAR, KING OF THE DANES
The water monster

HUCKSTERS
The ass carrying salt

Hudden and Dudden and Donald
O'Neary
Rugoff— *Harvest* p.494-499

HUDSON, GEOFFREY
Little people

HUDSON, HENDRIK
People of the sea

HUDSON, SAM
Sam Hudson the Great

Hughes, Arthur, illus.
The day boy and the night girl
The golden key

Hughes, Langston
Carol of the brown king
My people
The negro speaks of rivers
Thank you, M'am

HUICHOL MYTHS
The aunts

HULDERFOLK
The Faery folk

HUMILITY. See Meekness

Hummingbird of the South
Roy — *Serpent* p.41-46

HUMMINGBIRDS
The king of the hummingbirds
The legend of the hummingbird

HUMOR
The fabulous Wilson Mizner

HUMPBACKS. See Hunchbacks

Humpty Dumpty
Baum — *Mother* p.207-217

HUNCHBACKS
Chapkin the scamp
Foxglove
The garden of magic
The men who wouldn't stay dead
The miller's mule
The sunshade
The twin hunchbacks

Hung Vuong and the betel
Duong — *Beyond* p.13-17

Hung Vuong and the earth and sky
cakes
Duong — *Beyond* p.18-28

HUNGARY
See also **Magyars**
The enchanted prince
Hans and his master
The hero
The obedient servant
The singing tree

HUNGER
Coyote loses his dinner
The fast
Hans and Greta
The high-low jump
The peddlar of Ballaghadereen
The rich señora
Saint Fronto's camels
Saint Rigobert's dinner
Ubir

Hungry-for-battle
Higonnet-Schnopper — *Tales*

The hungry old witch
Shaw — *Witch* p.9-23

The hungry time
Carpenter — *People* p.33-40

The hunter and his wife
Ransome — *Old* p.189-195

The hunter, the Ukten and thunder
Bird — *Path* p.75-78

HUNTERS AND HUNTING
Ballad of Saint Giles and the deer
Brer Rabbit, businessman

HUNTERS AND HUNTING *(continued)*

Cooperation
The cowardly hunter and the
  woodcutter
Dag and Daga, and the flying troll
  of Sky Mountain
Deidre
Diana and Actaeon
The dog and the hunter
The draper who swallowed a fly
The foolish monkeys
The haunted plantation house
Jack's hunting trips
The Lamehva people
Leopard hunt
Lippo and Tapio
The little man and his little gun
Maiwasa
The ordeal of Hugh Glass
The rabbit huntress
The rascal crow
Roa Kabuwam
Saint Bridget and the king's wolf
The sportsman
The sunset
The tale of the huntsman
Trickery
The tsar and the angel
The twelve huntsmen
The voices at the window
The white doe
The wolf-mother of Saint Ailbe

The hunter's bargain
Heady — *Safiri* p.51-57

Hunting
Schwartz — *Whoppers* p.39-41

Hurrah for cats!
Shaw — *Cat* p.42

HURRICANES
The gray man
The stone dog
- *Warnings*
    The gray man's warning

The husband who was to mind the
  house
Minard — *Womenfolk* p.106-110

HUSBANDS
Gone is gone
The husband who was to mind
  the house

Now I should laugh if I were not
  dead
Princess Peridot's choice
Rip Van Winkle
The untamed shrew
What came of picking flowers
Women
Zalagi and the mari

The hut in the forest
Ransome — *Old* p.1-5

HUTS. See Houses

Hutton, Joan
Priscilla's witches
Some mice under ferns

HY-BRASAIL (island)
Kirwan's search for Hy-Brasail

Hyatt, Robert M.
The terrible stranger

Hyde, Douglas
The well of D'yerree-in-Dowan

HYDRA
Workers of evil — and a few good
  spirits

Hyena and hare
Manning — *Tortoise* p.67-74

The hyena and the fox
Levine — *Fables* p.92

HYENAS
Lion and hyena and rabbit

Hylten-Cavallues, Gunnar Olof
A cat for a cow

HYMAN, TRINA SCHART
Trina Schart Hyman (subject)
Greene — *Clever* p.159

HYPERTRICHOSIS
Halfway people

HYPOCRISY
The bear and the fox

I

I ate the loaf
Rugoff — *Harvest* p.708-709

I have a dream
    Corrigan — *Holiday* p.23-24

I hear America singing
    Corrigan — *Holiday* p.171

I know an owl
    Shaw — *Owl* p.48

I saw three witches
    Shaw — *Witch* p.199

I will leave it to the devil
    Raskin — *Ghosts* p.42-50

Ialbuz
    Lawrie — *Myths* p.9-10

Iawar
    Lawrie — *Myths* p.61

IB (IBKEP)
    - *Sacred ritual*
        Bai

ICARUS
    Daedalus, Icarus, and the wings

ICE
    One trick too many
    Silent Biana

The ice dragon, or Do as you are told
    Bland — *Complete* p.69-94

ICE FISHING
    Why the bear has a stumpy tail
        (and variants)

ICELAND
    Bjarni Sveinssen and his sister
        Salvör
    The boy in the secret valley
    Cow Bu-cola
    The gold knob
    The golden shoe
    Jon and the troll wife
    The man, the woman, and the
        fly
    Now I should laugh if I were not
        dead
    Sigurd the King's son
    The small red ox
    Tritil, Litil, and the birds
    The witch in the stone boat

Ichabod, Crook-Jaw and the witch
    Life — *Treasury* p.90-92

Shaw — *Witch* p.32-36

IDEAS
    Thousands of ideas

IDIOTS. See Fools and Foolishness

The idle boy. *See* Aladdin

IDLENESS. See Laziness

**IDOLS. See Gods and Goddesses;
    Statues**

If not still higher
    Hautzig — *Case* p.33-37

If you don't like it, don't listen
    Higonnet-Schnopper — *Tales* p.21-
        29

IGNORANCE
    The griffin and the wise old
        philosopher

Igowa
    Lawrie — *Myths* p.245-246

ILEX TREES
    Jason and the dragon of Colchis

The ill-shorn lamb
    Levine — *Fables* p.84

ILLEGITIMACY
    The invisible cloth

ILLNESS. See Sickness

ILLUSION
    The griffin and the wise old
        philosopher

**ILLUSTRATORS. See names of illus-
    trators**

I'm coming up the stairs
    Leach — *Whistle* p.57-58

I'm nobody
    Shaw — *Frog* p.46-47

Im
    Lawrie — *Myths* p.29-30

Imaginary twins
    Cott — *Beyond* p.252-257

Imermen and Kikmermer
    Lawrie — *Myths* p.291-292

118

IMITATION
The Khevsouri and the Eshmahkie

IMMIGRANTS
Ocean-born Mary

IMMORTALITY
The wish that came true

IMPERSONATIONS
See also Disguises; Magic;
Transformations; Witchcraft
The eitu who went as a man's wife
Hina and the eel
The white buffalo

IMPERTINENCE. See Discourtesy

The impious
Krylov — Tales p.89-91

IMPOSSIBILITY
The man who promises the
impossible

IMPOSSIBLE PEOPLE
- Origin
Introduction (Impossible
people)
Workers of evil — and a few
good spirits

IMPOSTERS
The Emperor's new clothes

IMPRISONMENT. See Prisons and
Prisoners

IMPS
Workers of evil — and a few good
spirits

Impulse
Hoke — Monsters p.53-68

In Abdul Kasim's palace. See Abdul
Kasim the rich

In Arkansas stick to bears; don't mess
with swampland skeeters
Jagendorf — Folk, South p.51-53

In just-/Spring
Corrigan — Holiday p.94

In Mexico the people say . . . Short
sayings based on long experience
Lyons — Tales p.80-81

In the Avu observatory
Hoke — Monsters p.110-119

In the beginning
Martin — Raven p.11-15

In the beginning there was no earth
Belting — Whirlwind n. pag.

The incubus
Rugoff — Harvest p.592-595

INDEPENDENCE. See Freedom

INDEPENDENCE DAY. See Fourth of
July

Independence Day
Corrigan — Holiday p.145-154

INDIA
The alligator and the jackal
The banyan deer
Big people
The blind man, the deaf man,
and the donkey
The cat and the parrot
Don't marry two wives
Greedy and Speedy
Halfway people
The hermit and the mouse
The horse-egg
Irani and the cuckoos
Little Hiram
The little jackals and the lion
The monkey gardeners
The noodlehead tiger
The princess of the mountain
Rama. The bow that could not be
bent
Sir Buzz
There are such people
The tiger, the Brahmen, and the
jackal
The valiant chattee-maker
Workers of evil — and a few good
spirits
- Benares
The best food
The company you keep
Cooperation
Decide for yourself
Don't try the same trick twice
Fearing the wind
The greedy cow
A handful of peas

How a wolf reforms
Learn and live
Leave well enough alone
The most beautiful of all
Responsibility
Rumors
Sweet tooth
The tortoise who talked too
  much
Using your head
The wonders of palace life
, East
  Bastianelo
  The Brahman and the pot of
    rice
  Devabhuti and the foolish
    magistrate
  The golden goose
  The greedy jackal caught
  Holding the truth
  The Judas tree
  The king who was fried
  The lion makers
  The loyal mongoose
  The merchant
  The mice that ate iron
  Mouse-maid made mouse
  Pinto Smalto
  Rāma and Sitā
  The robbers and the treasure
  Scissors they were
  The thoughtless abbot
  The three fastidious men
  - Folk tales
    Folk tales (subject)
      Rugoff — *Harvest*
        p.423-460
- *Varanasi.* See India —
  Benares

**INDIAN REORGANIZATION ACT OF
  1934**
The founding of Moencopi

INDIANS OF LATIN AMERICA
Tortoise and ogre
Tortoise and the children
- *Tribes*
  - *Aztec*
    The fifth son
    Hermit into scorpion
    Hummingbird of the South
    The king and the rain
      dwarfs

The monster we live on
People of the heron and
  the hummingbird
Plumed serpent in Tula
The warrior who shot
  arrows at a star
The wind's bride
- *Carib*
  The little blue light
  Yuisa and Pedro Mexias
- *Maya*
  The first flute
  The monkey musicians
  The warriors who shot
    arrows at a star
  Xibalba

INDIANS OF NORTH AMERICA
American Indians (subject)
  Rugoff — *Harvest* p.93-129
Benny's flag
The creation of man
The deceived blind men
The discontented grass plant
Grasshopper and fox
Gray moss on green trees
The hermit Mitsina
How red strawberries brought
  peace in the woods
Little Burnt-Face
The Negro speaks of rivers
Old Hildebrand
Outwitting the Indians
The Pleiades
Rabbit and the wolves
The rabbit huntress
The raven brings light
Raven's deed
The ring around the tree
The savage birds of Bald
  Mountain
The search for Little Water
The shining lodge
The silver doe
The silver snake of Louisiana
The son of the Cherokee rose
Specter of the Spanish castle
The tale of the daughters of the
  sun
Thunderbird
- *California*
  The evil eye
- *Canada*
  Hare running
  The little scared one

INDIANS OF NORTH AMERICA
(continued)

- *Captives*
  Drop Star
- *Clans*
  See also names of individual
  tribes
  Homolovi and the journey
  northward
  Lamehva people
  The migrations
  Tokonave: The snake and
  horn people
- *Dances and dancing*
  The Lalakon dance at
  Shongopovi
  - *Spruce tree dance*
  The flight from Huckovi
- *Fighters*
  Brady's leap
  Tom Quick, the Indian slayer
- *Folklore*
  Folklore (subject)
  Life — *Treasury* p.46-77
- *Holidays. See* **American Indian
  Day**
- *Mexico*
  The first tale of Alabama
- *Northwest coast*
  Cannibal
  Eagle boy
  The everlasting house
  The false shaman
  In the beginning
  The mountain goats
  The nose of the Konakadet
  The people who told the tales
  Raven lets out the daylight
  Strong-man
  The unlucky fisherman
- *Ohio River*
  Brady's leap
- *Songs*
  The destruction of Awatovi
- *Superstitions*
  The hole in the back wall
- *Tribes*
  Skeleton Cliff of Montana
  - *Apache*
    Homolovi and the journey
    northward
    The search for the Golden
    cities

- *Arawak. See Tainos*
- *Assiniboine*
  Coyote conquers the Iya
  Coyote loses his dinner
  Coyote rescues the ring-
  girl
  Coyote steals the summer
- *Bahanas*
  The four worlds
- *Bella Bella*
  Digger boy was hunting
  clams . . .
- *Bella Coola*
  A man sits in the ice . . .
  Not long ago after the
  earth was made . . .
- *Blackfoot*
  Blood Clot boy
  The shining lodge
- *Cherokee*
  The Cumins of Culter
  The dog and the hunter
  How fire came to the earth
  How the animals obtained
  fire
  How the rabbit lost his eye
  How the raccoon got rings
  on his tail
  The hunter, the Ukten, and
  the thunder
  The legend of the Chero-
  kee sweet shrub (and
  variants)
  The Little People
  The man who became a
  lizard
  The origin of corn and
  beans
  The panther and the crow
  The place of the beginning
  The rabbit and the honey-
  gum slide
  The seven-clan scribe
  society
  The squirrel and the craw-
  fish race
  The terrapin and the pos-
  sum outwit the fox
  Thunder appoints the
  eagle ruler of the earth
  Why the possum' tail is
  bare
- *Comanche*
  Bigfoot Wallace and the

hickory nuts
- *Crow*
  Pot-Tilter
- *Dakota*
  Coyote conquers the Iya
  Coyote loses his dinner
  Coyote rescues the ring-
    girl
  Coyote steals the summer
  Wind is a ghost
- *Delaware*
  Tom Quick, the Indian
    slayer
- *Hopi*
  The antelope boy of
    Shongopovi
  The arrival of the Tewas
  Black Mesa region and
    surrounding country
  The breakup of Oraibi
  The Castillas at Oraibi
  The destruction of Awatovi
  The destruction of Palat-
    kwapi
  The dispersal from Sik-
    yatki
  Escape from the Under-
    world
  The flight from Huckovi
  The founding of Moencopi
  The four worlds
  Homolovi and the journey
    northward
  Judgment by fire at Pivan-
    honkapi
  The Lalakon dance at
    Shongopovi
  The Lemehva people
  Maski, the land of the
    dead
  The migrations
  The Navajo attack on
    Oraibi
  Pakabva and the Kachinas
  The races between Pay-
    upki and Tikuvi
  Tokonave: The snake and
    horn peope
  - *Origin*
    The coming of the
      Hopis
- *Iroquois*
  Dew eagle, at night . . .
  Hiawatha
- *Karankawa*

The Karankawa from the
    gleaming oyster shells
- *Maidu*
  In the beginning there was
    no earth . . .
- *Menominee*
  The deceived blind men
  Manabozho, the trickster
- *Micmac*
  Little Burnt-Face
- *Navaho*
  The Indians' secret
  The Navajo attack on
    Oraibi
  The twins' journey to the
    sun
  The war god's horse song
    — Navaho Indian
- *Ojibway*
  Father Marquette and the
    manitou
- *Onondaga*
  The creation of man
  The Pleiades
  - *Origin*
    The four worlds
- *Paiute*
  The rocks of Bryce Canyon
- *Papago*
  Papago Indians (subject)
    Baker — *At* p.51-53
  Coyote drowns the world
  Earth magician
  The first war
  The killing of Eetoi
  The killing pot
  The monster eagle
- *Pascagoulas*
  The singing river
  The song in the sea
- *Pawnee*
  Coyote conquers the Iya
  Coyote loses his dinner
  Coyote rescues the ring-
    girl
  Coyote steals the summer
- *Pecos*
  Coronado and the Indian
    guide
- *Pueblo*
  The arrival of the Tewas
- *Quapaw*
  "Spook Light" of Devil's
    Promenade

INDIANS OF NORTH AMERICA
(continued)

- *Seneca*
 Evil-minded and good-
 minded
 Sky woman
- *Shoshoni*
 The sky is a bowl of
 ice . . .
- *Six Nations*
 Hiawatha
- *Tachi*
 Island of the dead
- *Tainos*
 The land of brave men
 The legend of the royal
 palm
- *Thompson River*
 Moon sits smoking his
 pipe . . .
- *Zuni*
 The dance of the corn
 maidens
 The hermit Mitsina
 The search for the Gold-
 en Cities
- *Folk Tales*
 The rabbit huntress

The Indians' secret
 Life — *Treasury* p.220-222

INDO-EUROPEAN MYTHOLOGY
Little people
Workers of evil — and a few good
 spirits

The inexperienced ghost
 Hoke — *Ghosts* p.132-148

INFIDELITY
Bata
What happened to Hadji
The wondrous wonder

INGRATITUDE
Abdallah the ungrateful
Catch-the-wind
The farmer and the ungrateful
 snake
Gratitude
The history of Little Mook
The kitchen pooka
The old man, the wolf, and the
vixen
The rat-catcher's daughter

INITIATION
Dead man

INJUSTICE
The sword

The inn that wasn't there
 Littledale — *Strange* p.9-11

INNS AND INNKEEPERS
The boy and the North Wind
The forest inn
The merchant's son who never
 smiled
The riddle of the room upstairs
The sad-lovely end of Wilhelmina
 Inn
Shish and the innkeeper
The tragedy of Potts' Hill
The wolf's eyelashes

INQUISITIVENESS. See Curiosity

INSANITY
A pair of wings

INSECTS
See also names of insects
A forest mansion
Wavouwuumira

INTELLIGENCE
Ricky with the tuft

INTERFERENCE
The test

INTOXICATION. See Alcoholism

The invasion and investment
 Cott — *Beyond* p.110-116

INVENTIONS
Down-to-earth dreamer

The invisible cloth
 Rugoff — *Harvest* p.709-712

INVISIBILITY
Hats to disappear with
Little Burnt-Face
The little scarred one

Invitation to a ghost
 Hoke — *Ghosts* p.150-156

IO (life essence)
Chant to Io

IRAN. *See* **Persia**

Irani and the cuckoos
Harris — *Sea Magic* p.81-98

IRAQ
The woman of the well

IRELAND AND IRISH
The adventures of Billy MacDaniel
The best laugh is the last laugh
Bottle Hill
Bran the blessed
The captive piper
Country-under-wave
Earl Desmond and the banshee
Edain the queen
The enchanted island
The Faery folk
Fair, brown, and trembling
The fairies
The fairy thorn
The fairy tree
Foxglove
Guleesh
Halfway people
The harp of the Dagda Mor
Hie over to England
The Isle of Satan's hand
Jamie Freel and the young lady
John O'Hara's lantern
The kitchen pooka
The lady of Gollerus
The leprechaun of Carrigadhroid
Little people
Maelduin's voyage
The magic lake
The magic shilling
A new way to boil eggs
Noodlehead Pat
The peddlar of Ballaghadereen
People of the sea
The Phouka
Princess Finola and the dwarf
Saint Bridget and the king's wolf
Sir Tristram in Ireland
The son of bad counsel
The swan-children of Lir
The terrible stranger
Two tales of leprechauns
Usheen in the Island of Youth
The voyage of St. Brandan
The well of D'yeeree-in-Dowan

The white fairy horse
The white hen
The wolf-mother of Saint Ailba
The wonders of Saint Berach
Workers of evil — and a few good
spirits
- *Bangor*
Saint Comgall and the mice
- *Folk tales*
Folk tales of Ireland (subject)
Rugoff — *Harvest* p.461-
512
- *Islands*
Kirwan's search for Hy-Brasail

IRON
People can't be made from iron

Iron Henry. *See* The frog-king, or Iron
Henry

The iron wolf
Bain — *Cossack* p.159-163

IRUAM
Lawrie — *Myths* (Version 1:p.350-
351; Version 2:p.352-354;
Version 3:p.354-357)

Irving, Washington
Rip Van Winkle

Irwin, Margaret
The book

IRWIN, MARGARET
Margaret Irwin (subject)
Manley — *Sisters* p.183-184,
219

ISEULT, QUEEN
Sir Tristram in Ireland

Isfendiār
Picard — *Tales* p.240-245

The Isinyandende
Rugoff — *Harvest* p.38-39

The island of demons
Higginson — *Tales* p.205-219

Island of the dead
Life — *Treasury* p.68-69

The Island of the Nine Whirlpools
Bland — *Complete* p.163-184

124

ISLANDS
See also names of islands
Antillia, the island of the seven
  cities
Dauan
The enchanted island
Fisherman's dream
The lost half-hour
Maelduin's voyage
St. Brendan's Isles of the Blest
The seven Simons (and variants)
Sisters who quarreled
Smartness for sale
The sporran full of gold
The shipwrecked sailor
The tale of the daughters of the
  sun
The tale of the men of Prach
The three hermits
Uncle James or the Purple
  stranger
The voyage of St. Brandan
- *Origin*
  Norinori

The islands of the Amazons
  Life — *Treasury* p.23

ISLE OF MAN
Halfway people
The water-bull

The Isle of Satan's hand
  Higginson — *Tales* p.134-142

Ispirescu, Petre
  Twelve dancing princesses

ISRAEL AND ISRAELITES
The cat's choice
Daniel and the dragon of Babylon
David and Goliath, the shepherd
  boy and the giant
Figs for gold, figs for folly
Tale of the devout Israelite

It
  Hoke — *Ghosts* p.149

ITALY
See also **Rome, Ancient; Sicily**
The baker's son and the king's
  daughter
The ballad of Saint Felix
Cesarino and the dragon
The cockerel-stone

Fanta-Ghiro
Fools' bells ring in every town
Gigi and the magic ring
The girl in the basket
Giufá and the judge
The joyful abbot
The months
The mysterious fig tree
Romulus and Remus. Sons of the
  the wolf
The shepherd who could not lie
The three mermaids
- *Folk tales*
  Italian folk tales (subject)
  Rugoff — *Harvest* p.513-
  546

It's a long time between drinks
  Life — *Treasury* p.177

It's only an owl
  Shaw — *Owl* p.32

Ivan the fool
  Whitney — *In* p.59-63

Ivan the fool and St. Peter's fife
  Bain — *Cossack* p.229-235

Ivan the peasant's son and the little
  man himself one-finger tall, his
  mustache seven versts in length
  Curtin — *Myths* p.37-46

Ivan Tsarevich, the fire-bird, and the
  gray wolf
  Curtin — *Myths* p.20-36

"IVANOV DAY"
A chapter of fish

Ivashko and the witch
  Hopkins — *Witching* p.62-70

IVIAHOCA
Belpré — *Once* p.34-44

IYAS (monsters)
Coyote conquers the Iya

J

Jabberwocky
  Greene — *Cavalcade* p.180-181

JACK AND (IN) THE BEANSTALK
Jack in the beanstalk (subject; and variants)
Opie — *Classic* p.162-163

Jack and the beanstalk
Bamberger — *My* p.58-65
Haviland — *Fairy* p.78-85
Manning — *Choice* p.39-48
Morel — *Fairy* p.60-64
Rugoff — *Harvest* p.242-247
Sekorová — *Europe* p.98-105

Jack and the varmints
Rugoff — *Harvest* p.47-53

Jack and the white cap
Colwell — *Round* p.97-101

Jack and the wizard
Manning — *Choice* p.268-275

Jack Buttermilk
Colwell — *Round* p.87-89

JACK THE GIANT KILLER
Jack the Giant Killer (subject; and variants)
Opie — *Classic* p.47-50

Jack the giant-killer
Fairy Tales p.1-14

JACKALS
The alligator and the jackal
Decide for yourself
Friends and neighbors
The greedy jackal caught
How blue crane taught jackal to fly
Lion and jackal
The little jackals and the lion
One trick too many
The tiger, the Brahman, and the jackal

The jackdaw and the fox
Levine — *Fables* p.16

JACKDAWS
The eagle, the jackdaw, and the shepherd
The peacock and the jackdaw

Jack's hunting trips
Rugoff — *Harvest* p.53-56

JACKSON, ANDREW ("Old Hickory")
The ghost that came to stay
White House ghosts

Jacobs, Joseph
The black bull of Norroway
Cap o'Rushes
Fair, brown, and trembling
Henny-Penny
The history of Tom Thumb
Jack and the beanstalk
Kate Crackernuts
The Laidly Worm
The Lambton worm
The little bull–calf
The little red hen and the grain of wheat
The miller, his son, and their donkey
Mr. Fox
Molly Whuppie
The old woman and her pig
The story of the three little pigs
Tattercoats
The three little pigs

JAGUARS
The giant and the rabbit
The rabbit and the barrel

JAILS. See Prisons and Prisoners

JAMAICA. See West Indies — Jamaica

JAMES, JESSE
Jesse James and the widow

Jamie Freel and the young lady
McGarry — *Great* p.9-14

JAPAN
See also **Korea**
The adventures of Little Peachling
A-e-oina, the demon, and the tattle-tale dog
Animals from heaven
The badger and the fox
The bats of Ru-pe-shi-pe
The bear's revenge
The chestnut tree
The cloth of a thousand feathers
Crafty Yasohachi and the flea medicine
Crafty Yasohachi climbs to heaven
The crusty old badger
The draper who swallowed a fly

JAPAN *(continued)*

Dull-witted Hikoichi and the duck soup
Dull-witted Hokoichi, the mortar and the worn-out horse
The farmer's secret
The fisherman and the Sea King's daughter
The five strange ghosts
The flying sword
The four sacred scrolls
Fox magic
The fox's wedding
The frog's tattoo
Gohei and the god of povetry
The golden mare
"Good-by, dear little bear god"
The grateful toad
Gratitude
The haunted palace
Hiroko
How the snake lost his voice
The hungry time
The little fox
The "little people" (and variants)
The longest story in the world
The mad dancers of Upo-pou-shi
The magic listening cap
Magic! Silly magic!
The mat-maker's adventure
Men from the village deep in the mountains
The merchant's son who never smiled
The mirror
Momotaro. The peach boy
Momotaro, the peach sprite
The monkey's Buddha
The moon maiden
The mountain lad and the forest witch
New Year's hats for the statues
The old man on the mountain
The old man who made the trees blossom
The old woman in the cottage
The one-eyed monster
One-inch fellow
Pan'ambe and pen'ambe
Patches
People from the sky
People of the sea
Picking mountain pears
Raw monkey livers

The rice cake that rolled away
The sacred sword
The salesman who sold his dream
Sankichi's gift
Schippeitaro
The silver bell
Stingy Kichiyomu and the iron hammer
Stingy Kichiyomu and the rice thieves
The stone statue and the grass hat
The story of O-Tei
The strange folding screen
The tea house in the forest
The three brothers
Three strong women
Tokutaro
The tongue-cut sparrow
The two statues of Kannon
Two terrible fish
The wandering monk and the tabby cat
The white crane
The wolf's eyelashes
Yoshi-tsuni, brave warrior from Japan
Yukiko and the little black cat

JARS
See also **Jugs**
The donkey of Abdera
The little house
, *Wine*
The old woman and the wine jar

Jason and the dragon of Colchis
Green — *Cavalcade* p.3-9

JATAKA TALES
The best food
Blackmail
The brave beetle
The company you keep
Cooperation
Decide for yourself
The dog who wanted to be a lion
Don't try the same trick twice
Fearing the wind
Friends and neighbors
The golden goose
The greedy crow
The greedy jackal caught
A handful of peas

Harsh words
Holding the truth
How a wolf reforms
How straws were invented
The Judas tree
King of his turf
Learn and live
Leave well enough alone
The monkey and the crocodile
The most beautiful of all
The oldest of the three
Popularity
Rāmā and Sitā
Responsibility
The robbers and the treasure
Rumors
Sweet tooth
A taste of his own medicine
The tortoise who talked too much
Trickery
Using your head
The wonders of palace life

JAVA
Big people

JAYS (birds)
Look on your back!
- *Canada*
Esau and the gorbey

JEALOUSY
The best food
Hallabau's jealousy
Podepode and Ngukurpodepode
Saint Kentigern and the robin
Snow-White (and variants)
The water monster

JEFFERSON, THOMAS
White House ghosts

JELLYFISH
Biu

Jenny Green Teeth
Leach — *Whistle* p.85

Jerome, Jerome K.
The haunted mill

JERUSALEM
The fox in the hole

Jesse James and the widow
Life — *Treasury* p.189-190

The jester who learned to cry
Wojciechowska — *Winter* p.41-48

**JESTERS. See Clowns; Fools and
Foolishness**

JESUS CHRIST
Little Mary
Watch

JEWELRY
See also **Bracelets; Lockets;
Necklaces; Rings**

JEWELS
Aladdin
The fairies
Sadko

Jewett, Eleanore M.
Tiger woman
Which was witch?

JEWS
See also **Litvaks; Rabbis**
Abraham and the idols
Alone with God
Big people
Bontche the silent
The buried money
The case against the wind
The fast
Father bird and fledglings
Figs for gold, figs for folly
The fox in the hole
The golden shoes
The great traveler of Chelm
The Helm goat mystery
Higher mathematics in Helm
If not still higher
Joseph and Potiphar's wife
King Solomon and the Queen of
Sheba
Know before you criticize
The Lord helpeth man and beast
The match
Miracles on the sea
The obsession with clothes
Pinya of Helm
The princess and Rabbi Joshua
Rabbi Eliezur enjoys an exception
Revealed
The seven good years
Song of the kid
Tale of the devout Israelite
The thoughtful father

JEWS *(continued)*

The treasure
The wife's one wish
The wise rogue
- *Folk tales*
Jewish folk tales (subject)
Rugoff — *Harvest* p.547-585
- *Holidays.* See **Hanukkah**

Jim Bridger overcomes gravity
Life — *Treasury* p.293

Jim gets murdered
Schwartz — *Whoppers* p.70

Jiménez, Juan Ramón
Watch

JINGLES. See **Nursery Rhymes; Repetitive Rhymes and Stories**

JINNIES (JINNIS). See **Genies**

JIZO
The old woman and her dumpling
The old woman who lost her dumpling
The stone statue and the grass hat

Joe Baldwin's light
Life — *Treasury* p.175-177
Roberts — *Ghosts* p.89-93

Joe Hamelin and the "Loup-Garou"
Life — *Treasury* p.135

Joe John and the carpenter
Life — *Treasury* p.174-175

Joe Magarac, the man of steel
Life — *Treasury* p.261-262

JOHN, SAINT
A chapter of fish
Cledog and the "Ceffyl-dwr"
Epilogue

John Henry
Life — *Treasury* p.168

John Henry and the machine in West Virginia
Rugoff — *Harvest* p.85-91

John in the storeroom
Jagendorf — *Noodle* p.284-286

John McGraw's jinx killer
Life — *Treasury* p.250-252

John O'Hara's lantern
Stuart — *Witch's* p.17-27

John Travail and the devil
Stuart — *Witch's* p.81-87

Johnny and the three goats
Great Children's p.74-80

Johnny and the witch-maidens
Manning — *Choice* p.81-88

Johnny Appleseed
Life — *Treasury* p.113-116

JOHNSON, SAMUEL
Halfway people

JOKES AND JOKESTERS. See **Clowns; Trickery**

The jolly miller
Baum — *Mother* p.119-127

Jon and the troll wife
Manning — *Ogres* p.91-100

JONES, HETTIE
Hetty Jones (subject)
Jones — *Coyote* p.50

JONES, JOHN LUTHER ("Casey")
Casey Jones

Jonson, Ben
Witches' charm

Jorinda and Joringel
Bamberger — *My* p.15-17
Morel — *Fairy* p.118-121

Joseph and Potiphar's wife
Rugoff — *Harvest* p.576-582

Joseph the Zulu
McDowell — *Third* p.13-16

Josiah, Henry W.
Makonaima returns

JOTUNS
Big people
Workers of evil — and a few good spirits

The journey in the dark
Vogel — *Rainbow* p.21-32

JOY. See Happiness; Laughter

Joyce, James
Golden hair

The joyful abbot
Spicer — *13 Rascals* p.17-26

Juan Bobo
Carter — *Greedy* p.112-118
Jagendorf — *Noodle* p.260-262

The judas tree
Rugoff — *Harvest* p.438

The judge and the baseball-pitching
Indian chief
Jagendorf — *Folk, South* p.47-49

JUDGES AND JUSTICE
Abdul Kasim the rich
The bull didn't have a chance
The Colonel teaches the judge a
lesson in good manners
Devabhuti and the foolish
magistrate
Dirty hands
Giufá and the judge
Harchand the Just
How far is it to Jacob Cooper's?
Only in Texas
The pig that went to court
Semrude the Fair and the Cadi
The theft of a smell

Judgment by fire at Pivanhonkapi
Courlander — *Fourth* p.133-138

The judgment of the Caliph. *See* Abdul
Kasim the rich

A jug of syrup
Hoke — *Ghosts* p.95-104

JUGS
See also **Jars**
The salesman who sold his dream
, *Vinegar*
The man and the wife in the
vinegar jug

Julia Bulette of Virginia City
Life — *Treasury* p.213-214

The jumper
Heady — *Safiri* p.62-65

JUMPING
Tortoise and elephant

Jumping Sam Patch
Life — *Treasury* p.141-142

JUNGLE
Ayaymama
The legend of the betel

The juniper tree
Segal — *Juniper (II)* p.314-332

JUNNE, I. K.
I. K. Junne (subject)
Junne — *Floating* p.136

JUPITER
The frogs asking for a king
The lion, Jupiter, and the elephant

JUSTICE. See Judges and Justice

JUSTICES OF PEACE
Roy Bean, necktie justice

K

Kabai
Lawrie — *Myths* p.132-134

KACHINAS (rain gods)
Pakabva and the Kachinas

Kae and the whale
Alpers — *Legends* p.203-210

Kahukura and the net-makers
Alpers — *Legends* p.331-334

KAILYARDS
The princesses who lived in a
kailyard

Kaka, Philomena Kessewa
My wish

KALANORO
Little people

Kaleeba
Serwadda — *Songs* p.11-15

The Kalevala
Rugoff — *Harvest* p.280-292

Kalibala, E. B.
   Wakaima and the clay man
KALMUKS
   Burun-Teges
Kama
   Lawrie — *Myths* p.85-118
Kamutnab
   Lawrie — *Myths* p.85-86
KANNON (goddess)
   The two statues of Kannon
KAPAS (musical shows)
   The coming of Tute
Kaperkaper the cannibal
   Lawrie — *Myths* p.316-317
KAPPAS (water sprites)
   Little people
Karakarkula
   Lawrie — *Myths* p.23-24
The Karankawa from the great gleaming
   oyster shells
   Jagendorf — *Folk, South* p.269-
   270
Karbai and Pukat
   Lawrie — *Myths* p.172-173
KARELIA (country)
   The lazy daughter
Karum
   Lawrie — *Myths* p.36-37
Kasakuik
   Lawrie — *Myths* p.177
KASHMIR
   The Prince of the flowery meadow
Kate Crackernuts
   Minard — *Womenfolk* p.65-70
Kate, the bell witch
   Jagendorf — *Folk, South* p.231-
   234
KATYDIDS
   Why the possum's tail is bare
KAVA (drink)
   The origin of kava

Kawai
   Lawrie — *Myths* Part I: p.255-256;
   Part II: p.256-257
KAZAKH TALES
   Unerbek
KEELBOATS
   The life of Annie Christmas
   Mike Fink, last keelboat-man
'Keenene
   Serwadda — *Songs* p.1-5
KELPIES. *See* **Water Spirits**
Kennedy, Patrick
   The kitchen pooka
KENETH, SAINT
   Saint Keneth of the gulls
KENSINGTON GARDENS (London)
   Peter Pan in Kensington Gardens
"KENSINGTON STONE"
   The Vikings and their traces
KENTIGERN, SAINT
   Saint Kentigern and the robin
KENYA. *See* **Africa — Kenya**
Kererum
   Lawrie — *Myths* p.222-223
Kerman, Kerman (illus.)
   Shaw — *Mouse* p.6
KETTLES
   Magic! Silly magic!
The key-flower
   De Bosschere — *Christmas* p.134-
   135
KEYS
   Fitcher's feathered bird
   The golden key
   Maraboe and Morsegat
   Mons Tros
   Why women always take advan-
   tage of men
The Khan's hawk. *See* **Turandot**
Khavroshechka
   Carey — *Baba* p.109-113

The Khevsouri and the Eshmahkie
Rugoff — *Harvest* p.653-654

Khosroes and Afrāsib
Picard — *Tales* p.143-155

Khusrau and the fisherman
Rugoff — *Harvest* p.146-147

Kiba
Lawrie — *Myths* p.209-210

Kibbe's shirt
Jagendorf — *Noodle* p.287-289

The kid and the flute — playing wolf
Levine — *Fables* p. 68

The kid and the wolf
Darrell — *Once* p.241-242

KIDNAPPING
The story of Almansor

Kiki, Albert Maori
A visit to Orokolo

KILLING. See Murder

The killing of Eetoi
Baker — *At* p.33-42

The killing pot
Baker — *At* p.16-24

Kind little Edmund, or the Caves and
the cockatrice
Bland — *Complete* p.141-161

KINDNESS
See also **Generosity**
Baba Yaga
The banyan deer
The fairies
The golden goose
The good man and the kind mouse
The haunted room
The house in the forest
Jon and the troll wife
Kind little Edmund, or the Caves
and the cockatrice
The King of Colchester's daughters
The lion and the mouse
The little turtle
The longest story in the world
The three heads of the well
The three wishes

King, Ben
That cat

**KING, MARTIN LUTHER, JR. —
BIRTHDAY**
Birthday (subject)
Corrigan — *Holiday* p.21-26
I have a dream
My people
The prize is won

The king and his wazir's wife
Rugoff — *Harvest* p.157-159

The king and the rain dwarfs
Roy — *Serpent* p.59-65

The king and the witch
Colwell — *Round* p.77-81

King Arthur at Avalon
Higginson — *Tales* p.83-95

King Bungo's measures
Cott — *Beyond* p.64-71

King Golden
Bamberger — *My* p.94-98

King Johnny
Manning — *Choice* p.171-182

King Malcolm and the herd-boy
Wyness — *Legends* p.85-93

The king of Cauliflower's castle
Kingsley — *Sesame* p.8-16

The King of Colchester's daughters
Opie — *Classic* p.158-161

King of his turf
DeRoin — *Jataka* p.68-70

The King of Scotland's sons
Stuart — *Witch's* p.55-65

The king o' the cats
Rugoff — *Harvest* p.231-233
Shaw — *Cat* p.16-17

The King of the Golden River or The
Black brothers
Cott — *Beyond* p.1-37

The king of the hummingbirds
Gardner — *King* p.1-16

132

King of the mice
Heady — *Safiri* p.71-74

The king of the toads
Curtin — *Myths* p.311-330

KING PHILIP'S WAR
The angel of Hadley

King Rumti's statue
Cott — *Beyond* p.48-55

King Solomon and the Queen of Sheba
Rugoff — *Harvest* p.569-574

King Solomon's ring
Fehse — *Thousand* p.79-97

The king who did not want to die
Bomans — *Wily* p.155-158

The king who was fried
Rugoff — *Harvest* p.455-460

King William's palace
Wyness — *Legends* p.66-71

The kingdom of the lion
Darrell — *Once* p.236

KINGMINGOARKULLUK (Eskimo dwarf)
Little people

KINGS AND QUEENS
The archer and the king
The baker's son and the king's
    daughter
Ballad of Saint-Giles and the deer
The battle of the birds
The bewitched cat
Bluebeard
The book of beasts
Boyislav, youngest of twelve
Brother and sister
The brown bear of the green glen
Cap o' rushes
The clever thief
The cloak of friendship
The clock that walked by itself
Constantes and the dragon
The cunning cat
Diem and Siem
Dragon, dragon
The dragon, sliced-in-two
Elephant wants to be king
Elf Hill
The Emperor's new clothes
Fanta-Ghiro

Ferdinand Faithful and Ferdinand
    Unfaithful
The fisherman and the gatekeeper
The fox and the goat
The frogs asking for a king
The garden of magic
Gifts of love
The girl in the basket
Go I know not whither and fetch
    I know not what
The good man and the kind mouse
The grandee
The half-chick
Hans my hedgehog
The history of Little Mook
How a tailor became a king
How the great Turisgale met his
    death
Humpty Dumpty
The invisible cloth
The Island of the Nine Whirlpools
The jester who learned to cry
The last balloon
Linda-Gold and the old king
Little Hiram
The little shepherd boy
The little turtle
Many-Fur
The miller, his cook, and the king
The miller's mule
Mirko, the king's son
Molly Whuppie
Old King Cole
Popularity
Prince Rabbit
Punished pride
Puss in boots
The Queen
Rāma and Sitā
Responsibility
The rooster who couldn't crow
The rose and the violinist
The sea gulls
The shepherd and the princess
The shepherd who could not lie
Sigurd the king's son
Silent Bianca
Sing a song o' sixpence
The sister queens
The six who went together
    through the world
The Sleeping beauty in the wood
    (and variants)
Snow-White (and variants)
The soldier with the wooden leg

The spice woman's basket
The sword
Tatterhood
"That's not true"
The three feathers
The three golden hairs
The three men of power — Evening,
  midnight, and sunrise
The three shirts of Cannach Cotton
The tinder box
The treasures of Rhampsinitus
Turtles of gold and bitter regrets
The twelve huntsmen
The two journeymen
The valiant little tailor
The water festival
The Well of D'yeree-in-Dowan
When Mother Troll took in the
  King's washing
The witch in the stone boat
The wonders of palace life
The yellow dwarf

The King's choice
  Olenius — *Great* p.50-58

The King's nose
  Kingsley — *Sesame* p.20-28

Kirk, Richard R.
  The mice

KIRKYARDS. See Cemeteries

Kirwan's search for Hy-Brasail
  Higginson — *Tales* p.125-133

Kiss Miklos, and the green daughter of
  the green king
  Curtin — *Myths* p.477-516

The kitchen pooka
  Littledale — *Strange* p.91-95

The kite
  Krylov — *Fables* p.88-89

KITES
  Lament on losing a kite
  Peter Pan in Kensington Gardens
  The toys

The kitten
  Shaw — *Cat* p.48

The kitten and the falling leaves
  Shaw — *Cat* p.28-29

KITTENS. See Cats

The Kiwai raiders
  Lawrie — *Myths* p.143-147

Kjellin, Helge
  Leap the elk and Little Princess
  Cottongrass

KNAPSACKS
  Brother Gaily
  The soldier and the demons

The knee-high man
  Lester — *Knee* p.27-29

The knight of the red shield
  MacFarlane — *Mouth* p.131-146

The knight of Wedderhill
  Wyness — *Legends* p.60-65

The knight with the stone heart
  Littledale — *Strange* p.97-101

KNIGHTS AND KNIGHTHOOD
  See also **Arthur, King**
  The bald knight
  The black charger
  The castle of Ker Glas
  The dragon at hide-and-seek
  The dragon at Loschy Hill
  Galahad. The Holy Grail
  The giant of the causeway
  The king and the witch
  The last balloon
  Maelduin's voyage
  The magic spider box
  The pear tree
  Prince Bajaja
  The princess and the three tasks
  Princess Finola and the dwarf
  The Red Cross knight and the
    dragons
  Sir James the Rose
  Sir Lancelot of the Lake
  Sir Launcelot and the dragon
  The wish that came true
  , *Humpbacked*
    The shape-shifters of Shorm

KNIVES
  The two princes
  , *Bowie*
    The lost treasure

KNOBS
The gold knob

"KNOCK-KNOCKS"
Tales from Tartari-Barbari

KNOCKERS (Cornwall little people)
Little people

Knoist and his three sons
Rugoff — *Harvest* p.361

Knoonie in the sleeping palace
Housman — *Rat* p.153-163

KNOTS
Three knots

Know before you criticize
Rugoff — *Harvest* p.558-559

KNOWLEDGE. *See* **Wisdom**

Knucklehead John
Jagendorf — *Noodle* p.122-124

KNUCKLEHEADS. *See* **Fools and Foolishness**

Knurremurre
Corrigan — *Holiday* p.204-208
Manning — *Choice* p.49-53

KOBOLDS (German fairies)
Little people

Kogia
Lawrie — *Myths* p.139-142

Kol
Lawrie — *Myths* p.324

KOLA NUTS
Breaking in a kola nut

KONAKADETS (sea monsters)
The false shaman
The nose of the Konakadet

Kongasau
Lawrie — *Myths* p.178-179

KOREA
Gifts of love
Hats to disappear with
The magic hammer
The tiger and the hare
Tiger woman

Korseim
Lawrie — *Myths* p.325

Kos and Abob
Lawrie — *Myths* p.342-343

Koshchei without-death
Curtin — *Myths* p.106-123,165-178

KOTOKELY
Little people

KRAMPUS
Workers of evil — and a few good spirits

Krasilovsky, Phyllis
Benny's flag

Kuaka
Lawrie — *Myths* p.62-63

Kuduluk and Kui
Lawrie — *Myths* p.37-38

Kuikueve
Alpers — *Legends* p.227-228

Kultani, the noodle gossip
Jagendorf — *Noodle* p.202-206

Kultut
Lawrie — *Myths* p.318-319

Kusa Kap
Lawrie — *Myths* p.127-132

L

LA SALLE, ROBERT CAVALIER DE
Ghost ship of the Great Lakes

LABOR DAY
Labor Day (subject)
Corrigan — *Holiday* p.170-175
Down-to-earth dreamer
I hear America singing

LABYRINTH, THE
Halfway people

Lac Long Quan and Au Co
Duong — *Beyond* p.6-11

The lad who stared everyone down
Yolen — *Girl* p.35-44

LADDERS
The gold knob

The lady and the lion
Darrell — *Once* p.38-42

The lady and the unjust judge
Rugoff — *Harvest* p.165-167

The Lady Dragonissa
Green — *Cavalcade* p.182-184

The lady in black of Boston harbor
Anderson — *Haunting* p.17-26

The lady of Gollerus
McGarry — *Great* p.92-98

LADY OF MONSERRATE
The miracle of Hormigueros

The Lady of Nam Xuong
Duong — *Beyond* p.81-88

LADY OF THE LAKE
Sir Lancelot of the Lake

The Lady of the Lake
Bomans — *Wily* p.9-20

The lady of the tower
Wyness — *Legends* p.55-59

LAFITTE, JEAN
Lafitte's great treasure
Three great men at peace

Lafitte's great treasure
Jagendorf — *Folk, South* p.292-294

The lagoon of Masaya
Carter — *Enchanted* p.37-39

The Laidly Worm
Green — *Cavalcade* p.103-108

The laidly worm of Spindlestone Heugh
Spicer — *13 Dragons* p.58-68

The laird's man
Wyness — *Legends* p.33-37

LAKES
How straws were invented
The Lady of the Lake
People of the heron and the
hummingbird
Sir Lancelot of the Lake
The twelve dancing princesses

, *Magic*
The magic lake

The Lalakon dance at Shongopovi
Courlander — *Fourth* p.111-117

The lamar who became a rainbow
Lawrie — *Myths* p.279-280

LAMASSU
Workers of evil — and a few good
spirits

Lamb, Charles and Mary
Three tales from Shakespeare

The lamb
Krylov — *Fables* p.155

The lambikin
Great Children's p.113-121

Lamborn, Florence, trans.
Pippi celebrates her birthday

LAMBS. See Sheep

The Lambton worm
Green — *Cavalcade* p.109-114

The Lamehva people
Courlander — *Fourth* p.43-55

Lament on losing a kite
Alpers — *Legends* p.188-189

LAMIA
Halfway people

Lamming, George
Boy Blue the crab-catcher

The lamp
Cott — *Beyond* p.431-433

LAMPS
See also **Lanterns**
Esben and the witch
, *Magic*
Aladdin

LANCELOT, SIR
Sir Lancelot of the Lake
Sir Launcelot and the dragon

LANCES
Usheen in the Island of Youth
, *Diamond*
The castle of Ker Glas

LAND. *See* **Earth**

Land! Land in sight!
  Corrigan — *Holiday* p.191-195

The land of brave men
  Belpré — *Once* p.9-12

"LAND WITHOUT MEN"
  Kae and the whale

LANDLORDS
  Anfy and the landlord
  Bottle Hill

LANDOWNERS
  Not bad — but it could be better

Lang, Andrew
  The forty thieves
  The half-chick
  The Lady Dragonissa
  The song of Orpheus

LANTERNS
  John O'Hara's lantern

LAOS
  The fig-tree beggar and the willful
    princess
  The little turtle
  Mister Lazybones

LAPLAND
  Little Lapp
  Stalo and Kaurus
  Why the bear sleeps all winter
  The woodpecker

LARKS (SKYLARKS)
  The lady and the lion

LARS
  Little people

The lass who went out at the cry of
    dawn
  Minard — *Womenfolk* p.83-92

The last adventure
  Rugoff — *Harvest* p.286-292

The last adventure of Thyl Ulenspiegel
  Fairy Tales p.112-122

The last balloon
  Bomans — *Wily* p.147-154

The last news of the pony
  Cott — *Beyond* p.145-146

The last of the dragons
  Bland — *Complete* p.185-198

The last of the spirits
  Darrell — *Once* p.218-222

The last piece of light
  Gardner — *Dragon* p.55-73

Lat take a cat
  Shaw — *Cat* p.40

LATIN (language)
  The book

LATIN AMERICA
  See also names of countries
  Lesson for lesson
  - *Folk tales*
    Latin American folk tales
      Rugoff — *Harvest* p.587-
      618

LATVIA
  The bird, the mouse, and the
    sausage
  The clever thief
  Three knots

LAUGHTER
  The best laugh is the last laugh
  Come and laugh with Bobby
    Gum
  The coyote and Juan's maguey
  The goblins giggle
  The golden goose
  Lizard and a ring of gold
  Peter's adventures
  The time of the ugly

LAUNCELOT, SIR. *See* **Lancelot, Sir**

LAUNOMAR, SAINT
  Saint Launomar's cow

LAWRENCE, JOHN
  John Lawrence (subject)
    MacFarlane — *Mouth* p.147

LAWYERS
  Clever Manka
  Richmuth of Cologne

Laye, Camara
  Visit to the village

LAZAREVICH, MILA
 Mila Lazarevich (subject)
  Littledale — *Strange* p.148

LAZINESS
 Aladdin
 Aukam and Tiai
 Ayoga
 Bartek the doctor
 The bird, the mouse, and the
  sausage
 The Chinese dragons
 The clever thief
 Ea and Eo
 Easy breed
 Faithful legs and lazy head
 The fig-tree beggar, and the willful
  princess
 The flower of happiness on Sunny-
  mount Crest
 Hiroka
 The maid in the mirror
 The miller's sons
 Mister Lazybones
 Nail stew (and variants)
 Oh: The Tsar of the forest
 The ox and the ass
 The princess who learned to work
 The seven wishes
 Sheidulla
 The talema
 Three knots
 Toast and honey
 The tricks of Hunahpú and
  Ixbalanqué
 Two frogs
 Wakaima and the clay man
 Wamin Ngurbum
 Who will row next?
 Who will wash the pot?
 Wooden Tony: an Anyhow story

The lazy daughter
 Ginsburg — *Lazies* p.49-55

The lazy farmer's tale
 Carrick — *Wise* n. pag.

Lazy Hans
 Hopkins — *Witching* p.103-116

Lazy Jack
 Morel — *Fairy* p.104-105

Leap the elk and Little Princess
 Cottongrass
 Olenius — *Great* p.123-134

Learn and live
 De Roin — *Jataka* p.35-37

LEARNING. See Scholarship; Wisdom

"Leave it there!"
 Robinson — *Singing* p.50-65

Leave well enough alone
 De Roin — *Jataka* p.41-42

LEAVES
 The kitten and the falling leaves
 Why evergreens keep their leaves
 - *Eating*
  The giraffe's neck
 , *Singing*
  The singing leaves

The leaves and the roots
 Krylov — *Fables* p.143-144

Lee, F. G.
 The mummer's play

Lee, Tanya
 The fish with hooked noses
 The fisherman and the gatekeeper
 Gifts of love
 Hats to disappear with
 The magic hammer
 The mystery maiden from heaven
 The tall tales
 The tiger and the hare

The legend of Augustín Lorenzo
 Rugoff — *Harvest* p.615-618

A legend of Knockmany
 Rugoff — *Harvest* p.615-618

A legend of Lake Okeefinokee
 Shaw — *Frog* p.24-27

The legend of Linda the lonely
 Kingsley — *Sesame* p.31-37

The legend of Lizzie Borden
 Life — *Treasury* p.256-258

The legend of Rara
 Alpers — *Legends* p.140-170

The legend of the betel
 Duong — *Beyond* p.13-17

The legend of the Ceiba of Ponce
 Belpré — *Once* p.51-54

The legend of the Cherokee sweet
  shrub
  Bird — *Path* p.33-37

The legend of the elephant
  Rugoff — *Harvest* p.35-37

The legend of the hummingbird
  Belpré — *Once* p.25-28

Legend of the perfect people
  Lyons — *Tales* p.8-11

The legend of the royal palm
  Belpré — *Once* p.13-17

Leland, Charles Godfrey
  The mysterious fig tree

Lemon, Mark
  Tinykin's transformations

LEMON, MARK
  Lemon Mark (subject)
    Cott — *Beyond* p.310

LEMURS
  Halfway people
  Little people

LENT
  The alms tale

Leodhas, Sorche Nic
  The lass who went out at the crack
    of dawn
  The stolen bairn and the Sidh
  The wild ride in the tilt cart
  The woman who flummoxed the
    fairies

Leopard hunt
  McDowell — *Third* p.35-43

LEOPARDS
  Dog and leopard
  The fox and the leopard
  Little hen eagle
  The tortoise
  Workers of evil — and a few good
    spirits

LEOU, YEHUDA, RABBI
  Big people

The leprechaun of Carrigadhroid
  McGarry — *Great* p.33-39

The leprechaun; or, Fairy shoemaker
  Corrigan — *Holiday* p.75-77

LEPRECHAUNS
  Leprechauns (subject)
    McGarry — *Great* p.29
  The magic shilling
  Two tales of leprechauns

Lepuha and the widow of Utumalama
  Alpers — *Legends* p.289

LESHY
  Little people

LESSING, DORIS
  Doris Lessing (subject)
    Manley — *Sisters* p.205-206,
    219-220

Lessing, Dorothy L.
  No witchcraft for sale

Lesson for lesson
  Rugoff — *Harvest* p.590-592

LESTER, JULIUS
  Lester Julius (subject)
    Lester — *Knee* p.32

Letter from Massachusetts: 1688
  Manley — *Sisters* p.128-140

Letters! Letters! Letters
  Cott — *Beyond* p.258-262

LETTUCE
  Mr. Rabbit and Mr. Bear

Lewis, C. S.
  The dragon speaks

The liar
  Krylov — *Fables* p.56-58

**LIARS. See Dishonesty; Falsehood;
  Tall Tales**

LIBAN
  People of the sea

LIBERTY. See Freedom

LIBRARIANS
  The "spirited" librarian

LIBRARIES
  , *School*
    Benno and the secret code

LICE
The message

LIES. *See* **Dishonesty; Falsehood; Tall Tales**

LIFE
See also **Immortality; Youth, Eternal**
- *Meaning*
Hung Vuong and the earth and sky cakes
- *Saving*
The noblest deed
, *Water of*
Water of youth, water of life, and water of death

The life of Annie Christmas
Jagendorf — *Folk, South* p.128-133

LIGHT
The four worlds
The raven brings light
Raven's deed
, *Blue*
The little blue light
, *Dancing*
The three brothers
, *Fading*
The last piece of light
, *Ghost*
Joe Baldwin's light

LIGHT ELVES
Little people

LIGHTHOUSES
The foghorn

LIGHTNING
The time lightning struck little Ida's umbrella

Like master, like servant
Jagendorf — *Noodle* p.75-77

LINCOLN, ABRAHAM
Abraham Lincoln, a mourning figure, walks
The ghosts in the White House
Nancy Hanks
"Peculiarsome" Abe
White House ghosts
- *Birthday*
Abraham Lincoln (subject) p.28-39

Corrigan — *Holiday* p.28-39
Abraham Lincoln (1809-1865)

LINCOLN, MARY TODD
White House ghosts

Lincolnshire moon
Stuart — *Witch's* p.67-79

Linda-Gold and the old king
Olenius — *Great* p.195-202

Lindgren, Astrid
Pippi celebrates her birthday

Lindholm, F. A.
Stalo and Kaurus

LINDWORMS
Prince Lindworm

LINEN
The shroud of Mari-Yvonne

The lion and ass go hunting
Rugoff — *Harvest* p.420

Lion and hyena and rabbit
Dolch — *Animal* p.81-87

Lion and jackal
Dolch — *Animal* p.63-69

The lion and the bull
Levine — *Fables* p.24

The lion and the farmer's daughter
Levine — *Fables* p.58

The lion and the fox
Krylov — *Fables* p.93

The lion and the goat
Dolch — *Animal* p.13-17

The lion and the grateful mouse
Levine — *Fables* p.62

The lion and the mouse
Morel — *Fairy* p.70-71
Piper — *Stories* n. pag.
Rockwell — *Three* p.14-15

The lion and the panther
Krylov — *Fables* p.77-78

The lion and the wild ass
Levine — *Fables* p.14

The lion and the wild boar
Levine — *Fables* p.64

The lion, Jupiter, and the elephant
Darrell — *Once* p.247

The lion makers
Rugoff — *Harvest* p.447-448

The lion, the ass, and the fox
Levine — *Fables* p.4

The lion, the bear, and the fox
Levine — *Fables* p.60

The lion, the chamois and the fox
Krylov — *Fables* p.113-115

The lion, the wolf, and the fox
Levine — *Fables* p.56

The lioness and the fox
Levine — *Fables* p.96

LIONS
    The aged lion
    The ass who passed for a lion
    Cesarino and the dragon
    The dog who wanted to be a lion
    Foni and Fotia
    The foolish lion and the silly
      rooster
    The fox and the lion
    Friends and neighbors
    Goat and lion and snake
    Godfather to skunks
    The herdsman and the lion
    The hunter's bargain
    The kingdom of the lion
    The lady and the lion
    Leave well enough alone
    The little jackals and the lion
    The man and the lion
    Rabbit and big rat and lion
    Rabbit and tortoise and lion
    Saint Gerasimus and the lion
    The stag and the lion
    This for that
    The twelve huntsmen
    Why the baboon has a shining seat
    The zebras who spoke the truth
  - *Cubs* — *Spots*
    Spots
  - *Teeth*
    Rabbit's long ears

Lippo and Tapio
Rugoff — *Harvest* p.295-300

Lipuniushka
Carey — *Baba* p.96-98

Lisalill
Sperry — *Scand.* p.238-246

The listeners
Hoke — *Ghosts* p.71-73

LITERATURE
    The book

LITHUANIA
    The shared reward

The little blacksmith Verholen
De Bosschere — *Christmas* p.42-60

The little blue light
Belpré — *Once* p.55-59

Little Bo-Peep
Baum — *Mother* p.151-159

Little Boy Blue. *See The story of
Little Boy Blue*

The little boy who wanted pancakes
Sperry — *Scand.* p.79-85

The little boy's secret
Harrison — *Book* p.7-18

The little bull-calf
Green — *Cavalcade* p.115-119

Little Bun Rabbit
Baum — *Mother* p.257-265

Little Burnt-Face
Stories From World p.30-33

Little cat and little hen
Manning — *Tortoise* p.75-79

The little daughter of the snow
Ransome — *Old* p.83-93

The little donkey
Bamberger — *My* p.47-49

The little engine that died
Piper — *Stories* n. pag.

Little Eva
Morel — *Fairy* p.20-21

Little Filipp
    Carey — *Baba* p.114-116

The little fisherman
    Bagley — *Candle* p.89-93

LITTLE FOLK. *See* **Little People**

The little fox
    Novák — *Fairy* p.131-137

The little girl and the hare
    Morel — *Fairy* p.84-85

The little glass slipper. *See* Cinderella
    (and variants)

The little golden fish
    Bamberger — *My* p.29-33
    Sekorová — *Europe* p.115-120

Li'l' Hannibal
    Piper — *Stories* n. pag.

Little head, big medicine
    Jagendorf — *Noodle* p.274-277

Little hen eagle
    Aardema — *Behind* p.3-10

Little Hiram
    Manning — *Choice* p.200-215

The little house
    Darrell — *Once* p.279-291
    Morel — *Fairy* p.106

The little jackals and the lion
    Haviland — *Favorite India* p.21-26

Little Lapp
    Sperry — *Scand.* p.261-276

Little Lodewyk and Annie the witch
    De Bosschere — *Christmas* p.123-125

The little man and his little gear
    Baum — *Mother* p.131-137

The little man in green
    Colwell — *Round* p.82-84

Little Mary
    Bamberger — *My* p.38-39

Little Master Misery
    Ransome — *Old* p.130-145

The little match-girl
    Bamberger — *My* p.175-177

Little Miss Muffet
    Baum — *Mother* p.233-241

A little mouse
    Shaw — *Mouse* p.17

LITTLE PEOPLE
    See also names and types, e.g.
        Fairies; Leprechauns; etc.
    Hiroko
    The little man in green
    The piper of Keil
    Skillywidden
    Thumbelina
    Tom Thumb
    , *Hairy*
        The little red hairy man
    - *Indians*
        The little people

The little people
    Carpenter — *People* p.104-107
    McHargue — *Impossible* p.47-73
    Roberts — *Ghosts* p.51-57

A little piece of thread
    Life — *Treasury* p.282-283

The little pig's way out
    Bagley — *Candle* p.49-56

The little pot
    Rockwell — *Three* p.110-112

Little Poucet (Hop o' my thumb)
    Opie — *Classic* p.130-136

The little red hairy man
    Colwell — *Round* p.90-94

The little red hen
    Great Children's p.9-15
    Morel — *Fairy* p.26-27

The little red hen and the grain of wheat
    Haviland — *Fairy* p.32-35

Little Red Riding Hood
    Little Red Riding Hood (subject)
    Opie — *Classic* P.93-94
    Haviland — *Fairy* p.146-151
    Morel — *Fairy* p.11-13
    Opie — *Classic* p.95-97
    Perrault — *Fairy* p.9-12

LITTLE RED RIDING HOOD (continued)
Rockwell — *Three* p.102-109
Sekorová — *Europe* p.68-72

The little scarred one
Sheehan — *Folk* p.141-148

The little shepherd boy
Bamberger — *My* p.69-70

Little sister fox
Manning — *Tortoise* p.51-59

Little step-mother
Bamberger — *My* p.192-195

The little tailor and the three dogs
Manning — *Ogres* p.101-109

Little Tuppens
Great Children's p.129-139

The little turtle
Junne — *Floating* p.85-87

LITTLEDALE, FREYA
Freya Littledale (subject)
Littledale — *Strange* p.148

LITVAKS
If not still higher

LIVERS
Raw monkey liver

The living colors of the Twenty-first
Jagendorf — *Folk, South* p.151-153

Living in the forest
McDowell — *Third* p.53-58

Lizard and a ring of gold
Sherlock — *Ears* p.89-103

Lizard-husband, scaly skin
Alpers — *Legends* p.335-336

Lizard who was always right
Dolch — *Animal* p.89-95

LIZARDS
The crocodile and the hen
Karum
The man who became a lizard
Ttimba

, *Monster*
The monster of Cakaudrove
- *Tongues, Scarred*
How fire was brought to Torres
Strait
, *White*
Uletka and the white lizard

Lizards and promises and Vue Cong
Due
Duong — *Beyond* p.31-38

(La) Llorona
Lyons — *Tales* p.12-18

Lloyd, Noel (and Geoffrey Palmer)
Invitation to a ghost

LLUDD, KING
The red dragon of Wales

Lludd and Llevelys
Fairy Tales p.28-33

LOAFING. See Laziness

The lobster and the flounder
Alpers — *Legends* p.314

The lobster-quadrille
Darrell — *Once* p.123-128

LOBSTERS
Alice's adventures in Wonderland
The tailor from the sea

A local haunting
Hoke — *Ghosts* p.43-46

LOCKETS
Petsetilla's pony

Lock-out time
Darrell — *Once* p.270-279

LOGGERS. See Lumbermen

LOGS
The frogs asking for a king
Lutyona
The wish that came true

LONDON, ENGLAND
Dick Whittington

LONDON BRIDGE
The peddlar of Swaffham

LONELINESS
The legend of Linda the Lonely

The lonely witch
Hopkins — *Witching* p.27-55

The long wait
Bagley — *Candle* p.77-81

The longest story in the world
Novák — *Fairy* p.31-37

LONGEVITY. See Old Age

Longfellow, Henry W.
Evangeline

Longnose the dwarf
Hauff — *Big* p.61-98

Lonopuha, or the origin of healing: and the story of Milu
Alpers — *Legends* p.257-261

Look on your back!
Bagley — *Candle* p.108-113

LOOKING GLASSES. See Mirrors

Lookit the little pig!
Bagley — *Candle* p.39-48

LORD, THE. See God; Jesus Christ

The Lord helpeth man and beast
Rugoff — *Harvest* p.551-553

LORELEI
The People of the sea

Lorenzo Dow raises the devil
Life — *Treasury* p.270

LOST
Hansel and Gretel
The little people
The miracle of Hormigueros
Saint Launomar's cow

"LOST ADAMS DIGGINGS"
The Indians' secret

"LOST COLONY"
The silver doe

The lost continent of Atlantis
Life — *Treasury* p.21-22

The lost half-hour
Provensen — *Book* p.13-23

The lost treasure
Jagendorf — *Folk, South* p.62-64

LOTUS
The suitors of Princess Fire-fly

LOUDNESS. See Noise

LOUISIANA
See also **New Orleans, Louisiana**
The bridal ghost dinner
Evangeline
Fairy web for Mr. Durand's daughters
Gossamer wedding
Gray moss or green trees
John in the storeroom
The life of Annie Christmas
One pair of blue satin slippers and four clever maids
The silver bell of Chênière Caminada
The silver snake of Louisiana
Three great men at peace

"LOUP-GAROUS"
Joe Hamelin and the "Loup-Garou"

Louse and flea go fishing
Alpers — *Legends* p.279

Love, Nat
Outwitting the Indians

LOVE
See also **Courtship; Lovers**
Answer to a child's question
Cap o' rushes
Crystal love
The Lady of the Lake
The legend of the betel
Monsoon
Moon snow
Orpheus and Eurydice
The spice woman's basket
The stolen heart
The test
Tiger woman
The yellow ribbon
, *Family*
Kuikueve
, *Frustrated*
Romeo and Juliet

144

LOVE *(continued)*

, *of animals*
Saint Blaise and his beasts
Saint Francis of Assisi

The love of a Mexican prince and
princess
Stories From World p.48-55

Lovecraft, H. P.
The outsider

LOVERS
The bridal chamber of Silver
Springs
Good Bishop Valentine
Hina and the eel
The legend of the Cherokee sweet
shrub (and variants)
The magic spider box
A midsummer night's dream
Romeo and Juliet
The song of the Cherokee rose
(and variants)
The tragic tale of Fenwick Hall

The lovers of Dismal Swamp
Life — Treasury p.166-167

The loyal mungoose
Rugoff — Harvest p.448-450

LOYALTY
The frog king, or Iron Henry
The Lady of Man Xuong
The legend of the betel
The travelers and the bear
The white crane

Lu-bo-bo
Manning — Monsters p.41-48

LUCERNE, SWITZERLAND
The dragons of Rhodes, Lucerne
and Somerset

LUCIFER. *See* **Devils**

LUCK
See also **Charms; Rings; Super-
stitions;** etc.
The clock that walked by itself
Good luck and bad luck
Mirko, the king's son
, *Bad*
Song of an unlucky man
The story of the unlucky days

The story of unlucky David
, *Good*
Go to the verge of destruc-
tion and bring back
Shmat-Razum
Hans in Luck
Noodlehead luck

Luck for fools
Jagendorf — Noodle p.216-221

Lucky Hans
Bamberger — My p.127-133

LULLABIES
, *African*
Ca, ca, ca

Lullaby
McDowell — Third p.46

LUMBERMEN
Paul Bunyan
Paul Bunyan's big griddle
Paul's cornstalk
Pecos Bill meets Paul Bunyan

LUTES AND LUTE PLAYERS
The little donkey
Vasilisa and Prince Vladimir
The wanderings of Arasmon

LUTINS
Lutins (subject)
McHargue — Impossible p.52

Lutonya
Jagendorf — Noodle p.235-240

LYCANTHROPY
Halfway people

The McCanles fight as Hickok told it
Life — Treasury p.202-205

M

McCord, David
Who wants a birthday?

McCOY FAMILY
The Hatfields and McCoys
The day boy and the night girls

McDonald, George
The golden key

MacDONALD, GEORGE
George MacDonald (subject)
Cott — *Beyond* p.392

MACEDON, KING
The dragon of Macedon

MACEDONIA
The monster in the mill
Pentalina

MacFARLANE, IRIS
Iris MacFarlane (subject)
MacFarlane — *Mouth* p.147

MacFarlane, Leslie
A Dominion Day to remember

McGarry, Mary
The fairy tree
Hie over to England
The leprechaun of Carrigadhroid
The magic shilling
The son of bad counsel
Two tales of leprechauns
The white hen

McGRAW, JOHN
John McGraw's jinx killer

McHARGUE, GEORGES
Georges McHargue (subject)
McHargue — *Impossible* p.170

MACHNOW (ghost)
Big people

McKemy, Kay
The frogs who wished for a king
Ms. Cat and I

Maclintock, Letitia
Jamie Freel and the young lady

MacManus, Dermott
The white fairy horse

MacManus, Seumas
Feather o' my wing

Macpherson's lament
Stuart — *Witch's* p.89-104

A mad tea-party
Darrell — *Once* p.104-110

MADAGASCAR (island)
Halfway people
Little people

Madam crab loses her head
McDowell — *Third* p.81-87

MADISON, DOLLY
White House ghosts

MADNESS. See Insanity

Madoc
Life — *Treasury* p.37

Maelduin's voyage
Higginson — *Tales* p.96-107

MAES KNOLL
Big people

MAGARAC, JOE
Joe Magarac, the man of steel

MAGI, THREE
The three Magi
Workers of evil — and a few
good spirits

MAGIC
See also **Magicians; Witch Doctors;
Witches; Witchcraft; Wizards**
Aniello
Bata
The bewitched cat
Bia
Blackberries in February
The boy with the hand of fire
The castle of Ker Glas
The castle of the active door
The cockleshell
Cow Bu-cola
The discontented grass plant
Dugama, maker of dugong magic
Feather o' my wing
The foam maiden
The forest bride
The garden of magic
The giant who was afraid of
butterflies
Go I know not whither and fetch
I know not what
The graveyard rose
The great bear of Orange
The hermit and the mouse
The horned women
The house in the forest
Irani and the cuckoos
The island of the Nine Whirlpools
Jorinda and Joringel
The lady and the lion

MAGIC (continued)

The Lady of the Lake
Lazy Hans
The little donkey
Little hen eagle
Maraboe and Morsegat
The merchant's son who never
  smiled
The nine doves
Oda and the snake
The old woman of the forest
Prince Monkey
Princess Finola and the dwarf
The princess under the earth
The princess's slippers
Rose Red
The saga of Kuiam
Sagerwazer
Sankichi's gift
Sea magic
The search for Little Water
Seven black crows
Sigai
The sleeping beauty in the wood
  (and variants)
The small red ox
Snow-White (and variants)
Sorcerer Kaldoon
The tailor and the treasure
Takise
The terrible stranger
Tiger woman
White orchid, red mountain
The wizard of Long Sleddale
The wife who talked too much
The wily wizard and the witch in
  the hollow tree
The wonderful shirt

The magic ball
  Hopkins — *Witching* p.117-127

The magic box
  Ficowski — *Sister* n. pag.

The magic egg
  Bain — *Cossack* p.239-251

The magic hammer
  Junne — *Floating* p.71-73

The magic horse
  Bamberger — *My* p.181-192

The magic lake
  Manning — *Choice* p.295-300

The magic listening cap
  Junne — *Floating* p.55-59

The magic mill
  Bamberger — *My* p.81-85

The magic monkeys
  Manning — *Sorcerers* p.112-121

The magic pot
  Spicer — *13 Rascals* p.101-109

The magic shilling
  McGarry — *Great* p.30-32

Magic! Silly magic!
  Jagendorf — *Noodle* p.97-99

The magic spider box
  Spicer — *13 Dragons* p.128-138

The magic table, the gold-donkey, and
  the cudgel in the sack
  Bamberger — *My* p.136-146

The magical spectacles
  Sperry — *Scand.* p.133-145

MAGICIANS
  See also **Witch Doctors; Witches;
    Wizards**

Beetle
Blodeuwed the betrayer
The Caliph turned stork
Conrad and the dragon
Earth magician
The enchanted cat
The history of Tom Thumb (and
  variants)
The Island of the Nine Whirlpools
Merlin the enchanter
Prince Ahmed and the fairy
  Peribanou
Prince Rabbit
The riddle of the room upstairs
Stan Bolovan
Stan Bolovan and the dragon
Uncle James, or the Purple
  stranger
Workers of evil — and a few good
  spirits

The magician's cape
  Olenius — *Great* p.19-28

The magician's cloak
  Sperry — *Scand.* p.113-122

The magpie with salt on her tail
Olenius — *Great* p.136-141

MAGPIES
The cane with a will of its own
Feather o' my wing

The magpie's nest
Morel — *Fairy* p.96

MAGUEYS (plants)
The coyote and Juan's maguey

MAGYARS
The hedgehog, the merchant, the
king, and the poor man
King Miklos, and the green daugh-
ter of the green king
The poor man, and the king of
the crows
The reed maiden
The useless wagoner

MAI TREES
Karum
Tubu and the seven sisters

The maid in the mirror
Sheehan — *Folk* p.118-126

Maida
Lawrie — *Myths* p.259

The maiden in the castle of rosy clouds
Olenius — *Great* p.221-229

The maiden stone
Wyness — *Legends* p.128-133

Maigi
Lawrie — *Myths* p.189-190

Mailer, Norman
The inexperienced ghost

Maiwasa
Lawrie — *Myths* p.107

Maizab Kau
Lawrie — *Myths* p.283-284

MAIZE. *See* Corn

The making of the hammer
Rugoff — *Harvest* p.662-666

Makonaima returns
McDowell — *Third* p.75-80

Malice, Bouki and Momplaisir
Carter — *Greedy* p.91-98

Malo
Lawrie — *Myths* p.326-336

Malo ra Gelar
Lawrie — *Myths* p.337-338

Malory, Sir Thomas
Sir Launcelot and the dragon

MAN
See also **Creation; Women**
Coyote drowns the world
The creation of man
How man began
Tiki the first man
, *Perfect*
Legend of the perfect people
- *Strength*
The power of woman and the
strength of man

The man and his boots
Rugoff — *Harvest* p.65-67

The man and his shadow
Krylov — *Fables* p.54-55

The man and the lion
Levine — *Fables* p.46

The man and the satyr
Rugoff — *Harvest* p.415-416

The man and the wife in the vinegar
jug
Bechstein — *Rabbit* p.22-34

The man bitten by a dog
Levine — *Fables* p.66

Man-crow
Carter — *Greedy* p.73-78

The man in the middle
Life — *Treasury* p.238-240

The man in the moon
Baum — *Mother* p.109-116

The man on Morvan's road
Leach — *Whistle* p.59-60

A man sits in the ice . . .
Belting — *Whirlwind* n. pag.

148

The man, the white steed, and the
wondrous wood
Jagendorf — *Folk, South* p.193-
198

The man, the woman, and the fly
Jagendorf — *Noodle* p.161-163

The man who became a lizard
Bird — *Path* p.71-73

The man who couldn't get married
MacFarlane — *Mouth* p.123-130

The man who promises the impossible
Levine — *Fables* p.22

The man who sold the winds
Pugh — *More* p.67-76

The man who tricked Sultan Otakul
Spicer — *13 Rascals* p.34-42

The man with three wives
Krylov — *Fables* p.109-110

Manabozho, the trickster
Life — *Treasury* p.61

Manaii and the spears
Alpers — *Legends* p.342-344

MANÁUS
The Yara

MANDARINS (tyrants)
The five brothers Li
A strange and rare friendship

Mandeville, John, Sir
Halfway people
Sir John Maunderville's dragon

MANGAIA (island)
Chant for a new tooth
The coming of Tute
Hina and the eel
How Tahaki lost his golden skin
Visitor's song

MANGAREVA
Kuikueve
A mother shames her son, Mapu-
kutaora
Onokura laments his old age
Tonga's lament for his daughter

MANGO TREES AND MANGOES
Prince monkey

MANGOSTEEN TREES
The Lady of Nam Xuong

MANGROVE TREES
Biu

Manhattan hoax
Life — *Treasury* p.155-156

MANIHIKI
Maui-of-a-thousand-tricks

MANIKINS
Sir Buzz

Manley, Seon
Letter from Massachusetts: 1688

MANLEY, SEON
Seon Manley (subject)
Manley — *Sisters* p.126-127,
219

MANNANAN MAC LIR (half-animal)
Halfway people

MANNERS. See Courtesy

Mannikin Spanalong
Manning — *Sorcerers* p.33-36

Manning-Sanders, Ruth
Knurremurre
Lazy Hans
The old witch
The seven Simons (and variants)

Man's first sight of the camel
Levine — *Fables* p.30

The mansion of the dead
Anderson — *Haunting* p.156-161

MANSIONS
The strange, sad spirit of the
Scioto
, *Governor's*
Ghost of the governor's man-
sion

MANTICORA
The book of beasts
Halfway people

MANTLES, SEA
Slime

MANUSCRIPTS
The Caliph turned stork

Many-Fur
Segal — *Juniper (II)* p.236-244

MAORIS
See also **New Zealand**
Hine and Tinirau
Lizard-husband, scaly skin
Mataora and Niwareka
Te Kanawa and the visitors by
firelight

A map of myths of early America
Life — *Treasury* p.40-45

MAPLE SUGAR
A jug of syrup

MARA (demon)
Workers of evil — and a few good
spirits

Maraboe and Morsegat
Bomans — *Wily* p.72-84

Marandenboni
Rugoff — *Harvest* p.29-33

MARCH (month)
The months

MARDI GRAS
The bridal ghost dinner

"MARE-LOCKS"
Elf hill

MARI. *See* **Ghosts**

MARIBUNDAS
Little people

Marie Laveau, queen of the voodoos
Anderson — *Haunting* p.85-92

MARINE DISASTERS. *See* **Disasters,
Marine**

MARINERS. *See* **Sailors**

"MARAKI." *See* **Ghosts**

The markai of Tawapagai
Lawrie — *Myths* p.108-109

Markep and Sarkep
Lawrie — *Myths* p.312-313

Marley's ghost
Darrell — *Once* p.173-186

MARMOSETS (monkeys)
Ears and tails and common sense

MARMOTS
The fox and the marmot

MARQUETTE, FATHER
Father Marquette and the Manitou

MARRIAGE
Onokura laments the old age

The marriage of Robin Redbreast and
the wren
Piper — *Stories* n. pag.

The marriage tale
Carrick — *Wise* n. pag.

Marriott-Watson, Ethel
The witch of the marsh

MARRIOTT-WATSON, ETHEL
Ethel Marriott-Watson (subject)
Manley — *Sisters* p.45-46, 217-
218

MARSHES
The witch of the marsh

Martens, Frederick H.
The inn that wasn't there

MARTYRS
Saint Prisca, the child martyr

"MARUTS" (ghosts)
Big people

The marvelous chirrionera
Lyons — *Tales* p.19-28

MARY, VIRGIN
Our Lady's tumbler

"Mary Celeste"
Life — *Treasury* p.154

Mary Culhane and the dead man
Bang — *Goblins* p.29-40

Marya Morevna
Curtin — *Myths* p.203-216
Whitney — *In* p.107-120

MARYLAND
Fifty years in chains
The ghost challenger
- *Silver Springs*
The bridal chamber of Silver
Springs

Marzipan (recipe)
Greene — *Clever* p.98-99

Masha and the bear
Carey — *Baba* p.117-120

Maski, the land of the dead
Courlander — *Fourth* p.101-110

MASKS
The destruction of Palatkwapi

MASSACHUSETTS
See also **Boston; Nantucket Island**
They called her a witch
- *Cape Cod*
Ichabod, Crook-Jaw and the
witch
The Witch of Wellfleet
- *Charlestown*
Letter from Massachusetts
- *Great Barrington*
Crossing the bridge
- *Hadley*
The angel of Hadley
- *New Bedford*
Thar she blows
- *Salem*
The midnight voyage of the
Seagull
A pot of trouble
The Salem witches and their
own voices: Examination
of Sarah Good

MASSACRES
Rebes and Id

The master and his pupil
Rugoff — *Harvest* p.233-235

The master cat (Puss in boots)
Opie — *Classic* p.113-116
Perrault — *Fairy* p.25-31
Stories From World p.88-95

Master Money and Madame Fortune
Bamberger — *My* p.33-37

Master Richard Bird
Cott — *Beyond* p.273-278

The master thief
Rugoff — *Harvest* p.676-689
Segal — *Juniper (I)* p.113-128

The master thief and the dragon
Green — *Cavalcade* p.133-137

MAT FAIRIES
Hiroko

The mat-maker's adventure
Novák — *Fairy* p.95-99

MAT-WEAVING
Aukam

Mataora and Niwareka
Alpers — *Legends* p.319-327

The match
Hautzig — *Case* p.45-53

MATCHES
The flying trunk
The little match-girl

MATHEMATICS
See also **Counting**
Higher mathematics in Helm
The island of the Nine Whirlpools

MATS
Raramai
, *Wishing*
The cat sat on the mat

Mau and Matang
Lawrie — *Myths* p.232-234

Maude's story
Wahl — *Muffletump* p.39-63

Maui and Tuna
Alpers — *Legends* p.107-112

Maui and Usuru
Lawrie — *Myths* p.230-232

Maui-of-a-thousand-tricks
Alpers — *Legends* p.92-105

Maundeville, John, Sir. **See** Mandeville,
John, Sir

MAY EVE
Faery folk

Workers of evil — and a few good spirits

MAYAS. *See* **Indians of Latin America — Tribes — Maya**

MAYORS
The dragon tamers
The four wizards
The wily wizard, and the witch in the hollow tree

MAZES
The wooing of the maze

MEAD (drink)
Salt

The meadow mouse
Shaw — *Mouse* p.26-27

MEADOWS
The Prince of the flowery meadow

MEANNESS. *See* **Cruelty; Evil; Wickedness**

MEASLES
The little boy's secret

MEAT
The dog and the piece of meat
The man who became a lizard
The old gray man of Spring

MECHANICS
The shape-shifters of Shorm

MEDDLESOMENESS. *See* **Interference**

MEDEA
Jason and the dragon of Colchis

Medea
Rugoff — *Harvest* p.394-397

MEDICINE
See also **Healing; Physicians**
No witchcraft for sale
Tshinyama heavenly maidens

MEDICINE MEN
The four worlds

MEDUSA
Halfway people

MEEKNESS
The proud pastor

The meeting
Bomans — *Wily* p.164-167

Meeting with a double
Hoke — *Ghosts* p.74-76

MELANCHOLY. *See* **Grief; Sadness**

MELUSINA
The People of the sea

MEMORIAL DAY
Memorial Day (subject)
Corrigan — *Holiday* p.103-110
"Old Abe" American eagle

Men from the village deep in the mountains
Bang — *Men* p.1-13

The men who wouldn't stay dead
Rugoff — *Harvest* p.331-333

MENDING
The magician's cape

Menu for a king
Greene — *Clever* p.108

The merchant
Corrigan — *Holiday* p.97
Krylov — *Fables* p.61-62
Rugoff — *Harvest* p.525-535

MERCHANTS
Beauty and the beast
Blackmail
The buried money
The division
The fox in the hole
Half of everything
The haunted palace
The hedgehog, the merchant, the king, and the poor man
Holding the truth
The inn that wasn't there
Little Master Misery
The mice that ate iron
Saint Fronto's camels
Salt
The singing leaves
The tale of the silver saucer and the transparent apple
The talema
The treasure of Li-Po
Vasilisa the beautiful
Vassilisa and Prince Vladimir

MERCHANTS *(continued)*

Vassilissa the cunning, and the
Tsar of the sea
What happened to Hadji
The wondrous wonder

The merchant's son who never smiled
Novák — *Fairy* p.108-118

MERCY
The banyan deer
Gudgekin, the thistle girl

MERLIN
The history of Tom Thumb

Merlin the enchanter
Higginson — *Tales* p.48-62

The mermaid
De Bosschere — *Christmas* p.69-
74

The mermaid and the monster
Sleigh — *Stirabout* p.79-89

MERMAIDS
See also **Mermen**
The fisherman and his soul
The magic lake
The People of the sea
Rake up!
Sven and Lilli
The three mermaids

Mermaids
Life — *Treasury* p.38-40

MERMEN
The People of the sea
The seal catcher and the Merman

MERRIMENT. *See* **Laughter**

MERROWS
The Lady of Gollerus
The People of the sea
Souls under the sea

The merry tale of Belle Boyd
Jagendorf — *Folk, South* p.304-306

The message
Carter — *Enchanted* p.70-74

MESSENGERS
Why there is death in the world

Metarawai
Lawrie — *Myths* p.182

MEXICO
Ashes for sale
The aunts
Brother sun and sister moon
The coyote and Juan's maguey
The fifth sun
The flea
The giant and the rabbit
Godfather to skunks
Good advice
Hermit into scorpion
Hummingbird of the South
In Mexico the people say . . .
Short sayings based on long
experience
The king and the rain dwarfs
The legend of Agustín Lorenzo
Legend of the perfect people
(La) Llorona
The love of a Mexican prince
and princess
The marvelous Chirrionera
The monkey musicians
The monster we live on
The noblest deed
People of the heron and the
hummingbird
Plumed serpent in Tula
Repaying good with evil
The rich señora
Riddles
The sombreros of the men of Lagos
The talema
A time for everything
The wind's bride
Wine and the devil
Witches
Xibalba
, *Language, glossary of*
Glossary of Mexican language
(subject)
Lyons — *Tales* p.83-86

Meyer, Michael, trans.
The tinder-box

Mibu and the coconut
Lawrie — *Myths* p.198-199

MICE
See also **Dormice**
Aniello

The bird, the mouse, and the
sausage
Blackmail
The castle of the active door
Cat and mouse in partnership
The cat and the mice
The cat and the mouse
Cinderella or The little glass
slipper (and variants)
The city mouse and the garden
The cock and the mouse and the
little red hen (and variants)
The cockerel-stone
The country mouse and the city
mouse
Daughter and stepdaughter
Dick Whittington
Don't foul the well — you may
need its waters
The dormouse
The elf and the doormouse
The forest bride
The goblins at the bath house
The good man and the kind
mouse
He who likes to bite and kiss will
always go astray and miss
The hermit and the mouse
Hickory, Dickory, Dock
King of the mice
The lion and the grateful mouse
The lion and the mouse
The little house
A little mouse
The meadow mouse
Minching and munching mouseling
"Not a creature was stirring . . ."
The protector of the mice
Saint Comgall and the mice
Some mice under ferns
The three butterflies
Titty mouse and Tatty mouse
The town mouse and the country
mouse
The troll's little daughter
When the mouse laughs . . .

Mice
Shaw — *Mouse* p.29

The mice
Shaw — *Mouse* p.21

The mice and the cat
Morel — *Fairy* p.94-95

The mice in council
Krylov — *Fables* p.38-39
Shaw — *Mouse* p.22

Mice never . . .
Shaw — *Mouse* p.9

The mice that ate iron
Rugoff — *Harvest* p.451-452

Mice under snow
Shaw — *Mouse* p.43

MICHAEL, SAINT
The vampire and St. Michael

MICHIGAN
See also **Detroit**
Blood stoppers

MIDAS, KING
The golden touch

The middle-aged man and his two
mistresses
Levine — *Fables* p.30

MIDDLE EAST
Ali Baba

Middlemore, S. G. C.
The werewolf

Middleton, Thomas
A witch's song

MIDGETS
Ivan the peasant's son and the
little man himself one-finger tall,
his mustache seven versts in
length
Lipsuniushka
The little man and his little gun
Little people
Little Poucet
One-inch fellow
Tom Thumb (and variants)

MIDNIGHT
The three men of power —
evening, midnight and sunrise

The midnight voyage of the Seagull
Manley — *Sisters* p.146-182

MIDSUMMER EVE
A chapter of fish
Faery folk

A midsummer night's dream
Darrell — *Once* p.147-157

MIGRATIONS
Polynesian migrations (subject)
Alpers — *Legends* p.2-5
The migrations
Courlander — *Fourth* p.34-42

Mike Fink, last keelboatman
Life — *Treasury* p.116-118

Mike Hooter and the smart bear in
Mississippi
Jagendorf — *Folk, South* p.162-164

MIKOLAYCAK, CHARLES
Charles Mikolaycak, illus. (subject)
Ficowski — *Sister* n. pag.

MILK
Lutonya
The story of Tremsin the bird Zhar
and Nastasia, the lovely maid
of the sea
- *Charms*
Cushy cow, bonny
- *Cream*
A tale of two frogs

The milkmaid and her pail
Morel — *Fairy* p.69

MILKYWAY (constellations)
How the Milky Way came to be
How the moon came to be
The little scarred one

The miller, his cook and the king
Greene — *Clever* p.101-107

The miller, his son, and their donkey
(and variants)
Haviland — *Fairy* p.102-103

MILLERS
The devil and his three golden
hairs
The jolly miller
The magic pot
The poor miller's boy and the
little cat
The test
The three golden hairs

The miller's mule
Gardner — *Dragon* p.37-54
The miller's sons
Ginsburg — *Lazies* p.64-70
The miller's tale
Carrick — *Wise* n. pag.

MILLET
A-e-oine, the demon, and the
tattle-tale dog
Tweriire
- *Dumplings*
The adventures of Little
Peaching

MILLINERY. See Hats

MILLS
The haunted mill
I will leave it to the devil
The monster in the mill
The Phouka
, *Hand*
The magic mill
Why the sea is salt

Milne, A. A.
Prince Rabbit

Mimer, the master
Stories From World p.74-87

Minching and munching mouseling
Sleigh — *Stirabout* p.61-69

MIND-READING
The queen

MINISTERS. See Clergymen

MINNESOTA
The Vikings and their traces

MINOTAUR
The halfway people

MINSTRELS
The blind singer, Saint Hervé
The first flute
The men who wouldn't stay dead
, *Welsh*
Taliessin of the radiant brow

The miracle of Hormigueros
Belpré — *Once* p.72-75

The miracle of the mail
Life — *Treasury* p.215-216

MIRACLES
The purchased miracle
Saint Kentigern and the robin
The wonders of Saint Berach

Miracles on the sea
Hautzig — *Case* p.55-63

Mirko, the king's son
Curtin — *Myths* p.434-456

The mirror
Bang — *Men* p.67-69

The mirror and the monkey
Krylov — *Fables* p.84

MIRRORS
The basilisk
The fox's daughter
The Isinyandende
The last balloon
The maid in the mirror
The moon in the donkey
The mouse-hole, and the under-
ground kingdom
Narcissus
Snow-White and the seven dwarfs
Sven and Lilli
Taikoko
The time of the ugly
The valiant chattee-maker
The water-nixie

**MISCHIEF AND MISCHIEF-MAKERS.
See Trickery**

The miser
Krylov — *Fables* p.81-82
Levine — *Fables* p.86

The miser who received his due
Carter — *Greedy* p.125-131

MISERS
See also **Greed**
The Brahman and the pot of rice
A Christmas carol
The fox and the dragon
The haunted mill
The last piece of light
Stingy Kichiyomu and the iron
hammer

Stingy Kichiyomu and the rice
thieves

MISERY
The enchanted apple-tree
Why misery remains in the world

**MISFORTUNE. See Disasters; Luck,
Bad**

Miss Peabody
Sleigh — *Stirabout* p.28-37

The mission ended
Carter — *Enchanted* p.81-82

MISSIONARIES
The breakup of Oraibi
The destruction of Awatovi
Gé of Dabangai
, *Jesuit*
Father Marquette and the
manitou

MISSIONS
, *California* — *Soledad*
The miracle of the mail

MISSISSIPPI
The ghost wedding in Everhope
Guess who!
The harp player of Pitcher's Point
The living colors of the Twenty-
first
Mike Hooter and the smart bears
in Mississippi
The ring around the tree
The sad tale of the half-shaven
head
The song in the sea
Tar-wolf tale
- *Natchez*
Goat castle
- *Pascagoala River*
The singing river

MISSISSIPPI RIVER
Blue Johnny and the pilot
Corpse maker and Calamity's child

MISSOURI
"Spook Light" of Devil's Prom-
enade
- *Pike County*
Sweet Betsy
- *Wayne County*
Can't rust

Missouri stubborn — that's what it is!
Calhoun — *Three* p.4-5

Mr. and Mrs. Vinegar
Piper — *Stories* n. pag.

Mr. Cuttlefish's love story
Orczy — *Old* p.39-50

Mr. Fox
Minard — *Womenfolk* p.30-35

Mister Lazybones
Junne — *Floating* p.83-84

Mr. Rabbit and Mr. Bear
Lester — *Knee* p.12-20

The mistress and her two maids
Krylov — *Fables* p.120-122

Mistress Crispin's story
Cott —*Beyond* p.233-238

Mrs. Gertrude
Segal — *Juniper (II)* p.310-313

The mistress in black
Hoke — *Ghosts* p.77-94

Mistress Mary
Baum — *Mother* p.75-86

Mrs. Scruby and the Spanish spider
Sleigh — *Stirabout* p.90-97

Ms. Cat and I
Shaw — *Cat* p.22-24

MITTENS
The three little kittens who lost
their mittens

MIWOK LEGENDS
The creation of man

MIXE MYTHS
Brother sun and sister moon

MIZNER, WILSON
The fabulous Wilson Mizner

The mock turtle's story
Darrell — *Once* p.117-122

MOCKINGBIRDS
Nobody sees a mockingbird on
Friday

MODESTY
Zeus and modesty

Modupe, Prince
Leopard hunt

Moe, Jorgen Engerbretsen (jt. author).
See Asbjornsen, Peter Christian

MOFSIE, LOUIS
Louis Mofsie (subject)
Jones — *Coyote* p.50

Moggie Mewling
Sleigh — *Stirabout* p.139-143

Möibu and Bazi
Lawrie — *Myths* p.219-221

Mokan
Lawrie — *Myths* p.251-252

Molasses milk shake (recipe)
Greene — *Clever* p.89

MOLDAVIAN TALES
Toast and honey

MOLES
The eagle and the mole
The thrush girl
Thumbelina
- *Origin*
The origin of the mole

Molly Whuppie
Haviland — *Fairy* p.152-157
Minard — *Womenfolk* p.20-29

MOLOCH
Workers of evil — and a few good
spirits

Momotaro, The peach boy
Stories From World p.146-151

Momotaro, the peach sprite
Novák — *Fairy* p.6-15

MONASTERIES
The great bell of Bosham
Saint Gerasimus and the lion

MONEY
The brave flute-player
The buried money
Can't rust
The ducat

The golden touch
The good ogre
The history of Little Mook
Master Money and Madam Fortune
The star money
The tinder box
- *Shillings*
  The magic shilling
- *Sixpence*
  Sing a song o' sixpence
- *Strings of*
  Tiger woman

MONGOOSES
The loyal mongoose

The monkey and the crocodile
De Roin — *Jataka* p.38-40

The monkey and the spectacles
Krylov — *Fables* p.147

The monkey gardeners
Junne — *Floating* p.50-51

The monkey musicians
Roy — *Serpent* p.79-85

The monkey princes
Heady — *Safiri* p.11-16

MONKEYS
The adventures of Little Peachling (and variants)
Brer Rabbit's trickery
The creation of man
Don't try the same trick twice
The dragon and the monkey
The foolish monkeys
The fox and the monkey who was elected king
Greedy and Speedy
A handful of peas
How straws were invented
The mirror and the monkey
Momotaro, the peach boy (and variants)
The oldest of the three
Popularity
Prince Monkey
Raw monkey liver
Responsibility
Riddle me riddle, riddle me ree
Semrude the Fair and the Cadi
Sorcerer Kaldoon

The wagers
The wonders of palace life
- *Capuchins*
  Brown owl plans a party
  Ears and tales and common sense
  The grass-cutting races
- *Chimpanzees*
  Brown owl plans a party
  Riddles one, two, three
- *Colobus*
  The monkey princes
- *Hearts*
  The dragon and the monkey
  The monkey and the crocodile
  The monkey's heart
, *Red tail*
  The monkey princes

The monkey's Buddha
Novák — *Fairy* p.145-151

The monkey's heart
Heady — *Safiri* p.93-96
Sheehan — *Folk* p.93-99

MONKS
The four sacred scrolls
The haunted palace
A pair of wings
Saint Fronto's camels
Saint Gerasimus and the lion
The silver bell
The wandering monk and the tabby cat

MONOPODS
Halfway people

Mons Tro
Manning — *Choice* p.148-167

Monsoon
Duong — *Beyond* p.39-44

MONSOONS
Turtles of gold and bitter regrets

Monster copper forehead
Manning — *Monsters* p.17-28

The monster eagle
Baker — *At* p.25-32

The monster in the mill
Manning — *Monsters* p.60-66

The monster of Cakaudrove
  Hoke — *Monsters* p.88-93

The monster of Leeds
  Life — *Treasury* p.92-93

"MONSTER OF THE FIELDS"
  The gratified toad

The monster we live on
  Roy — *Serpent* p.15-20

MONSTERS
  The basilisk
  Beauty and the beast
  The book of beasts
  Coyote conquers the Iya
  Dunber
  The foghorn
  Gabriel-Ernest
  The golden valley
  The great golloping wolf
  The horror of the heights
  Impulse
  In the Avu observatory
  King Solomon's ring
  Lu-bo-bo
  Moxon's master
  Negotium perambulans
  The one-eyed monster
  The outsider
  Pentalina
  Picking mountain pears
  Prince Lindworm
  The river monster
  The sea maiden
  The seven monsters
  The singing leaves
  The sisimiqui
  Sister of the birds
  Slime
  The sphinx
  The story of the three young
    shepherds
  Tusi and the great beast
  Ubir
  The vampire of Tempassuk
  The water monster
  What came of picking flowers

MONTANA
  - *Anaconda*
      The sisy from Anaconda
  - *Billings*
      Skeleton Cliff of Montana

Montejo, Esteban
  Living in the forest

The months
  Bamberger — *My* p.91-94

MONTHS OF THE YEAR
  See also **Seasons;** names of months
  The twelve months

MONUMENTS
  See also **Statues**
  Washington monument by night

MOON
  A-e-oina, the demon, and the
    tattle-tale dog
  Brother sun and sister moon
  The buried moon
  The cinnamon tree in the moon
  The flea
  The four worlds
  Gray moss on green tree
  How the moon came to be
  How the moonfish came to be
  How three mighty heroes saved
    the sun and the moon from the
    dragon
  Hummingbird of the South
  Iruam
  Kabai
  Kiss Miklos, and the green daugh-
    ter of the green king
  Lincolnshire moon
  The man in the moon
  Why the sun and moon are in the
    sky
  The woman in the moon

The moon in the donkey
  Jagendorf — *Noodle* p.249-252

The moon maiden
  Morel — *Fairy* p.72-75

The moon on the ground
  Jagendorf — *Noodle* p.73-74

Moon sits smoking his pipe
  Belting — *Whirlwind* n. pag.

Moon snow
  Pugh — *More* p.89-94

MOONFISH
  How the moonfish came to be

Moore, Lilian
The witch's garden

Moore, Rosalie
Catalogue

MOORSOM, SASHA
Sasha Moorsom (subject)
Perrault — *Fairy* p.96

Moozipoo
Housman — *Rat* p.68-85

MORAVIA
The match

Mordaunt, Elinor
The prince and the goose girl

MORDVINIAN TALES
Syre-Varda

The morning glory
Morel — *Fairy* p.80

MOSQUITOES
In Arkansas stick to bears, don't
mess with swampland skeeters
The origin of mosquitoes

Mosquitoes
Schwartz — *Whoppers* p.76-79

MOSS
, *Spanish*
Gray moss on green trees

The most beautiful of all
De Roin — *Jataka* p.43-44

The most haunted house
Anderson — *Haunting* p.35-39

MOTHER GOOSE
Mother Goose (subject)
Baum — *Mother* p.9-15
The black sheep
The cat and the fiddle
Hickory, dickory, dock
How the beggars came to town
Humpty Dumpty
The jolly miller
Little Bo-Peep
Little Bun Rabbit
The little man and his little gun
Little Miss Muffet
The man in the moon
Mistress Mary

Old King Cole
Pussy-cat Mew
Sing a song o' sixpence
The story of Little Boy Blue
The story of Tommy Tucker
Three wise men of Gotham
Tom, the piper's son
What Jack Horner did
The woman who lived in a shoe
The wondrous wise man

"Mother-in-law, today is shake-head
day!"
Robinson — *Singing* p.66-74

MOTHER-OF-PEARL
Gammelyn, the dressmaker

The mother of the sun
Ficowski — *Sister* n. pag.

A mother shames her son, Mapukutaora
Alpers — *Legends* p.230

MOTHERS
The goblins giggle
Iviahoca
The king who did not want to die
Lock-out time
Maud's story
The mermaid
The three kingdoms (and variants)

MOTHER'S DAY
Mother's Day (subject)
Corrigan — *Holiday* p.96-102
The cap that Mother made
The flute
The merchant

MOTHERS-IN-LAW
Don Demonio's mother-in-law
"Mother-in-law, today is shake-
head day!"
A pot of trouble
The twelve brothers

MOTHS
The ice dragon, or Do as you are
told
Korseim

MOTTE, REBECCA
The tale of Rebecca Motte

The mountain goats
Martin — *Raven* p.53-59

The mountain lad and the forest witch
Novák — *Fairy* p.66-71

MOUNTAIN LIONS
Pecos Bill and the mountain lion

MOUNTAINS
See also names of mountains
The hen that saved the world
The love of a Mexican prince and
princess
Makonaima returns
The miracle of Hormigueros
The old man on the mountain
The three kingdoms
The three sisters who were en-
trapped into a mountain
Three strong women
, *Glass*
The frog
, *King of*
Monsoon

The mouse
Shaw — *Mouse* p.24-25

The mouse and the rat
Krylov — *Fables* p.91

The mouse-hole, and the underground
kingdom
Curtin — *Myths* p.331-355

The mouse in the wainscot
Shaw — *Mouse* p.10

Mouse-maid made mouse
Rugoff — *Harvest* p.443-446

A mouse must not think . . .
Shaw — *Mouse* p.43

Moxon's master
Hoke — *Monsters* p.164-176

MUD
The golden shoes

MUFFLETUMPS. See Dolls, Victorian

The Muiar
Lawrie — *Myths* p.319

Mukeis
Lawrie — *Myths* p.302-303

MULATTOES. See Blacks — Mulattoes

MULES
Ali Baba
The miller's mule
Not on the Lord's Day
The time cousin Emmett out-
stubborned his mules

The mummer's play
Green — *Cavalcade* p.87-92

MURDER
Burumnaskai
The dispersed from Sikyatki
Garuge
The legend of Lizzie Borden
Retribution

Murgatroyd, the Kluge maker
Life — *Treasury* p.267

MURYANS
Little people

MUSEUMS
The ghost of Captain Flint

MUSHROOMS
Dirty hands

MUSIC
Elsie's story
The smith, the weaver, the harper
- *Animals*
The quartet

MUSICAL INSTRUMENTS
See also names of instruments
The girl in the basket

MUSICIANS
See also types of musicians
- *Animals*
The Bremen town musicians
, *Traveling*
A bed for the night
The wanderings of Arasmon

MUSKETS. See Guns and Gunnery

MUSTANGS. See Horses — Mustangs

Muta
Lawrie — *Myths* p.39-41

Mutuk
Lawrie — *Myths* p.68-69

My cat Jeoffry
Shaw — *Cat* p.44-45

My people
Corrigan — *Holiday* p.24

My wish
McDowell — *Third* p.45

Myself
Bamberger — *My* p.66-69

The mysterious fig tree
Littledale — *Strange* p.31-33

The mysterious fire of Frendraught
Wyness — *Legends* p.134-140

The mysterious Ticonderoga curse
Anderson — *Haunting* p.27-34

The mysterious traveller
Colwell — *Round* p.43-45

The mystery maiden from heaven
Junne — *Floating* p.40-41

The mystery of Bigfoot
Anderson — *Haunting* p.162-164

The mystery of Theodosia Burr
Jagendorf — *Folk, South* p.199-202

A mystical rhyme
Cott — *Beyond* p.279-285

N

Naga
Lawrie — *Myths* p.19-20

NAGAS (Naginis)
Halfway people

Nageg and Geigi
Lawrie — *Myths* p.306-311

NAGGING
The woman of the well

NAGINIS. See Nagas

Nail broth
Morel — *Fairy* p.109-111

Nail stew
Spicer — *13 Rascals* p.121-127

NAMES
A good name gives strength
The white hen
, *Russian*
- *Pronunciation*
Higonnet-Schnopper —
Tales p.9-11

NANAI (Asiatic tribe)
Ayoga

Nancy Hanks
Corrigan — *Holiday* p.30-31

Nandayure and his magic rod
Carter — *Enchanted* p.27-30

NANDI
Workers of evil — and a few good
spirits

Nandris, Mabel, trans.
Twelve dancing princesses

Nanny goat with nuts
Manning — *Tortoise* p.90-95

NANTUCKET ISLAND, MASSACHU-SETTS
Ichabod, Crook-Jaw and the witch
The silver bullet

Narcissus
Rugoff — *Harvest* p.397-398

Nas-ed-Din Hodja in the pulpit
Rugoff — *Harvest* p.173-174

NATURE
See also related subjects
Come out and look!
Leave well enough alone
The sightseer

NAUDI BEAR
Workers of evil — and a few good
spirits

NAUGHTINESS. See Trickery

The Navajo attack on Oraibi
Courlander — *First* p.185-190

A necklace of raindrops
Aiken — *Necklace* p.9-20

NECKLACES
, *Jade*
The treasure of Li-Po

NECROMANCERS. See Fortune Tellers

The needle crop of Sainte-Dodo
Jagendorf — *Noodle* p.133-135

NEEDLES
The lass who went out at the cry of dawn
The longest story in the world
Spindle, shuttle, and needle
Through the needle's eye

NEEDLEWORK
See also types of needlework
The lazy daughter
Through the needle's eye

NEEDY. See Poverty

NEGLECT
Why the sea moans

Negotium perambulans
Hoke — *Monsters* p.69-87

The negro speaks of rivers
McDowell — *Third* p.105

NEGROES. See Blacks; Africa; etc.

NEIGHBORS
The Colonel teaches the judge a lesson in good manners
Dancing stones
Friends and neighbors

Nemcová, Bozena
Prince Bajaja
Punished pride

NENETZ (Samoyeds)
How Wilka went to sea

NEPHEWS
Saurkeke

NERGAL
Workers of evil — and a few good spirits

Nerucci, Gherardo
Fanta-Ghiro

Nesbit, Edith. See Bland, Edith Nesbit

NETHERLANDS
The three rascals and the magic cap
- *Zeeland*
Knurremurre

NEVADA
The sky is a bowl of ice
- *Virginia City*
Julia Bulette of Virginia City

NEW ENGLAND
See also names of states
Kibbe's shirt

NEW GUINEA
The cycle of A'Aisa
The eagle
The first woman
How man began
Song of a hen
Tee Kuntee
A visit to Orokolo
Why the sun and moon are in the sky

NEW HAMPSHIRE
- *Appledore Island*
The golden girl of Appledore Island
- *Henniker*
Ocean-born Mary
- *Isles of Shoals*
The golden girl of Appledore Island

NEW JERSEY
The young witch-horse
- *Leeds*
The monster of Leeds

New lamp for old. See Aladdin

The new law
Carey — *Baba* p.61-62

NEW MEXICO
The black cat's eyes

NEW ORLEANS, LOUISIANA
Marie Laveau, queen of the voodoos

A new way to boil eggs
Jagendorf — *Noodle* p.130-132

NEW YEAR'S
New Year's day (subject)
Corrigan — *Holiday* p.14-21
Gohei and the god of poverty
Hung Vuong and the earth and
sky cakes
The little match-girl
A round for the New Year
The stone statue and the grass hat
Through the fire

New Year's hats for the statues
Corrigan — *Holiday* p.16-20

NEW YORK (state)
Dew eagle, at night . . .
- *Catskill mountains*
Rip Van Winkle
- *Genesee River valley*
Drop star
- *Gibbet Island*
The ghosts of Gibbet Island

NEW YORK CITY, N.Y.
- *Bowery*
Big Mose, the bowery boy
- *Manhattan*
Black Sam and the haunted
treasure
Manhattan hoax
- *Subways*
The man in the middle
- *Ticonderoga*
The mysterious Ticonderoga
curse

NEW ZEALAND
Chant to Io
The cockleshell
Confirmation of a warrior
Creation
Kahukura and the net-makers
When the sky lay on the earth
- *Rotorua*
Hine and Tu
- *Tuhoe*
Mataora and Niwareka
- *Waikato*
Te Kanawa and the visitors
by firelight
- *Whanganui*
Lizard-husband, scaly skin

NEWSPAPER REPORTERS
The golden girl of Appledore Island

Next turn to the right
Leach — *Whistle* p.103-104

NICARAGUA
The lagoon of Masaya

NICHOLAS, SAINT
Workers of evil — and a few good
spirits
, *Polynesian*
The origin of kava

NIGERIA. *See* **Africa — Nigeria**

NIGHT
See also **Darkness**
The three men of power — Eve-
ning, midnight and sunrise

The nightingale
Provensen — *Book* p.25-32

NIGHTINGALES
The ass and nightingale
Jorinda and Joringel
The swine-herd (and variants)

The nightingales
Krylov — *Fables* p.62-64

Nilar Makrem
Lawrie — *Myths* p.363-365

Nils in the forest
Manning — *Ogres* p.123-127

Nima and Poipoi
Lawrie — *Myths* p.157-160

The nine doves
Manning — *Choice* p.63-73

The nine-headed bird
Fehse — *Thousand* p.107-114

"NINE-PINS"
Rip Van Winkle

NITTAEWO
Little people

NIXIES (NIX)
The People of the sea
The water-nixie

Nnoonya Mwana Wange
Serwadda — *Songs* p.7-9

Nnyonyi
    Serwadda — *Songs* p.27-31

No witchcraft for sale
    Manley — *Sisters* p.207-216

NOBEL PEACE PRIZE
    My people

NOBILITY
    See also **Kings and Queens;**
        Princes and Princesses; etc.
    Iviahoca

The noblest deed
    Lyons — *Tales* p.54-57

Nobody and Polyphemus
    Rugoff — *Harvest* p.386-392

Nobody here but you and me
    Leach — *Whistle* p.28

Nobody sees a mockingbird on Friday
    Jagendorf — *Folk, South* p.69-71

NOISE
    The foolish lion and the silly
        rooster
    The sad victory
    The Woman in the moon
    The woman who flummoxed the
        fairies

Nollichucky Jack
    Jagendorf — *Folk, South* p.184-187

Noodlehead Jack
    Jagendorf — *Noodle* p.281-283

Noodlehead Pat
    Jagendorf — *Noodle* p.263-267

The noodlehead tiger
    Jagendorf — *Noodle* p.30-33

NOODLEHEADS. *See* **Fools and Foolish-**
    ness; stories in Jagendorf —
    Noodle

Norinori
    Lawrie — *Myths* p.370-372 (appen-
    dix)

NORTH
    The dragon of the North

NORTH AMERICA
    See also **Indians of North America;**
        names of countries
    Big people
    Halfway people
    Little people
    People of the sea
    The search for Little Water

NORTH CAROLINA
    It's a long time between drinks
    The man, the white steed, and the
        wondrous wood
    The mystery of Theodosia Burr
    Nollichucky Jack
    Pirate Blackbeard's deep-sea end
    The revolution of the Ladies of
        Edenton
    The tale of the hairy toe
    The ways of the Lord
    The white doe
    - *Bald Mountain*
        The savage birds of Bald
            Mountain
    - *New Bern*
        The pirates and the Palatines
    - *Roanoke Island*
        The silver doe
        The white doe
    - *Southport*
        Tony and the harp
    - *Wilmington*
        Joe Baldwin's light

NORTH DAKOTA
    Wind is a ghost . . .

NORTH POLE
    The ice dragon or Do as you are
        told

NORTH STAR
    The shining lodge
    , *Lady of*
        The last piece of light

The North wind and the sun
    Darrell — *Once* p.236-237
    Levine — *Fables* p.44

NORTHERN LIGHTS. *See* **Aurora**
    Borealis

Norton, Andre
    Through the needle's eye

NORTON ANDRE
Andre Norton (subject)
Manley — *Sisters* p.29-30,217

NORUMBEGA (island)
The search for Norumbega

NORWAY
The archer and the king
The bewitched cat
Big people
The boy and the North Wind
The Christmas bear
The Faery folk
The hen that saved the world
How Thor found his hammer
The magic mill
The making of the hammer
The master thief
Odin's search for wisdom
The pig that went to court
The proud pastor
The rooster that fell in the brew
  vat
Silly Matt
Tatterhood
The three billy-goats-gruff
The twelve wild ducks
Why the bear's tail is short
Why the sea is salt
Widow Fox and her four suitors

The nose of the Konakadet
Martin — *Raven* p.37-43

NOSES
Baba Yaga
Dwarf long nose
The King's nose
The three wishes
, *Long*
  East of the sun and West of
    the moon
  Longnose the dwarf

NOSINESS. See Curiosity

"Not a creature was stirring . . ."
Shaw — *Mouse* p.44

Not bad — but it could be better
Higonnet-Schnopper — *Tales* p.49-
57

Not long after the earth was made . . .
Belting — *Whirlwind* n. pag.

Not of school age
Corrigan — *Holiday* p.113-114

Not on the Lord's Day
Jagendorf — *Noodle* p.253-255

Not one more cat
Shaw — *Cat* p.11-12

Notes on fairy faith and the idea of
  childhood
Cott — *Beyond* p.xxi-1

NOVA SCOTIA. See Canada — Nova Scotia

Now every child
Corrigan — *Holiday* p.234

Now I should laugh if I were not dead
Rugoff — *Harvest* p.694-696

Nsangai
Serwadda — *Songs* p.45-49

NUCKELAVEE
The halfway people

Nuiumma-kwiten
Leach — *Whistle* p.88

NUMBERS
- *Seven*
  The place of the beginning

NUMBSKULLS. See Fools and Foolishness

NUNS
The mat-maker's adventure

NURSERY RHYMES
A pavane for the nursery
Wanted — a king

NURSES AND NURSING
The book of beasts
The fiery dragon, or the Heart of
  stone and the heart of gold
Little Miss Muffet
The Prince of the flowery meadow

NUTS AND NUT TREES
Kate Crackernuts
Little cat and little hen
Nanny goat with nuts
The ogre

NUTS AND NUT TREES *(continued)*

- *Hickory*
Bigfoot Wallace and the
hickory nuts
, *of knowledge*
Country-under-wave

Nyangara the python
McDowell — *Third* p.25-28

Nyblom, Helena
The changelings
The ring

Nycteris
Cott — *Beyond* p.428

NYMPHS
See also types of nymphs
Diana and Actaeon
The yellow dwarf
, *Forest*
People of the sea
Workers of evil — and a few
good spirits
, *Water*
Halfway people
People of the sea
Workers of evil — and a few
good spirits

O

The oak and the reed
Krylov — *Fables* p.46-47

OAK TREES
The golden mare
The tinder box

OANNES
People of the sea

OBEDIENCE
The untamed shrew

The obedient servant
Jagendorf — *Noodle* p.207-211

OBSERVATORIES
In the Avu observatory

The obsession with clothes
Hautzig — *Case* p.9-17

OBSTINACY. *See* **Stubbornness**

OCCUPATIONS
Guess who?

Ocean-born Mary
Anderson — *Haunting* p.7-16

October
Corrigan — *Holiday* p.203

OCTOPUS
Old Stormalong and the octopus

Oda and the snake
Bamberger — *My* p.13-14
Manning — *Sorcerers* p.65-68

ODALA (fruit)
The stepchild and the fruit trees

Odin's search for wisdom
Rugoff — *Harvest* p.658-662

ODYSSEUS
Big people
Nobody and Polyphemus

Of Sam Bass
Jagendorf — *Folk, South* p.287-289

Of the Peace congress and bootinter
Cott — *Beyond* p.104-109

The offspring of the sky and earth
Alpers — *Legends* p.47-50

The ogre
De Bosschere — *Christmas* p.136-145

OGRES AND OGRESSES
See also **Onis**
The adventures of Little Peachling
(and variants)
Big people
The children on the pillar
The girl in the basket
The good ogre
The green bird
How straws were invented
Jack and the beanstalk
Little Poucet
The magic pot
The master cat (and variants)
Puss in boots
The rice cake that rolled away
The sea gulls

The sleeping beauty
The sleeping beauty in the wood
The three Ivans
Tom Thumb
Tortoise and ogre

The ogres
Manning — *Sorcerers* p.69-82

The ogre's breath
Manning — *Ogres* p.32-37

Oh: The Tsar of the forest
Bain — *Cossack* p.15-26

OHDOWAS
Little people

OHIO
Johnny Appleseed
- *Crawford Co.*
Sam'l Dany, noodlehead
- *Portage Co.*
Brady's leap
- *Scioto river*
The strange, sad spirit of the Scioto

OIL
The last balloon
- *West Virginia*
Snake Magee's rotary broiler

OINTMENT
The doctor's servant

Ojumiri and the giant
Robinson — *Singing* p.34-43

"Old Abe" American eagle
Corrigan — *Holiday* p.104-110

OLD AGE
The golden key
The old man, the wolf, and the vixen
The old man's wen
The oldest of the three
Onokura laments his old age
Sergevan
Usheen in the Island of Youth

The old barn owl
Shaw — *Owl* p.46

Ol' Clackety teeth
Shaw — *Witch* p.116-125

The old dog
Bain — *Cossack* p.129

Old Gally Mander
Rugoff — *Harvest* p.56-59

The old gray man of Spring
McFarlane — *Mouth* p.31-37

"Old Hickory" and the Bell witch
Anderson — *Haunting* p.93-103

Old Hildebrand
Rugoff — *Harvest* p.358-362

Old King Cole
Baum — *Mother* p.65-72

The old lion and the fox
Levine — *Fables* p.18

The old man and death
Levine — *Fables* p.34
Rugoff — *Harvest* p.419-420

The old man and the bears
Schwartz — *Whoppers* p.49-50

The old man, his son, and the donkey
Piper — *Stories* n. pag.

The old man on the mountain
Carpenter — *People* p.49-54

The old man, the wolf, and the vixen
Ginsburg — *One* p.10-13

The old man who made the trees blossom
Novák — *Fairy* p.184-191

The old man's wen
Bang — *Goblins* p.1-13

Old Mister Smoothback
Bagley — *Candle* p.34-38

Old spells and charms
Hopkins — *Witching* p.97

Old Stormalong and the octopus
Life — *Treasury* p.156-157

Old Sultan
Bamberger — *My* p.42-43

Old Tom comes home
Leach — *Whistle* p.33

The old troll of Big Mountain
Olenius — *Great* p.114-121

Old Verlooka
Manning — *Choice* p.301-306

The old wife and the ghost
Hoke — *Ghosts* p.111-113

Old wine in new bottles
Hoke — *Ghosts* p.123-131

The old witch
Hopkins — *Witching* p.74-81
Shaw — *Witch* p.200-203

The old woman
Rugoff — *Harvest* p.4-25

The old woman and her dumpling
Minard — *Womenfolk* p.44-50

The old woman and her pig
Great Children's p.48-58
Haviland — *Fairy* p.28-31
Morel — *Fairy* p.122-124

The old woman and the doctor
Levine — *Fables* p.34

The old woman and the physician
Rugoff — *Harvest* p.418-419

The old woman and the tramp
Greene — *Clever* p.145-152

The old woman and the wine jar
Rugoff — *Harvest* p.417

The old woman in the cottage
Bang — *Men* p.55-59

The old woman of the forest
Bamberger — *My* p.10-13

The old woman who lost her dumpling
Greene — *Clever* p.32-38

The oldest of the three
De Roin — *Jataka* p.1-3

Ole Sis Goose
Life — *Treasury* p.280

Oliver Stanley is kidnumped
Schwartz — *Whoppers* p.51-53

OLIVES AND OLIVE TREES
The girl who cried flowers
The reed and the olive tree

OLOKUN
The People of the sea

Once upon a great holiday
Corrigan — *Holiday* p.133-134

The one-eyed monster
Carpenter — *People* p.66-70

One handful
Leach — *Whistle* p.41-42

One-inch fellow
Haviland — *Fairy* p.162-169

The one-legged crane
Greene — *Clever* p.117-123

One pair of blue satin slippers and
four clever maids
Jagendorf — *Folk, South* p.138-140

One trick too many
Ginsburg — *One* p.17-20

"ONE WITH THE WHITE HAND"
Workers of evil — and a few good
spirits

"1001 NIGHTS"
The barber's tale of his sixth
brother
The fifth voyage of Sindbad the
seaman
The first Kalander's tale
Khusrau and the fisherman
The king and the wazir's wife
The ruined man who became rich
again through a dream
Tale of the devout Israelite

ONIONS
- *Skins*
The rich señora

ONIS (ogres)
Momotaro, The peach boy (and
variants)
The old woman and her dumpling
The old woman who lost her
dumpling
One-inch fellow

Only in Texas
Jagendorf — *Folk, South* p.281-283

Onokura laments his old age
Alpers — *Legends* p.199

The open window
Hoke — *Ghosts* p.105-110

OPOSSUMS
Full moon a-shining
The terrapin and the possum
outwit the fox
- *Tails*
Why the possum's tail is bare

The oracle
Krylov — *Fables* p.132-133

ORANG PENDEK
Little people

ORANGES AND ORANGE TREES
The yellow dwarf
, *Golden*
Three golden oranges

ORCHARDS. *See* **Trees**

The ordeal of Hugh Glass
Life — *Treasury* p.226-229

Ordinary people
Schwartz — *Whoppers* p.15-21

Ordinary things
Schwartz — *Whoppers* p.22-45

OREADS (nymphs)
Workers of evil — and a few good
spirits

ORGAN-GRINDERS
Budulinek

ORIENT. *See* names of countries

The origin of corn and beans
Bird — *Path* p.27-31

The origin of kava
Alpers — *Legends* p.271-272

The origin of mosquitoes
Lawrie — *Myths* p.349

The origin of the Magellan clouds
Alpers — *Legends* p.273-276

The origin of the mole
Bain — *Cossack* p.207-208

ORPHANS
Alenoushka and her brother

The dragon, sliced-in-two
Foni and Fotia
Johnny and the witch-maiden
Khavroshechka
Mannikin Spanalong
The obsession with clothes
Old Verlooka
Pippi celebrates her birthday
Sing a song o' sixpence
Yukiko and the little black cat

ORPHEUS
The song of Orpheus; The song
that Orpheus sang to charm the
dragon

Orpheus and Eurydice
Rugoff — *Harvest* p.398-401

Osbarn, the smith
Wyness — *Legends* p.106-113

Ostenson, Harald
Dag and Daga, and the flying
troll of Sky Mountain
The maiden in the castle of rosy
clouds

OSTRICHES
This for that

OTTERS
Decide for yourself
Sea magic
The unlucky fisherman

Our goodman
Rugoff — *Harvest* p.272-276

Our Lady's tumbler
Rugoff — *Harvest* p.333-336

Out
Cott — *Beyond* p.433-436

OUTLAWS
See also **Bandits**
Jesse James and the widow
The McCanles fight as Hickock
told it
Macpherson's lament
Of Sam Bass
Railroad Bill

The outside man
Leach — *Whistle* p.54-56

The outsider
Hoke — *Monsters* p.177-187

Outwitting the Indians
McDowell — *Third* p.98-105

OVENS
See also **Earth-ovens**
Brer Rabbit, businessman
Dunber
Hansel and Gretel (and variants)
Karum

Over in the meadow
Shaw — *Owl* p.33

Over the turnstile with Topleaf
Cott — *Beyond* p.222-227

OVINNIK
Little people

The owl (Aiken)
Shaw — *Owl* p.26-27

The owl (Hubbell)
Shaw — *Owl* p.42

The owl (Smith)
Shaw — *Owl* p.30

The owl and the eagle
Shaw — *Owl* p.40-41

The owl and the grasshopper
Shaw — *Owl* p.16-18

OWLS
Blodeuwed and the betrayer
Brown owl plans a party
The caliph turned stork
Coyote steals the summer
The grouchy old owl
How wise is an owl
I know an owl
It's only an owl
The knee-high man
Look on your back!
Over in the meadow
Riddles one, two, three
Song for a gluttonous owl
The tragic tale of Hooty the owl
Two little owls
The ugly duck
Who says, who says?
Whooooo?
A wise old owl

Wisky, wasky, weedle
, *Barn*
The old barn owl

Owls are like this
Shaw — *Owl* p.38-39

Owls aren't so smart
Shaw — *Owl* p.29

The ox and the ass
Ginsburg — *Lazies* p.33-35

The ox and the frog
Darrell — *Once* p.241

OXEN
The best food
The frog and the ox
Pecos Bill meets Paul Bunyan
The small red ox
The tortoise
- *Bulls*
Harsh words
- *Hides*
The thoughtless abbot
, *King of*
Big people
, *Straw*
The straw ox

The oxen and the axle
Levine — *Fables* p.38

OYSTERS
- *Shells*
The Karankawa from the
gleaming oyster shells

OZARKS. See Arkansas — Ozarks

P

Pablo and the pirate's ghost
Belpré — *Once* p.91-96

PACKS
The table, the pack, and the bag

PADDLES
, *Magic*
The old woman and her
dumpling
The old woman who lost her
dumpling

PADDOCK, ICHABOD, Captain
Ichabod, Crook-Jaw and the witch

"PADUTU". *See* **Ghosts**

Paehr, Gunbild
The lonely witch

PAGE BOYS
Beauty
The good man and the kind mouse
The lost half-hour
Witzenspitzel

Paimi a Nawanawa
Lawrie — *Myths* p.320-321

PAIN
See also **Sickness**
The flower of happiness on Sunny-
mount Crest

Painted skin
Stories From World p.112-121

Painter, George D.
Meeting with a double

PAINTERS AND PAINTINGS
A Chinese fairy tale
The mystery maiden from heaven
The strange sad spirit of the
Scioto
- *Portraits*
Mons Tro

Painting
Schwartz — *Whoppers* p.42

A pair of wings
Bomans — *Wily* p.46-50

Pakabva and the Kachinas
Courlander — *Fourth* p.96-100

The palace of the seven little hills
Manning — *Sorcerers* p.45-55

PALACES
Abdul Kasim the rich
Beauty and the beast
The golden slippers
The haunted palace
Knoonie in the sleeping palace
Pussy-cat Mew
, *Life in*
The wonder of palace life

, *Underground*
Aladdin
The fisherman and the Sea
King's daughter
The three men of power —
Evening, midnight and sun-
rise
, *Undersea*
Sadko

PALATINES
The pirates and the Palatines

PALLADINI, DAVID
David Palladini, illus. (subject)
Yolen — *Girl* p.56

PALM TREES
, *Royal*
The legend of the royal palm

Palmer, Geoffrey, and Noel Lloyd
Invitation to a ghost

PALMISTRY
Revealed

PANAMA
The rabbit and the barrel
The wagers

Pan'ambe and pen'ambe
Carpenter — *People* p.76-80

Pancake (recipes)
Greene — *Clever* p.127-128

Pancake day
Greene — *Clever* p.125-126

PANCAKES
The frying-pan
The little boy who wanted pan-
cakes

PANDANUS
- *Leaves*
Raramai

PANSIES
Little step-mother
Petsetilla's posy

PANTALEONI, HEWITT
Hewitt Pantaleoni (subject)
Serwadda — *Songs* n. pag.

The panther and the crow
  Bird — *Path* p.79-81
PANTHERS
  The lion and the panther
PAPAWS
  The terrapin and the possum out-
  wit the fox
PAPUA. *See* **New Guinea**
PARADISE
  See also **Heaven**
  The soldier and the demons
PARCHMENT
  King Solomon's ring
PARENTS
  Nnoonya Mwana Wange
  Why the baboon has a shining seat
  - *Child hostility*
    Hans and Greta
The parishioner
  Krylov — *Fables* p.145-146
PARKER, ISAAC C.
  The judge and the baseball-pitch-
  ing Indian chief
PARKIN
  The dragon and the square-round
  parkin
Parradiddle Pete
  Sleigh — *Stirabout* p.70-78
The parrot who couldn't say Cataño
  Belpré — *Once* p.85-90
PARROTS
  Brown owl plans a party
  The cat and the parrot
  The Emperor's parrot
  Forty men I see, forty men I do
    not see
  Little Hiram
  Popularity
  Riddles one, two, three
PARSONS. *See* **Clergymen**
PARTIES
  Brown owl plans a party

, *Tea*
  Alice's adventures in Won-
    derland
PARTRIDGES
  The oldest of the three
Paslag
  Lawrie — *Myths* p.365
PASSOVER, FEAST OF
  Song of the kid
PATCH, SAM
  Jumping Sam Patch
Patches
  Bang — *Men* p.15-19
The patchwork quilt
  Aiken — *Necklace* p.84-94
PATIENCE
  The three wishes
Patient Griselda
  Perrault — *Fairy* p.75-80
PATRICK, SAINT
  Saint Patrick (subject)
    Corrigan — *Holiday* p.66-77
  The leprechaun; or, Fairy shoe-
    maker
  The peddler of Ballaghadereen
  The swan-children of Lir
Paul Bunyan
  Life — *Treasury* p.285-286
Paul Bunyan's big griddle
  Rugoff — *Harvest* p.79-81
Paul's cornstalk
  Rugoff — *Harvest* p.81-85
A pavane for the nursery
  Corrigan — *Holiday* p.120-121
PEACE
  Hiawatha
  How red strawberries brought
    peace in the woods
  The kingdom of the lion
  Saint Francis of Assisi
  Three great men at peace
  - *Birds*
    Saint Cuthbert's peace

- *Polynesia*
  Alpers — *Legends* p.22-23

PEACHES AND PEACH TREES
  The adventures of Little Peachling
  Momotaro, the peach sprite (and
  variants)

The peacock and the jackdaw
  Levine — *Fables* p.60

PEACOCKS
  The golden apple-tree and the
  nine peahens
  The prince with the nine sorrows
  The tortoise who flew to heaven

The pear tree
  Gardner — *King* p.31-43

PEARLS
  The cinnamon tree in the moon
  The cock and the pearl

PEARS AND PEAR TREES
  Dunber
  The girl in the basket
  Picking mountain pears
  Planting a pear tree
  The swan maiden
  Why misery remains in the world

PEAS
  Five in a pod
  Five peas in a pod
  A handful of peas
  How the rabbit lost his eye
  The real princess

The peasant and snake
  Krylov — *Fables* p.94-95

The peasant and the bear
  Carey — *Baba* p.84-85

The peasant and the robber
  Krylov — *Fables* p.76-77

The peasant and the sheep
  Krylov — *Fables* p.44-45

The peasant in trouble
  Krylov — *Fables* p.140-141

The peasant, the bear, and the fox
  Higonnet-Schnopper — *Tales* p.76-81

PEASANTS
  The cat who became head-forester
  The dragon and the peasant
  The Emperor's parrot
  The fool of the world and the
  flying ship
  Little Master Misery
  Old Hildebrand
  The red fox and the walking stick
  The rich woman and the poor
  woman
  The serpent and the peasant
  Three peasants
  The workman and the peasant

The peasants and the river
  Krylov — *Fables* p.100-101

Peattie, Donald Culross
  Come out and look!

Pecos Bill and the mountain lion
  Life — *Treasury* p.274-275

Pecos Bill meets Paul Bunyan
  Stories From World p.122-129

"Peculiarsome" Abe
  Corrigan — *Holiday* p.34-39

The peddlar of Ballaghadereen
  Corrigan — *Holiday* p.67-74

PEDDLERS
  The Caliph turned stork
  George Piney-Woods peddler
  Yankee peddlers

The pedlar of Swaffham
  Colwell — *Round* p.61-63

Pedro the trickster
  Rugoff — *Harvest* p.722-728

PELE (goddess)
  The eruption of Pele's anger
  Ghostly goddess of the volcano

PELICANS
  Amipuru
  Damak and Daram

PENANCE. See Punishment

PENNSYLVANIA
  How hoop snakes can sting
  The swapper

PENNSYLVANIA *(continued)*
- *Berks Co.*
  How Daniel Boone met his
    wife
Pentalina
  Manning — *Monsters* p.118-128
PEOPLE
  See also **Man; Women**
  Ordinary people
People can't be made from iron
  McDowell — *Third* p.29-30
People from the sky
  Carpenter — *People* p.1-8
PEOPLE OF THE DANA. *See* **Dana,**
  People of
People of the heron and the humming-
  bird
  Roy — *Serpent* p.66-75
People of the sea
  McHargue — *Impossible* p.135-158
The people who told the tales
  Martin — *Raven* p.1-9
The perambulatin' pumpkin
  Greene — *Clever* p.137-142
Percy the wizard, nicknamed Snail
  De Bosschere — *Christmas* p.86-93
PERETZ, ISAAC LOEB
  Isaac Loeb Peretz (subject), and
    stories
  Hautzig — *Case* p.ix-xiv
PERFECTION
  The princess with freckles
PERFUME
  Tahia the fragrant girl
PERIL. *See* **Danger**
The perpetual motion in the sea
  Jagendorf — *Folk, South* p.224-226
Perrault, Charles
  Cinderella (and variants)
  Little Red Riding-Hood
  The master cat
  Puss in Boots (and variants)

PERRAULT, CHARLES
  Charles Perrault (subject)
  Perrault — *Fairy* p.96
PERSEA TREES
  Anpu and Bata
PERSEVERANCE
  Good advice
  A tale of two frogs
PERSIA
  Afrāsib
  The birth and boyhood of Rustem
  Bizhān and Manizha
  The death of Rustem
  The defeat of Persia
  The departure of Khosroes
  The earliest kings
  The forty thieves
  Forud of Jalāt
  Gushtāsp
  Halfway people
  How Rustem found Raksh
  Infendiār
  Klosroes and Afrāsaib
  Prince Ahmed and the fairy Peri-
    banou
  The river monster
  Rustem and Akvān the demon
  Rustem and Isfendiār
  Rustem and Tahmina
  Rustem's battle with Pulādvend
  Rustem's journey to Māzendarān
  Siyāvush the unfortunate
  Sohrāb and Rustem
  The sons of Feridun
  Who is who?
  Workers of evil — and a few good
    spirits
  Zāl and Rudāda
  Zāl the white-haired
  Zohāk and Feridun
  Zohāk the monster
- *Defeat*
  The defeat of Persia
PERSISTENCE. *See* **Perseverance**
PERSUASION
  The North wind and the sun
PERU
  Ayaymama
PERVERSITY. *See* **Stubbornness**

The pet crocodile
    Lawrie — *Myths* p.190-194

PETER, SAINT
    Brother Gaily
    Ivan the fool and St. Peter's fife
    The key-flower
    The rich woman and the poor
        woman
    The tortoise who flew to
        heaven

Peter and the Witch of the wood
    Hopkins — *Witching* p.82-96

Peter Klaus
    Rugoff — *Harvest* p.371-373

PETER OF GREECE, Prince
    Big people

Peter Pan
    Darrell — *Once* p.256-263

Peter Pan in Kensington Gardens
    Darrell — *Once* p.249-296

Peter Rugg
    Life — *Treasury* p.130-133

Peter's adventures
    Jagendorf — *Noodle* p.147-155

Peter's goat
    Darrell — *Once* p.291-296

PETS. See types of pets

Petsetilla's posy
    Cott — *Beyond* p.39-146

Petsetilla's youth, and Bungo's bothers
    Cott — *Beyond* p.72-75

The phantom of the loch
    Wyness — *Legends* p.38-44

The phantom train of Marshall Pass
    Life — *Treasury* p.188-189

The phantom vaquero of the Texas
        plains
    Anderson — *Haunting* p.137-142

PHANTOMS. See Ghosts

PHARAOHS
    Anpu and Bata

Bata
    The three dooms

PHARMACISTS
    The silver bell

PHEASANTS
    The clever thief
    Momotaro, the peach boy (and
        variants)

PHILIPPINE ISLANDS
    Little people

PHILOSOPHERS
    Do you know?
    The griffin and the wise old phil-
        osopher
    Pinya of Helm

Photogen
    Cott — *Beyond* p.427-428

The Phouka
    McGarry — *Great* p.40-44

PHYSICIANS
    Bartek the doctor
    The draper who swallowed a fly
    Godfather Death
    Gratitude
    How the clever doctor tricked
        death
    The old woman and the doctor
    The old woman and the physician
    The sick man and the doctor
    The warlock
    , *Quack*
        The quack frog
    - *Women*
        The daring of yellow doc

Piatt, Sara Morgan Bryant
    The witch in the glass

Picard, Barbara Leonie
    Richmuth of Cologne
    The three wishes

Picking mountain pears
    Bang — *Men* p.71-77

The Pied Piper of Hamelin
    Piper — *Stories* n. pag.

PIES
Sing a song o' sixpence
A very great curiosity
, *Plum*
What Jack Horner did

PIETY
Harchand the Just

Pig and Pepper
Darrell — *Once* p.97-104

The pig and the sheep
Levine — *Fables* p.52

The pig-headed wife
Rugoff — *Harvest* p.292-294

The pig that went to court
Sperry — *Scand.* p.44-48

The pig with gold bristles, the deer
with golden horns, and the
golden-maned steed with golden
tail
Curtin — *Myths* p.59-71

PIGEONS
Anansi and turtle and pigeon
The finch and the pigeon
The greedy crow
The prince and the dragon
The tortoise who flew to heaven
The Zamay who hid his life

The piglet and the fairy
Colwell — *Round* p.108-109

PIGS. See Hogs

The pike
Krylov — *Fables* p.40-41

The pike and the cat
Krylov — *Fables* p.141-142

PILGRIMS AND PILGRIMAGES
The purchased miracle
Why misery remains in the world

PILLARS
Uncle James or the Purple stranger
, *Ivory*
The children on the pillar

PINE TREES
The saga of two trees
The wishing-ring

PINCKNEY, JERRY
Jerry Pinckney, illus. (subject)
Shaw — *Mouse* p.15

PINTO, RALPH
Ralph Pinto (subject)
Lester — *Knee* p.32

Pinto Smalto
Greene — *Clever* p.90-97
Rugoff — *Harvest* p.535-540

Pinya of Helm
Rugoff — *Harvest* p.565-569

Pipe and Pitcher
Carey — *Baba* p.121-126

The piper of Keil
Littledale — *Strange* p.3-7

PIPERS
The captive pigeon
The Pied Piper of Hamelin
Tom, the piper's son
The young piper

PIPES (musical)
The kid and the wolf
Peter Pan
A red, ripe apple, a golden saucer

Pippi celebrates her birthday
Corrigan — *Holiday* p.158-168

Pirate Blackbeard's deep-sea end
Jagendorf — *Folk, South* p.187-190

The pirate women
Life — *Treasury* p.94-95

PIRATES
Blackbeard's treasure
The ghost of Captain Flint
The ghosts of Gibbet Island
Lafitte's great treasure
The mystery of Theodosia Burr
Ocean-born Mary
Pablo and the pirate's ghost
The tale of Lura Lous
The tired ghost

The pirates and the Palatines
Life — *Treasury* p.86-88

The Piskeys on Selena Moor
Rugoff — *Harvest* p.256-261

PISKIES (Pisgies). *See* **Pixies**

PISTOLS. *See* **Guns and Gunnery**

Pitai
    Lawrie — *Myths* p.78-79

PITCHERS
    The crow and the pitcher

PITHECANTROPUS
    Big people

PITY. *See* **Mercy**

PIXIES
    Little people
    The piskeys on Selena Moor

The pixy visitors
    Colwell — *Round* p.114-116

The place of the beginning
    Bird — *Path* p.11-15

PLAGUES
    Lludd and Llevelys
    , *Children's*
        They called her a witch

PLAINS
    - *Climate*
        Febold Feboldson

Planting a pear tree
    Rugoff — *Harvest* p.182-183

PLANTS
    See also **Flowers; Gardens and**
        Gardening; Herbs; names of
        plants
    - *Mitrewort ("Bishop's cap")*
        The Cumins of Cutter
    - *Roots*
        No witchcraft for sale
    , *Useless*
        The poorest man in the world

The Pleiades
    Rugoff — *Harvest* p.99-100

PLINY
    People of the sea

PLOUGHS AND PLOUGHING
    Lipuniushka

PLOUTOS
    Heracles and Ploutos

Plumed serpent in Tula
    Roy — *Serpent* p.47-58

PLUMS AND PLUM TREES
    Amagi
    Dirty hands
    Dunber
    Visitor

PLUTO
    Workers of evil — and a few good
        spirits

Podepode and Ngukurpodepode
    Lawrie — *Myths* p.229-230

Poe, Edgar Allan
    The sphinx

Poem of a girl whose young sister
        loves the same man she does
    Alpers — *Legends* p.191

POETICAL
    See also **Chants; Songs**
    Abraham Lincoln (1809-1865)
    Afternoon by a pond in the heart
        of Vermont
    The aged lion
    The ant
    The ape
    Apelles and the young ass
    April
    As the tadpole said
    The ass and the nightingale
    The ballad of Saint Athracta's stags
    The ballad of Saint Felix
    The ballad of Saint Giles and the
        deer
    The barrel
    The bear among the bees
    Beware
    A boasting chant in war
    The boy and the snake
    The brook
    Broomstick train
    By whose command?
    Carol of the brown king
    Cat! (Eleanor Farjeon)
    Cat (J.R.R.Tolkien)
    The cat heard the cat-bird
    Catalogue
    Cat's menu

POETICAL (*continued*)

The chest
The Christmas gift
A Christmas wish
The city mouse and the garden
The cloud
The cock and the pearl
Confirmation of a warrior
The cornflower
Creation
The cuckoo and the eagle
The cycle of A'Aisa
Demyán's fish soup
Dew eagle, at night . . .
Digger boy was hunting clams . . .
The division
The dormouse
The dragon speaks
The dragon tamers
The drum
The ducat
The eagle
The eagle and the bee
The eagle and the fowls
The eagle and the mole
The eagle and the spider
Earl Desmond and the banshee
The elephant and the pug
The elephant as governor
The elf and the dormouse
The enchanted island
The fairies (Allingham)
The fairy thorn
The false accusation
The fiddling cat
The finch and the pigeon
Fireworks
The flute
The fly and the bee
Fortune and the beggar
The fox
The fox and the marmot
The frog (anonymous)
The frog (by Hilaire Belloc)
The frog (by Oliver Herford)
The frog and the ox
The frogs who wished for a king
The funeral
The geese
The gnat and the shepherd
Goblin market
Goldenhair
Good Bishop Valentine

The grandee
The great discovery
Grimelda
The grouchy old owl
The hag
Haiku
The hare at the hunt
Havaiki the land
The hermit and the bear
The hoard
Hopping frog
How wise is an owl
Hurrah for cats!
I hear American singing
I know an owl
I saw three witches
I'm nobody
The impious
In just-/Spring
In the beginning there was no
  earth . . .
Iruam
It's only an owl
Jabberwocky
John Henry
The kite
The kitten
The kitten and the falling leaves
The lamb
Lament on losing a kite
Lat take a cat
The leaves and the roots
A legend of Lake Okeefinokee
The leprechaun; or, Fairy shoe-
  maker
The liar
The lion and the fox
The lion and the panther
The lion, the chamois and the fox
The listeners
A little mouse
A local haunting
Louse and flea go fishing
Lullaby
Malo ra Gelar
The man and his shadow
A man sits in the ice . . .
The man with three wives
The meadow mouse
Meeting with a double
The merchant
Mice
The mice in council
Mice never . . .

Mice under snow
The mirror and the monkey
The miser
The mistress and her two maids
Ms. Cat and I
The monkey and the spectacles
Moon sits smokin his pipe . . .
A mother shames her son, Mapu-
    kutaora
The mouse
The mouse and the rat
The mouse in the wainscot
The mummer's play
My people
My wish
Nancy Hanks
The negro speaks of rivers
The nightingales
"Not a creature was stirring"
Not long after the earth was
    made . . .
Not of school age
Not one more cat
Not every child
The oak and the reed
October
The old barn owl
Old spells and charms
The old wife and the ghost
Once upon a great holiday
Onokura laments his old age
The oracle
Over in the meadow
The owl (Aiken)
Owl (Hubbell)
The owl (Smith)
Owls are like this
Owls aren't so smart
The parishioner
A pavana for the nursery
The peasant and snake
The peasant and the robber
The peasant and the sheep
The peasant in trouble
The peasants and the river
The pike
The pike and the cat
The pond and the river
Prayer for Thanksgiving
Priscilla's witches
Puss leaves home
Pussy-cat Mew
The quartet
Rao's dirge for herself

The raven and the fox
The Red Cross knight and the
    dragon
The ride-by-nights
A round for the New Year
The sack
The sheep and the dogs
The shepherd of the Giant Moun-
    tains
The sightseer
The sky is a bowl of ice . . .
The slanderer and the snake
The snake and the lamb
Some mice under ferns
Song for a gluttonous owl
Song of a hen
Song of an unlucky man
The song of Orpheus; The song
    that Orpheus sang to charm the
    dragon
The sportsman
Squatter's rights
The steed and his rider
Suppose you met a witch
The swan, the pike and the crayfish
The swimmer and the sea
Tee Kuntee
That cat
This witch
Three peasants
To a cat
Tommy
Tonga's lament for his daughter
The tragic tale of Hooty the owl
The tree
Trishka's coat
Twenty froggies
Two casks
Two cats of Kilkenny
Two little owls
The two peasants
The unwelcome cat
The war god's horse song
Washington monument by night
Watch
What is a witch?
When the sky lay on the earth
Who says, who says?
Who wants a birthday?
Whoooo?
A widow's funeral chant
Wind is a ghost . . .
A wise old owl
Wisky, wasky, weedle

POETICAL (continued)

The witch in the wintry wood
The witch of Willowby Wood
The witches are flying
Witches' chant
Witches' charm
The witch's garden
A witch's song
Witch's song from Hansel & Gretel
The wolf and the cat
The wolf and the stork
The wolf in the kennel
The wolves and the sheep
The workmen and the peasant
- Narratives
     The consequence

POISON

Conrad and the dragon
Texas centipede coffee
The witch: a tale of the Dark
   Ages
- Polynesia (subject)
     Polynesia poison
          Alpers — Legends p.23

POKER (game)

The fireplace

POLAND

The angel
Bartek the doctor
The basilisk
Big people
The freak
How a tailor became a king
The jester who learned to cry
Seven black crows
The sorcerer and his apprentice
The test
The time of the ugly
- Chelm
     The golden shoes
     The great traveler of Chelm

POLECATS. See Skunks

POLEVIK

Little people

POLITENESS. See Courtesy

POLITICIANS

Demedes the politician

POLLYWOGS. See Frogs

POLO, MARCO

Halfway people

POLTERGEIST

Little people

POLYNESIA

Polynesia (subject)
   Alpers — Legends p.1-42
- Colors
   - Red (subject)
        Alpers — Legends p.16-18
- Crafts (subject)
     Alpers — Legends p.7
- Life (subject)
     Alpers — Legends p.10-23
- Sexual customs (subject)
     Alpers — Legends p.19-20

POLYPHEMUS

Big people
Nobody and Polyphemus

POMEGRANATES

- Seeds
     The wise rogue

PONCE DE LEON, DON JUAN

Bimini and the fountain of youth
The fountain of youth
Iviahoca

The pond and the river
   Krylov — Fables p.59-61

PONDS. See Pools

"POOKAS"

The halfway people
The kitchen pooka

The pool of tears
   Darrell — Once p.76-80

POOLS

Ataraga at the pool
Hine and Tu
Jenny Green Teeth
The legend of the hummingbird
Mokan
The pond and the river
, Wishing
     The witch's wish

POOR. See Poverty

The poor man, and the king of the
crows
Curtin — *Myths* p.409-423

The poor miller's boy and the little cat
Segal — *Juniper (II)* p.178-186

The poorest man in the world
Spicer — *13 Rascals* p.110-120

Pop and Kod
Lawrie — *Myths* p.303

POPES
The meeting

"POPOL VUH"
The creation of man
The message
The mission ended
The revenge
The tricks of Hunahpú and
Ixabalanqué

Popularity
De Roin — *Jataka* p.48-50

PORAPORA
Turtle, fowl and pig

PORPHYRIA (disease)
The halfway people

PORRIDGE
The little pot
The story of the three young
shepherds
The three bears
The wonderful shirt

PORTERS
The seven good years
The theft of a smell

PORTRAITS
The mouse-hole, and the under-
ground kingdom
Punished pride

PORTUGAL
The magic spider box
Not on the Lord's Day
What came of picking flowers

POSSUMS. See Opossums

POSTMEN
The girl in the lavender dress
Snake the postman

A pot of trouble
Raskin — *Ghosts* p.7-15

Pot-Tilter
Leach — *Whistle* p.88

Potikain and Ngiangu
Lawrie — *Myths* p.5

POTS AND PANS
See also Cauldrons
The Hedley Kow
Juan Bobo
The killing pot
Pot-Tilter
Who will wash the pot?
Who'll wash the porridge pot?
, *Broken*
Kaleeba
, *Magic*
The little pot
The magic pot
The wonderful porridge pot

POULTRY. See names of poultry

POVERTY
See also titles beginning with Poor
The alms tale
Aniello
The cloth of a thousand feathers
The echo well
Little Master Misery
The magic mill
Mons Tro
The poor man, and the king cf
the crows
The rich woman and the poor
woman
Saint Rigobert's dinner
The stone statue and the grass hat
The straw ox

POWAKAS (witches)
The four worlds

POWER
Monsoon

The power of woman and the strength
of man
Jagendorf — *Folk, South* p.254-256

**PRANKSTERS. See Clowns; Fools and
Foolishness; Trickery**

PRAYER
The hermit and the mouse
, *Procession*
The Rogativa

Prayer for Thanksgiving
Corrigan — *Holiday* p.212

PREACHERS. *See* **Clergymen**

PRECAUTION
The ant and the grasshopper

PRECEPTS. *See* **Sayings**

PREPAREDNESS. *See* **Precaution**

PRESENTS. *See* **Gifts**

Pretutssky, Jack
A little mouse

PRIDE
See also **Braggarts**
Ayoga
The gnat and the bull
How the frog lost his tale (tail)
The proud pastor
Punished pride
The Tsar and the angel
The ugly duck
, *Madness of*
The lad who stared everyone
down

PRIESTS
An ancient curse
The fisherman and his soul
Guleesh
The meeting
The miracle of the mail
Painted skin
Painting a pear tree
A Taoist priest
The two chickens or the two ears
The wizard's revenge

Prince Ahmed and the fairy Peribanou
Junne — *Floating* p.91-114

The prince and the dragon
Green — *Cavalcade* p.148-156

The prince and the goose girl
Provensen — *Book* p.68-81

Prince Bajaja
Sekorová — *Europe* p.33-45

Prince Ivan, the witch baby and the
little sister of the sun
Ransome — *Old* p.94-108

Prince Lindworm
Manning — *Monsters* p.49-59

Prince Loaf
Manning — *Choice* p.216-223

Prince Monkey
Fehse — *Thousand* p.66-78

The prince of the flowery meadow
Fehse — *Thousand* p.7-14,188-209

Prince Rabbit
Provensen — *Book* p.93-104

The prince with the nine sorrows
Housman — *Rat* p.100-115

PRINCES AND PRINCESSES
Aladdin
The badger and the fox
Beauty
Beauty and the beast
The bird witch
The boy and the trolls, of The
adventure
Boyislav, youngest of twelve
Briar Rose
Broad, Tall and Sharp-eyes
The cap that mother made
The changelings
Cinderella, or The little glass slip-
per (and variants)
Cinderelma
The clock that walked by itself
Conrad and the dragon
The crystal ball
Dag and Daga, and the flying troll
of Sky Mountain
The dancing princesses
Don Demonio's mother-in-law
Donkey skin
The doomed prince
The dragon-king and the twin
horses
Dragon thieves of Peking
East of the sun and West of the
moon
The enchanted prince
The enchanted princess
Fair, brown, and trembling
A feather of Finist the bright
falcon

Feather o' my wing
The fiery dragon
The fig-tree beggar and the willful
  princess
The firebird and Princess Vasilisa
The fire-bird, the horse of power
  and the Princess Vasilissa
The first flute
The fish with hooked noses
The fisherman and the Sea King's
  daughter
The forest bride
Forget-me-not
The frog
The frog king or Iron Henry
The frog prince
The frog princess
The golden apple-tree and the
  nine peahens
The golden bird
The golden goose
The golden slippers
The golden valley
The graveyard rose
The green bird
Gudgekin, the thistle girl
Guleesh
Hag-of-the-mist
The happy prince
The house in the forest
How the beggars came to town
Ivan Golik and the serpents
Ivan Tsarevitch, the fire-bird, and
  the gray wolf
Jack the giant-killer
Jason and the dragon of Colchis
Kate Crackernuts
The King of Colchester's daughters
The king of the hummingbirds
King Solomon's ring
Knoonie in the sleeping palace
The lady and the lion
The Lady of the Lake
The Laidly Worm
The last balloon
The last of the dragons
The last piece of light
Leap the elk and Little Princess
  Cottongrass
Linda-Gold and the old king
The little donkey
The little red hairy man
The love of a Mexican prince and
  princess
The magic horse

Marya Moryevna
The master cat, or Puss in boots
Mimer the master
Mons Tro
Moon snow
The mouse-hole, and the under-
  ground kingdom
The nine doves
The nine-headed bird
Oda and the snake
The ogre's breath
The old woman of the forest
One-inch fellow
The one-legged crane
The palace of the seven little hills
Patient Griselda
The pear tree
Peter's adventures
Petsetilla's posy
Pinto Smalto
The psaltery that played by itself
The Queen
The rabbit catcher
Rama, The bow that could not
  be bent
Rapunzel
The rat-catcher's daughter
The real princess
Ricky with the tuft
The ring
Rocking-horse land
Rose Red
Saint Werburgh and her goose
Salt
The sea gulls
The sea maiden
Semrude the Fair and the Cadi
The seven Simons (and variants)
The sharp gray sheep
The shepherd and the princess
Sigurd the dragon-slayer
Sigurd the King's son
Sir Buzz
The sleeping beauty
The small kingdom
Snow-White and the seven dwarfs
  (and variants)
Song for a princess
Spindle, shuttle, and needle
The swan maiden
The swineherd
The tall tales
Tattercoats
Tatterhood
Ten miles at each step

184

PRINCES AND PRINCESSES *(continued)*

The test
The three butterflies
The three dooms
The three golden hairs
The three heads of the well
The three Ivans
The three riddles
Through the fire
The tinder box (and variants)
Tinykin's transformations
The traveller's shoes
The troll's little daughter
The true enchanter
Turandot
Turtles of gold and bitter regrets
The twelve dancing princesses
The twelve wild ducks
The two princes
Uncle James or The Purple
   stranger
Vasilisa and Prince Vladimir
Why the sea moans
A witch and her servants
The wonder-working steeds
The wooing of the maze
The yellow dwarf
The youth who wanted to shiver
, *Green*
   Kiss Miklos, and the green
     daughter of the green
     king
, *Horned*
   The cuirassier and the horned
     princess
, *Sea*
   Sadko

The princess. *See* Aladdin

The princess
   Manning — *Sorcerers* p.82-90

The princess and Rabbi Joshuah
   Rugoff — *Harvest* p.553-554

The princess and the peas (The real
   princess)
   Opie — *Classic* p.218

The princess and the three tasks
   Gardner — *Dr.* p.7-37

Princess Finola and the dwarf
   Sheehan — *Folk* p.37-50

The princess of the mountain
   Sheehan — *Folk* p.100-111

"THE PRINCESS ON THE PEA"
   "The princess on the pea" (subject)
   Opie — *Classic* p.216-217

The princess on the pea
   Rugoff — *Harvest* p.696-697

Princess Peridot's choice
   Sleigh — *Stirabout* p.38-47

The princess under the earth
   Bamberger — *My* p.79-81

The princess who learned to work
   Ginsburg — *Lazies* p.36-41

The princess with freckles
   Bomans — *Wily* p.64-71

The princess with unruly thoughts
   Sperry — *Scand.* p.60-69

The princess's christening
   Cott — *Beyond* p.56-63

The princess's slippers
   Manning — *Choice* p.256-267

The princesses who lived in a kailyard
   Sheehan — *Folk* p.22-31

PRISCA, SAINT
   Saint Prisca, the child martyr

Priscilla's witches
   Shaw — *Witch* p.190-191

PRISONS AND PRISONERS
   The battle of Bay Minette
   Daddy Mention
   The forest inn
   Macpherson's lament
   The outsider
   , *of war*
     The lady in black of Boston
     harbor

PRIVATEERS. *See* **Pirates**

The prize is won
   Corrigan — *Holiday* p.25-26

PROMETHEUS
   The two sacks

PROMISES
Dagmet
Half of everything
The King's choice
The man who promises the
 impossible
Pentalina

PROPHETS AND PROPHECIES
See also **Fortune Tellers**
The doomed prince
The sleeping beauty
The three golden hairs
The voices at the window

Prospecting for silver
 Schwartz — *Whoppers* p.43

The protector of the mice
 Carey — *Baba* p.55-57

The proud pastor
 Spicer — *13 Rascals* p.63-72

The proud tale of David Dodd
 Jagendorf — *Folk, South* p.35-41

PROVERBS
See also **Sayings**
- *Africa*
 When the mouse laughs . . .
- *England*
 A mouse must not think . . .

"PRYDAIN" TALES
The foundling
The rascal crow
The smith, the weaver, and the
 harper
The stone
The sword
The true enchanter

The psaltery that played by itself
 Whitney — *In* p.79-82

PSYCHE
Cupid and Psyche

PSYCHIC PHENOMENA
See also **Ghosts**
Little people

"PUCAS". See "POOKAS"

PUERTO RICO
Amapola and the butterfly

The chapel on Cristo Street
The cistern of San Cristobal
Compae Rabbit's ride
Guani
Iviahoca
Juan Bobo
The land of brave men
The legend of the Ceiba of Ponce
The legend of the hummingbird
The legend of the royal palm
The little blue light
Pablo and the pirate's ghost
The parrot who wouldn't say
 Cataño
The shepherd and the princess
The stone dog
The three fairies
Why misery remains in the world
Yuisa and Pedro Mexias
- *San Juan*
 The Rogativa
 Three tales of old San Juan

PUGH, ELLEN
Ellen Pugh (subject)
 Pugh — *More* p.125

Pulling teeth
 Schwartz — *Whoppers* p.43-45

Pumpkin
 Leach — *Whistle* p.80-81

Pumpkin chiffon pie (crust recipe)
 Greene — *Clever* p.143

PUMPKINS
Cinderella, or The little glass
 slipper (and variants)
The perambulatin' pumpkin
Who is who?

PUNCTUALITY. See Time

Punished pride
 Sekorová — *Europe* p.25-32

PUNISHMENT
The creation of man
The fish with hooked noses
The half-chick
Joseph and Potiphar's wife
Judgment by fire at Pivanhonkapi
The kitchen pooka
Mr. Rabbit and Mr. Bear
Mutuk

PUNISHMENT *(continued)*

    Retribution
    Saint Comgall and the mice
    The tiger story
    Waiaba
    Why dog lost his voice

The purchased miracle
    Carter — *Enchanted* p.115-121

Purple stranger. *See* Uncle James, or
    the Purple stranger

Purrr Ce!
    Serwadda — *Songs* p.33-39

PURRS. *See* **Hogs**

PURSES
    The magic shilling
    - *Snatchers*
        Thank you, Ma'am

Puss in boots
    See also The Master cat
    Puss in boots (subject)
        Opie — *Classic* p.110-112
    Bamberger — *My* p.210-213
    Haviland — *Fairy* p.122-127
    Morel — *Fairy* p.78-79
    Sekorová — *Europe* p.20-24

Puss leaves home
    Shaw — *Cat* p.38

Pussy-cat Mew
    Baum — *Mother* p.175-180

Putrefactions and the wonders
    Schwartz — *Whoppers* p.82-86

A putrified forest
    Schwartz — *Whoppers* p.82-83

PUZZLES. *See* **Mathematics; Riddles**

PYGMIES. *See* **Africa — Tribes — Pygmies**

Pyle, Katharine
    The dreamer
    The swan maiden

PYTHONS. *See* **Snakes**

Q

The quack frog
    Darrell — *Once* p.246

QUAIL
    Cooperation
    The fox and the quail
    King of his turf
    Using your head

Quaise, Thomas
    Hurrah for cats!

QUARRELING
    Cooperation
    Deibui and Teikui
    Don't marry two wives
    Heracles and Athena
    The McCanles fight as Hickock
        told it
    The sack of grain
    Sisters who quarreled
    The test

The quartet
    Krylov — *Fables* p.70-72

The queen
    Olenius — *Great* p.230-238

"QUEEN OF THE WOODS"
    The three wishes

QUEENS. *See* **Kings and Queens**

The Queen's croquet-ground
    Darrell — *Once* p.110-116

QUERNS. *See* **Mills**

QUESTIONS
    See also **Riddles**
    The convent free from care
    The little shepherd boy
    The miller, his cook, and the king
    The proud pastor
    The story of Ivan and the daughter
        of the sun
    The wondrous story of Ivan Golik
        and the serpents

QUICK, TOM
    Tom Quick, the Indian slayer

QUILTS
    Aili's quilt
    The patchwork quilt

R

Rabbi Eliezer enjoys an exception
Rugoff — *Harvest* p.557

RABBIS
Alone with God
The Helm goat mystery
If not still higher
The Princess and Rabbi Joshuah
The wife's one wish

Rabbit and antelope
Dolch — *Animal* p.103-111

Rabbit and big rat and lion
Dolch — *Animal* p.19-28

Rabbit and elephant
Dolch — *Animal* p.155-167

Rabbit and our old woman
Manning — *Tortoise* p.30-35

The rabbit and the barrel
Carter — *Enchanted* p.87-90

The rabbit and the honey-gum slide
Bird — *Path* p.55-61

Rabbit and the wolves
Manning — *Tortoise* p.36-46

Rabbit and tortoise and lion
Dolch — *Animal* p.25-29

The rabbit catcher
Bechstein — *Rabbit* p.2-12

The rabbit huntress
Rugoff — *Harvest* p.119-126

The rabbit sends in a little bill
Darrell — *Once* p.86-91

RABBITS
See also titles beginning with Hare
The bamboo cutter
Big for me, little for you
Brer Rabbit, businessman
Brer Rabbit's trickery
The cloak of friendship
Compae Rabbit's ride
Coyote steals the summer
Ears and tails and common sense
The fox, the rabbit and the rooster
Full moon a-shining

The giant and the rabbit
Greedy and Speedy
Horns for a rabbit
The hound and the hare
Hyena and hare
Lion and hyena and rabbit
Little Bun Rabbit
The little house
Mr. Rabbit and Mr. Bear
Prince Rabbit
The right drumstick
Rumors
The seven Swabians
The Sisimiqui
The smart rabbit
The smartest one in the woods
Snake the postman
The story of the brave little rabbit,
  Squirt Eyes — Flop Ears —
  Stub Tail
The tar baby
Tar-wolf tale
This for that
The tiger and the hare
Tío Rabbit and the barrel
The tortoise and the hare (and
  variants)
The useless wagoner
Visitor
Wakaima and the clay man
What is trouble
Why the baboon has a shining
  seat
Why the possum's tail is bare
Widow Fox and her four suitors
The wishing-skin
- *Eyes*
  How the rabbit lost his eye
, *Golden*
  The magic egg
- *Holes*
  Alice adventures in Wonder-
    land
- *Hunting*
  The antelope boy of Shongo-
    povi
, *White*
  Moozipoo

Rabbit's bride
Segal — *Juniper (II)* p.275-277

Rabbit's long ears
Carter — *Greedy* p.62-67

RACCOONS
The deceived blind man
- *Tails*
How the raccoon got rings
on his tail

RACES, ATHLETIC
Alice's adventures in Wonderland
The dispersal from Sikyatki
The squirrel and the crawfish race
The tortoise and the hare (and
variants)

The races between Payupki and Tikuvi
Courlander — *Fourth* p.147-157

RACES OF MAN
The eruption of Pele's anger
- *Easter Island*
How the Short-ears conquered
the Long-ears

Rackham, Arthur
Arthur Rackham, illus. (subject)
Darrell — *Once* p.7-12
Beauty and the beast

RADISHES
Dull-witted Hikoichi and the duck
soup

Raggatti a reformer
Cott — *Beyond* p.127-134

Ragnar Shaggy-Legs and the dragons
Green — *Cavalcade* p.54-57

RAGWEED
The field of boliauns

RAIDS. See Battles

Railroad Bill
Jagendorf — *Folk, South* p.13-15

RAILWAY STATIONS
The three travelers

RAIN
Do what you can
A necklace of raindrops
Pakabva and the Kachinas
A safe home

The rain
Schwartz — *Whoppers* p.95

RAIN GODS
The river monster

The rainbow dress
Vogel — *Rainbow* p.1-12

RAINBOWS
The golden key
The lamar who became a rainbow
The little scarred one
The sky is a bowl of ice
The twins' journey to the sun

Rake up!
Manning — *Choice* p.166

RAKSHAWS (demons)
Blind man, deaf man, and the
donkey

Rāma and Sitā
Rugoff — *Harvest* p.439-442

Rama. The bow that could not be bent
Stories From World p.100-105

Rao's dirge for herself
Alpers — *Legends* p.351-352

Rapunzel
Bamberger — *My* p.7-10
Darrell — *Once* p.47-50
Segal — *Juniper (II)* p.247-255
Shaw — *Witch* p.192-198

Raramai
Lawrie — *Myths* p.41-42

RARATONGA (island)
Rao's dirge for herself

RARITIES (treasures)
Prince Ahmed and the fairy Peribanou

The rascal crow
Alexander — *Foundling* p.45-59

RASCALS
Ashes for sale
The baker's son and the king's
daughter
The bear's revenge
Beetle
Boastful Aulus and the sly thief
Chapkin the scamp
The joyful abbot
The magic pot

Malice, Bouki and Momplaisir
The men who tricked Sultan
Otakul
Nail stew
The poorest man in the world
The proud pastor
The shared reward
The shepherd who could not lie
Tandala and Pakala
The three rascals and the magic
cap
The wife who talked too much

RASPBERRIES
'Keenene

The rat-catcher's daughter
Housman — *Rat* p.3-12

RATS
Chant for a new tooth
The mouse and the rat
The Pied Piper of Hamelin
The story of the rat and the flying-
fox
The tricks of Hunahpú and
Ixbalanqué
The war between the rats and the
weasels
Xibalba

The rattlesnake that played "Dixie"
Life — *Treasury* p.164-166

**RATTLESNAKES. See Snakes —
Rattlesnakes**

RAVANA (demon)
Workers of evil — and a few good
spirits

The raven and the fox
Krylov — *Fables* p.148-149

The raven brings light
Rugoff — *Harvest* p.100-102

Raven lets out the daylight
Martin — *Raven* p.17-25

RAVENS
The battle of the birds
Cannibal
Eagle boy
The everlasting house
The false shaman
Monster copper forehead

Mons Tro
The mountain goats
The nose of the Konakadet
The palace of the seven little hills
The people who told the tales
The pig that went to court
Strong-man
True tears
The twelve brothers
The unlucky fisherman
- *Color*
In the beginning

Raven's deed
Life — *Treasury* p.71-72

Raw head and Bloody Bones
Leach — *Whistle* p.91

Raw monkey liver
Bang — *Men* p.33-37

Rawlings, Marjorie Kinnan
A boy and his pa

READ, MARY
The pirate women

The real princess
Haviland — *Fairy* p.170-173
Morel — *Fairy* p.18-19

REASON. See Wisdom

The rebel belle
Life — *Treasury* p.161

Rebes and Id
Lawrie — *Myths* p.284-287

REBIRTH. See Reincarnation

RECIPES. See names of recipes

The Red Cross knight and the dragons
Green — *Cavalcade* p.167-172

The red dragon of Wales
Green — *Cavalcade* p.61-67

The red fox and the walking stick
Ginsburg — *One* p.3-7

"RED RIDING HOOD"
The Chinese red riding hoods
Little Red Riding-Hood

Red Riding Hood
Darrell — *Once* p.55-58

A red, ripe apple, a golden saucer
Higonnet-Schnopper — *Tales*
p.118-128

Reed, A. W., and Inez Hames
The monster of Cakaudrove

The reed and the olive tree
Levine — *Fables* p.96

The reed maiden
Curtin — *Myths* p.457-476

REEDS
How straws were invented
The message
The mission ended
The oak and the reed
A red, ripe apple, a golden saucer
The tale of the silver saucer
and the transparent apple

REEFS
Gigi

Rees, Ennis
As the tadpole said

Reeves, James
Fireworks
The old wife and the ghost

REFLECTION. See Mirrors

REFORM
How a wolf reforms

Refuge
Cott — *Beyond* p.456-460

A regional guide to American folklore
Life — *Treasury* p.297-299

REINCARNATION
The story of O-Tei

REINDEER
Little Lap

RELIGION
See also **Bible; God;** etc.
Malo

Remsky in raptures
Cott — *Beyond* p.84-89

RENT
The hare

Repaying good with evil
Rugoff — *Harvest* p.598-601

REPETITIVE RHYMES AND STORIES
See also **Games and Rhythms**
Chicken Licken
The gingerbread boy
Henny-Penny
The house that Jack built
The little red hen
The little red hen and the grain of
wheat
Little Tuppens
The old woman and her pig
The turnip

**REPTILES. See Alligators and
Crocodiles; Lizards; Snakes**

Rescue of Ivan Tsarevich and the
winning of the colt (and variants)
Curtin — *Myths* p.217

RESCUES
Friends and neighbors
Jamie Freel and the young lady
What Jack Horner did

Responsibility
De Roin — *Jataka* p.14-15

RESURRECTION
Cesarino and the dragon

RETALIATION. See Revenge

RETRIBUTION. See Punishment

Retribution
Rugoff — *Harvest* p.189-191

Revealed
Hautzig — *Case* p.25-31

REVENGE
The bear's revenge
Deirdre
The dragon of Macedon
Medea
The old woman in the cottage
Pitai
The witch: a tale of the Dark Ages

The revenge
Carter — *Enchanted* p.75-80

The revolution of the ladies of Edenton
Jagendorf — *Folk, South* p.182-184

REVOLUTIONARY WAR. *See* **United
States — History — Revolution**

REWARDS
The chestnut tree
The dwarf and the blacksmith
The Emperor's parrot
The fisherman and the gatekeeper
The shared reward
The tale of the huntsman
The valiant little tailor

RHINOCEROS
Greedy and Speedy

RHODE ISLAND
- *Block Island*
Block Island wreckers

RHODES (island)
The dragons of Rhodes, Lucerne
and Somerset

The rhyme-shop
Cott — *Beyond* p.297-301

RHYMES. *See* **Nursery Rhymes;
Poetical; Reptitive Rhymes and
Stories**

RHYTHMS. *See* **Games and Rhythms;
Repetitive Rhymes and Stories**

RIBBONS
The yellow ribbon

RICE
The Brahman and the pot of rice
The grateful toad
The old woman and her dumpling
The old woman who lost her
dumpling

The rice cake that rolled away
Junne — *Floating* p.60-65

RICE-CAKES
The mountain lad and the forest
witch

RICH. *See* **Wealth**

The rich Athenian in distress
Levine — *Fables* p.20

The rich man and the hired mourners
Levine — *Fables* p.80

The rich señora
Lyons — *Tales* p.29-33

The rich woman and the poor woman
De Bosschere — *Christmas* p.1-7

Richards, Laura E.
A legend of Lake Okeefinokee

Richmuth of Cologne
Littledale — *Strange* p.57-61

Ricky with the tuft
Perrault — *Fairy* p.44-49

Riddle me riddle me, riddle me ree
Sherlock — *Ears* p.69-73

The riddle of the room upstairs
Raskin — *Ghosts* p.32-41

Riddle upon riddle. *See* Turandot

RIDDLES
Riddles (subject)
Greene — *Clever* p.27,31,40,55,
86,100,116,129,136,144,154
Clever Manka
The devil's granny
The dragon and his grandmother
Footless and blind champions
The golden valley
Hag-of-the-mist
Humpty Dumpty
Prince Rabbit
Russian riddles
The test
The three riddles
Turandot

Riddles
Lyons — *Tales* p.82

Riddles one, two, three
Sherlock — *Ears* p.11-17

The ride-by-nights
Shaw — *Witch* p.168

RIDERS. *See* **Horsemen and Horsemanship**

RIDICULE
The purchased miracle

The ridiculous wishes
  Perrault — *Fairy* p.81-83

The right drumstick
  Bagley — *Candle* p.12-18

RIGOBERT, SAINT
  Saint Rigobert's dinner

The ring
  Olenius — *Great* p.99-113

The ring around the tree
  Jagendorf — *Folk, South* p.155-156

"RING-A-ROUNDS"
  A round for the New Year

The ring with twelve screws
  Curtin — *Myths* p.137-148

RINGS
  Beetle
  The cockerel-stone
  Coyote rescues the ring-girl
  Elf Hill
  The fish and the ring
  The fish with hooked noses
  Jack and the wizard
  King Solomon's ring
  The last balloon
  The magic lake
  Richmuth of Cologne
  The singing leaves
  The sorcerer and his apprentice
  The three feathers
  , *Copper*
      The old woman of the forest
  , *Gold*
      Half of everything
  , *Iron*
      The bird witch
  , *King Solomon's*
      The dragon of the North
  , *Magic*
      Aladdin
      Gigi and the magic ring
      The princess and the three tasks
      Ten miles at each step
  , *Ruby*
      Cap o' rushes
      Cinderelma
  , *Wishing*
      The wishing-ring

Rip Van Winkle
  Darrell — *Once* p.13-36
  Life — *Treasury* p.142-149

Ritchie, Alice
  The fox's daughter

RIVALRY
  Boigu
  The fight with Oroi and the killing of Oroi
  Poem of a girl whose young sister loves the same man she does

The river monster
  Junne — *Floating* p.115-116

RIVER MONSTERS. See Sea Monsters

The river-road ramble
  Bagley — *Candle* p.62-69

RIVERS
  The king of the Golden River
  The miller's mule
  The negro speaks of rivers
  The peasants and the river
  The pond and the river
  Sadko
  The singing river
  Why the bear sleeps all winter

RIVETS
  The dragon tamers

Roa Kabuwam
  Lawrie — *Myths* p.182-184

Roach, Eloise, trans.
  Watch

ROADS
  The giant of the causeway
  The man on Moran's road

ROANES
  The People of the sea

ROANOKE ISLAND. See North Carolina — Roanoke Island

Roast chicken (recipe)
  Greene — *Clever* p.115-116

ROBBERS. See Bandits; Thieves and Thievery

The robbers and the treasure
  Rugoff — *Harvest* p.431-435

ROBERTS, BRUCE
Bruce Roberts (subject)
Roberts — *Ghosts* p.95

ROBERTS, NANCY
Nancy Roberts (subject)
Roberts — *Ghosts* p.95

ROBIN HOOD
Of Sam Bass

Robin Hood and the beggar
Rugoff — *Harvest* p.249-251

Robin Hood and the butcher
Rugoff — *Harvest* p.247-249

"ROBIN HOODS"
Sam Bass, Texas Robin Hood

ROBINS
The marriage of Robin Redbreast
and the wren
Saint Kentigern and the robin

ROBOTS
Moxon's master

Rocking-horse land
Housman — *Rat* p.13-23

ROCKS AND STONES
See also Statues
An ancient curse
Dag and Daga, and the flying troll
of Sky Mountain
Dancing stones
Fiddler's rock
Foni and Fotia
Havaiki the land
Im
Imermen and Kikmermer
Kamutnab
Karakarkula
The king and the witch
Korseim
The maiden stone
The miller's mule
Paimi a Nawanawa
Pötikain and Ngiangu
The seven monsters
Umi Markail
Waubin
, *Black*
Kol

- *Carvings*
The warrior who shot arrows
at a star
, *Glowing*
The story of Ait Kadal
, *Green*
The hungry old witch
, *Magic*
Aniello
The cockerel-stone
The stone
- *Pebbles*
The story of three young
shepherds
The tiger and the hare
, *White*
The legend of the betel

The rocks of Bryce Canyon
Life — *Treasury* p.74

ROCKY MOUNTAINS
- *Colorado*
The phantom train of Marshall
Pass

RODEGAST, ROLAND
Roland Rodegast, illus. (subject)
Shaw — *Mouse* p.17

RODS. See Sticks

Roethke, Theodore
The meadow mouse

The Rogativa
Belpré — *Once* p.66-71

ROGUES. See Rascals

ROLLING PINS
The fox and the rolling pin

ROME, ANCIENT
Little people
Romulus and Remus, sons of the
wolf

Romeo and Juliet
Darrell — *Once* p.158-169

Romulus and Remus, sons of the wolf
Stories From World p.66-73

Room for one more
Life — *Treasury* p.259

ROOMS
, *Haunted*
The enchanted prince
, *Secret*
The widow and her daughters

The rooster and the bean
Carey — *Baba* p.15-16

The rooster that fell in the brew vat
Sperry — *Scand.* p.15-20

The rooster who couldn't crow
Sperry — *Scand.* p.99-112

ROOSTERS. *See* **Chickens — Roosters**

ROOTS
Havaiki the land
The leaves and the roots

ROPE AND ROPING
Tyll Ulenspiegel. The tale of a
merry dance

The rose and the violinist
Ficowski — *Sister* n. pag.

Rose Red
Morel — *Fairy* p.88-91

ROSEMARY
The midnight voyage of the Seagull

ROSES
Beauty and the beast
The graveyard rose
The pear tree
The song of the Cherokee rose
The swine-herd
, *Magic*
The rose and the violinist

Rossetti, Christina
The city mouse and the garden
Goblin market

ROSSETTI, CHRISTINA
Christina Rossetti (subject)
Cott — *Beyond* p.466

ROUMANIA. *See* **Rumania**

A round for the New Year
Corrigan — *Holiday* p.15

"ROUNDS." *See* **"Ring-A-Rounds"**

The rout
Cott — *Beyond* p.123-126

Route taken by Nima in Binibin
Lawrie — *Myths* p.159-160

ROWBOATS
Who will row next?

Roy Bean, necktie justice
Life — *Treasury* p.205-207

RUADH, ANGUS
People of the sea

RUBIES
The island of the Nine Whirlpools
The miller's mule

RUGS. *See* **Carpets**

The ruined man who became rich
again through a dream
Rugoff — *Harvest* p.147-148

RULERS. *See* **Kings and Queens;**
Pharaohs; etc.

RUMANIA
Prince Loaf
Stan Bolovan (and variants)
Tandala and Pakala
Twelve dancing princesses
- *Transylvania*
The story of three young
shepherds
Rumors
De Roin — *Jataka* p.80-83

Rumpelstiltskin
Rumpelstiltskin (subject)
Opie — *Classics* p. 195-196
Little people (subject)
McHargue — *Impossible* p.47-
73
Haviland — *Fairy* p.158-161
Morel — *Fairy* p.50-52
Opie — *Classic* p.197-198

Rumti Redivus
Cott — *Beyond* p.135-138

The run of the forest
Bagley — *Candle* p.114-119

RUNNERS AND RUNNING
See also **Races, Athletic**
The gingerbread man

The hare
Hare running
The six who went together through
the world
- *Runaways*
Edward's story
Li'l Hannibal
Little Miss Muffet
Painted skin

RURAL LIFE. *See* **Country Life**

RUSHLIGHTS
The farthing rushlight

RUSHES
The adventures of Billy MacDaniel

Ruskin, John
The Black brothers
The King of the Golden River

RUSKIN, JOHN
John Ruskin (subject)
Cott — *Beyond* p.2

Russell, Eric Frank
Impulse

RUSSELL, GERALD
Big people

RUSSIA
See also **Armenia; Estonia; Latvia;
Lithuania**
An adventure with Eveseika
Afterword
Alenoushka and her brother
Alyosha Popovich
Anfy and his landlord
Ayoga
Baba Yaga
Baba Yaga's geese
The beautiful birch
Beetle
Big people
The bird, the mouse, and the
sausage
Boiled axe
Burun-Teges
The cat and the she-fox
The cat who became head-forester
Catch-the-wind
A chapter of fish
The children on the pillar

The christening in the village
The clever Durmian
The clever soldier and the stingy
woman
The clever thief
The cuckoo and the eagle
Daughter and stepdaughter
The dog and the horse
Don't foul the well — you may
need its waters
Ea and Eo
Easy bread
The enchanted princess
The feather of Bright Finist the
falcon
A feather of Finist the bright falcon
The firebird
The firebird and Princess Vasilisa
The fire-bird, the horse of power
and the Princess Vasilissa
The fool of the world and the
flying ship
The footless and blind champions
The footless and the blind
A forest mansion
The fox and the rolling pin
The fox, the rabbit, and the
rooster
The frog princess
Frost
Go I don't know where and bring
back I don't know what
Go to the verge of destruction
and bring back Shmat-Razum
Going fishing
The golden cock
The golden cockerel
The golden fish
The good ogre
The great golloping wolf
He who likes to bite and kiss will
always go astray and miss
The heron and the crane
How fire took water to wife
How three mighty heroes saved
the sun and the moon from the
dragon
How Wilka went to sea
Hungry-for-battle
The hunter and his wife
The hut in the forest
If you don't like it, don't listen
Ivan the fool
Ivan the peasant's son and the
little man himself one-finger tall,

RUSSIA *(continued)*

his mustache seven versts in
length
Ivan Tsarevich, the fire-bird, and
the gray wolf
Khavroshechka
Koshchēi without-death
The lazy daughter
Lipuniushka
Little cat and little hen
The little daughter of the snow
Little Filipp
The little golden fish
Little Master Misery
Little people
Little sister fox
Lutonya
Marya Moryevna
Masha and the bear
The miller's sons
Nanny goat with nuts
The new law
Not bad — but it could be better
Old Verlooka
The ox and the ass
The peasant and the bear
The peasant, the bear, and the fox
The pig with gold bristles, the
deer with golden horns, and the
golden-maned steed with
golden tail
Pipe and Pitcher
Prince Ivan, the witch baby and
the little sister of the sun
The princess who learned to work
The protector of the mice
The psaltery that played by itself
A red, ripe apple, a golden saucer
Rescue of Ivan Tsarevich and the
winning of the colt (variant)
The ring with twelve screws
The rooster and the bean
Sadko
Salt
Sergevan
The seven Simeons
The seven Simeons and the
trained Siberian cat
The seven Simeons, full brothers
(and variants)
Sheidulla
Shish and the innkeeper
A shrewd woman
The soldier and the demons

The soldier's fur coat
Spring in the forest
The stolen turnips, the magic
tablecloth, the sneezing goat
and the wooden whistle
The story of the brave little rabbit,
Squirt Eyes — Flop Ears —
Stub Tail
The swan-geese
Syre-Varda
The tailor, the bear, and the devil
The tale of the silver saucer and
the transparent apple
A tale of two frogs
Terenti, the black grouse
Thousands of ideas
The three hermits
The three kingdoms
The three kingdoms — The cop-
per, the silver, and the golden
Three knots
The three men of power — Eve-
ning, midnight and sunrise
Toast and honey
The traveling frog
True or false
Two frogs
Unerbek
Vasilisa and Prince Vladimir
Vasilisa the beautiful
Vassilissa golden tress, bareheaded
beauty
Vassilissa the cunning, and the
Tsar of the sea
Water of youth, water of life, and
water of death
Who lived in the skull?
Who will row next?
Who'll wash the porridge pot?
Who will wash the pot?
A witch and her servants
The wolf and the cat
The wonder-working steeds
The wonderful shirt
The wondrous wonder
Yelena the wise
- *Caucasia*
The earth will have its own
- *Folk tales*
Rugoff — *Harvest* p.619-654
- *Georgia*
The Khevsouri and the Esh-
mahkie
The serpent and the peasant
A witty answer

- *Siberia*
  Halfway people
  Workers of evil — and a few
    good spirits
, *South*
  Monster copper forehead
- *Ukraine*
  The frog
- *Volga river*
  The christening in the village

Russian riddles
  Carey — *Baba* p.86-88

RUSTEM
  Afrāsib
  The birth and boyhood of Rustem
  How Rustem found Raksh
  Sohrāb and Rustem

Rustem and Akvān the demon
  Picard — *Tales* p.193-202

Rustem and Isfendiār
  Picard — *Tales* p.246-262

Rustem and Tahmina
  Picard — *Tales* p.97-105

Rustem's battle with Pulādvend
  Picard — *Tales* p.186-192

Rustem's journey to Māzendarān
  Picard — *Tales* p.75-96

Rutter, Owen
  The vampires of Tempassuk

Ryan, H. J., trans.
  Fanta-Ghiro
  The little golden fish

RYE
  The peasant and the bear
  Sing a song o' sixpence

S

SABBATH
  Fisherman's dream
  Not on the Lord's Day

SABBATS
  Halfway people

SABRES. See Swords

The sack
  Krylov — *Fables* p.137-139

The sack of grain
  Carrick — *Wise* n. pag.

SACKS
  Jack Buttermilk
  The table, the pack, and the bag
  The travels of a fox
  The two sacks
  The wolf in the sack

The sacred sword
  Spicer — *13 Dragons* p.69-78

SACRIFICE
  The revenge
  A strange and rare friendship
  The twelve wild ducks

The sad-lonely end of Wilhelmina Inn
  Jagendorf — *Folk, South* p.44-47

The sad tale of the half-shaven head
  Jagendorf — *Folk, South* p.164-167

The sad victory
  Jagendorf — *Noodle* p.78-82

Sadko
  Ransome — *Old* p.22-32

SADNESS
  See also **Grief**
  The first flute
  The girl who cried flowers
  The prince with the nine sorrows

A safe home
  Heady — *Safiri* p.58-61

"SAFE-KEEPS" (charms)
  The dead hand

The saga of Kuiam
  Lawrie — *Myths* p.88-101

The saga of two trees
  Sperry — *Scand.* p.247-257

SAGAS. See Story-tellers and Story-telling

Sagerwazer
  Lawrie — *Myths* p.269-270

SAGES. See Scholars; Wise Men

SAHARA DESERT
Workers of evil — and a few good spirits

SAILORS
The fifth voyage of Sindbad the seaman
The Island of the Nine Whirlpools
Mistress Mary
The parrot who wouldn't say Cataño
The seafaring wizard
The shipwrecked sailor
Three knots
- *Souls*
Souls under the sea

Saint Blaise and his beasts
Brown — *Book* p.88-94

St. Brendan's Isles of the Blest
Life — *Treasury* p.24-26

Saint Bridget and the king's wolf
Brown — *Book* p.1-10

Saint Comgall and the mice
Brown — *Book* p.148-155

Saint Cuthbert's peace
Brown — *Book* p.95-107

St. Elmo's fire
Life — *Treasury* p.23

Saint Francis of Assisi
Brown — *Book* p.211-225

Saint Fronto's camels
Brown — *Book* p.114-125

SAINT GEORGE. See George, Saint

St. George and the dragon
Green — *Cavalcade* p.82-86

Saint Gerasimus and the lions
Brown — *Book* p.11-29

SAINT JOHN'S DAY. See John, Saint

Saint Keneth of the gulls
Brown — *Book* p.30-41

Saint Kentigern and the robin
Brown — *Book* p.77-87

Saint Launomar's cow
Brown — *Book* p.42-52

SAINT LAWRENCE RIVER
The guardians of the St. Lawrence

St. Monire of Crathie
Wyness — *Legends* p.114-120

St. Nathalan of Tullich
Wyness — *Legends* p.29-32

SAINT NICHOLAS. See Nicholas, Saint

SAINT PATRICK'S DAY. See Patrick, Saint

SAINT PETER. See Peter, Saint

Saint Prisca, the child martyr
Brown — *Book* p.166-175

Saint Rigobert's dinner
Brown — *Book* p.199-210

SAINT VALENTINE'S DAY. See Valentine Day

Saint Werburgh and her goose
Brown — *Book* p.53-68

SAINTS
See also names of Saints
- *Calendar of days*
A Calendar of Saints' days

SAKALAVA
Little people

Saki
Gabriel-Ernest
The open window

SALEM, MASSACHUSETTS. See Massachusetts — Salem

The Salem witches and their own voices: Examination of Sarah Good
Manley — *Sisters* p.141-143

The salesman who sold his dream
Novák — *Fairy* p.153-155

Salkey, Andrew
The barracuda

SALT
The ass and the load of salt
The ass carrying salt
Cap o' rushes
Gathering salt

The heavenly sandwich
The Lalakon dance at Shongopovi
The magic mill
Why the sea is salt

Salt
Ransome — *Old* p.214-229

Sam Bass, Texas Robin Hood
Life — *Treasury* p.192-195

Sam Hudson the Great
Jagendorf — *Folk, Song* p.49-51

Sammelkin
Sleigh — *Stirabout* p.98-111

SAMOA
Why the sea-slug has two mouths
- *Manu'a*
Fiti au mua, who was born in
the sea
- *Savai'i*
The dolphins at Fagasa

Samoan gift, Tongan payment
Alpers — *Legends* p.290

SAMOYEDS. See Nenetz (people)

Sam'l Dany, noodlehead
Jagendorf — *Noodle* p.278-280

**SAN JUAN, PUERTO RICO. See Puerto
Rico — San Juan**

SAND
Andrusz who disliked beans
Rake up!
- *Banks*
Maizab Kaur
- *Walls*
The fish who helped Saint
Gudwall

Sandburg, Carl
"Peculiarsome" Abe
Washington monument by night

SANDIN, JOAN
Joan Sandin (subject)
Pugh — *More* p.125

SANDWICHES
The heavenly sandwich

SANKHASHURNIS (ghosts)
The wicked Sankhashurni

Sankichi's gift
Harris — *Sea Magic* p.117-134

SANTA CLAUS
See also **Nicholas, Saint**
Little Bun Rabbit

Saso and Gogwana the witch
Aardema — *Behind* p.66-73

SATAN. See Devil(s)

SATIRES
, *Political*
Petsetilla's posy

SATISFACTION. See Contentment

SATYRS
The halfway people
The man and the satyr

SAUM TALES
Sergevan
True or false

Saurkeke
Lawrie — *Myths* p.110-113

SAUSAGES
The bird, the mouse, and the
sausage
The three wishes

The savage birds of Bald Mountain
Jagendorf — *Folk, South* p.175-
177

SAWDUST
Blackberries in February

Sawyer, Ruth
The peddler of Ballaghadereen
Schnitzle, Schnotzle, and
Schnootzle

Sayers, Dorothy L.
The Cyprian cat

SAYERS, DOROTHY L.
Dorothy L. Sayers (subject)
Manley — *Sisters* p.11-12,217

SAYINGS
See also **Proverbs**
, *Mexican*
In Mexico the people say

200

SCANDINAVIA
See also names of countries
The Emperor's new clothes
Faery folk
Little people
People of the sea
, Folk tales
Folk Tales (subject)
Rugoff — Harvest p.655-
703

SCARECROWS
The little pig's way out
The monkey's Buddha

SCARVES (SCARFS)
- Bands
The treasure of Li-Po

Schaffgotsch
The little golden fish

The Schilda town hall
Jagendorf — Noodle p.184-188

The Schildbürger build a council house
Rugoff — Harvest p.374-375

Schippeitaro
Sheehan — Folk p.112-117

Schnitzle, Schnotzle, and Schnootzle
Corrigan — Holiday p.235-244

SCHOLARS
Barefoot in bed
Like master, like servant
The maid in the mirror
A strange and rare friendship
The wish that came true
, Chinese
Which was witch?

SCHOLARSHIP
The lion makers

SCHOOLMASTERS. See Teachers

SCHOOLS
Little Filipp
The ungrateful children and the
old father who went to school
again

SCISSORS
The rich woman and the poor
woman

Scissors they were
Rugoff — Harvest p.545-546

SCORN. See Ridicule

SCORPIONS
Hermit into scorpion

SCOTLAND
See also **Hebrides, Scottish; Shet-
land Isles**
The battle of the birds
The Faery folk
Halfway people
The King of Scotland's sons
Little people
The piper of Keil
The princess who lived in a
kailyard
Saint Cuthbert's peace
The seal catcher and the merman
A sheep can only bleat
Workers of evil — and a few good
spirits
- Clans
- Campbell
The mysterious Ticonder-
oga curse
- Highlands
The wild ride in the tilt
cart
, North Eastern
The black colonel
Brechannock of Monymusk
The crooked Mary
The Cumins of Culter
Donald Oig of Monaltrie
Edom o' Gordon
A good name gives
strength
King Malcolm and the
herdyboy
King William's palace
The knight of Wedderhill
The lady of the tower
The laird's man
The maiden stone
The mysterious fire of
Frendraught
Osbarn, the smith
The phantom of the loch
St. Monire of Crathie
St. Nathalan of Tullich
Sir James the rose
The spectre of the tower

The trumpeter of Fyvie
Castle
The warlock of Glen Dye
The wicked lard of
Balquhain
The witch of Findrack

SCREENS
The strange folding screen

SCROLLS
The four sacred scrolls
The mystery maiden from heaven

SEA
See also **Boats; Sailors; Ships and
Shipbuilding**; etc.
How Wilka went to sea
The shepherd and the sea
The swimmer and the sea
- Bottom
See also **Palaces, Undersea**
An adventure with Eveseika
, King of
Monsoon

The sea captain at the door
Leach — Whistle p.63

SEA CAPTAINS. See **Captains, Sea**

SEA FOLK
See also **Mermaids; Mermen**
The people of the sea
The sea maiden
The story of Tremsin the bird
Zhar, and Nastasia, the lovely
maid of the sea

SEA GULLS
The bat, the bramblebush, and
the gull
Saint Keneth of the gulls
Umi Markail

The sea gulls
Gardner — Gudgekin p.53-59

SEA LIONS
Strong-man

Sea magic
Harris — Sea Magic p.1-19

The sea maiden
MacFarlane — Mouth p.6-21

SEA MAIDENS. See **Mermaids; Sea Folk**

SEA MONSTERS
See also names of sea monsters
The false shaman
The foghorn
The Gloucester sea serpent
Lac Long Quan and Au Co
The mermaid and the monster
The monster we live on
The nose of the Konakadet
Plumed serpent in Tula
The shipwrecked sailor
The water monster
Why the sea moans
The wind's bride

SEA-NYMPHS. See **Sea Folk**; names of
sea nymphs

Sea of Darkness
Life — Treasury p.14-16

SEA PEOPLE. See **Mermaids; Mermen;
Sea Folk**

SEA SERPENTS. See **Sea Monsters;
Snakes**

SEA-SHELLS. See **Shells**

SEA-TROWS. See **Sea Folk**

SEA VOYAGES
Hine and Tu
Maelduin's voyage
The voyage of St. Brandon

SEA-WITCHES. See **Sea Folk**

The Seabees
Life — Treasury p.293

The seafaring wizard
Raskin — Ghosts p.69-79

"SEAGULL" (ship)
The midnight voyage of the
Seagull

The seal catcher and the merman
Littledale — Strange p.75-81

SEALS
People of the sea
- Skins
The woman from the sea

SEAMEN. See **Sailors**

SEAMSTRESSES. *See* **Dressmakers**

The search for Little Water
Harris — *Sea Magic* p.143-158

The search for Norumbega
Higginson — *Tales* p.186-195

The search for the Golden Cities
Life — *Treasury* p.28-33

SEASONS
See also names of seasons
and months
Coyote steals the summer

Sebgugugu the glutton
Aardema — *Behind* p.42-47

The second of three spirits
Darrell — *Once* p.201-217

SECRETS
Bai
The farmer's secret
The invisible cloth
The little boy's secret
The master and his pupil
The treasures of Rhampsinitus
The twelve dancing princesses

Sedna and the fulmar
Life — *Treasury* p.66-67

SEEDS
Tommy

SELCHIES
The people of the sea

SELF-DEFENSE
Hans and Greta

SELFISHNESS
Dunber
Saint Comgall and the mice
The soldier's fur coat
Why dogs hate cats

Sellar, May, trans.
The dragon and his grandmother

Semrude the Fair and the Cadi
Fehse — *Thousand* p.154-176

A sensible suitor?
Sperry — *Scand.* p.179-183

SENTIMENT. *See* **Love**

SEPTUPLETS
The seven Simeons and the trained
Siberian cat (and variants)

SERBIA
The dragon king and the twin
horses
The golden apple-tree and the
nine peahens
The Zamay who hid his life

Seredy, Kate
The singing tree

Sergevan
Ginsburg — *How* p.21-25

The serpent and the peasant
Rugoff — *Harvest* p.650-652

The serpent-Tsarevich and his two
wives
Bain — *Cossack* p.197-204

The serpent-wife
Bain — *Cossack* p.105-108

SERPENTS. *See* **Lindworms; Sea
Monsters; Snakes**

Serraillier, Jan
The mouse in the wainscot
Suppose you met a witch

SERVAN, SAINT
Saint Kentigern and the robin

SERVANTS
The adventures of Billy MacDaniel
Ali Baba
Baba Yaga
Donkey skin
The dragon and his grandmother
The fish with hooked noses
Hans and his master
The iron wolf
The kitchen pooka
Like master, like servant
The lost half-hour
The mistress and her two maids
The obedient servant
The old woman of the forest
The thoughtless abbot
A time for everything
A witch and her servants

SERWADDA, WILLIAM MOSE
William Mose Serwadda (subject)
Serwadda — *Songs* n. pag.

SESAME STREET
Big Bird's story hour

Sesere
Lawrie — *Myths* p.57-60

Seven black crows
Wojciechowska — *Winter* p.49-54

The seven blind brothers
Lawrie — *Myths* p.30-33

"SEVEN CITIES"
Antillia, the island of the seven cities

The seven-clan scribe society
Bird — *Path* p.83-87

Seven fairy tales (Grimm brothers)
Darrell — *Once* p.37-70

The seven good years
Hautzig — *Case* p.19-23

The seven monsters
Manning — *Monsters* p.98-101

The seven ravens
Darrell — *Once* p.66-70

The seven Simeons (Simons)
Provensen — *Books* p.57-67
Rugoff — *Harvest* p.639-645

The seven Simeons and the trained Siberian cat
Whitney — *In* p.123-129

The seven Simeons, full brothers
Curtin — *Myths* p.228-237

The seven Swabians
Carle — *Eric* p.89-93

The seven wishes
Olenius — *Great* p.39-48

Seven with one blow
Carle — *Eric* p.61-74

SEWING
The frog (by Leonora Alleyne)
The three fairies

SEXTONS
The proud pastor

SHADOWS
The ass's shadow
The man and his shadow

Shake hands with a Yankee
Jagendorf — *Folk, South* p.205-207

Shakespeare, William
A midsummer night's dream
Romeo and Juliet
The taming of the shrew
Witches' chant

SHAKESPEARE, WILLIAM
- *Plays*
Cap o' rushes

SHAME
Wamaladi

SHAPE-SHIFTERS
Halfway people
People of the sea

The shape-shifters of Shorm
Gardner — *Gudgekin* p.41-52

The shared reward
Spicer — *Rascals* p.54-62

SHARING. See Generosity

SHARKS
Beizam
The monkey's heart
The story of Peibri

The sharp gray sheep
MacFarlane — *Mouth* p.77-81

SHAVING
The haunted room

Shaw, Jennifer
Ol' Clackety teeth

Shaw, Richard
Mice never
Not one more cat
Squatter's rights
The Wellfleet witch
Who but a tadpole?
The witches are flying

SHEBA, QUEEN OF
King Solomon and the Queen of Sheba

SHEEHAN, ETHNA
Ethna Sheehan (subject)
Sheehan — *Folk* p.152

SHEEP
Bjarni Sveinssen and his sister Salvör
The deceitful leopard
The peasant and the sheep
The pig and the sheep
The sharp gray sheep
The shepherd who could not lie
The wise men of Gotham
The wolves and the sheep
, *Black*
The black sheep
- *Lambs*
Alenoushka and her brother
The costly feast
The ill-shorn lamb
The lamb
The lambikin
The princess under the earth
The snake and the lamb
The wolf and the lamb
- *Tails*
Little Bo-Peep

The sheep and the dogs
Krylov — *Fables* p.98

A sheep can only bleat
Jagendorf — *Noodle* p.127-129

Sheidulla
Ginsburg — *Lazies* p.1-7

SHELLEY, KATE
How Kate Shelley saved the Express

SHELLS
The little scarred one
- *Armshells*
Gaibida
- *Bu*
Adba
Aib

The shepherd and the princess
Carter — *Greedy* p.119-124

The shepherd and the sea
Levine — *Fables* p.32

The shepherd and the Giant Mountains
Green — *Cavalcade* p.173-179

The shepherd who could not lie
Spicer — *13 Rascals* p.73-81

The Shepherd who liked practical jokes
Levine — *Fables* p.82

SHEPHERDS AND SHEPHERDESSES
Bahhh!
Clever Manka
The convent free from care
David and Goliath. The shepherd boy and the giant
The dragon, sliced-in-two
The eagle, the jackdaw, and the shepherd
The gnat and the shepherd
Little Bo-Peep
The little shepherd boy
The mystery maiden from heaven
Prince Loaf
The rabbit catcher
The red fox and the walking stick
A red, ripe apple, a golden saucer
The sack of grain
Saint Cuthbert's peace
The sharp gray sheep
The story of Little Boy Blue
The story of the three young shepherds
The sword
The tale of the silver saucer and the transparent apple
The test
The wolf in the sack

The shepherd's choice
Littledale — *Strange* p.47-49

SHERIFFS
How the sheriff's posse and the hold-up men sat down to dinner together

Sherlock, Philip
From tiger to Anansi

SHERLOCK, HILARY
Hilary Sherlock (subject)
Sherlock — *Ears* p.124

SHERLOCK, PHILIP MANDERSON
Philip Manderson Sherlock (subject)
Sherlock — *Ears* p.123-124

SHERMAN, WILLIAM TECUMSEH
Young Sherman and the girl from Charleston

Sherwood, Lorraine
"Old Abe" American eagle

SHETLAND ISLES
The woman from the sea

SHIELDS, CHARLES
Charles Shields (subject)
Gardner — *Dragon* p.75

SHIELDS AND SHIELD-MAKERS
The knight of the red shield

Shimin, Symeon, illus.
Shaw — *Mouse* p.2, frontispiece

Shingebiss
Piper — *Stories* n. pag.

The shining lodge
Rugoff — *Harvest* p.108-111

The ship that sailed on sea and land
MacFarlane — *Mouth* p.95-101

SHIPS AND SHIPBUILDING
See also **Boats**; etc.
The chestnut tree
Dick Whittington
The Laidly worm of Spindlestone Heugh
Salt
- *Disappearances*
"Mary Celeste"
, *Ghost*
Ghost ship of the Great Lakes
The pirates and the Palatines
The tale of Lura Lou
- *Voyages*
The midnight voyage of the Seagull
The warlock
- *"Wreckers"*
Block Island wrecker

SHIPTON, ERIC
Big people

The shipwrecked sailor
Rugoff — *Harvest* p.208-212

Shish and the innkeeper
Carey — *Baba* p.79-80

SHIVA
Harchand the Just

SHIVERING
The boy who wanted to learn to shudder
The youth who wanted to shiver

The shoemaker and the elves
Rockwell — *Three* p.71-77

SHOEMAKERS
The battle of the birds
Dragon, dragon
Dwarf long nose
The elves and the shoemaker
The fish and the ring
The frying-pan
The giant and the Wrekin
The golden slippers
The King of Colchester's daughters
The leprechaun; or, Fairy shoemaker
Longnose the dwarf
Schnitzle, Schnotzle, and Schnootzle
The seafaring wizard
Semrude the Fair and the Cadi
The sorcerer and his apprentice
The three heads of the well
The three kingdoms
Tokutaro
The traveller's shoes
The two journeymen

SHOES
The great traveler of Chelm
Pinya of Helm
Sammelkin
The shoemaker and the elves
The three kingdoms
The woman who lived in a shoe
- *Boots*
Boots
Like master, like servant
The man and his **boots**
Puss in boots
Ten miles at each step
What came of picking flowers

SHOES *(continued)*

, *Dancing*
　The traveller's shoes
, *Golden*
　The golden shoe
　The golden shoes
　The golden slippers
　The princess of the mountain
, *Magic*
　The history of Little Mook
　The lost half-hour
- *Slippers*
　Cinderella (and variants)
　Fair, Brown, and Trembling
　The match
　One pair of blue satin slippers
　　and four clever maids
　The princess's slippers
　Rāma and Sitā

SHOPKEEPERS. *See* **Merchants**

A shrewd woman
　Carey — *Baba* p.75-78

SHREWS
　The taming of the shrew
　"That's once"
　The untamed shrew

SHRIEKS
　Lludd and Llevelys

The shroud of Mari-Yvonne
　Rugoff — *Harvest* p.316-320

SHROVE TUESDAY
　Pancake day

SHRUBS
　The legend of the Cherokee sweet
　　shrub

Shub, Elizabeth, trans.
　Hanukkah

SHUDDERING. *See* **Shivering**

SHUTTLES
　Spindle, shuttle, and needle

SIBERIA. *See* **Russia — Siberia**

SICILY
　Aniello

Cesarino and the dragon
The golden valley
The green bird
The ogre's breath
Scissors they were
The thoughtless abbot

The sick man and the doctor
　Levine — *Fables* p.66

SICKNESS
　How ailments were put in their
　　proper place

SIDHE (SIDHEAN)
　The stolen bairn of the Sidh

SIEGEL, HELEN
　Helen Siegel (subject)
　　Ginsburg — *One* p.40

SIEGFRIED
　Mimer, the master

SIERRA LEONE. *See* **Africa — Sierra
　　Leone**

Sigai
　Lawrie — *Myths* p.252-254

The sightseer
　Krylov — *Fables* p.83

SIGN PAINTERS
　Slappy Hooper

Sigourd the dragon-slayer
　Green — *Cavalcade* p.37-44

Sigurd the King's son
　Manning — *Ogres* p.53-65

Sik
　Lawrie — *Myths* p.27-29

SILENCE
　Bontche the silent
　Who'll wash the pot?

SILENI
　Halfway people

Silent Biana
　Yolen — *Girl* p.45-55

Silent Cal
　Life — *Treasury* p.241

"SILENT MOVING ONES"
　Faery folk

SILESIA. *See* Bohemia

SILLINESS. *See* Fools and Foolishness

Silly Matt
  Jagendorf — *Noodle* p.180-183

SILVER AND SILVER MINES
  The legend of Agustín Lorenzo
  Prospecting for silver
  The three kingdoms
  The wife who talked too much

The silver bell
  Novák — *Fairy* p.193-196

The silver bell of Chênière Caminada
  Jagendorf — *Folk, South* p.140-143

The silver bullet
  Manley — *Sisters* p.54-59

The silver doe
  Anderson — *Haunting* p.57-63

The silver snake of Louisiana
  Jagendorf — *Folk, South* p.123-124

Simeli Hill
  Bamberger — *My* p.23-27

Simnel cake (recipe)
  Greene — *Clever* p.134-136

Simon and the unicorn
  Sleigh — *Stirabout* p.48-60

Simple John
  De Bosschere — *Christmas* p.94-99

SIMPLETONS. *See* Fools and Foolish-
    ness

SIN
  Tantalus

Sing a song o' sixpence
  Baum — *Mother* p.19-28

Singer, Issac Bashevis, trans.
  Zlateh the goat

SINGERS AND SINGING
  See also Songs
  The blind singer, Saint Hervé
  The first flute
  Grasshopper and fox
  I hear America singing
  The jolly miller

The legend of the royal palm
  Miracles on the sea
  Nanny goat with nuts
  Sadko
  The story of Tommy Tucker
  The wanderings of Arasmon
  - *Christmas*
    Now every child

The singing leaves
  Manning — *Monsters* p.102-117

The singing river
  Life — *Treasury* p.70-71

The singing tree
  Corrigan — *Holiday* p.197-201

Sir Buzz
  Haviland — *Favorite, India* p.63-82

Sir James the rose
  Wyness — *Legends* p.72-75

Sir Lancelot of the Lake
  Higginson — *Tales* p.63-73

Sir Launcelot and the dragon
  Green — *Cavalcade* p.77-81

Sir Maundeville's dragon
  Green — *Cavalcade* p.93-95

Sir Tristram in Ireland
  Green — *Cavalcade* p.68-76

SIRENIA
  The people of the sea

SIRENS
  Halfway people
  The people of the sea

The Sisimiqui
  Carter — *Enchanted* p.91-96

The sissy from Anaconda
  Life — *Treasury* p.283

Sister of the birds
  Ficowski — *Sister* n. pag.

The sister queens
  Duong — *Beyond* p.73-79

SISTERS
  Apimini and Sidipuar
  Beauty and the beast

SISTERS (continued)

Bjarni Sveinssen and his sister
Salvör
Brother and sister
Dag and Daga, and the flying troll
of Sky Mountain
The enchanted prince
Fair, brown and trembling
The feather of Bright Finist the
falcon
Feather o' my wing
Geinau and Jeiai
Goblin market
Hallabau's jealousy
Hansel and Gretel
Karum
Kate Crackernuts
Kuaka
The lass who went out at the
cry of dawn
The little scarred one
Marya Moryevna
Nima and Poipoi
Poem of a girl whose young sister
loves the same man she does
The Prince with the nine
sorrows
A red, ripe apple, a golden saucer
The sleeper
Susui and Dengam
The tale of the silver saucer and
the transparent apple
The three sisters who were
entrapped into a mountain
Tubu and the seven sisters
The twelve brothers
The twelve wild ducks
The twin sisters

Sisters who quarreled
Lawrie — *Myths* p.85

SIVA
Workers of evil — and a few
good spirits

The six who went together through the
world
Bamberger — *My* p.161-168

Siyāveesh the unfortunate
Picard — *Tales* p.123-131

SIZE
Big John the conqueror

The giant who was afraid of
butterflies
How a tailor became a king
The king of Cauliflower castle
Uncle James, or the Purple stranger

Skeleton Cliff of Montana
Life — *Treasury* p.190-191

SKIING
Lippo and Tapio

SKILL. *See* **Cleverness**

Skillywidden
Colwell — *Round* p.122-125

SKIN
- *Color, Sacred*
How Tahaki lost his golden
skin
Tahaki of the golden skin
- *Sores*
Tshinyama heavenly maidens
, *Wishing*
The wishing skin

SKIPPERS, SEA. *See* **Captains, Sea**

Skull race
Leach — *Whistle* p.27

SKULLS
, *Horse's*
Who lived in the skull?

SKUNKS
Godfather to skunks

SKY
Havaiki the land
There's some sky in this pie
When the sky lay on the earth

The sky is a bowl of ice
Belting — *Whirlwind* n. pag.

Sky Woman
Life — *Treasury* p.48-50

SKYLARKS
Animals from heaven

SLANDER. *See* **Gossip**

The slanderer and the snake
Krylov — *Fables* p.134-135

Slappy Hooper
  Life — *Treasury* p.291-293

The slave of the lamp. *See* Aladdin

The slave of the ring. *See* Aladdin

SLAVES AND SLAVERY
  Fifty years in chains
  The man and his boots
  The miser who received his due
  The thoughtful father
  , *Runaway*
  Bras coupé

SLAVIC MYTHS
  See also individual countries;
  Yugoslavia — Slavonia
  Little people
  People of the sea

SLEEP
  Knoonie in the sleeping palace
  Peter Klaus
  Rip Van Winkle
  Willie Winkie
  , *Hymn to*
    Jason and the dragon of
    Colchis
    The song of Orpheus; The
    song that Orpheus sang to
    charm the dragon

The sleeper
  Manning — *Sorcerers* p.24-32

The sleeping beauty
  Fairy Tales p.53-65
  Sekorová — *Europe* p.83-86

The sleeping beauty in the wood
  Perrault — *Fairy* p.61-72

SLEIGH, BARBARA
  Barbara Sleigh (subject)
    Sleigh — *Stirabout* p.144

Slime
  Hoke — *Monsters* p.11-41

SLINGSHOTS
  David and Goliath. The shepherd
  boy and the giant

SLIPPERS. *See* Shoes — Slippers

SLOVAKIA
  The twelve months

SLUGS, SEA
  Why the sea-slug has two mouths

The sly fox
  Ginsburg — *One* p.21-27

SLYNESS. *See* Trickery

SMALL FOLK. *See* Fairies; Little
  People; etc.

The small kingdom
  Bomans — *Wily* p.21-27

The small red ox
  Harris — *Sea Magic* p.159-178

SMALLPOX
  Skeleton Cliff of Montana

Smart, Christopher
  My cat Jeoffrey

The smart rabbit
  Dolch — *Animal* p.123-131

The smartest one in the woods
  Jagendorf — *Folk, South* p.22-24

Smartness for sale
  Jagendorf — *Noodle* p.244-248

Smedberg, Alfred
  The boy who was never afraid
  The flower of happiness on Sun-
  nymount Crest
  The seven wishes
  The trolls and the youngest
  Tomte

Smedley, Menella Bute
  The shepherd of the Giant Mountains

SMELL, SENSE OF
  The theft of a smell

Smith, William Jay
  A pavane for the nursery

The smith, the weaver, and the harper
  Alexander — *Foundling* p.75-87

SMITHS. *See* Blacksmiths

SMOKY MOUNTAINS
  The place of the beginning

SMUGGLING
The crooked Mary

SNAILS
Percy the wizard, nicknamed Snail

The snake and the lamb
Krylov — *Fables* p.158-159

Snake Magee's rotary boiler
Life — *Treasury* p.240-241

The snake of Apro
Lawrie — *Myths* p.276

Snake the postman
Carter — *Greedy* p.79-83

SNAKES
See also **Sea Monsters**
Agburug
All on a summer's day
The boy and the snake
The boy with the hand of fire
The crow and the snake
The doomed prince
The draper who swallowed a fly
The farmer and the poisonous
snake
The farmer and the snake
The farmer and the ungrateful
snake
The flower of happiness on Sun-
nymount Crest
From tiger to Anansi
Gratitude
Halfway people
He who likes to bite and hiss will
always go astray and miss
How the snake lost his voice
The hunter and his wife
Ivan the peasant's son and the
little man himself one-finger tall,
his mustache seven versts in
length
Kogie
Kongasau
The lagoon of Masaya
The legend of Agustín Lorenzo
The little turtle
Maiwasa
The marvelous chirrionera
Nyangara, the python
Oda and the snake
Patches
The peasant and snake

The ring with twelve screws
The serpent-Tsarevich and his
two wives
The serpent-wife
The seven wishes
The silver snake of Louisiana
The slanderer and the snake
The story of little Tsar Novishny,
the false sister, and the faithful
beasts
Susui and Dungam
A taste of his own medicine
Tokonave: The snake and horn
people
Ttimba
Vassilissa golden tress, bare-
headed beauty
The wondrous story of Ivan Golik
and the serpents
Zohăk the monster
- *Bites*
No witchcraft for sale
- *Eggs*
Rabbit's long ears
, *Hoop*
How hoop snakes can sting
- *Rattlensnakes*
Fiddler's rock
How Joe became Snaky Joe
The rattlesnake that played
"Dixie"

Snakes
Schwartz — *Whoppers* p.80-81

SNEEZING
The adventures of Billy MacDaniel

Sneezy Snatcher and Sammy Small
Manning — *Choice* p.144-147

Snipy hunters
Life — *Treasury* p.289-290

SNOBBERY
The Hodja visits Halil

SNOW
See also **Ice**
The gladiator, the belle, and the
good snowstorm
The hut in the forest
The little daughter of the snow
The love of a Mexican prince and
princess
Moozipoo

New Year's hats for the statues
- *Queen*
    Where blonde people came
    from

Snow Drop
    See also Snow White and the
    seven dwarfs
    Opie — *Classic* p.176-182

Snow-White (and variants)
    Bamberger — *My* p.107-118
    Haviland — *Fairy* p.128-137
    Sekorová — *Europe* p.73-82

**SNOW WHITE AND THE SEVEN
    DWARFS**
    Snow White and the Seven Dwarfs
    (subject)
    Opie — *Classic* p.175
    Kingsley — *Sesame* p.38-41
    Segal — *Juniper (II)* p.256-274

SOAP
    Pentalina

Sobol, Donald J.
    George Washington, the torch-
    bearer

A soccer game on Dung-ting Lake
    Bang — *Goblins* p.41-46

SOCRATES
    The story of Atlantis

SOFTNESS
    Rabbit's long ears

Sohrãb and Rustem
    Picard — *Tales* p.106-122

The soldier and the demons
    Rugoff — *Harvest* p.630-639

The soldier with the wooden leg
    Bomans — *Wily* p.112-119

SOLDIERS
    Bearskin
    Brother Gaily
    The castle in the silver wood
    The clever soldier and the stingy
    woman
    The dancing princesses
    Devil-may-care
    Fanta-Ghiro
    The horse and the soldier

The Lady of Nam Xuong
The tinderbox (and variants)
The twelve dancing princesses
Yelena the wise
, *Deserted*
    The dragon and his grand-
    mother

The soldier's fur coat
    Higonnet-Schnopper — *Tales* p.1-
    20

SOLOMON, KING
    The case against the wind
    King Solomon and the Queen of
    Sheba
    A time for everything
    - *Ring*
    King Solomon's ring

SOLON
    The story of Atlantis

The sombreros of the men of Lagos
    Jagendorf — *Noodle* p.268-270

Some mice under ferns
    Shaw — *Mouse* p.31

Something quite new
    Cott — *Beyond* p.444-447

The son of bad counsel
    McGarry — *Great* p.86-91

The son of the king of the city of straw
    MacFarlane — *Mouth* p.82-94

Song for a gluttonous owl
    Shaw — *Owl* p.12-14

Song for a princess
    Sperry — *Scand.* p.86-98

The song in the sea
    Jagendorf — *Folk, South* p.149-150

Song of a hen
    McDowell — *Third* p.136

Song of an unlucky man
    McDowell — *Third* p.44

The song of Orpheus; The song that
    Orpheus sang to charm the
    dragon
    Green — *Cavalcade* p.10

The song of the Cherokee rose
Jagendorf — *Folk, South* p.93-94

Song of the kid
Rugoff — *Harvest* p.584-585

SONGS
See also **Chants; Indians of North
America — Songs; Singers and
Singing**
The arrival of the Tewas
By whose command?
Canoe-launching song
Norinori
Visitor's song
The winning of Kwelanga
Wooden Tony; and Anyhow story
, *African*
Akanyonyi
Awo!
Ayele and the flowers
Ca, ca, ca
Kaleeba
'Keenene
"Leave it there!"
"Mother-in-law, today is
shake-head day!"
Nnoonya Mwana Wange
Nnyonyi
Nsangi
Ojumiri the giant
Purrr Ce!
The stepchild and the fruit
trees
Ttimba
Tweriire
Wavvuuvuumira
Why the baboon has a shining
seat
Why there is death in the
world
Woowooto
- *Dirges*
Rao's dirge for herself
, *Fatal*
The Yara
- *"Frankie and Johnnie"*
Frankie and Albert
- *"The song of Hiawatha"*
Hiawatha
- *Trees*
Lisalill
The saga of two trees

SONINKE TALES
Marandenboni

SONS
See also titles beginning with Son
Apukura's mourning for her son
Burum
The crystal ball
Dragon, dragon
The fool of the world and the
flying ship
Half of everything
Iviahoca
Knoist and his three sons
Lac Long Quan and Au Co
The longest story in the world
Moozipoo
A mother shames her son,
Mapukutaora
Oh: the Tsar of the forest
The sea maiden
The seven Simeons and the
trained Siberian cat
The ship that sailed on sea and
land
The stolen heart
The three Ivans
The wondrous story of Ivan Golik
and the serpents

The sons of Feridun
Picard — *Tales* p.30-42

SOOT
Moon snow

SOOTHSAYERS. See Fortunetellers

The sorcerer and his apprentice
Bamberger — *My* p.75-79

Sorcerer Kaldoon
Manning — *Sorcerers* p.99-111

The sorcerer of the White Lotus Lodge
Rugoff — *Harvest* p.191-193

**SORCERY. See Enchanters; Magic;
Magicians; Witchcraft; Witches;
Wizards**

SORROW. See Grief; Sadness

Soule, Jean Conder
Grimelda

SOULS
The basket of souls

The fisherman and his soul
The hole in the back wall
The princess of the mountain
The stolen heart

Souls under the sea
Stuart — *Witch's* p.119-126

SOUNDS
The magic listening cup

SOUP
See also **Porridge**
Balten and the wolf
Boiled axe
The clever soldier and the stingy
woman
Don't drop into my soup
Nail broth
, *Fish*
Demyàn's fish soup

SOUTH
Alas for Theodosia
The army of the dead
Blue Johnny and the pilot
Bras coupé
The brave drummer boys
Daddy Mention
De witch woman
Gossamer wedding
The Hatfields and McCoys
It's a long time between drinks
Joe Baldwin's light
Joe John and the carpenter
John Henry
The lovers of Dismal Swamp
The rattlesnake that played
"Dixie"
The rebel belle
The traveling frog
- *Folklore*
Southerners, folklore
Life — *Treasury* p.158-185

SOUTH AFRICA. See Africa, South

SOUTH AMERICA
See also **Latin America;** names of
countries
(El) Enano
The flying fool
Halfway people
Little people
People of the sea

SOUTH CAROLINA
Ah-Dunno Ben
Chickens come home to roost
Emily's famous meal
The ghost dog
It's a long time between meals
The perpetual motion in the sea
Shake hands with a Yankee
The tale of Rebecca Motte
The tragic tale of Fenwick Hall
Young Sherman and the girl from
Charleston
- *Charleston*
The army of the dead
- *Pawleys Island*
The gray man
The gray man's warning

SOUTH DAKOTA
Wind is a ghost . . .
- *Deadwood*
Calamity Jane, the loud canary

Southey, Robert
The story of the three bears

SPACE
The conflict of the gods

SPAGHETTI
How a tailor became a king

SPAIN AND SPANIARDS
Antillia, the island of the seven
cities
The black charger
Don Demonio's mother-in-law
Good luck and bad luck
I ate the loaf
The invisible cloth
Iviahoca
The legend of the Ceiba of Ponce
Little Mary
Master Money and Madame Fortune
The moon in the donkey
Pedro the trickster
The strange, sad spirit of the Scioto
Three golden oranges
The werewolf
The wish that came true
What happened to a young man
on his wedding day
The witches' cellar
Yuisa and Pedro Mexias

SPAIN AND SPANIARDS (continued)
- *Folk tales*
    Spain, folk tales
        Rugoff — *Harvest* p.705-
            728
- *Madrid*
    The half-chick

The sparrow and the bush
    Bain — *Cossack* p.123-125

SPARROWS
    The prince and the dragon
- *Tongues*
    The tongue-cut sparrow

SPEARS
    Bia
    Galahad. The Holy Grail
    Manaii and the spears
    Mibu and the coconut
    Sisters who quarreled

SPECTACLES. See Glasses, Eye

Specter of the Spanish castle
    Roberts — *Ghosts* p.67-74

The spectre of the tower
    Wyness — *Legends* p.94-99

SPEECH
    See also **Talk**
    The clock that walked by itself
        (Luck or wisdom)
    The old man on the mountain

SPEED
    Greedy and Speedy
    Rabbit's long ears
    The wonderful jug of wild-cherry
        wine

SPELLS. See Magic; Witchcraft

Spenser, Edmund
    The Red Cross knight and the
        dragons

Sperry, Armstrong
    Land! Land in sight!

The sphinx
    Hoke — *Monsters* p.94-100

SPHINXES
, *The Great*
    Halfway people
, *Greek*
    Halfway people

The spice woman's basket
    Corrigan — *Holiday* p.43-53

SPICER, DOROTHY GLADYS
    Dorothy Gladys Spicer (subject)
        Spicer — *13 Rascals* p.128

The spider and the sky god's stories
    Dolch — *Animal* p.143-153

"SPIDER GRANDMOTHER"
    The flight from Huckovi
    The four worlds
    Homolovi and the journey
        northward
    Judgment by fire at Pivanhonkapi
    The Lalakon dance at Shongopovi
    The Lamehva people
    The Navajo attack on Oraibi
    The races between Payupki and
        Tikuvi
    Tokonowei: The snake and horn
        people
- *Webs*
    Gossamer wedding

"SPIDER WOMAN"
    See also **"Spider Grandmother"**
    Escape from the Underworld
    The twins' journey to the sun

SPIDERS
    See also **"Anansi" Stories**
    The eagle and the spider
    A forest mansion
    From tiger to Anansi
    Gar-room!
    The girl who got a fairy in her eye
    Little Miss Muffet
    The magic spider box
    "Mother-in-law, today is shake-
        head day"
    The tea house in the forest
    The tortoise who flew to heaven
    Why the spider has a small head
, *Spanish*
    Mrs. Scruby and the Spanish
        spider

- *Webs*
    Fairy web for Mr. Durand's
      daughters
    The killing of Eetoi

Spiders
    Schwartz — *Whoppers* p.81

SPIES
- *Women*
    Emily's famous meal
    The merry tale of Belle Royal
    The rebel belle

SPINA, ALPHONSE DE
    Workers of evil — and a few good
      spirits

Spindle, shuttle, and needle
    Segal — *Juniper (I)* p.55-62
    Sheehan — *Folk* p.32-36

SPINNING
    Briar Rose
    The frog (by Leonora Alleyne)
    The horned women
    Mannikin Spanalong
    The three fairies

SPINNING-WHEELS
    A sheep can only bleat
    , *Golden*
      East of the sun and West of
        the moon

The "spirited" librarian
    Anderson — *Haunting* p.122-125

SPIRITS
    See also **Ghosts; Soul;** names
      of spirits
    , *Evil*
      Ayamama
      The master and his pupil
      Workers of evil — and a few
        good spirits
    - *Girls*
      Bila
      Ug
    , *of the well*
      The horned women
    - *Women*
      The lamar who became a
       rainbow

The two spirit women of
    Daoma Kes
    Umi Markail

SPITE. *See* **Revenge**

"Spook Light" of Devil's Promenade
    Anderson — *Haunting* p.133-136

SPOOLS
    The ghostly spools

SPOONS
    , *Silver*
      The tale of the huntsman
    , *Wooden*
      Tatterhood

SPORN, MICHAEL
    Michael Sporn (subject)
      Gardner — *Gudgekin* p.60
      Gardner — *King* p.58

The sporran full of gold
    MacFarlane — *Mouth* p.22-30

SPORTS. *See* **Athletes and Athletics;**
    names of sports

The sportsman
    Krylov — *Fables* p.112-113

Spots
    Heady — *Safiri* p.67-70

SPRING
    April (John Updike)
    The cuckoo
    The cuckoo of Borrowdale
    In just-/Spring
    True or false

Spring in the forest
    Ransome — *Old* p.81-82

SPRINGS (WATER)
    Aib
    Bia
    , *Magical*
      The fountain of youth

"SQUATTERS"
    The Arkansas traveler

Squatter's rights
    Shaw — *Cat* p.46

The squirrel and the crawfish race
  Bird — *Path* p.39-42
SQUIRRELS
  Longnose the dwarf
SRI LANKA. *See* **Ceylon**
STAFFORD, JEAN
  Jean Stafford (subject)
  Manley — *Sisters* p.71-72,218-219
  The warlock
STAFFS. *See* **Sticks**
The stag and the lion
  Levine — *Fables* p.42
STAGECOACHES
  - *Robberies*
    Black Bart, bandit and "Po8"
STAGS. *See* **Deer**
STAIRWAYS
  I'm coming up the stairs
Stalo and Kaurus
  Olenius — *Great* p.170-173
Stamm, Claus
  Three strong women
STAMMERING. *See* **Stuttering**
Stan Bolovan
  Manning — *Choice* p.307-319
Stan Bolovan and the dragon
  Green — *Cavalcade* p.138-147
The star money
  Rockwell — *Three* p.113-117
Staring at you!
  Leach — *Whistle* p.61-62
STARLINGS
  His very best friend
  The story of three young shepherds
STARS
  See also **Constellations**
  Dogai I
  The joyful abbot
  The Pleiades
  The shining lodge
  The thoughtless abbot

The warrior who shot arrows at a
  star
  , *of Bethlehem*
    The three wise men
STARVATION. *See* **Famine; Hunger**
Stasiak, Krystyna
  The basilisk
The statue vendor
  Levine — *Fables* p.46
STATUES
  Abdul Kasim the rich
  Abraham and the idols
  The ass bearing an idol
  The happy prince
  The man and the lion
  New Year's hats for the statues
  The oracle
  Pinto Smalto
  The stone statue and the grasshat
  The two statues of Kannon
  - *Shrines*
    The badger and the fox
STEALING. *See* **Thieves and Thievery**
STEAM
  How fire took water to wife
  - *Drills*
    John Henry
STEAMBOATS (Steamships)
  - *Pilots*
    Blue Johnny and the pilot
The steed and his rider
  Krylov — *Fables* p.156-157
Steel, Flora Annie
  The story of the three bears
STEEL-WORKERS
  John Henry
  , *Hungarian*
    Joe Magarac, the man of
    steel
STEEP HOLME
  Big people
Stenström, Walter
  The boy and the trolls, or The
  adventure

The stepchild and the fruit trees
Robinson — *Singing* p.24-33

STEPDAUGHTERS
Cinderella (and variants)
Daughter and stepdaughter

STEPFATHERS
The little bull-calf

STEPMOTHERS
Baba Yaga
Blackberries in February
The blue falcon
Brother and sister
Cinderella (and variants)
Cinderelma
Diem and Siem
Don't foul the well — you may
need its waters
The enchanted cat
The enchanted princess
Frost
The golden shoe
The golden slipper
Gudgekin, the thistle girl
Hans and Greta
The juniper tree
The King of Colchester's daughters
The Laidly Worm
Little Hiram
Little step-mother
The monster in the mill
The palace of the seven little hills
The sharp gray sheep
The small red ox
Snow-white (and variants)
The swan-children of Lir
The three heads of the well
The three mermaids
The three shirts of Cannach Cotton
The twelve months
Vasilisa the beautiful
The wolf's eyelashes

STEW
Nail stew (and variants)

**STICK-TO-IT-TIVENESS. See Persever-
ance**

STICKS
Esben and the witch
, *Magic*
The boy and the North Wind

The magic table, the gold-
donkey, and the cudgel in
the sack
Nandayure and his magic rod

STINGINESS
See also **Greed; Misers**
The clever soldier and the stingy
woman
The marvelous chirrionera
Nail broth (and variants)
Old Gally Mander
The rich señora

Stingy Kichiyomu and the iron hammer
Bang — *Men* p.12-13

Stingy Kichiyomu and the rice thieves
Bang — *Men* p.4-5

The stolen bairn and the Sidh
Minard — *Womenfolk* p.1-13

The stolen heart
Bomans — *Wily* p.134-146

The stolen turnips, the magic tablecloth, the sneezing goat and
the wooden whistle
Ransome — *Old* p.109-129

The stone
Alexander — *Foundling* p.17-30

The stone-cold heart
Hauff — *Big* p.167-224

STONE-CRUSHERS. See Stonemasons

The stone dog
Belpré — *Once* p.80-84

The stone people and the alderman
Sleigh — *Stirabout* p.124-131

The stone statue and the grass hut
Bang — *Man* p.21-25

STONEHENGE
Faery folk
- *Origin*
Merlin the enchanter

STONEMASONS
Blackmail

STONES. See Rocks and Stones

Stonor, Charles
 Big people

STOREKEEPERS. *See* **Merchants**

STOREROOMS
 John in the storeroom

STORKS
 The Caliph turned stork
 The fox and the stork
 The frogs asking for a king
 The story of Caliph Stork
 The two journeymen
 The wolf and the stork

The story of a man who was going to
 mind the house. *See* **Gone is
 Gone**

The story of Ait Kadal
 Lawrie — *Myths* p.161-165

The story of Almansor
 Hauff — *Big* p.101-117

The story of Atlantis
 Higginson — *Tales* p.1-4

The story of Caliph Stork
 Bamberger — *My* p.200-209

The story of Ivan and the daughter
 of the sun
 Bain — *Cossack* p.183-187

The story of Little Boy Blue
 Baum — *Mother* p.31-42

The story of little Tsar Novishny, the
 false sister, and the faithful
 beasts
 Bain — *Cossack* p.57-80

The story of Meidu
 Lawrie — *Myths* p.314-315

The story of O-Tei
 Littledale — *Strange* p.127-131

The story of one who set out to study
 fear
 Segal — *Juniper (I)* p.23-41

The story of Peibri
 Lawrie — *Myths* p.301

The story of Seppy who wished to
 manage his own house
 De Bosschere — *Christmas* p.8-13

The story of the brave little rabbit,
 Squint-Eyes — Flop Ears —
 Stub Tail
 Carey — *Baba* p.23-26

The story of the forty-first brother
 Bain — *Cossack* p.255-258

The story of the little half-cock
 De Bosschere — *Christmas* p.75-
 79

The story of the rat and the flying-fox
 Alpers — *Legends* p.298-300

The story of the three bears
 See also **Goldilocks and the three
 bears**
 Haviland — *Fairy* p.36-43
 Opie — *Classic* p.201-205

The story of the three little pigs
 Haviland — *Fairy* p.22-27

The story of the unlucky days
 Bain — *Cossack* p.261-263

The story of the wind
 Bain — *Cossack* p.29-45

The story of the wooden images
 Alpers — *Legends* p.243-246

The story of three young shepherds
 Manning — *Monsters* p.75-84

The story of Tommy Tucker
 Baum — *Mother* p.163-171

The story of Tremsin, the bird Zhar,
 and Nastasia, the lovely maid
 of the sea
 Bain — *Cossack* p.95-102

The story of Unlucky Daniel
 Bain — *Cossack* p.111-120

STORYTELLERS AND STORYTELLING
 Big for me, little for you
 Brown owl plans a party
 Ears and tails and common sense
 The flying trunk
 Forty men I see, forty men I do
 not see

The grass-cutting races
Horns for a rabbit
Kind little Edmund, or the Caves
and the cockatrice
Lizard and a ring of gold
The longest story in the world
The old man on the mountain
The prince of the flowery meadow
Riddle me riddle, riddle me ree
Riddles one, two, three
Sister of the birds
The smartest one in the woods
A time for everything
- *Africa, East*
Author's note (Safiri the singer)

The stove and the town hall
Jagendorf — *Noodle* p.189-191

A strange and rare friendship
Duong — *Beyond* p.64-72

The strange folding screen
Bang — *Men* p.79-84

The strange, sad spirit of the Scioto
Anderson — *Haunting* p.112-121

STRANGERS
The terrible stranger

STRATTON, CHARLES SHERWOOD
Little people

The straw ox
Bain — *Cossack* p.139-148
Great Children's p.36-47

STRAWBERRIES
The girl who picked strawberries
Pipe and Pitcher
- *Origin*
How red strawberries brought
peace in the woods

STREAMS. See Fields and Streams

STRENGTH
See also **Giants;** titles beginning
with Strong
The boy in the secret valley
Clever Oonagh
The giant of the Fens
Hercules of Virginia
How El Bizarrón fooled the devil
Joe Magarac, the man of steel

John Henry and the machine in
West Virginia
John Travail and the devil
The man and the lion
The North wind and the sun
Rabbit and our old woman
The six who went together
through the world
Stalo and Kauru
The sun and the wind
Three strong women
The turnip
Why women always take advan-
tage of men

STRING
The tea house in the forest
- *Figures*
Wameal

The strong chameleon
Heady — *Safiri* p.31-35

Strong-man
Martin — *Raven* p.61-67

The strong voice
Sperry — *Scand.* p.70-78

STUBBORNNESS
The pig-headed wife
Scissors they were
The time Blue Louisey put a hex
on the house
The time cousin Emmett out-
stubborned his mules
The time lightning struck little
Ida's umbrella
- *Missouri*
Missouri-stubborn — that's
what it is!

STUTTERING
A sensible suitor?

SUGAR CANE
Usius

Sui
Lawrie — *Myths* p.173-176

SUICIDE
Romeo and Juliet
, *Mass*
The song in the sea

SUITORS
See also **Courtship**
Marya Morevna
Monsoon
Moon snow
A sensible suitor?
Song for a princess
The true enchanter
Turandot
Widow Fox and her four suitors

The suitors of Princess Fire-fly
Orczy — Old p.25-32

SULTANS
Abdul Kasim the rich
Aladdin
The enchanted cat
The man who tricked Sultan
Otakul
Prince Ahmed and the fairy
Peribanou

SUMATRA
Little people

SUMMER
Coyote steals the summer

SUN
Brother sun and sister moon
Dawn-strider
How the moon came to be
How three mighty heroes saved
the sun and the moon from the
dragon
Hung Vuong and the earth and
sky cakes
Kabai
The killing of Eetoi
Kiss Miklos, and the green daugh-
ter of the green king
The lad who stared everyone down
Makonaima returns
The North wind and the sun
Photogen
The Sunday child
The twins' journey to the sun
Why the sun and moon are in the
sky
- Daughter
The story of Ivan and the
daughter of the sun
- Festival
Little Lapp

- King
Mother of the sun

The sun
Cott — Beyond p.447-452

The sun and the wind
Haviland — Fairy p.100-101
Morel — Fairy p.49

SUNDAY
See also **Sabbath**
Revealed
The treasure

The Sunday child
Bomans — Wily p.105-111

SUNFLOWERS
The Sunday child

Sunrise
Leach — Whistle p.108

SUNRISES
The three men of power —
Evening, midnight and sunrise

The sunset
Cott — Beyond p.439-442

The sunshade
Bamberger — My p.177-180

SUPERNATURAL LEGENDS
See also **Ghosts**
Workers of evil — and a few good
spirits

SUPERSTITION
John McGraw's jinx killer

Suppose you met a witch
Shaw — Witch p.24-31

SURFING
The basket of souls
Chant to dump a surfer
Lonopuha, or the origin of healing:
and the story of Milu

SURGEONS. See Physicians

SURVIVAL
Learn and live

Susui and Dengam
Lawrie — Myths p.171

Sven and Lilli
  Manning — *Choice* p.89-94

SWABIANS
  The seven Swabians

SWALLOWS
  The happy prince
  Thumbelina

SWAMPS
  Boigu
  The buried moon
  The dead hand
  The lovers of Dismal Swamp
  Slime
  Wakemab
  Warupudamaizinga
  Way deep down in the Okefenokee
    swamps
  The witch of the marsh

The swan-children of Lir
  Higginson — *Tales* p.17-24

The swan-geese
  Whitney — *In* p.65-68

The swan maiden
  Provenson — *Book* p.117-124

The swan, the pike and the crayfish
  Krylov — *Fables* p.131

SWANS
  Halfway people
  Manabozho, the trickster
  Saint Comgall and the mice
  True or false
  The ugly duckling

The swapper
  Life — *Treasury* p.273-274

"SWAPPING". See Traders and Trading

SWEDEN
  The barrel bung
  Beowulf and the dragon
  The boy and the trolls, or The
    adventure
  The boy who was never afraid
  The can with a will of its own
    (and variants)
  The cap that mother made
  A cat for a cow
  The changelings

Dag and Daga, and the flying
    troll of Sky Mountain
  The flower of happiness on
    Sunnymount Crest
  The four big trolls and Little Peter
    Pastureman
  His very best friend
  The King's choice
  Leap the elk and Little Princess
    Cottongrass
  Linda — Gold and the old king
  The little boy who wanted pan-
    cakes
  Little people
  The magical spectacles
  The magician's cape
  The magnificent cloak
  The magpie with salt on her tail
  The maiden in the castle of rosy
    clouds
  Nail stew (and variants)
  The old troll of Big Mountain
  Prince Lindworm
  The princess with unruly thoughts
  The Queen
  Ragnar Shaggy-Legs and the
    dragons
  The ring
  The rooster who couldn't crow
  The seven wishes
  Song for a princess
  Stalo and Kauras
  The strong voice
  The troll ride
  The trolls and the youngest Tomte
  The twin sisters
  When Mother Troll took in the
    King's washing
  - *Pioneers*
  Febold Feboldson

Sweet Betsy
  Life — *Treasury* p.218-220

Sweet tooth
  De Roin — *Jataka* p.4-5

SWIFTNESS. See Speed

The swimmer and the sea
  Krylov — *Fables* p.128

The swine-herd
  Bamberger — *My* p.214-220
  Opie — *Classic* p.232-235

SWINEHERDS
The swineherd (subject)
Opie — *Classic* p.230-231

SWITZERLAND
See also **Lucerne, Switzerland**
Belmont antics
The dragon, sliced-in-two
The knight with the stone heart
The shepherd's choice
The tailor and the treasure
Wooden Tony: an Anyhow story

The sword
Alexander — *Foundling* p.61-74

SWORDS
Boastful Aulus and the sly thief
The flying sword
How the Great Turisgale met his
death
Mimer the master
, *of sharpness*
The cloak of friendship
, *Sacred*
The sacred sword
, *White*
The blue falcon

Syre-Varda
Ginsburg — *How* p.55-65

SYRIA
Donkeys all

SZEKERES, CINDY
Cyndy Szekeres, illus. (subject)
Wahl — *Muffletump* p.127

T

The table, the pack, and the bag
Curtin — *Myths* p.295-310

TABLECLOTHS
The boy and the North Wind
The stolen turnips, the magic
tablecloth, the sneezing goat
and the wooden whistle

TABLES
King Johnny
The magic table, the gold-donkey,
and the cudgel in the sack
Ten miles at each step

TABLETS
, *Stone*
The breakup of Oraibi
The four worlds

TABOOS
Esau and the gorbey
- *Polynesia*
Polynesian taboos (subject)
Alpers — *Legends* p.16

TADPOLES. *See* **Frogs**

Tagai
Lawrie — *Myths* p.304-305

Tagore, Rabindranath
The merchant

Tahaki of the golden skin
Alpers — *Legends* p.118-129

Tahia the fragrant girl
Alpers — *Legends* p.211-226

TAHITI
Anointing of a new-born child
Baptismal chant
A boasting chant in war
Chant on the dying of an only
child
Havaiki the land
Tahaki of the golden skin
The woman in the moon
- *Gods*
Tangawa maker of all things

Taikoko
Lawrie — *Myths* p.138

TAILED MEN
Halfway people

The tailor and the fairies
Colwell — *Round* p.51-53

The tailor and the giant
Gardner — *Dragon* p.19-35

The tailor and the treasure
Bamberger — *My* p.44-45

The tailor from the sea
Jagendorf — *Noodle* p.192–195

The tailor, the bear, and the devil
Ginsburg — *How* p.81-87

TAILORS
The dreamer
How a tailor became a king
The little tailor and the three dogs
The magic table, the gold-donkey,
and the cudgel in the sack
Seven with one blow (and variants)
The two journeymen
The valiant and the little tailor
Voices in the night

TAILS
The fox who lost his tail

"Tain't so"
Leach — *Whistle* p.34-37

Takise
Rugoff — *Harvest* p.25-29

The tale of a merry dance
Rugoff — *Harvest* p.375-377

The tale of Lura Lou
Jagendorf — *Folk, South* p.71-77

The tale of Rebecca Motte
Jagendorf — *Folk, South* p.219-224

A tale of steep-stair town
Jagendorf — *Folk, South* p. 57-59

The tale of the daughters of the sun
Jagendorf — *Folk, South* p.97-99

Tale of the devout Israelite
Rugoff — *Harvest* p.144-145

The tale of the doctor's secret. *See*
Abdul Kasim the rich

The tale of the gardener's boy. *See*
Abdul Kasim the rich

The tale of the hairy toe
Jagendorf — *Folk, South* p.180-182

The tale of the huntsman
Bomans — *Wily* p.127-133

The tale of the men of Prach
Jagendorf — *Noodle* p.241-243

The tale of the silver saucer and the
transparent apple
Ransome — *Old* p.6-21

The tale of the three wishes
See also The three wishes
Opie — *Classic* p.153-155

A tale of two frogs
Carey — *Baba* p.58-60

The talema
Wolkstein — *Lazy* p.14-23

Tales from Tartari-Barbari
Jagendorf — *Noodle* p.142-146

Taliessin of the radiant brow
Higginson — *Tales* p.5-16

TALK
A sensible suitor?
The tortoise who talked too much
The wife who talked too much
(and variants)

Talk
Rugoff — *Harvest* p.39-41

The talking turtle
Life — *Treasury* p.270-271

TALL TALES
Animals and insects
Fancy clothes, and narrow escapes
If you don't like it, don't listen
John Henry and the machine in
West Virginia
Ordinary people
Ordinary things
Putrefactions and other wonders
The Seabees
Slappy Hooper
Three strong women
The weather
Yarns, tall tales and practical jokes

The tall tales
Junne — *Floating* p.3-5

TAMARISK (TAMARIND) TREES
How the sneaky waterstealer set
the cattlemen and the sheepmen against each other

The taming of the shrew
Darrell — *Once* p.140-146

Tandala and Pakala
Jagendorf — *Noodle* p.222-226

Tangaroa maker of all things
  Alpers — *Legends* p.51-54

Tantalus
  Rugoff — *Harvest* p.392-393

A Taoist priest
  Rugoff — *Harvest* p.183-186

TAPA CLOTH
  The woman in the moon

TAPAS. *See* Hermits

TAPESTRIES
  Prince Ahmed and the fairy
    Peribanou

TAR
  Hyena and hare
  The straw ox

The tar baby
  Rugoff — *Harvest* p.60-64

Tar-wolf tale
  Jagendorf — *Folk, South*
    p.157-162

TARTARS. *See* Tatars

TARTARY
  The sparrow and the bush
  Ubir

TARTS. *See* Cakes — Tarts

TASKS. *See* Tests

A taste of his own medicine
  De Roin — *Jataka* p.71-73

TATARS
  The tailor, the bear, and the devil

Tattercoats
  Sekorová — *Europe* p.111-114

Tatterhood
  Manning — *Choice* p.246-255

Tattle-tale dog. *See* Ae-e-oina, the
    demon, and the tattle-tale dog

TATTOOING
  The frog's tattoo
  Mataora and Niwareka
  - *Japan, girls of*
    People from the sky

TAVERNS
  The ghosts of Gibbet Island

Tawaka, the greedy man
  Lawrie — *Myths* p.119

TAXATION
  How the beggars came to town

Te Kanawa and the visitors by firelight
  Alpers — *Legends* p.328-330

TEA
  The revolution of the ladies of
    Edenton

The tea house in the forest
  Novák — *Fairy* p.138-144

TEACHERS
  Kind little Edmund, or the Caves
    and the cockatrice
  Miss Peabody
  The mistress in black
  The strong voice
  The wisdom of the Lord

TEAKETTLES
  The little fox

TEARS
  Alice's adventures in Wonderland
  The girl who cried flowers
  The jester who learned to cry
  (La) Llorona
  Nuinumma-Kiviten
  Pot-Tilter
  Stan Bolovan

TEASING
  The ugly duck

Tee Kuntee
  McDowell — *Third* p.136

Teeny-Tiny
  Piper — *Stories* n. pag.
  Rockwell — *Three* p.78-80

The teeny-tiny woman
  Morel — *Fairy* p.58-59

TEETH
  Chant for a new tooth
  The knight of the red shield
  Ol' Clackety teeth
  , *Ghostly*
    An apparition

Teig O'Kane and the corpse
  Rugoff — *Harvest* p.499-512

TEKA (game)
  Tu'i Tofua

TELESCOPES
  Prince Ahmed and the fairy
    Peribanou

The telltale seaweed
  Life — *Treasury* p.248-250

TEMPER
  Garuge
  The giant who threw tantrums
  Good advice
  Greedy Mariani
  The taming of the shrew
  The water-bull

TEMPLES
  The mat-maker's adventure
  The white crane

Ten miles at each step
  Sperry — *Scand.* p.184-199

TENNESSEE
  Beale street folks
  The best laugh is the last laugh
  Big sixteen
  Come and laugh with Bobby
    Gum
  Fiddler's rock
  The ghost that came to stay
  The ghost the whole town knew
  The ghost who wasn't a ghost
  The gladiator, the belle, and the
    good snowstorm
  Kate, the bell witch
  The Little people
  The power of woman and the
    strength of man
  Trust not a new friend
  - *Robertson Co.*
    "Old Hickory" and the Bell
      witch

TEPICTOTON
  Little people

Terenti, the black grouse
  Carey — *Baba* p.51-53

Terer
  Lawrie — *Myths* p.322-323

The terrapin and the possum outwit
  the fox
  Bird — *Path* p.63-65

TERRAPINS
  How the raccoon got rings on
    his tail

The terrible stranger
  Littledale — *Strange* p.133-146

TERROR. See Fear

The test
  Wojciechowska — *Winter* p.22-31

TESTS (tasks, trials)
  Burun — Teges
  The frog (by Leonora Alleyne)
  Guess who!
  Marya Moryevna
  The master thief
  The princess and the three tasks
  The rabbit catcher
  The sea maiden
  The shepherd and the princess
  A shrewd woman
  The three feathers
  The winning of Kwelanga

TEUTONIC MYTHS
  Big people
  Little people
  People of the sea

TEXAS
  Bigfoot Wallace and the hickory
    nuts
  The ghosts of Stampede Mesa
  Horse trading in Wichita Falls
  How Joe became Snaky Joe
  The Karankawa from the great
    gleaming oyster shells
  Lafitte's great treasure
  Of Sam Bass
  Only in Texas
  The phantom vaquero of the
    Texas plains
  Roy Bean, necktie justice
  Sam Bass, Texas Robin Hood
  The white buffalo
  - *German settlers*
    Gretchen and the white stallion

Texas centipede coffee
  Jagendorf — *Folk, South* p.284-
    286

THAILAND
    The tiger and the cow
    The water festival

Thank you M'am
    McDowell — *Third* p.106-111

"THANK YOU'S". *See* **Gratitude**
    Thanks to Patrick Henry
    Jagendorf — *Folk, South* p.314-317

THANKSGIVING DAY
    Thanksgiving (subject)
        Corrigan — *Holiday* p.210-222
    Give my love to Boston
    Prayer for Thanksgiving
    The right drumstick

Thar she blows
    Life — *Treasury* p.134

That cat
    Shaw — *Cat* p.30

"That's not true"
    Orczy — *Old* p.93-95

"That's once"
    Life — *Treasury* p.277

The theft of a smell
    Rugoff — *Harvest* p.314-315

There are such people
    Jagendorf — *Noodle* p.34-36

There's some sky in this pie
    Aiken — *Necklace* p.35-42

They called her a witch
    Raskin — *Ghosts* p.22-31

THIEVES AND THIEVERY
    Ali Baba
    Beetle
    Boastful Aulus and the sly thief
    Brother Mike
    The buried money
    The clever thief
    Dagmet
    The dogai of Zurat
    The enchanted apple-tree
    The forest inn
    The forty thieves
    Greedy Goba
    The herdsmen and the lion
    The Hodja and the burglar
    Hok Lee and the dwarfs

    Karum
    Kultut
    The master thief
    The master thief and the dragon
    A necklace of raindrops
    The old gray man of Spring
    The old woman and the physician
    The peasant and the robber
    Percy the wizard nicknamed Snail
    The piglet and the fairy
    The robbers and the treasure
    Saint Gerasimus and the lion
    Saint Launomar's cow
    Saurkeke
    Semrude the Fair and the Cadi
    The seven blind brothers
    The shroud of Mari-Yvonne
    The swan maiden
    There are such people
    Tokutaro
    Tom, the piper's son
    The trail of the white cat
    Wakaima and the clay man
    The wise rogue

The thieving child and his mother
    Levine — *Fables* p.78

THIRST
    The crow and the pitcher
    Dokere
    Goba
    The King of the Golden River
    Mokan

This for that
    Aardema — *Behind* p.48-56

This witch
    Hopkins — *Witching* p.61

THISTLES
    Gudgekin, the thistle girl
    The prince of the flowery meadow
    - *Thistledown*
        The twelve wild ducks

THONGA TALES
    This for that

THOR
    How Thor found his hammer
    The making of the hammer

THORNBUSHES
    The winning of Kwelanga

THORNS
The fairy thorn
The king of the hummingbirds
Saint Gerasimus and the lion

The thoughtful father
Rugoff — *Harvest* p.555-557

The thoughtless abbot
Rugoff — *Harvest* p.543-545

The thousand and one days
Fehse — *Thousand* p.210-213

Thousands of ideas
Carey — *Baba* p.21-22

THREAD
The cow and the thread
A little piece of thread

The three bears
Great Children's p.27-35
Rockwell — *Three* p.1-13

The three billy goats gruff
Great Children's p.122-128
Haviland — *Fairy* p.56-57
Rockwell — *Three* p.56-62

Three bits of advice
Pugh — *More* p.107-114

The three brothers
Bain — *Cossack* p.167-170
Novák — *Fairy* p.54-60

The three butterflies
Pugh — *More* p.13-28

The three dooms
Fehse — *Thousand* p.177-187

The three fairies
Carter — *Greedy* p.106-111

The three fastidious men
Rugoff — *Harvest* p.453-455

The three feathers
Segal — *Juniper (I)* p.3-10

The three golden hairs
Carle — *Eric* p.25-38

Three golden oranges
Sheehan — *Folk* p.61-71

Three great men at peace
Jagendorf — *Folk, South* p.143-145

Three heads in the well
See also The King of Colchester's
daughters (subject)
Opie — *Classics* p.156-157
Sheehan — *Folk* p.1-7

The three hermits
Stories From World p.56-65

The three Ivans
Manning — *Sorcerers* p.65-90

The three kingdoms
Curtin — *Myths* p.97-105

The three kingdoms, — The copper,
the silver, and the golden
Curtin — *Myths* p.1-19

Three knots
Ginsburg — *Lazies* p.21-25

The three little kittens who lost their
mittens
Kingsley — *Sesame* p.29-30

The three little pigs
Great Children's p.59-65
Kingsley — *Sesame* p.5-7
Morel — *Fairy* p.37-39
Rockwell — *Three* p.81-91
Sekorová — *Europe* p.94-97

The three Magi
Corrigan — *Holiday* p.247-252

The three men of power — Evening,
midnight and sunrise
Ransome — *Old* p.196-213

The three mermaids
Manning — *Choice* p.280-290

Three peasants
Krylov — *Fables* p.129-130

The three rascals and the magic cap
Spicer — *13 Rascals* p.9-16

The three riddles
See also Turandot
Bomans — *Wily* p.174-180

The three shirts of Cannach Cotton
MacFarlane — *Mouth* p.65-76

The three sisters who were entrapped
   into a mountain
   Minard — *Womenfolk* p.156-163

Three strong women
   Minard — *Womenfolk* p.93-105

Three tales from Shakespeare
   Darrell — *Once* p.139-169

Three tales of Old San Juan
   Belpré — *Once* p.60-71

The three travelers
   Aiken — *Necklace* p.55-64

The three wise men
   Bomans — *Wily* p.120-126

Three wise men of Gotham
   Baum — *Mother* p.245-254

THE THREE WISHES
   The three wishes (subject)
      Morel — *Fairy* p.86-87
      Opie — *Classic* p.151-152
      Provensen — *Book* p.105-116

THRIFT
   The wives' tale

Through the fire
   Cott — *Beyond* p.163-191

Through the needle's eye
   Manley — *Sisters* p.31-44

The thrush girl
   Bomans — *Wily* p.99-104

THRUSHES
   Peter Pan in Kensington gardens

The thrush's nest
   Darrell — *Once* p.264-270

THUMB, TOM. See "Tom Thumb"

"THUMBELINA"
   See also **Tommelise**
   "Thumbelina" (subject)
      Opie — *Classic* p.219
      Morel — *Fairy* p.97-103

THUNDER
   The hunter, the Ukton, and thunder
   Thunderbird
   True or false

Thunder appoints the eagle ruler of
   the earth
   Bird — *Path* p.21-25

The thunder god
   Rugoff — *Harvest* p.186-189

Thunderbird
   Corrigan — *Holiday* p.179-186

TIBET
   Two foolish friends

Tick, tick, tick
   Leach — *Whistle* p.79

The tiger and the cow
   Junne — *Floating* p.121-122

The tiger and the hare
   Junne — *Floating* p.79-80

The tiger story
   Junne — *Floating* p.133-134

The tiger, the Brahman, and the jackal
   Haviland — *Favorite India* p.83-90

Tiger woman
   Littledale — *Strange* p.35-45

TIGERS
   Anansi and turtle and pigeon
   Animals from heaven
   Big for me, little for you
   Compae Rabbit's ride
   Ears and tails and common sense
   The elves in the shelves
   From tiger to Anansi
   Gar-room!
   The goat and the tiger
   The grass-cutting races
   Horns for a rabbit
   Leave well enough alone
   The little turtle
   The noodlehead tiger
   Riddles one, two, three
   Sir Buzz
   The Sisimiqui
   The valiant chattee-maker

Tiki the first man
   Alpers — *Legends* p.68-72

TIME
   See also **Clocks; Watches**

Happy returns
The lost half-hour

The time Blue Louisey put a hex on
the house
Calhoun — *Three* p.33-48

The time cousin Emmett out-stubborned
his mules
Calhoun — *Three* p.7-17

A time for everything
Rugoff — *Harvest* p.601-602

The time lightning struck little Ida's
umbrella
Calhoun — *Three* p.18-32

The time of the ugly
Wojciechowska — *Winter* p.61-65

Timperley, Rosemary
The mistress in black

The tinder box
The tinder box (subject)
Opie — *Classic* p.206
Opie — Classic p.207-215
Rugoff — *Harvest* p.697-703
Sekorová — *Europe* p.46-53

"TINKERBELLE" (of Peter Pan)
Little people

TINKERS
See also Peddlers
John O'Hara's lantern
The lass who went out at the
cry of dawn

Tinykin's transformations
Cott — *Beyond* p.309-390

Tio Rabbit and the barrel
Carter — *Enchanted* p.87-90

The tired ghost
Leach — *Whistle* p.48-49

TIROL. See Austria — Tyrol

TITANS
Big people
Workers of evil — and a few good
spirits

TITMICE
Lippo and Tapio

Titty mouse and Tatty mouse
Great Children's p.66-73

TLALOC (rain god)
The king and the rain dwarfs

To a cat
Shaw — *Cat* p.36-37

TOADS
The enchanted princess
The grateful toad
Guani
The king of the toads
The mouse-hole, and the under-
ground kingdom
The seven monsters
The three feathers
Thumbelina
The witch's wish

Toast and honey
Ginsburg — *Lazies* p.42-45

TOES. See Feet — Toes

Tokelau moetonga
Alpers — *Legends* p.277-278

Tokonave: The snake and horn people
Courlander — *Fourth* p.82-95

Tokutaro
Littledale — *Strange* p.13-21

TOLERANCE
Ugly-ugly! Frizzled-heads, frizzled
heads

Tolkein, J.R.R.
Cat
The hoard

Tolstoy, Aleksei
The turnip

Tolstoy, Leo
The three hermits

Tom Quick, the Indian slayer
Life — *Treasury* p.88-90

Tom, the piper's son
Baum — *Mother* p.199-204

"TOM THUMB"
Tom Thumb (subject)
Opie — *Classic* p.30-32

"TOM THUMB" *(continued)*
The history of Tom Thumb
Little people

Tom Thumb
Carle — *Eric* p.49-58
Perrault — *Fairy* p.50-60

Tom Tit Tot
Little people

Tommelise
See also "Thumbelina"
Opie — *Classic* p.220-229

Tommy
Corrigan — *Holiday* p.84

TOMORROW. *See* **Future**

TOMTES
The trolls and the youngest Tomte

TONGAN GROUP (Islands)
- *Ha'apai*
The origin of Kava
The origin of the Magellan
clouds
Tokelau moetonga
Tu'i Tofua
- *Tongatapu*
The consequence
Lepuha and the widow of
Utumualama
Louse and flea go fishing
Samaon gift, Tongan payment

Tonga's lament for his daughter
Alpers — *Legends* p.197

The tongue-cut sparrow
Fairy Tales p.89-91

Tony and his harp
Leach — *Whistle* p.71-72

TOOTEGA (Eskimo little people)
Little people

TOOTHPICKS
Hiroko

Topelius, Zacharias
Fisherman's dream
Lisalill
Little Lapp
The saga of two trees

Why the bear sleeps all winter
The woodpecker

TOPS
The toys

TORRES STRAIT
- *Badu* (Mulgrave Island)
Beug and the sarap
Bia
Biu
The dogai of Zurat
Dokere
The four beautiful daughters
Greedy Goba
Iawar
Kuaka
Mutuk
Norinori
Pitai
Sesere
Tubu and the seven sisters
Wad and Zigin
Waii and Sobai
Wawa
- *Boigu* (Talbot Island)
Ausi and Dubua
Babaia and Sagewa
Boigu
Bukia
Damak and Daram
Darak and Göidan
The discovery of the garden
land of Padrin
Doigu Metakurab
Dugama, maker of dugong
magic
Ganalai Dogai
Garuge
Geinau and Jeiai
Kererum
Kiba
- *Map*
Lawrie — *Myths* p.206
Mau and Matang
Maui and Usuru
Möibu and Bazi
Podepode and Ngukurpode-
pode
Waireg
Wawa
- *Dauan*
Gabai
Kabai
The Kiwai raiders

Kogia
Kusa Kap
- *Map*
    Lawrie — *Myths* p.126
Taikoko
- *Dauar and Waier*
- *Map*
    Lawrie — *Myths* p.294
-*Erub* (Darnley Island)
  Aib
  Didipapa and Gorarasiasi
  Imerman and Kikmermer
  Maizab Kaur
- *Map*
    Lawrie — *Myths* p.282
  Rebes and Id
- *Gialag* (Friday Island)
  Dugama
  Dupul and Mumag
- *Iama* (Turtlebacked Island or
  Yam Island)
  Kawai
  Maida
- *Map*
    Lawrie — *Myths* p.250
  Mokan
  Sigai
  Uzu, the white dogai
- *Mabuiag* (Jervis Island)
  Amipuru
  Crocodile play
  Deibui and Teikui
  Dogai I
  Gi of Dabangai
  Gigi
  How fire was brought to Torres
    Strait
  Kama
  Kamutnab
  Maiwasa
- *Map*
    Lawrie — *Myths* p.82
  The markai of Tawapagai
  The saga of Kuiam
  Saurkeke
  Sisters who quarreled
  Tawaka, the greedy man
  Ug
  Waiaba
  Waiat
  Wameal
- *Maps*
  See *also* under individual
    islands
  Lawrie — *Myths* p.xvi

- *Muralag, Gialag, Nurupai*
    Lawrie — *Myths* p.4
- *Nagi, Mua, Badu*
    Lawrie — *Myths* p.18
- *Masig* (York Island)
  The diamond fish
  Gaibida
  Igowa
- *Map*
    Lawrie — *Myths* p.244
  Umi Markail
- *Mer* (Murray Island)
  Adba (part I,2)
  Apinini and Sidipuar
  Bai
  Beizam
  Bila
  Deumer
  Ganomi and Palai
  Gedor of Leiwag
  Gelam
  Iruam (version 1,2,3)
- *Map*
    Lawrie — *Myths* p.294
  Kaperkaper the cannibal
  Kol
  Korseim
  Kos and Abob
  Kultut
  Malo
  Malo ra Gelar
  Markep and Sarkep
  The Muiar
  Mukeis
  Nageg and Geigi
  Nilar Makrem
  The origin of mosquitoes
  Paimi a Nawanawa
  Paslag
  Pop and Kod
  The story of Meidu
  The story of Peibri
  Tagai
  Terer
  Waiat
  Wakai and Kuskus
- *Mua* (Banks Island)
  Aukam and Tiai
  Burum
  Burumnaskai
  Goba
  Gora and the buk
  Im
  Karakarkula
  Karum

232

TORRES STRAIT *(continued)*

  Kuduluk and Kui
  Muta
  Raramai
  The seven blind brothers
  Sik
  Usius
  Wamin Ngurbum
  Yelub and his dog
- *Muralag* (Prince of Wales Island)
  Ialbuz
  Potikan and Ngiangu
  Utua Ninia
  Waubin
  Zalagi and the mari
- *Muri* (Mt. Adolphus Island)
  Aiwali of Muri
- *Nagi*
  Naga
- *Nurupai* (Horn Island)
  Waiaba
- *Sabai*
  Agburug
  Amagi
  Aukam
  Biu
  Dagmet
  Dauan
  The first man at Saibai (version A,B)
  Girbar
  How Baira got a wife
  Karbai and Pukat
  Kasakuik
  Kongasau
  Maigi
  - *Map*
    Lawrie — *Myths* p.150
  Metarawai
  Mibu and the coconut
  Nima and Poipoi
  The pet crocodile
  Roa Kabuwam
  Route taken by Nima in Binibin
  The story of Ait Kadal
  Sui
  Susui and Dengam
  Wakemab
  Wamaladi
  Warupudamaizinga
- *Ugar* (Stephens Island)
  Badi and the sabei

  The Iamar who became a rainbow
  - *Map*
    Lawrie — *Myths* p.274
  The snake of Apro
  The two spirit women of Daoma Kes
  Zub and the Iamar
  - *Waraber* (Sue Island)
  - *Map*
    Lawrie — *Myths* p.268
  Sagerwazer

The tortoise
  Dolch — *Animal* p.133-141

Tortoise and elephant
  Manning — *Tortoise* p.15-24

Tortoise and ogre
  Manning — *Tortoise* p.25-29

Tortoise and the children
  Manning — *Tortoise* p.9-14

The tortoise and the hare
  Levine — *Fables* p.88

The tortoise who flew to heaven
  Carter — *Greedy* p.46-61

The tortoise who talked too much
  De Roin — *Jataka* p.10-11

TORTOISES
  The bamboo cutter
  Dirty hands
  Elephant and tortoise
  Faster than thunder
  Full moon a-shining
  Gathering salt
  The hare and the tortoise
  The jumper
  The long wait
  The most beautiful of all
  Rabbit and tortoise and lion
  Visitor
  The wagers
  Warupudamaizinga
  Why there is death in the world
  The wonderful jug of wild-cherry wine
  Zeus and the tortoise

TOTEMS
  - *Haida and Tlingit*
    Martin — *Raven* p.64-65

TOWERS
The island of the Nine Whirlpools
The lady of the tower
The last adventure of Thyl Ulen-
spiegel
Merlin the enchanter
Rapunzel
The spectre of the tower

TOWN HALLS
The Schilda town hall
The stove and the town hall

The town mouse and the country
mouse
Darrell — *Once* p.238
Shaw — *Mouse* p.19-20

TOYS AND TOY SHOPS
See also **Dolls**
Rocking-horse land

The toys
Bomans — *Wily* p.85-92

**TRADERS AND TRADING (bargaining,
swapping)**
George Piney-Woods peddler
Hudden and Dudden and Donald
O'Neary
Luck for fools
Lucky Hans
Mr. and Mrs. Vinegar
Red fox and the walking stick
Simple John
The swapper
This for that
Tom Thumb

TRADES
Hans in luck
The seven Simons (and variants)

The tragedy of Potts' Hill
Life — *Treasury* p.123-136

The tragic tale of Fenwick Hall
Jagendorf — *Folk, South* p.207-210

The tragic tale of Hooty the owl
Shaw — *Owl* p.19-22

The trail of the white cat
Life — *Treasury* p.258-259

TRAINS
, Ghost

Eerie iron horse of the Arizona
desert
The phantom train of Marshall
Pass
- *Lights*
Joe Baldwin's light
- *Wrecks*
Casey Jones

TRAITORS
See also **Betrayal**
Dan McGirth and his Gray Goose
mare

TRAMPS
A little piece of thread
Nail broth (and variants)
The old woman and the tramp

TRANSCENDANT PIG (Chinese giant)
Big people

TRANSFORMATIONS
See also **Disguises; Impersona-
tions;** names of animals and
birds
The antelope boy of Shongopovi
Ayoga
The beautiful birch
Blodeuwed the betrayer
The castle of the active door
The cat and Aphrodite
De witch woman
The frog prince
Joe Hamelin and the "Loup-Garou"
The King's choice
Kuaka
The Lady Dragonisse
The legend of the hummingbird
The magic egg
The magpie with salt on her tail
The man who became a lizard
Nima and Poipoi
Route taken by Nima in Binibin
The story of Ait Kadal
The story of Caliph Stork
The swan children of Lir
Taliessin of the radiant brow
Tinykin's transformations
The Tsar and the angel
Tubu and the seven sisters
The twelve wild ducks
Unerbek

TRANSYLVANIA. *See* **Rumania —
Transylvania**

The trap
  Schwartz — *Whoppers* p.54-55

TRAPPERS AND TRAPPING
  The coyote and Juan's maguey
  The tortoise

TRAVELERS
  The Arkansas traveler
  A bed for the night
  The great traveler of Chelm
  King Solomon's ring
  Lincolnshire moon
  The listeners
  The mysterious traveller
  The North wind and the sun
  Peter Rugg
  The three travelers
  The two journeymen

The travelers and the bear
  Levine — *Fables* p.38
  Rugoff — *Harvest* p.417-418

The travelers and the crow
  Levine — *Fables* p.98

The travel(l)er's shoes
  Housmen — *Rat* p.33-56

The traveling frog
  Carey — *Baba* p.33-38

The travels of a fox
  Great Children's p.16-26

The treacherous brothers
  Curtin — *Myths* p.370-405

**TREACHERY. See Betrayal; Deception;
  Traitors; Trickery**

TREASURE
  See also **Gold; Jewels; Silver;** etc.
  Abdallah the ungrateful
  Abdul Kasim the rich
  The basilisk
  Blackbeard's treasure
  The blind man, the deaf man, and
    the donkey
  The cloak of friendship
  Coronado and the Indian guide
  The dragon's egg
  The fox and the dragon
  The ghost the whole town knew
  The giant of the Fens
  The haunted palace

  The Indians' secret
  Lafitte's great treasure
  The leprechaun of Carriaghroid
  The little red hairy man
  The monster in the mill
  The pedlar of Swaffham
  The robbers and the treasure
  The salesman who sold his dream
  The sea maiden
  The six who went together through
    the world
  The tailor and the treasure
  The tired ghost
  The wife's one wish
  , *Guardians of. See* **Dragons**
  , *Pirates'*
      Black Sam and the haunted
        treasure
  - *Thirteen, of England*
      Merlin the enchanter

The treasure
  Hautzig — *Case* p.3-7

The treasure of Li-Po
  Junne — *Floating* p.17-31

The treasure of Nosara
  Carter — *Enchanted* p.31-36

The treasures of Rhampsinitus
  Rugoff — *Harvest* p.215-219

The tree
  Krylov — *Fables* p.85-86

TREES
  See also names of trees
  The fairy tree
  The Judas tree
  The man, the white steed, and the
    wondrous wood
  Pop and Kod
  The ring around the tree
  The wondrous story of Ivan Golik
    and the serpents
  , *as houses*
      Kererum
  - *Blossoms*
      The old man who made the
        trees blossom
  - *Branches*
      Hyena and hare
      , *Gold*
          The enchanted prince

- *Carvings*
  The cloud tree
, *Chopping of*
  The forest bride
, *Evergreen*
  The fir tree
  The fir tree and the bramble
    bush
  Why evergreens keep their
    leaves
, *Fruit*
  The stepchild and the fruit
    trees
- *Ghosts*
  The tragic tale of Fenwick
    Hall
, *Hollow*
  The wily wizard and the witch
    in the hollow tree
, *Nut*
  The chestnut tree
- *Orchards, Enchanted*
  The enchanted orchard
- *Persea*
  Bata
- *Sprites*
  Leave well enough alone

TREWHELLA, MATHEY
People of the sea

**TRIBES. See Africa — Tribes; Indians
of North America — Tribes**

The trick on the trek
  Aardema — *Behind* p.11-18

TRICKERY
See also **Betrayal; Deception**
Trickery (subject)
  Higonnet-Schnopper — *Tales*
    p.13-90
The adventures of Renard
Ashes for sale
The ass carying salt
The baker's son and the king's
  daughter
The bamboo cutter
The barred bung
The bear's revenge
The best laugh is the last laugh
Boastful Aulus and the sly thief
Brer Rabbit's trickery
Coyote conquers the Iya
Coyote loses his dinner
Coyote rescues the ring-girl

Coyote steals the summer
Crafty Yasohachi and the flea
  medicine
Crafty Yasohachi climbs to heaven
The crusty old badger
The deceived blind men
Donkey and scholars
Don't try the same trick twice
Elephant wants to be king
The Emperor's new clothes
(El) Enano
The field of bloiauns
The fox and the cat
The fox and the rolling pin
The fox and the stork
The gnome and the dragons
Gudgekin, the thistle girl
The haunted mill
The Helm goat mystery
Horse trading in Wichita Falls
How far is it to Jacob Cooper's?
I ate the loaf
The invisible cloth
Lesson for lesson
Little Mastery Misery
Little Red Ridinghood (and
  variants)
The magic pot
Malice, Bouki and Momplaisir
Man-crow
The man who tricked Sultan Otakul
Manabozho, the trickster
Maraboe and Morsegat
Maui and Tuna
Maui-of-a-thousand-tricks
Mr. Rabbit and Mr. Bear
The old lion and the fox
One trick too many
The peasant, the bear, and the fox
Pedro the trickster
Raw monkey liver
The red fox and the walking stick
The sad-tale of the half-shaven
  head
Samoan gift, Tongan payment
The seven blind brothers
The shepherd who could not lie
The shepherd who liked practical
  jokes
The sly fox
The smart rabbit
Snipe hunters
The sorcerer of the White Lotus
  Lodge
The story of the three little pigs

TRICKERY *(continued)*
>The tall tales
>The terrapin and the possum out-
>   wit the fox
>The tiger story
>Tubu and the seven sisters
>The two journeymen
>Why the bear has a stumpy tail
>Why the bear is stumpy-tailed
>Why the bear's tail is so short
>The wife who talked too much

Trickery
>De Roin — *Jataka* p.54-55

The tricks of Hunahpú and Ixbalanqué
>Carter — *Enchanted* p.62-69

Trishka's coat
>Krylov — *Fables* p.122-123

TRISTRAM, SIR
>Sir Tristram in Ireland

Tritii, Litii, and the birds
>Manning — *Ogres* p.20-31

TRITONS
>People of the sea

The troll ride
>Olenius — *Great* p.78-86

TROLLS
>Big people
>Billy Goat Gruff
>The boy and the trolls, or The
>   adventure
>The boy who was never afraid
>The Christmas bear
>Cow Bu-cola
>Dag and Daga, and the flying troll
>   of Sky Mountain
>East of the sun and West of the
>   moon
>The flower of happiness on Sun-
>   nymount Crest
>The four big trolls and Little
>   Peter Pastureman
>The gold knob
>Jon and the troll's wife
>Little people
>The magician's cloak
>Nils in the forest
>The old troll of Big Mountain
>The ring

>Sigurd the king's son
>The three billy goats gruff
>The three sisters who were en-
>   trapped into a mountain
>Tritil, Litil, and the birds
>When Mother Troll took in the
>   king's washing
>, *Mountain*
>   Little Lapp
>, *Sea*
>   Fisherman's dream

The trolls and the youngest Tomte
>Olenius — *Great* p.87-98

The troll's little daughter
>Manning — *Ogres* p.110-122

TROUBADOURS. *See* **Minstrels**

TROUBLE
>The convent free from care
>What is trouble

TROWS (sea people)
>The woman from the sea

TRUANCY
>Kind little Edmund, or the caves
>   and the cockatrice

The true enchanted
>Alexander — *Foundling* p.31-44

True or false
>Ginsburg — *How* p.15-17

True tears
>Heady — *Safiri* p.46-50

The trumpeter of Fyvie Castle
>Wyness — *Legends* p.50-54

TRUNKS
>, *Magic*
>   The flying trunk

Trust not a new friend
>Jagendorf — *Folk, South* p.239-241

TRUTH
>*See also* **Honesty**
>Abdul Kasim the rich
>The graveyard rose
>Holding the truth
>How the true facts started in
>   Simpsonville
>The weaver of tomorrow

TRYSTAN. *See* **Tristram, Sir**

The Tsar and the angel
Bain — *Cossack* p.173-180

TSARS. *See* **Tzars**

TSHINDAO TALES
Saso and Gogwana the witch
Tshinyama heavenly maidens

Tshinyama heavenly maidens
Aardema — *Behind* p.19-25

Ttimba
Serwadda — *Songs* p.61-69

TUAMOTU (ISLANDS)
Ataraga at the pool
The conflict of the gods
Maui and Tuna
Tiki the first man

TUATHA DE DANAAN. *See* **Dana, People of**

Tubu and the seven sisters
Lawrie — *Myths* p.63-65

Tu'i Tofua
Alpers — *Legends* p.281-284

Tuke, George
The eagle

"TUMBLERS" (entertainers)
Our Lady's tumbler

TUNA
Maui and Tuna

TUNNELS
The ghost of Captain Flint

Turandot
Fehse — *Thousand* p.115-154

TURKEY
See also **Turks**
Chapkin the scamp
The costly feast
The Hodja and the burglar
The Hodja and the caldron
The Hodja visits Halil
The lady and the unjust judge
The man who tricked Sultan Otakul
Nast-ed-Din Hodja in the pulpit
What happened to Hadji

The wisdom of the Lord
- *Folk tales (subject)*
Rugoff — *Harvest* p.134, 165-178

TURKEYS
Give my love to Boston
The right drumstick

TURKISTAN
The poorest man in the world

TURKS
The flying trunk

The turnip
Haviland — *Fairy* p.44-47
Morel — *Fairy* p.114-115

TURNIPS
The peasant and the bear
The psaltery that played by itself
The stolen turnips, the magic tablecloth, the sneezing goat and the wooden whistle

Turtle, fowl and pig
Alpers — *Legends* p.78-79

TURTLES
See also **Tortoises**
Anansi and turtle and pigeon
The fisherman and the Sea King's daughter
Greedy Goba
In the beginning there was no earth . . .
Karakarkula
Little head, big medicine
The little turtle
Maida
The place of the beginning
Raw monkey liver
The talking turtle
Waiat
Wakai and Kuskus
Warupudamaizinga
Wawa
- *Hunting*
Dokere
The four beautiful daughters
Wad and Zigin

Turtles of gold and bitter regrets
Duong — *Beyond* p.50-62

Tusi and the great beast
  Aardema — *Behind* p.57-65

TUTORS. See Teachers

Twain, Mark. *See* Clemens, Samuel

The twelve brothers
  Minard — *Womenfolk* p.36-43

THE TWELVE DANCING PRINCESSES
  The twelve dancing princesses
    (subject)
  Opie — *Classic* p.188
  Opie — *Classic* p.190-194
  Sekorová — *Europe* p.54-67

The twelve huntsmen
  Segal — *Juniper (I)* p.63-70

The twelve months
  Sekorová — *Europe* p.87-93

The twelve wild ducks
  Sheehan — *Folk* p.14-21

Twenty froggies
  Shaw — *Frog* p.40-41

Tweriire
  Serwadda — *Songs* p.21-25

The twin hunchbacks
  Orczy — *Old* p.33-37

The twin sisters
  Sperry — *Scand.* p.123-132

TWINS
  Brewery of eggshells
  Burum
  The eitu who went as a man's
    wife
  Evil-minded and good-minded
  The legend of the betel
  The monkey musicians
  Prince Bajaja
  Romolus and Remus, sons of the
    wolf
  Sorcerer Kaldoon
  Woowooto
  Xibalba

The twins' journey to the sun
  Life — *Treasury* p.75-77

Two casks
  Krylov — *Fables* p.144-145

Two cats of Kilkenny
  Shaw — *Cat* p.40

The two chickens or the two ears
  De Bosschere — *Christmas* p.100-102

The two enemies
  Levine — *Fables* p.40

Two foolish friends
  Junne — *Floating* p.125-126

Two foxes
  Jagendorf — *Folk, South* p.306-308

Two frogs
  Ginsburg — *Lazies* p.26-27
  Morel — *Fairy* p.17

The two journeymen
  Segal — *Juniper (II)* p.278-297

Two little owls
  Shaw — *Owl* p.34

Two love songs
  Alpers — *Legends* p.191-192

Two peasants
  Krylov — *Fables* p.92-93

The two princes
  Bain — *Cossack* p.211-216

The two roosters and the eagle
  Levine — *Fables* p.82

The two sacks
  Levine — *Fables* p.98

The two spirit women of Daoma Kes
  Lawrie — *Myths* p.278-279

The two statues of Kannon
  Bang — *Men* p.61-65

Two tales of leprechauns
  McGarry — *Great* p.29

Two terrible fish
  Carpenter — *People* p.98-103

The two wizards
  Manning — *Choice* p.276-279

Tyll proves to fools how great is their
    folly
  Rugoff — *Harvest* p.377-379

Tyll Ulenspiegel; the tale of a merry
dance
Rugoff — *Harvest* p.375-381

Tyll's last prank
Rugoff — *Harvest* p.380-381

TYROL. *See* **Austria — Tyrol**

"TZAR OF THE SEA"
Saako

TZARS
Beetle
The firebird
The firebird, the horse of power
and the Princess Vasilissa
The fool of the world and the
flying ship
The golden cock
The golden cockerel
A red, ripe apple, a golden saucer
The shared reward
The story of the little Tsar Novish-
ny, the false sister and the
faithful beasts
The story of unlucky Daniel
The tale of the saucer and the
transparent apple
The vampire and St. Michael

U

U.F.O.'s
The horror of the heights

Ubir
Manning — *Monsters* p.9-16

Uchida, Yoshiko
The magic listening cap
New Year's hats for the statues
The rice cake that rolled away

UDMART TALES
The beautiful birch

Ug
Lawrie — *Myths* p.104-107

UGANDA. *See* **Africa — Uganda**

UGLINESS
The sunshade
The time of the ugly

The ugly duck
Gardner — *Dr.* p.57-73

The ugly duckling
Haviland — *Fairy* p.180-191
Morel — *Fairy* p.34-36
Piper — *Stories* n. pag.

Ugly-ugly! Frizzled-heads, frizzled
heads!
Alpers — *Legends* p.345-347

UKTENS (snakes)
The hunter, the Ukten, and thunder

Uletka and the white wizard
Orczy — *Old* p.11-23

ULYSSES. *See* **Odysseus**

UMBRELLAS
The princess with freckles
The time lightning struck little
Ida's umbrella
, *Magic*
The sunshade

Umeasiegbu, Rems Nna
Breaking a kola nut
Burial of a titled man

Umi Markail
Lawrie — *Myths* p.248

Unanana and the elephant
Minard — *Womenfolk* p.127-134

Uncle Davy Lane loses his underwear
Schwartz — *Whoppers* p.60-61

Uncle James, or the Purple stranger
Bland — *Complete* p.23-45

"UNCLE REMUS STORIES"
The doodang
Fables of animals and friends
Old Sis Goose

UNCLES
Bukia
The vampire and St. Michael

UNDERGROUND. *See* **Underworld**

The underground palace. *See* Aladdin

The underground treasure chamber.
See Abdul Kasim the rich

UNDERSEAS
Sea magic
Souls under the sea

UNDERWORLD
See also **Hell**
Escape from the Underworld
Island of the dead
The killing of Eetoi
Xibalba

Unerbek
Ginsburg — How p.103-113

The ungrateful children and the old
father who went to school again
Bain — Cossack p.219-225

UNGRATEFULNESS. See Ingratitude

UNHAPPINESS. See Grief; Sadness

UNICORNS
Simon and the unicorn

**UNION OF SOUTH AFRICA. See
Africa — South**

**UNION OF SOVIET SOCIALIST
REPUBLICS. See Russia**

UNITED STATES
See also **America; Eskimos; In-
dians of North America; Blacks;
Tall Tales;** names of states and
areas
The "Foolish people"
John in the storeroom
Kibbe's shirt
Little head, big medicine
Noodlehead luck
Sam'l Dany, noodlehead
The yellow ribbon
- History
- Revolution
Ah-dunno Ben
Fearless Nancy Hart
Hoozah for fearless ladies
and fearless deeds
The revolution of the
Ladies of Edenton
The tale of Rebecca
Motte
- Heroines
They called her a
witch

- Spies
Emily's famous meal
- Civil War
The daring of yellow doc
Fearless Emma
The lady in black of
Boston harbor
The proud tale of David
Dodd
Trust not a new friend
- Captains
Dixie, the knight of
the silver spurs
- Confederacy
The army of the dead
- Drummer boys
The brave drummer
boys
, Post
The sad state of the
half-shaven head
- Spies
The merry tale of
Belle Boyd
- "Twenty-first"
The living colors of
the Twenty-first
- World War I
The singing tree
- World War II
Murgatroyd, the kluge
maker

UNKINDNESS. See Meanness

The unlucky fisherman
Martin — Raven p.27-35

UNRELIABILITY
The dragon's egg
The griffin and the wise old owl

**UNSELFISHNESS. See Generosity;
Kindness**

The untamed shrew
Rugoff — Harvest p.516-520

UNTIDINESS. See Carelessness

UNTRUTH. See Falsehood; Tall Tales

The unwelcome cat
Shaw — Cat p.34

Updike, John
April
October

URISKA
Halfway people

URUGUAY
The hungry old witch

The useless wagoner
Curtin — *Myths* p.424-433

Usheen in the Island of Youth
Higginson — *Tales* p.25-31

Using your head
De Roin — *Jataka* p.27-28

Usius
Lawrie — *Myths* p.43-44

UTAH
The sky is a bowl of ice

UTENSILS. See Pots and Pans

Uttley, Alison
The spice woman's basket

Utua Ninia
Lawrie — *Myths* p.11-12

UYGUR TALES
The ox and the ass

Uzu, the white dogai
Lawrie — *Myths* p.257-258

V

VAGABONDS
Xibalba

VAGABONES. See Minstrels

VALENTINE DAY
Valentine Day (subject)
Corrigan — *Holiday* p.40-54
Answer to a child's question
Goldenhair
Good Bishop Valentine
The spice woman's basket

The valiant chattee-maker
Haviland — *Favorite India* p.5-20

The valiant little tailor
Rugoff — *Harvest* p.350-357

VALLEYS
The King of the Golden River

The vampire and St. Michael
Bain — *Cossack* p.83-91

VAMPIRES
Halfway people
Sir Buzz

The vampires of Tempassuk
Hoke — *Monsters* p.101-109

VANITY
The Emperor's new clothes

Vasilisa and Prince Vladimir
Higonnet-Schnopper — *Tales* p.141-160

Vasilisa the beautiful
Whitney — *In* p.45-57

VASILIU, MIRCEA
Mircea Vasiliu (subject)
Sheehan — *Folk* p.152

Vassilissa golden tress, bareheaded beauty
Curtin — *Myths* p.124-136

Vassilissa the cunning, and the Tsar of the sea
Curtin — *Myths* p.249-270

VEILS
The Queen

Veirs, Frances
The witches' birthday party

VENGEANCE. See Revenge

VENUS
Cupid and Psyche

VERMONT
Afternoon by a pond in the heart of Vermont
- *Rutland*
Frozen people

A very great curiosity
Greene — *Clever* p.124

Vesper
Cott — *Beyond* p.426-427

VETERAN'S DAY
    Veteran's Day (subject)
        Corrigan — *Holiday* p.196-201
    The singing tree

VIETNAM
    Crystal love
    Diem and Siem
    Hung Vuong and the betel
    Hung Vuong and the earth and
      sky cakes
    The Lady of Nam Xuong
    The legend of the betel
    Lizards and promises and Vue
      Cong Due
    Monsoon
    The sister queens
    A strange and rare friendship
    The tiger story
    Turtles of gold and bitter regrets
    - *Customs and rituals* (subject)
        Duong — *Beyond* p.92-96
    - *History* (subject)
        Duong — *Beyond* p.91
        La Long Quan and Au Co
    - *Map* (subject)
        Duong — *Beyond* p.90
    - *Origin*
        Lac Long Quan and Au Co
    - *Warriors*
      - *Women*
        The sister queens

VIKINGS
    Harald the Viking

The Vikings and their traces
    Life — *Treasury* p.16-21

VILLAINS. See Rascals

VINEGAR
    Mr. and Mrs. Vinegar

VINES
    The doe and the vine
    The legend of the betel
    , *Pea*
        Five peas in a pod

VIOLINISTS AND VIOLINS
    The cat and the fiddle
    Dicey and Orpus
    The fiddlers of Tomnafurach
    Fiddler's rock
    Macpherson's lament

    Old King Cole
    The rose and the violinist
    - *Origin*
        The magic box

VIRGIN, HOLY. See Mary, Virgin

VIRGINIA
    All on a summer's day
    The black ghost dog
    Dance of the ghosts
    Grace Sherwood, the woman
      none could scare
    Hercules of Virginia
    The merry tale of Belle Boyd
    Thanks to Patrick Henry
    Two foxes
    - *Governors*
        Ghost of the governor's man-
        sion
    - *Portsmouth*
      - *Dismal Swamp*
        The lovers of Dismal
        Swamp

Virginia's ghostly aristocrat
    Anderson — *Haunting* p.49-56

VIRTUES
    King Solomon and the Queen of
      Sheba

VISIONS
    Saint Cuthbert's peace

A visit to Orokolo
    McDowell — *Third* p.137-146

Visit to the village
    McDowell — *Third* p.17-22

Visitor
    Heady — *Safiri* p.22-26

Visitor's song
    Alpers — *Legends* p.357-361

The vixen and her cub
    Ginsburg — *One* p.39

VIXENS. See Foxes

VODYANOI
    The people of the sea

VOICES
    The crow and the fox

The first woman
The strong voice
The visitor

The voices at the window
Bain — *Cossack* p.49-53

Voices in the night
Raskin — *Ghosts* p.80–88

VOLCANOES
- *Goddesses*
  Ghostly goddess of the volcano
- *Hawaii*
  The eruption of Pele's anger

VOLGA RIVER. See **Russia — Volga River**

Volkmann-Leander
The wishing-ring

"VOODOOS"
Marie Laveau, queen of the voodoos

The voyage of St. Brandan
Higginson — *Tales* p.108-124

VULTURES
Brother sun and sister moon

W

Wad and Zigin
Lawrie — *Myths* p.53-54

WADDELL, L.A., MAJOR
Big people

WAGERS (BETS)
Compae Rabbit's ride
Harsh words
If you don't like it, don't listen
John Travail and the devil
The making of the hammer
The miser who received his due
The sea gulls

The wagers
Carter — *Enchanted* p.83-86

WAGONS
See also **Carts**

- *Drivers*
  The obedient servant

WAGTAILS (birds)
Animals from heaven

WAHL, JAN
Jan Wahl (subject)
Wahl — *Muffletump* p.127

Wahlenberg, Anna
The barrel bung
The cane with a will of its own
His very best friend
The King's choice
Linda-Gold and the old king
The little boy who wanted pancakes
The magical spectacles
The magician's cape
The magician's cloak
The magpie with salt on her tail
The old troll of Big Mountain
Peter and the Witch of the wood
The princess with unruly thoughts
The queen
The rooster who couldn't crow
Song for a princess
The strong voice
The troll ride
The twin sisters

Waiaba
Lawrie — *Myths* p.15,121-122

Waiat
Lawrie — *Myths* p.115-117,344

WAIFS
The story of Tommy Tucker

Waii and Sobai
Lawrie — *Myths* p.76-77

Waireg
Lawrie — *Myths* p.216-217

Wakai and Kuskus
Lawrie — *Myths* p.346-348

Wakaima and the clay man
Haviland — *Fairy* p.104-109

Wakemab
Lawrie — *Myths* p.166-170

WALES
See also **WELSH(MEN)**
Blodeuwed the betrayer
The buried moon
Cledog and the "Ceffyl-dwr"
The dead hand
Dewi and the devil
Faery folk
The foundling
The garden of magic
Hag-of-the-mist
Jack and the wizard
Lludd and Llevelys
Madoc
The man who sold the winds
Moon snow
Saint Keneth of the gulls
Three bits of advice
The three butterflies
The rascal crow
The red dragon of Wales
The smith, the weaver, and the
    harper
The stone
The sword
Taliessin of the radiant brow
The true enchanter
- *Islands*
    Bran the blessed
    The castle of the active door
    The fish who helped Saint
        Gudwall

WALKING
Alenoushka and her brother

WALKING-STICKS
The history of Little Mook
The red fox and the walking stick

The wall and the battering ram
    Levine — *Fables* p.86

WALLACE, "BIGFOOT"
Bigfoot Wallace and the hickory
    nuts

WALLETS. *See* **Purses**

WALLS
The cuckoo of Borrowdale
Humpty Dumpty
, *Shell-shaped*
    Turtles of gold and bitter
        regrets

Wamaladi
    Lawrie — *Myths* p.180-181

Wameal
    Lawrie — *Myths* p.87

Wamin Ngurbum
    Lawrie — *Myths* p.33-34

WANDERERS. *See* **Travelers**

The wandering monk and the tabby cat
    Novák — *Fairy* p.72-80

The wanderings of Arasmon
    Cott — *Beyond* p.192-213

Wanted — a king
    Cott — *Beyond* p.215-307

The war between the rats and the
        weasels
    Levine — *Fables* p.94

War declared
    Cott — *Beyond* p.97-103

The war god's horse song — Navaho
        Indians
    Corrigan — *Holiday* p.178-179

The warlock
    Manley — *Sisters* p.73-104

The warlock of Glen Dye
    Wyness — *Legends* p.21-28

WARLOCKS
See also **Witchcraft; Wizards**
Workers of evil — and a few good
    spirits

The warrior who shot arrows at a star
    Carter — *Enchanted* p.18-23

WARRIORS
Alyosha Popovich
A boasting chant in war
Confirmation of a warrior
The firebird and Princess Vasilisa
Ganomi and Palai
Hungry-for-battle
Ivan the fool
Mau and Matang
Vasilisa and Prince Vladimir
, *Japanese*
    Yoshi-tsuni, brave warrior
        from Japan

, *Miniature*
    Hiroko
, *Sleeping*
    The wizard of Alderley Edge

WARS
    See also **United States — History,**
        subdivisions; names of wars
    A boasting chant in war
    The first war
    The freak

Warupudamaizinga
    Lawrie — *Myths* p.197-198

"WASHER," THE
    Workers of evil — and a few good
        spirits

WASHING AND WASHERWOMEN
    When Mother Troll took in the
        King's washing

WASHINGTON, GEORGE
    George Washington, the torch-
        bearer
    - *Birthday (subject)*
        Corrigan — *Holiday* p.55-64

WASHINGTON (state)
    - *Skamania county*
        The mystery of Bigfoot

Washington monument by night
    Corrigan — *Holiday* p.63-64

WASPS
    The blacksmith's tale
    The salesman who sold his dream

Watch
    Corrigan — *Holiday* p.245

WATCHES
    Tick, tick, tick

WATER
    The brown bear of the green glen
    Coyote drowns the world
    The crow and the pitcher
    The half-chick
    Holding the truth
    How fire took water to wife
    How the sneaky waterstealer set
        the cattlemen and the sheep-
        men against each other

In the beginning there was no
    earth
The rabbit and the honey-gum
    slide
Raven lets out the daylight
This for that
, *as cure*
    The Well of D'yererr-in-Dowan
, *Holy*
    Aib
    Mary Culhane and the dead
        man
- *Reflection. See* **Mirrors**
- *Waves*
    Why the waves have whitecaps

WATER BUFFALOS
    The tiger story

The water-bull
    Littledale — *Strange* p.23-29

WATER-CARRIERS
    Retribution

WATER DEMONS. See Demons, Water

The water festival
    Junne — *Floating* p.119-120

WATER-HORSES. See Horses, Water

WATER-LILIES
    Uletka and the white lizard

The water monster
    Hoke — *Monsters* p.120-131

The water-nixie
    Rockwell — *Three* p.53-55

WATER OF WISDOM
    The lost half-hour

"WATER OF LIFE"
    Mons Tro

Water of youth, water of life, and water
    of death
    Curtin — *Myths* p.72-81

WATER OGRES. See Ogres, Water

WATER SPIDERS
    How fire came to the earth

WATER SPIRITS (Sprites)
    See also **Kapas**
    Introduction *(Impossible people)*

WATERCRESS
The sporran full of gold

WATERHOLES
Iruam
The saga of Kuiam

WATERING
The monkey gardeners

WATERMELONS
The horse-egg

WATERSPOUTS
Im
Sik

Watho
Cott — *Beyond* p.425

Watho's wolf
Cott — *Beyond* p.453-456

Waubin
Lawrie — *Myths* p.6-8

Wavvuuvuumira
Serwadda — *Songs* p.17-19

Wawa
Lawrie — *Myths* p.70-72,225-227

Way deep down in the Okefenokee
swamps
Jagendorf — *Folk, South* p.79-81

The ways of the Lord
Jagendorf — *Folk, South* p.190-192

WEALTH
See also **Treasure;** etc.
Abdul Kasim the rich
Boastful Aulus and the sly thief
Catch-the-wind
The deliverers of their country
Dick Whittington
Little Master Misery
The rat-catcher's daughter
The rich Athenian in distress
The rich man and the hired
mourners
The rich señora
The rich woman and the poor
woman
The ruined man who became rich
again through a dream
The seven good years
The shoemaker and the elves

Simeli Hill
The stolen heart
The stone-cold heart
The tale of the huntsman
Tantalus
The three wise men
The wishing-ring

WEASELS
The war between the rats and
the weasels

WEATHER
See also names of seasons; types
of weather
High winds and funny weather

The weather
Schwartz — *Whoppers* p.87-102

WEATHERCOCKS
The foolish weathercock

The weaver of tomorrow
Yolen — *Girl* p.23-34

WEAVERS AND WEAVING
The Emperor's new clothes
Khavroshechka
Mataora and Niwareka
Raramai
The smith, the weaver, the harper
Vasilisa the beautiful
The white crane

WEDDINGS
Fairy web for Mr. Durand's
daughters
The fox's wedding
Gossamer wedding
The marriage tale
Not on the Lord's Day
Patient Griselda
The taming of the shrew
, *Ghost*
The ghost wedding in
Everhope
Invitation to a ghost
- *Processions*
The badger and the fox

WEE FOLK. *See* names of various types

WEEDS
Why dog lost his voice

- "*Teosinte*"
The beginning of maize

The well of D'yerree-in-Dowan
McGarry — *Great* p.52-62

The Wellfleet witch
Shaw — *Witch* p.152-156

Wells, H.G.
In the Avu observatory
The inexperienced ghost

WELLS
The bees in the well
Country-under-wave
Damak and Daram
Echo well
The foam maiden
The fox and the goat
The frog prince
The king of Colchester's daughters
The noodlehead tiger
Scissors they were
The son of the king of the city
of straw
The three heads of the well
The water-nixie
The wolf and the seven little kids

WELLS FARGO
- *Stagecoach robberies*
Black Bart, bandit and "Po8"

WELSH(MEN)
- *Language*
- *Pronunciation of names*
Pugh — *More* p.123-124

WENLOCK EDGE
Big people

WENS
The old man's wen

WERBURGH, SAINT
Saint Werburgh and her goose

WEREBEASTS
See also **Werewolves**
Halfway people

The werewolf
Cott — *Beyond* p.460-461
Littledale — *Strange* p.51-55

WEREWOLVES
Halfway people
Joe Hamelin and the "Loup-Garou"

WEST
Bigfoot Wallace and the hickory
nuts
Black Bart, bandit and "Po8"
Calamity Jane, the loud canary
The death of Billy the Kid
Gretchen and the white stallion
The hole in the back wall
How ailments were put in their
proper place
How Bart Winslow single handed
wiped out the Jimson gang,
which was known as the
scourge of the West
How Kate Shelley saved the express
How Matt Carney retired and
raised chickens
How the ranchers of Windy
Canyon built the biggest fence
the West has ever seen
How the sheriff's posse and the
hold-up men sat down to dinner
together
How the sneaky waterstealer set
the cattlemen and the sheep-
men against each other
How the true facts started in
Simpsonville
The Indians' secret
Jesse James and the widow
Julia Bulette of Virginia City
The McCanles fight as Hickok
told it
The miracle of the mail
The ordeal of Hugh Glass
The phantom train of Marshall Pass
Roy Bean, necktie justice
Sam Bass, Texas Robin Hood
Skeleton Cliff of Montana
Sweet Betsy
Wise, wise burros
- *Folklore* (subject)
Life — *Treasury* p.186-235

WEST AFRICA. See Africa, West

WEST INDIES
Anansi and turtle and pigeon
The barracuda
Boy Blue and crab-catcher
Living in the forest

WEST INDIES *(continued)*
   Madam Crab loses her head
   Makonaima returns
   - *Cuba*
      How El Bizarrón fooled the
         devil
      The miser who received his
         due
      Rabbit's long ears
   - *Jamaica*
      Brother Arrancy fools brother
         Fire
      From tiger to Anansi
      Gar-room!
      Man-crow
      Snake the postman
      Wheeler

WEST VIRGINIA
   John Henry and the machine in
      West Virginia
   The wizard's revenge

WESTERN ISLANDS. *See* **Hebrides,
   Scottish**

"WESTOVER" (Byrd home)
   Virginia's ghostly aristocrat

Wette, Adelheid
   Witch's song from Hansel & Gretel

WEYER, JOHAN
   Workers of evil — and a few good
      spirits

WHALES AND WHALING
   Fair, brown, and trembling
   Ichabod, Crook-Jaw and the witch
   Kae and the whale
   Mons Tro
   Mukeis
   Sven and Lilli
   Thar she blows
   The witch of Wellfleet

What came of picking flowers
   Fairy Tales p.77-83

What happened to a young man on
   his wedding day
   Rugoff — *Harvest* p.712-716

What happened to Hadji
   Rugoff — *Harvest* p.171-173

What is a witch?
   Shaw — *Witch* **p.42**

What is trouble
   Lester — *Knee* p.5-8

What Jack Horner did
   Baum — *Mother* p.99-106

What Merle found in the box
   Cott — *Beyond* p.228-232

What's the matter?
   Leach — *Whistle* p.30

WHEAT
   Brother Mike
   The little red hen

Wheeler
   Carter — *Greedy* p.84-90

When Mother Troll took in the King's
      washing
   Olenius — *Great* p.1-18

When Noodlehead marries Noodlehead
   Jagendorf — *Noodle* p.85-88

When the mouse laughs . . .
   Shaw — *Mouse* p.28

When the sky lay on the earth
   Alpers — *Legends* p.63

Where blond people came from
   Ficowski — *Sister* n. pag.

Where Joe Merriweather went to
   Schwartz — *Whoppers* p.46-48

Which was witch?
   Hopkins — *Witching* p.98-102

WHINING. *See* **Grumbling**

WHIPS AND WHIPPINGS
   , *Magic*
      The dragon and his grand-
         mother

WHIRLPOOLS
   The fiery dragon (and variants)
   The island of the Nine Whirlpools

WHIRLWINDS
   Terer
   The three kingdoms
   Wind is a ghost . . .

WHISTLES AND WHISTLING
Alone with God
The echo well
The giant who was afraid of
butterflies
The golden slippers
, *Magic*
The rabbit catcher
- *Pipes*
The stolen turnips, the magic
tablecloth, the sneezing goat
and the wooden whistle
The tale of the silver saucer
and the transparent apple

WHITCOMB, JAMES (Indiana governor)
The "spirited" librarian

The white blackbird: an Easter story
Corrigan — *Holiday* p.88-93

The white buffalo
Jagendorf — *Folk, South* p.275-
277
Life — *Treasury* p.62-63

The white crane
Novák — *Fairy* p.156-164

The white doe
Housman — *Rat* p.116-129
Jagendorf — *Folk, South* p.178-180
Life — *Treasury* p.104-105

The white fairy horse
McGarry — *Great* p.109-111

White ghosts
Leach — *Whistle* p.27

The white hen
McGarry — *Great* p.99-108

WHITE HOUSE
Abraham Lincoln, a mourning
figure, walks

White House ghosts
Leach — *Whistle* p.17-19

"WHITE LADY"
Feather o' my wing

White orchid, red mountain
Harris — *Sea Magic* p.99-116

Whitehead, Henry S.
The fireplace

Whitman, Walt
I hear America singing

WHITNEY, THOMAS P.
Thomas P. Whitney (subject)
Whitney — *On* p.131-136

Who but a tadpole?
Shaw — *Frog* p.44-45

Who can tell a bigger lie?
Bamberger — *My* p.39-41

Who is who?
Jagendorf — *Noodle* p.93-96

Who lived in the skull?
Ransome — *Old* p.164-167

Who says, who says?
Shaw — *Owl* p.10-11

Who stole the tarts?
Darrell — *Once* p.129-132

Who wants a birthday?
Corrigan — *Holiday* p.157

Who will row next?
Ginsburg — *Lazies* p.18-20

Who'll wash the porridge pot?
Higonnet-Schnopper — *Tales* p.30-
33

Who will wash the pot?
Ginsburg — *Lazies* p.8-11

Whoooo?
Shaw — *Owl* p.8-9

"WHOPPERS." See Tall Tales

Why cats always wash themselves after
eating
Shaw — *Cat* p.19-20

Why dog lost his voice
Carter — *Greedy* p.14-17

Why dogs hate cats
Lester — *Knee* p.9-11

Why evergreens keep their leaves
Morel — *Fairy* p.112-113

Why misery remains in the world
Carter — *Greedy* p.18-22

"WHY" TALES
The first tale of Alabama
The power of woman and the
strength of man
The silver snake of Louisiana

Why the baboon has a shining seat
Robinson — *Singing* p.8-15

Why the bat flies at night
Dolch — *Animal* p.7-11

Why the bear has a stumpy tale (and
variants)
Piper — *Stories* n. pag.

Why the bear is stumpy-tailed
Morel — *Fairy* p.65

Why the bear sleeps all winter
Sperry — *Scand.* p.258-259

Why the bear's tail is so short
Sperry — *Scand.* p.27-28

Why the possum's tail is bare
Bird — *Path* p.43-46

Why the sea is salt
Rugoff — *Harvest* p.672-676

Why the sea moans
Sheehan — *Folk* p.127-137

Why the sea-slug has two mouths
Alpers — *Legends* p.301

Why the spider has a small head
McDowell — *Third* p.31-34

Why the sun and moon are in the sky
McDowell — *Third* p.129-130

Why the waves have white-caps
Lester — *Knee* p.21-23

Why there is no death in the world
Robinson — *Singing* p.16-23

Why women always take advantage
of men
Rugoff — *Harvest* p.71-74

The wicked laird of Balquhain
Wyness — *Legends* p.80-84

A wicked plan. **See** Semrude the
Fair and the Cadi

The wicked Sankhashurni
Fehse — *Thousand* p.104-106

WICKEDNESS
See also **Cruelty; Evil**
The farmer and the snake
The loyal mungoose
Yukiko and the little black cat

WIDGETS
Little people

The widow and her daughters
Rugoff — *Harvest* p.267-270

Widow Fox and her four suitors
Sperry — *Scand.* p.38-43

WIDOWS
The case against the wind
The fairies
Lepuha and the widow of
Utumalama
Lu-bo-bo
The mermaid
Myself
Pentalina
The ship that sailed on sea and
land
The story of Little Boy Blue

A widow's funeral chant
Alpers — *Legends* p.198

The wife who talked too much
Spicer — *13 Rascals* p.43-53

The wife's one wish
Rugoff — *Harvest* p.554-555

WIGS
The bald knight
The little man and his little gun

The wild boar and the fox
Levine — *Fables* p.62

The wild ride in the tilt cart
Hoke — *Ghosts* p.114-122

Wilde, Lady
Edain the queen
The horned woman
The Phouka

WILDE, LADY
Lady Wilde (subject)
Manley — *Sisters* p.60-61,218

Wilde, Oscar
  The fisherman and his soul
  The happy prince

Wilder, Laura Ingalls
  Independence Day

Wilkinson, Anne
  Once upon a great holiday

WILL. *See* **Determination**

WILL-O'-THE-WISPS
  The Faery folk
  Last adventure of Thyl Ulenspiegel

WILLIAM THE LION, King of Scots
  King William's palace

Williams-Ellis, Amabel
  Baba Yaga

Willie Winkie
  Leach — *Whistle* p.89-90

WILLOW TREES
  The golden slipper
  Syre-Varda

WILLS (legal)
  The thoughtful father

Wilson, Barbara Ker
  The piper of Keil

The wily wizard, and the witch in the
  hollow-tree
  Bomans — *Wily* p.1-8

"WINCHESTER HOUSE"
  The mansion of the dead

WIND
  The case against the wind
  East of the sun and West of the
    moon
  Fearing the wind
  The foolish weathercock
  The half-chick
  High winds and funny weather
  The man who sold the winds
  Mother of the sun
  The story of the wind
  The sun and the wind
  There are such people
  Why the waves have white-caps

, *North*
  The boy and the North Wind
  East of the sun and West of
    the moon
  A necklace of raindrops
  The north wind and the sun
  Shingebiss
  Why evergreens keep their
    leaves
, *Song of*
  Taliessin of the radiant brow
, *South*
  East of the sun and West of
    the moon
, *Southwest*
  The King of the Golden River
    or The Black brothers

The wind
  Schwartz — *Whoppers* p.96

Wind is a ghost . . .
  Belting — *Whirlwind* n. pag.

The wind man
  Bomans — *Wily* p.159-163

A winding way and a crooked house
  Cott — *Beyond* p.263-266

WINDOWS
  The Schilda town hall
  The Schildbürger build a council
    house
, *Breaking of*
  Know before you criticize
, *Open*
  The open window

The wind's bride
  Roy — *Serpent* p.36-40

WINE
  Clever Grethel
  John in the storeroom
  Rabbi Eliezer enjoys an exception
, *Wild-cherry*
  Faster than thunder
  The long wait
  The wonderful jug of wild-
    cherry wine

Wine and the devil
  Rugoff — *Harvest* p.603

WINGS
 Daedalus, Icarus, and the wings
 A pair of wings
 Tshinyama heavenly maidens

The winning of Kwelanga
 Aardema — *Behind* p.34-41

WISDOM
 See also titles beginning with Wise
 The clock that walked by itself
 The foam maiden
 The foundling
 The griffin and the wise old
  philosopher
 How wise is an owl
 The joyful abbot
 The little shepherd boy
 Monsoon
 Owls aren't so smart
 The Princess and Rabbi Joshuah
 Saint Launomar's cow
 Silent Bianca
 Taliessin of the radiant brow
 The thoughtful father
 Three golden oranges
 Turandot
 - *Old age*
  Sergevan

The wisdom of the Lord
 Jagendorf — *Noodle* p.102-104

The wise man of Gotham
 Morel — *Fairy* p.16

WISE MEN
 Carol of the brown king
 The golden shoes
 Rama
 Sheidulla
 The three wise men
 Three wise men of Gotham (and
  variants)
 The wond'rous wise man

The wise men of Gotham
 Jagendorf — *Noodle* p.115-118

A wise old owl
 Shaw — *Owl* p.36

The wise rogue
 Rugoff — *Harvest* p.559-560

Wise, wise burros
 Life — *Treasury* p.209-210

The wish that came true
 Littledale — *Strange* p.111-115

WISHES
 Aniello
 The beautiful birch
 Brother Gaily
 Dewi and the devil
 The enchanted apple-tree
 The fisherman and his wife
 Gigi and the magic ring
 The golden slipper
 The great bear of Orange
 John O'Hara's lantern
 The little blacksmith Verholen
 The little golden fish
 Little Mary
 The magpie with salt on her tail
 The man and the wife in the
  vinegar jug
 My wish
 One-inch fellow
 Peter Pan in Kensington Gardens
 The ridiculous wishes
 The seven wishes
 Stan Bolovan and the dragon
 The stone-cold heart
 Ten miles at each step
 The three wishes
 The tinder box (and variants)
 Why misery remains in the world
 The wife's one wish
 The witch's wish
 The wonderful fish

The wishing-ring
 Bamberger — *My* p.19-23

The wishing skin
 Orczy — *Old* p. 83-91

Wisky, wasky, weedle
 Shaw — *Old* p.36

WIT. See Humor

Wit, wisdom and whoppers (folklore)
 Life — *Treasury* p.268-299

The witch: a tale of the Dark Ages
 Manley — *Sister* p.107-125

A witch and her servants
 Shaw — *Witch* p.126-151

WITCH DOCTORS
 Elephant wants to be king
 Nsangi

The witch in the glass
   Shaw — *Witch* p.31

The witch in the stone boat
   Shaw — *Witch* p.43-50

The witch in the wintry wood
   Hopkins — *Witching* p.71-73

The witch of Findrack
   Wyness — *Legends* p.100-105

The witch of the marsh
   Manley — *Sisters* p.47-52

The Witch of Wellfleet
   Life — *Treasury* p.102-104

The witch of Willowby Wood
   Hopkins — *Witching* p.56-58

The witch who spoke in many tongues
   Raskin — *Ghosts* p.60-68

WITCHCRAFT
   See also **Warlocks; Witch Doctors; Witches; Wizards**
   Babaia and Sagewa
   Bai
   The book
   Bukia
   The Caliph turned stork
   The coyote and Juan's maguey
   The Cyprian cat
   Dupul and Mumag
   The four beautiful daughters
   Gi of Dabangai
   The Laidly worm
   Letter from Massachusetts, 1688
   Maida
   Mutuk
   Nilas Makrem
   Roa Kabuwam
   Through the needle's eye
   Utuah Minia
   Waiat

WITCHES
   See also **Warlocks**
   Alenoushka and her brother
   Andrusz who disliked beans
   Baba Yaga
   Beware
   The black cat's eyes
   Blackberries in February
   Broad, Tall and Sharp-eyes
   Broomstick train
   Brother and sister
   The buried moon
   The castle in the silver wood
   The cat and the Captain
   The crystal ball
   The day boy and the night girl
   The dragon of the North
   Dwarf long nose
   East of the sun and West of the
      moon
   The enchanted journey
   Esben and the witch
   The firebird
   The fisherman and his soul
   The flower of happiness on Sunnymount Crest
   Foni and Fotia
   The frog
   The frog (by Leonora Alleyne)
   The giant who was afraid of
      butterflies
   The giants of Castle Treen
   The golden cockerel
   Grimelda
   The hag
   Hag-of-the-mist
   Hans and Greta
   Hansel and Gretel
   The Horned women
   How to become a witch
   The hungry old witch
   I saw three witches
   Ichabod, Crook-jaw and the witch
   The island of the Nine Whirlpools
   Ivashko and the witch
   Jack Buttermilk
   Johnny and the witch-maidens
   Jorinda and Joringel
   Kate, the bell witch
   The Lady of the Lake
   The last balloon
   Lazy Hans
   Lincolnshire moon
   The little boy who wanted pancakes
   Little Lodewyk and Annie the witch
   The lonely witch
   Longnose the dwarf
   The magic ball
   The magic spectacles
   Mannikin Spanalong
   Maraboe and Morsegat
   Marandenboni
   The midnight voyage of the Seagull
   Mrs. Gertrude
   Ol' Clackety teeth

WITCHES *(continued)*

"Old Hickory" and the Bell witch
Old spells and charms
The old witch
The old woman of the forest
Painted skin
The palace of the seven little hills
Peter and the Witch of the wood
Pot-Tilter
The princess and the three tasks
The princess with freckles
Priscilla's witches
Rapunzel
The ride-by-nights
The Salem witches and their own
    voices; Examination of Sarah
    Good
Saso and Gogwana the witch
The sea gulls
The sea maiden
The ship that sailed on sea and
    land
The sleeper
Snow-White and the seven
    dwarfs (and variants)
Sorcerer Kaldoon
Suppose you met a witch
The swan maiden
Syre-Varda
Tatterhood
This witch
Three golden oranges
The three Ivans
The three shirts of Cannach Cotton
Thumbelina
The tinder box (and variants)
The toys
The twelve wild ducks
The two statues of Kannon
The Wellfleet witch
What is a witch?
Which was witch?
The wily wizard and the witch in
    the hollow-tree
The wishing-ring
Workers of evil — and a few good
    spirits
The young witch-horse
, *Accused*
    Grace Sherwood, the woman
        none could scare
    A pot of trouble
    The Salem witches and their
        own voices: Examination

of Sarah Good
They called her a witch
Voices in the night
- *Babies*
    Prince Ivan, the witch baby
        and the little sister of the
        sun
, *Bird*
    The bird witch
, *Blue*
    Workers of evil — and a few
        good spirits
- *Definition* (subject)
    Shaw — *Witch* p.198
    What is a witch?
, *Forest*
    Amapola and the butterfly
    The boy who was never
        afraid
    The four sacred scrolls
    Leap the elk and Little
        Princess Cottongrass
    The mountain lad and the
        forest witch
- *Skins*
    De witch woman
- *Queens*
    The laidly worm of Spindle-
        stone Hugh

Witches
    Lyons — *Tales* p.49-53

The witches are flying
    Shaw — *Witch* p.177

The witches' birthday party
    Hopkins — *Witching* p.16-19

The witch's bridle
    Stuart — *Witch's* p.1-8

The witches' cellar
    De Bosschere — *Christmas* p.21-24

Witches' chant
    Hopkins — *Witching* p.128

Witches' charm
    Shaw — *Witch* p.151

The witch's daughter
    Shaw — *Witch* p.178-189

The witch's garden
    Hopkins — *Witching* p.26

A witch's song
    Shaw — *Witch* p.125

Witch's song from Hansel & Gretel
    Shaw — *Witch* p.169-176

The witch's wish
    Garden — *King* p.17-30

A witty answer
    Rugoff — *Harvest* p.652-653

Witzenspitzel
    Bamberger — *My* p.147-155

WIVES
    See also **Bigamy;** titles beginning
        with Wife
    Don't marry two wives
    Frederick and the Katelizabeth
    How Baira got a wife
    Imermen and Kikmermer
    Island of the dead
    Kamutnab
    The Lady of Nam Xuong
    Markep and Sarkep
    The pig-headed wife
    Scissors they were
    The serpent-Tsarevich and his
        two wives
    The serpent-wife
    "That's once"
    Tshinyama heavenly maidens
    The untamed shrew
    Women
    The wonderful fish

The wives' tale
    Carrick — *Wise* n. pag.

The wizard of Alderley Edge
    Colwell — *Round* p.15-18

The wizard of Long Sleddale
    Colwell — *Round* p.27-29

WIZARDS
    See also **Magicians**
    Aladdin
    Aniello
    The cockerel-stone
    The crystal ball
    Dragon, dragon
    Dwarf long nose
    The fish and the ring
    Fitcher's feathered bird

The four wizards
The golden cock
The great golloping wolf
Jack and the wizard
Jason and the dragon of Colchis
The lass who went out at the cry
    of dawn
The magic horse
Percy the wizard nicknamed Snail
The seafaring wizard
The shape-shifters of Shorm
The sorcerer and his apprentice
The sorcerer of the White Lotus
    Lodge
The three butterflies
The three riddles
The two wizards
Unerbek
The wily wizard and the witch in
    the hollow tree
Workers of evil — and a few good
    spirits
, *Weather*
    The man who sold the winds

The wizard's gillie
    MacFarlane — *Mouth* p.57-64

The wizard's revenge
    Anderson — *Haunting* p.104-111

WOJCIECHOWSKA, MAIA
    Maia Wojciechowska (subject)
        Wojciechowska — *Winter* p.67

The wolf and the cat
    Carey — *Baba* p.18-19
    Krylov — *Fables* p.101-103

The wolf and the crane
    Rugoff — *Harvest* p.415

The wolf and the fox
    Great Children's p.140-146

The wolf and the heron
    Levine — *Fables* p.70

The wolf and the lamb
    Levine — *Fables* p.72

The wolf and the old woman
    Levine — *Fables* p.92

The wolf and the seven little kids
    Haviland — *Fairy* p.16-21

The wolf and the stork
    Krylov — *Fables* p.131-132

The wolf in the kennel
    Krylov — *Fables* p.78-79

The wolf in the sack
    Jagendorf — *Noodle* p.256-259

WOLF-BOYS
    Gabriel-Ernest

The wolf-mother of Saint Ailbe
    Brown — *Book* p.190-198

The wolf's eyelashes
    Novák — *Fairy* p.174-183

WOLVERINES
    The discontented grass plant

WOLVES
    See also **Lycanthropy; Werewolves**
    Animal friendship
    Balten and the wolf
    The blind singer, Saint Hervé
    The boy who cried "Wolf"
    The cat and the she-fox
    The cat who became head-forester
    Cesarino and the dragon
    The children on the pillar
    The Chinese red riding hoods
    Coyote steals the summer
    The discontented grass plant
    Easy bread
    Farmer Broom, Farmer Leaves,
        and Farmer Iron
    Going fishing
    The great golloping wolf
    The hero
    The house dog and the wolf
    How a wolf reforms
    How the Great Turisgale met his
        death
    Ivan Tsarevich, the fire-bird, and
        the gray wolf
    The kid and the wolf
    The lion, the wolf, and the fox
    Little Lapp
    Little Red Riding Hood (and
        variants)
    The old dog
    The old man, the wolf, and the
        vixen
    Old Sultan
    Rabbit and the wolves

Red Riding Hood (and variants)
The right drumstick
Saint Bridget and the king's wolf
Saint Francis of Assisi
Sheidulla
The sparrow and the bush
The story of the three little pigs
    (and variants)
Tar-wolf tale
Widow-Fox and her four suitors
, *Iron*
        The iron wolf
- *Mothers*
        Romulus and Remus
        The wolf mother of Saint Ailbe

The wolves and the sheep
    Krylov — *Fables* p.51-52

The woman from the sea
    Stuart — *Witch's* p.29-35

The woman in the moon
    Alpers — *Legends* p.80

The woman married to a drunkard
    Levine — *Fables* p.6

The woman of the well
    Rugoff — *Harvest* p.159-164

The woman who flummoxed the fairies
    Greene — *Clever* p.13-24
    Minard — *Womenfolk* p.135-145

The woman who lived in a shoe
    Baum — *Mother* p.221-229

WOMEN
    Cap o' rushes
    The Chinese red riding hoods
    Clever Grethel
    Clever Manka
    East of the sun and West of the
        moon
    Fanta-Ghiro
    The first woman
    The forty thieves
    The husband who was to mind
        the house
    Kate Crackernuts
    The lass who went out at the cry
        of dawn
    A legend of Knockmany
    Mr. Fox
    Molly Whuppie

The old woman and her dumpling
The stolen bairn and the Sidh
The three sisters who were
    entrapped into a mountain
Three strong women
The twelve brothers
Unanana and the elephant
Why women always take advantage
    of men
, *Beautiful*
    Three feathers
- *Duties, difficult*
    The races between Payupki
        and Tikuvi
- *Pirates*
    The pirate women
- *Power*
    The power of woman and the
        strength of man
- *Revolutionary war heroines*
    The tale of Rebecca Motte
, *Strong*
    The life of Annie Christmas
, *Tiny*
    Teeny-Tiny
, *Wicked*
    The old woman

Women
    Rugoff — *Harvest* p.195-196

The women and the bats
    Alpers — *Legends* p.315

The wonderful fish
    De Bosschere — *Christmas* p.105-
    114

The wonderful jug of wild-cherry wine
    Bagley — *Candle* p.85-88

The wonderful porridge pot
    Morel — *Fairy* p.76-77

The wonderful shirt
    Manning — *Choice* p.13-25

The wonderful-working steeds
    Whitney — *In* p.97-104

The wonders of palace life
    De Roin — *Jataka* p.56-59

The wonders of Saint Berach
    Brown — *Book* p.156-165

The wondrous story of Ivan Golik and
    the serpents

Bain — *Cossack* p.267-288

The wondrous wise man
    Baum — *Mother* p.89-95

The wondrous wonder
    Rugoff — *Harvest* p.645-646

WOOD
    George Piney-Woods peddler
    Maraboe and Morsegat

**"WOODBURN" (Virginia governor's
    mansion)**
    The most haunted house

**WOOD-CARVERS AND WOOD-
    CARVING**
    Gelam
    The statue vendor
- *House*
    Mons Tro
- *Images*
    - *Easter Island*
        The story of the wooden
            images

WOODCHUCKS
    The hedgehog, the merchant, the
    king, and the poor man

WOODCUTTERS
    The adventures of Little Peachling
    The cowardly hunter and the
        woodcutter
    The dragon of Shervage Wood
    The golden goose
    The golden-horned dragon
    The great golloping wolf
    Hans and Greta
    Hansel and Gretel (and variants)
    The house in the forest
    The King's choice
    Little Red Riding Hood (and
        variants)
    The ridiculous wishes
    The shape-shifters of Shorm
    The three riddles
    The three wishes
    Tom Thumb
    The treasure
    The twin hunchbacks
    The wife who talked too much
        (and variants)
    The wishing skin

Wooden Tony: an Anyhow story
Cott — *Beyond* p.147-161

The woodpecker
Sperry — *Scand.* p.260

WOODPECKERS
Lizard and a ring of gold

WOODS. *See* **Forests**

WOODSMEN
See also **Woodcutters**
The cat who became head-forester
The moon maiden
The prince with the nine sorrows
Ten miles at each step
- *Backwoodsmen and borderers*
  - *Folklore* (subject)
    Life — *Treasury* p.108-127

The wooing of the maze
Housman — *Rat* p.57-67

Woowooto
Serwadda — *Songs* p.71-75

Word, wit, and merry game
Rugoff — *Harvest* p.379

WORDS
Silent Bianca

Wordsworth, William
The kitten and the falling leaves

Workers of evil — and a few good
spirits
McHargue — *Impossible* p.74-104

The workman and the peasant
Krylov — *Fables* p.115-116

WORLD, BEGINNING OF. *See* **Creation**

WORLD, END OF
Mons Tro

WORMS
The cock and the dragon
How the snake lost his voice
The Lambton worm

WORSHIP. *See* **Religion**

WREKIN
The giant and the wrekin

WRENS
Elsie's story
The marriage of Robin Redbreast
and the wren
The morning glory
The white blackbird: an Easter
story

WRESTLERS AND WRESTLING
The half-man
John Travail and the devil
Sankichi's gift
Three strong women
Who is who?

Wrestling in Iboland
McDowell — *Third* p.7-8

Wyndham, Lee
Ivashko and the witch

X

Xibalba
Roy — *Serpent* p.86-97

Y

YAMS
Gigi
Talk

Yankee peddlers
Life — *Treasury* p.150-151

YANKEES
Shake hands with a Yankee
- *Folklore (subject)*
  Life — *Treasury* p.128-157

The Yara
Rugoff — *Harvest* p.612-614

Yarns, tall tales and practical jokes
Life — *Treasury* p.294-296

YARTHKINS
Little people

"THE YEARLINGS"
A boy and his pa

Yelena the wise
Curtin — *Myths* p.218-227

"YELLOW DWARF"
The yellow dwarf (subject)
Opie — *Classic* p.66-67

The yellow dwarf
Opie — *Classic* p.68-80

The yellow ribbon
Sheehan — *Folk* p.138-140

YELLOWSTONE
Jim Bridger overcomes gravity

Yelub and his dog
Lawrie — *Myths* p.42

YETI (giant)
Big people

YMIR
Big people
Little people

YOLEN, JANE
Jane Yolen (subject)
Yolen — *Girl* p.56

Yosji-tsuni, brave warrior from Japan
Carpenter — *People* p.41-48

The young piper
Stuart — *Witch's* p.37-44

Young Sherman and the girl from
Charleston
Jagendorf — *Folk, South* p.226-228

The young witch-horse
Shaw — *Witch* p.37-42

YOUNGERS FAMILY
Jesse James and the widow

YOUTH
Happy returns
The stone
, *Eternal*
The fountain of youth
- *Strength*
Sergevan
, *Water of*
Water of youth, water of life,
and water of death

The youth who wanted to shiver
Carle — *Eric* p.75-88

YUGOSLAVIA
See also **Serbia**
Smartness for sale
The tale of the men of Prach

The turnip
- *Slavonia*
King Johnny

Yuisa and Pedro Mexias
Belpré — *Once* p.45-50

Yukiko and the little black cat
Novák — *Fairy* p.44-53

Z

Zāl and Rudāba
Picard — *Tales* p.50-60

Zāl the white-haired
Picard — *Tales* p.43-49

Zalagi and the mari
Lawrie — *Myths* p.10-11

The zamay who hid his life
Spicer — *13 Dragons* p.32-46

The zebra who spoke the truth
Dolch — *Animal* p.31-37

Zeitlin, Ida
The golden cockerell

ZEMACH, MARGOT
Margot Zemach (subject)
Alexander — *Foundling* p.88

ZEUS
The asses complain to Zeus

Zeus and men
Levine — *Fables* p.50

Zeus and modesty
Levine — *Fables* p.36

Zeus and the tortoise
Levine — *Fables* p.58

ZHARS (birds)
- *Feathers*
The story of Tremsin the
bird Zhar, and Nastasia,
the lovely maid of the sea

Zlateh the goat
Corrigan — *Holiday* p.225-231

Zohāk and Feridun
Picard — *Tales* p.17-29